DARK TRIUMPH

His Fair Assassin BOOK II

DARK TRIUMPH

by ROBIN LaFEVERS

HOUGHTON MIFFLIN HARCOURT
BOSTON   NEW YORK

For information about permission to reproduce selections from this book, write to trade.permissions@
hmhco.com or to Permissions, Houghton Mifflin Harcourt Publishing Company, 3 Park Avenue,
19th Floor, New York, New York 10016.

hmhco.com

The text of this book is set in Adobe Garamond.

Map by Cara Llewellyn

The Library of Congress Cataloging-in-Publication data is on file.

ISBN: 978-0-547-62838-7 hardcover
ISBN: 978-1-328-56766-6 paperback

Printed in the United States of America
DOC 10 9 8 7 6 5 4 3 2 1
4500724672

This is a work of fiction. Names, characters, and incidents are the product of the author's imagination,
except in the case of historical figures and events, which are used fictitiously.

To my own patron saints:

Nancy Warner,
for patching me back together time and again
so I could leap once more into the fray;

Erin Murphy,
who sometimes saw this story more clearly than I did;

Kate O'Sullivan,
for her unwavering support and enthusiasm;

and Mary Hershey,
for creating a safe place
where we could have all the hard and scary conversations.

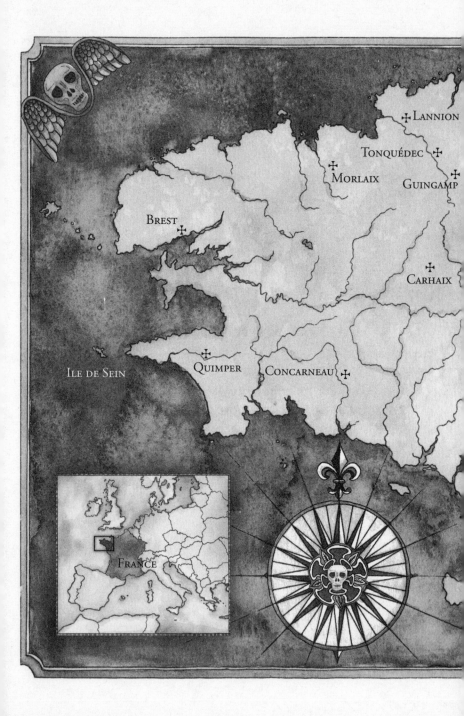

LANNION

TONQUÉDEC

MORLAIX

GUINGAMP

BREST

CARHAIX

ILE DE SEIN

QUIMPER

CONCARNEAU

FRANCE

DRAMATIS PERSONAE

LADY SYBELLA, handmaiden to Death

ISMAE RIENNE, handmaiden to Death

ANNITH, a novitiate of Mortain

ABBESS OF SAINT MORTAIN

ALAIN D'ALBRET, a Breton noble with extensive holdings in France

PIERRE D'ALBRET, his son

JULIAN D'ALBRET, his son

CHARLOTTE D'ALBRET, his ten-year-old daughter

LOUISE D'ALBRET, his seven-year-old daughter

BERTRAND DE LUR, captain of d'Albret's guard

JAMETTE DE LUR, his daughter

TEPHANIE, lady in waiting to Lady Sybella

MADAME FRANÇOISE DINAN, the duchess's former governess

JEAN RIEUX, marshal of Brittany and the duchess's former tutor

TILDE, a maid

ODETTE, her younger sister

BARON JULLIERS, a Breton noble

BARON VIENNE, a Breton noble

BARON IVES MATHURIN, a Breton noble

BENEBIC DE WAROCH, the Beast of Waroch and a knight of the realm

YANNIC, the jailor

GUION, a Breton farmer

BETTE, his wife

JACQUES, their son

ANTON, their son

The Charbonnerie

ERWAN, their leader

GRAELON, a charbonnerie man

LAZARE, a charbonnerie man

WINNOG, a charbonnerie youth

MALINA, a charbonnerie woman

The Breton Court and Nobility

ANNE, Duchess of Brittany, Countess of Nantes, Montfort, and Richmont

ISABEAU, her sister

DUKE FRANCIS II (Anne's father, deceased)

GAVRIEL DUVAL, a Breton noble

JEAN DE CHALON, Prince of Orange

MICHAULT THABOR, commander of the Rennes city guard

CAPTAIN DUNOIS, captain of the Breton army

PHILLIPE MONTAUBAN, chancellor of Brittany

BISHOP OF RENNES

CHARLES VIII, king of France

ANNE DE BEAUJEU, regent of France

MAXIMILIAN OF AUSTRIA, the Holy Roman emperor, one of Anne's suitors

SIR DE BROSSE, man-at-arms

SIR LORRIL, man-at-arms

SIR LANNION, man-at-arms

SIR GAULTIER, man-at-arms

ABBESS OF SAINT MER

SAMSON, a blacksmith's son

CLAUDE, a woodcutter's son

DARK TRIUMPH

Chapter One

I DID NOT ARRIVE AT the convent of Saint Mortain some green stripling. By the time I was sent there, my death count numbered three, and I had had two lovers besides. Even so, there were some things they were able to teach me: Sister Serafina, the art of poison; Sister Thomine, how to wield a blade; and Sister Arnette, where best to strike with it, laying out all the vulnerable points on a man's body like an astronomer charting the stars.

If only they had taught me how to watch innocents die as well as they taught me how to kill, I would be far better prepared for this nightmare into which I've been thrust.

I pause at the foot of the winding steps to see if I am being watched. The scullery woman scrubbing the marble hall, the sleepy page dozing against the doorway — either one of them could be a spy. Even if neither has been assigned to watch me, someone is always willing to tattle in the hopes of earning a few crumbs of favor.

Caution prevails and I decide to use the south stairs, then double back through the lower hall to approach the north tower from that side. I am very careful to step precisely where the maid has just washed, and I hear her mutter a curse under her breath. Good. Now I can be certain she has seen me and will not forget if she is questioned.

In the lower hall, there are few servants about. Those who have not been driven out are busy with their duties or have gone to ground like wise, clever rats.

When at last I reach the north wing of the palace, it is empty. Quickening my pace, I hurry toward the north tower, but I am so busy looking behind me that I nearly stumble over a small figure sitting at the base of the stairs.

I bite back an oath of annoyance and glare down to see it is a child. A young girl. "What are you doing here?" I snap. My nerves are already tightly strung, and this new worry does them little good. "Where is your mother?"

The girl looks up at me with eyes like damp violets, and true fear clutches at my gut. Has no one thought to warn her how dangerous it is for a pretty child to wander these halls alone? I want to reach down and shake her — shake her mother — and shout at her that she is not safe, not on these steps, not in this castle. I force myself to take a deep breath instead.

"Mama is dead." The child's voice is high and quivery.

I glance to the stairs, where my first duty lies, but I cannot leave this child here. "What is your name?"

"Odette," she says, uncertain whether to be frightened of me or not.

"Well, Odette, this is no place to play. Have you no one to look after you?"

"My sister. But when she is working, I am to hide like a little mouse."

At least her sister is no fool. "But this is not a good place to hide, is it? Look how easily I found you!"

For the first time, the girl gives me a shy smile, and in that moment, she reminds me so much of my youngest sister, Louise, that I cannot breathe. Thinking quickly, I take her hand and lead her back to the main hallway.

Hurry, hurry, hurry nips at my heels like a braying hound.

"See that door?" She nods, watching me uncertainly. "Go through

2

that door, then down the stairs. The chapel is there, and it is a most excellent hiding place." And since d'Albret and his men never visit the chapel, she will be safe enough. "Who is your sister?"

"Tilde."

"Very well. I will tell Tilde where you are so she may come and get you when her work is done."

"Thank you," Odette says, then skips off down the hall. I long to escort her there myself, but I already risk being too late for what I must do.

I turn back around and take the stairs two at a time. The thick wooden door on the landing has a new latch, stiff with disuse. I lift it slowly to be certain it will not creak out an alarm.

As I step into the cold winter sunshine, a bitter wind whips at my hair, tearing it from the net that holds it in place. All my caution has cost me precious time, and I pray that I have not been brought up here only to see those I love slaughtered.

I hurry to the crenellated wall and look down into the field below. A small party of mounted knights waits patiently while an even smaller party confers with that braying ass Marshal Rieux. I recognize the duchess immediately, her dainty figure poised on her gray palfrey. She looks impossibly small, far too small to carry the fate of our kingdom on her slender shoulders. That she has managed to hold off a French invasion for this long is impressive; that she has done so in spite of being betrayed by a full half of her councilors is close to a miracle.

Behind her and to the right is Ismae, sister of my heart and, possibly, my blood, if what the nuns at the convent told us is true. My pulse begins to race, but whether in joy that I am not too late or in panic at what I know is coming, I cannot tell.

Keeping my gaze fixed on Ismae, I gather up all my fear and dread and hurl them at her, like stones in a catapult.

She does not so much as glance in my direction.

From deep in the bowels of the castle, off toward the east, comes a faint rumble as the portcullis is raised. This time when I cast my warning, I fling my arms out as well, as if I am shooing away a flock of ducks. I hope—pray—that some bond still exists between us that will allow her to sense me.

But her eyes remain fixed on the duchess in front of her, and I nearly scream in frustration. *Flee,* my mind cries. *It is a trap.* Then, just as I fear I must throw myself from the battlements to gain her attention, Ismae looks up. *Flee,* I beg, then sweep my arms out once more.

It works. She looks away from me to the eastern gate, then turns to shout something to the soldier next to her, and I grow limp with relief.

The small party on the field springs to life, shouting orders and calling to one another. Ismae points again, this time to the west. Good. She has seen the second arm of the trap. Now I must only hope that my warning has not come too late.

Once Marshal Rieux and his men realize what is happening, they wheel their mounts around and gallop back to the city. The duchess and her party move to fall into a new formation but have not yet left the field.

Flee! The word beats frantically against my breast, but I dare not utter it, afraid that even though I stand on this isolated tower, someone from the castle might hear. I lean forward, gripping the cold, rough stone of the battlements so hard that it bites into my gloveless fingers.

The first line of d'Albret's troops rides into my sight, my half brother Pierre in the vanguard. Then, just when I am certain it is too late, the duchess's party splits in two, and a paltry dozen of the duchess's men turn their mounts to meet the coming onslaught. Twelve against two hundred. Hollow laughter at the futility of their actions escapes me but is snatched up by the wind before anyone can hear it.

As the duchess and two others gallop away, Ismae hesitates. I bite my lip to keep from shouting. She cannot think she can help the doomed knights? Their cause is hopeless, and not even our skills can help the twelve who so valiantly ride to their deaths.

"Flee." This time I do utter the word aloud, but just like my laughter, it is caught up by the cold, bitter wind and carried high above, where no one can hear it. Not the one it is meant to warn, nor those who would punish me for the betrayal.

But perhaps something has carried my warning to Ismae all the same, for she finally wheels her mount around and gallops after the duchess. The iron band squeezing my lungs eases somewhat, for while it is hard enough to watch these men meet their deaths, I could not bear to watch Ismae die.

Or worse, be captured.

If that happened, I would kill her myself rather than leave her to d'Albret, for he will grant her no mercy. Not after she ruined his plans in Guérande and nearly gutted him like a fish. He has had many days to hone his vengeance to a razor-sharp edge.

It is folly for me to linger. I should leave now while there is no chance of being discovered, but I cannot turn away. Like the rushing water of a swollen river, d'Albret's forces swarm the duchess's guard. The resounding clash is like thunder as armor crashes into armor, pikes break through shields, and swords meet.

I am astounded at the ferocity of the duchess's men. They all fight as if they have all been possessed by the spirit of Saint Camulos himself, slashing through their attackers much as farmers scythe through stalks of grain. By some miracle, they hold the oncoming line, and their efforts delay d'Albret's forces long enough for the duchess's party to reach the safety of the trees. D'Albret's greater number of men will be less of an advantage if they all must duck and dodge branches and bracken.

From the east, a trumpet sounds. I frown and look that way, fearing d'Albret has thought to arrange for a third mounted force. But no, the black and white banner of the Rennes garrison stands in stark relief against the crisp blue sky as an additional dozen men ride into the melee. When the duchess and the others finally disappear over the horizon, I allow myself to draw my first full breath.

But even with the infusion of new troops, it is a crushing defeat. The duchess's guards have no chance, not against so many. My hand itches for a weapon, but the knives I carry will do no good from this distance. A crossbow would work, but they are nigh unto impossible to conceal, and so I watch helplessly.

D'Albret had only ever planned for a trap—a quick in-and-out, thrust and parry, and then return with the prize. Once he realizes the quarry has escaped and he no longer has the element of surprise, he gives the signal for his soldiers to fall back behind the castle walls. Better to cut his losses than waste any more men in this failed gambit.

The battle below is nearly over. Only one soldier continues to fight, a great big ox of a man who doesn't have the sense to die quickly like the others. His helm has been knocked from his head, and three arrows pierce his armor, which is dented in a dozen places. His chain mail is torn, and the cuts beneath it bleed profusely, but still he fights with a nearly inhuman strength, stumbling ever forward into the mass of his enemies. *It is all right,* I long to tell him. *Your young duchess is safe. You may die in peace, and then you will be safe as well.*

His head jerks up from the blow he has just taken, and across the distance our eyes meet. I wonder what color they are and how quickly they will film over once Death claims him.

Then one of d'Albret's men lunges forward and cuts the knight's horse out from under him. He gives a long, despairing bellow as he goes down, then like ants swarming a scrap of meat, his enemies are upon him. The man's death cry reaches all the way up to the tower and wraps itself around my heart, calling for me to join it.

A fierce wave of longing surges through me, and I am jealous of that knight and the oblivion that claims him. He is free now, just like the gathering vultures who circle overhead. How easily they come and go, how far above danger they fly. I am not sure I can return to my own cage, a cage built of lies and suspicions and fear. A cage so full of darkness and shadow it may as well be death.

I lean forward, pushing my body out past the battlements. The wind plucks at my cloak, buffets me, as if it would carry me off in flight, just like the birds or the knight's soul. *Let go,* it cries. *I will take you far, far away.* I want to laugh at the exhilarating feeling. *I will catch you,* it whistles seductively.

Would it hurt? I wonder, staring down at the jagged rocks below. Would I feel the moment of my landing? I close my eyes and imagine hurtling through space, rushing down, down, down, to my death.

Would it even work? At the convent, the sisters of Mortain were as stingy with their knowledge of our deathly skills and abilities as a miser is with his coin. I do not fully understand all the powers Death has bestowed upon me. Besides, Death has already rejected me twice. What if He did so a third time and I had to spend the rest of my life broken and helpless, forever at the mercy of those around me? That thought has me shuddering violently, and I take a step away from the wall.

"Sybella?"

Fresh panic flares in my breast, and my hand reaches for the cross nestled among the folds of my skirt, for it is no ordinary crucifix but a cunningly disguised knife designed for me by the convent. Even as I turn around, I widen my eyes as if excited and curve the corners of my mouth up in a brazen smile.

Julian stands in the doorway. "What are you doing out here?" he asks.

I let my eyes sparkle with pleasure—as if I'm glad to see him rather than dismayed—then turn back around to the battlement to compose myself. I shove all my true thoughts and feelings deep inside, for while Julian is the kindest of them all, he is no fool. And he has always been skilled at reading me. "Watching the rout." I am careful to make my voice purr with excitement. At least he did not find me until *after* I warned Ismae.

He joins me at the wall, so close that our elbows touch, and casts me a look of wry admiration. "You wanted to watch?"

I roll my eyes in disdain. "It matters not. The bird slipped the net."

Julian tears his gaze away from me and looks out onto the field for the first time. "The duchess got away?"

"I'm afraid so."

He glances quickly back at me, but I keep the look of contempt plastered to my face like a shield. "He will not be happy," Julian says.

"No, he will not. And the rest of us will pay the price." I look at him as if just now noticing he is not dressed for battle. "Why are you not on the field with the others?"

"I was ordered to stay behind."

A brief spasm of fear clutches my heart. Is d'Albret having me watched so very closely, then?

Julian offers me his arm. "We need to get back to the hall before he returns."

I dimple at him and cozy up to his arm, letting it almost but not quite brush against my breast. It is the one power I have over him — doling out favors just often enough that he does not need to grab for them.

As we reach the tower door, Julian glances back over his shoulder at the battlement then turns his unreadable gaze on me. "I will not tell anyone that you were up here," he says.

I shrug, as if it is of no difference to me. Even so, I fear he will make me pay for this kindness of his.

Already I regret not jumping while I had the chance.

Chapter Two

I HURRY ALONGSIDE JULIAN, REFUSING to let my mind pick and fret at possibilities. I hold my head high, my scorn of those around me plain on my face. In truth, it is no act, for I loathe nearly everyone here, from d'Albret's courtiers and attendants to the spineless Breton lordlings who showed no resistance when he seized their duchess's castle for his own. Craven, lickspittle lackeys, the lot of them.

Julian pauses just outside the great hall, waits for a small cluster of retainers to pass, then slips in behind them, minimizing the chances that our entrance will be noted. And while I am glad he is committed to keeping my secret, I can only wonder what payment he will demand for doing so.

Inside the hall, quiet servants hurry to and fro, carrying flagons of wine, stoking the fire, trying to anticipate every need before they can be scolded or punished for not seeing to it quickly enough. Small knots of people are scattered throughout the hall, talking furtively among themselves. Clearly, word has reached them that d'Albret's gambit has failed and he will not be returning in triumph.

The only person in the hall who does not have the good sense to cloak himself in caution is the idiot Marshal Rieux. He paces before the fireplace, railing at Madame Dinan that d'Albret has destroyed his honor by springing a trap while under Rieux's flag of truce. He is a fine one to talk about honor as he was the duchess's own tutor and guardian—up until the day he betrayed her and joined forces with d'Albret, certain their combined might would convince the young duchess she had no choice but to do what they wished.

But she surprised them all.

There is a deafening clatter of hooves out in the courtyard as the men return, followed by the sound of soldierly chaos—the rattle of discarded weapons, the creak of leather, the clang of mail and armor. Usually, there are shouts of victory and coarse laughter, but not today. Today the men are eerily silent.

There is a thud as a door is flung open. Quick, heavy footsteps stride down the hall accompanied by the jingle of spurs. The entire room—even Rieux—falls quiet as we await the approaching storm. Servants make themselves scarce, and a few of the more cowardly retainers find excuses to leave the hall.

The desire to be elsewhere is overwhelming. It is all I can do to keep my feet anchored to the floor and not turn on my heel and run back up the stairs to the safety of the upper chambers. But my very guilt requires that I stay and show d'Albret that I have nothing to hide. Instead of fleeing as I wish, I lean toward Julian's ear. "Do you think Madame Dinan and Marshal Rieux are lovers?"

Even though Julian smiles in amusement, he also gives my arm a reassuring squeeze. I frown in annoyance and shrug my arm away from him. He knows me too well. Far, far too well.

And then the force of d'Albret's presence is upon us, swirling into the room with all the heat and destruction of a firestorm. With him comes the stench of blood and mud and sweat. His face is white with fury, making his beard look all the more unnaturally black. Close on his heels is his main henchman, Bertrand de Lur, captain of the guard, followed by a dozen lords and retainers. Two of them, Barons Julliers and Vienne, were the duchess's own vassals, but they were so eager to prove their loyalty to d'Albret that they agreed to ride with him to set this trap, even though they knew full well what he had in mind for their liege.

It therefore brings me a great joy to see that Mortain has marqued them both for death—each has a dark shadowy smear across his brow. Between that and the duchess getting away, this day has not turned out half bad.

"Why are you smiling?" Julian asks.

I pull my gaze away from the two men. "Because this should prove most entertaining," I murmur, just before d'Albret's voice cracks through the hall like a whip. "Get men up in all the towers. See if anyone is there who shouldn't be. If a warning was sent, it most likely came from the north tower."

I press my back against the wall and wish the nuns had taught us a cantrip to call down invisibility.

"Bring Pierre to me!" d'Albret continues. "His charge from the west gate should have come sooner. His laziness may well have cost me my prize." He thrusts his hands out, and his squire darts forward and removes his right gauntlet. Before the boy can take off the left, d'Albret turns to shout another order. The squire leaps back out of reach and waits warily, afraid to draw closer but even more afraid of not being there when needed. "I also want a detail of men to ride after the duchess and report on her movements and the forces protecting her. If a chance presents itself to snatch her, do it. Any man who brings her to me will find himself richly rewarded."

As de Lur repeats these orders to his men, a second squire hovers nearby, ready to place a goblet of wine in d'Albret's hand before he has to ask. Without looking, d'Albret reaches for it, then we all wait in pinprick anticipation while he slakes his thirst. Madame Dinan steps forward as if to calm him, then thinks better of it.

When the count has drained the goblet, he stares at it a long moment, then hurls it into the fireplace. The violent shatter of crystal echoes in the quiet hall. Slowly, he turns back to the room, wielding the silence with as much skill and cunning as he does his sword, letting it grow until it is stretched tighter than a drum skin. "How did the soldiers from Rennes manage to arrive just then, hmm?" His voice is deceptively soft and far more terrifying than his shouting. "How is that possible? Do we have a traitor in our midst?"

The room is silent, each of us knowing better than to risk answering that question. We know we have many traitors in our midst, but it is easy enough to betray a young girl. Whether any of them dared to betray d'Albret is another matter.

Marshal Rieux clenches his fists and takes a step toward d'Albret. Dinan reaches out to stop him, but he is too quick. *Mon Dieu,* he is either the bravest man I have ever met or the greatest fool.

"How can you have a traitor when no one knew of your plans?" Rieux asks.

D'Albret's gaze flicks lazily at Rieux's clenched fists. "It was a last-minute decision."

"Even so, I should have been told. I gave my word that the duchess would be granted safe parley." *Merde.* Does the idiot not feel the sands of his life slipping through the hourglass as he taunts d'Albret?

D'Albret turns his full attention to Rieux. Beside me, Julian tenses. "That is precisely why you were not told. You had given your word and would have clucked and scolded like an old woman."

Rieux says nothing. Whether because he is stunned by d'Albret's answer or because he is finally wise to his danger, I do not know.

"Besides"—d'Albret's voice takes on a mocking note—"look at how well your arguments won her over. It would be a poor commander who had only one tactic for winning a war." Then, faster than quicksilver, the look on d'Albret's face shifts and is no longer merely disdainful, but terrible. "You did not learn of this plan and warn her, did you? To protect your honor?"

Rieux recoils. Whatever he sees in d'Albret's eyes has finally given him pause. "No," he says shortly.

D'Albret holds his gaze for a long moment before turning back to the room. "How did the garrison from Rennes come to ride to her rescue? Why now? Why today, at this hour?" The count's eyes glitter dangerously. "The only explanation is that we have a traitor in our midst."

At least the arrival of the Rennes troops has distracted him from the north tower. For the moment.

"The duchess and Dunois brought news of the French." Rieux changes the subject abruptly.

D'Albret cocks his head, waiting.

"They say the French have crossed the border into Brittany and have taken three Breton towns, Ancenis among them."

Ancenis is Marshal Rieux's own holding. D'Albret purses his mouth, studying the marshal. "No doubt Dunois wished to divert your attention." D'Albret calls out to Bertrand de Lur. "Send a scouting party to confirm this report."

De Lur nods, but before he can give the order, d'Albret calls out additional instructions. "When that is done, question the men. See if any have departed for Rennes in the last week. If so, be sure to bring them to me for questioning when they return."

The men-at-arms grow silent—a few grow pale—for the methods d'Albret uses for questioning are the well-known stuff of nightmares. De Lur nods curtly, then goes to carry out his lord's orders. On his way out of the hall, he glances at me and winks. I pretend I do not see and instead focus on my brother Pierre as he strides past the departing captain. His helmet is under his arm, his chin is raised, and he has an ugly expression on his face. The white scar through his left eyebrow stands out like a brand. "What happened?" he calls as he strips out of his gloves. "How did she get away?"

D'Albret's head snaps up. "You were late with your men."

The accusation stops Pierre cold, and the rush of conflicting emotions that flutter across his face would be humorous if his situation were not so dire. "We were delayed by citizens who tried to jam the gates to prevent our joining you on the field."

D'Albret studies him a long moment, trying to see if he is lying. "You should have killed them."

"I did," Pierre says, his full, ripe mouth sullen.

"You should have killed them faster," d'Albret mutters, and a bitter laugh nearly escapes my throat. My brother does not murder quickly enough for him. In the end, however, d'Albret gives a brusque nod, which is as close as he ever comes to praise.

A commotion disrupts the tense moment as the returning soldiers herd a half a dozen men into the hall, naught but the dregs of the servants, by the looks of them.

D'Albret taps a finger to his lips. "They were found in the tower?"

De Lur kicks one of the men, who is not groveling enough to suit him. "No, but they were not on duty and have no witnesses to say where they were during the attack."

D'Albret cocks his head like a curious vulture. Slowly, he approaches the small group of the duchess's servants. "Are you such very loyal men, then?" he asks, his voice as soft and gentle as the finest velvet.

When no one answers, he smiles. It sends chills down my back. "You can tell me, for I am a great admirer of loyalty."

The oldest of them does his best to stand tall, but it is clear that he has been beaten and his leg will not work properly. "Aye, my lord," he says proudly. "We have served our duchess from the moment she was born and do not intend to stop now."

"The French were not able to buy you off with their gold?"

I close my eyes and pray briefly that the old fool will watch his tongue and look to his own safety, but he is too wrapped up in his honor. "Not us, sire."

D'Albret takes a step closer, his great bulk towering over the man, his gaze sweeping over the group. "Which of you learned of our little surprise greeting and crept out to warn the duchess?"

"None of us knew," the old man says, and I start to breathe a sigh of relief. But the fool is still riding high on his great loyalty and adds, "But we'd have told her if we did."

Annoyed, d'Albret looks over at Pierre. "How did we miss this one?"

My brother shrugs. "Even the best traps don't catch all the rats the first time, my lord."

Without word or warning, d'Albret hauls back his steel-gauntleted hand and strikes the old man across the face. The servant's neck snaps back with an audible crack. Julian squeezes my hand—hard—warning me to stay silent and still. And even though I want to fly at d'Albret, I do not move. Just as that last valiant knight held his position, so must I hold mine. As Death's handmaiden, I must be in place so I may strike when the time comes. Especially now, when d'Albret's bold treachery has assuredly earned him the very marque I have been waiting to see for six long months.

Besides, the old man is dead; my anger will do him no good. I utter a prayer for his departing soul. It is the least I can do, although it is not nearly enough.

Marshal Rieux steps forward with a look of outrage on his face, but before he can speak, d'Albret roars out, "I spared your miserable lives." His voice reverberates through the room like thunder, and the other servants finally have the sense to cower in fright. "And this is how you repay me?" There is a ring of steel as he draws his sword. My stomach shrivels into a tight little knot and tries to crawl up my throat, but before I can so much as call out a warning, the sword cuts through the huddled men. Blood splatters over the floor, then a second blow dispatches the rest.

I do not even realize I have taken a step forward until I feel Julian's arm snake around my waist to hold me in place. "Careful," he murmurs.

I close my eyes and wait for the roiling in my gut to pass. Julian nudges me, and my eyes snap open, a carefully neutral expression on my face. D'Albret's shrewd gaze is on us and I curl my lip, as if faintly amused by the carnage he has just wrought. "Fools," I mutter. It is a good thing that I no longer have a heart, because if I did, it would surely break.

"Julian!" d'Albret calls out, and I feel Julian flinch. He steps away from my side. "Yes, my lord father?"

"See to the cleanup here. And you, daughter." D'Albret's flat black eyes zero in on me and I force myself to meet his gaze with naught but amusement on my face. "See to Madame Dinan. I fear she has fainted."

As I step away from the safety of the stone wall to do as my father bids, I wish again—so very much—that Julian had not found me up on that tower. If our father finds out what I did, he will kill me as easily as he killed those men.

Although perhaps not as quickly.

Chapter Three

I FOLLOW THE FOOTMEN CARRYING Madame Dinan to her room, my thoughts and movements sluggish, as if I am wading through mud. It takes every last crumb of discipline I possess to keep myself together. I do not dare stumble about half-witted now.

When we reach the chamber, I have the footmen put her on the bed, then order them from the room. I stare down at the older woman. We are not allies, Madame Dinan and I; we merely share each other's secrets, which is an entirely different thing.

She came into our lives only occasionally, when she would escape her duties as governess to the duchess, the very duchess she has so thoroughly betrayed. D'Albret relied on her to oversee his daughters' upbringing. Much of that oversight was conducted across distances, with letters and go-betweens, except when some tragedy struck — then she would make an effort to come in person and smooth things over.

She looks older in repose, her face missing the false gaiety she wears like a mask. I unlace her bodice to ease her breathing, then remove the heavy, cumbersome headdress she wears. Not because it has contributed to her fainting, but because I know it eats at her vanity that she has white hair like an old woman's. It is a small enough punishment, but it is one I can afford.

I reach down and slap her cheek — perhaps harder than necessary — to rouse her. Her breath catches in her throat as she startles awake. She blinks twice, orienting herself, then begins to sit up. I push her back down. "Easy now, madame."

Her eyes widen when she sees who attends her. Her gaze flutters around the room and notes that we are alone. That gaze lands once more on me, then skitters away like a nervous lark. "What happened?" she asks.

Her voice is low and throaty, and I wonder if that is part of what draws d'Albret to her. Some say their union began when she was in the flower of her youth, a full two years younger than I am now. "You fainted."

Her long skinny fingers pluck at her bodice. "It grew warm in there."

Her quick and easy lie pricks my temper. I lean down close and put my face next to hers, forcing my voice to be as light and sweet as if we were talking about the latest fashion. "It was not warmth that caused you to faint, but the slaughter of innocents. Do you not remember?"

She closes her eyes again, and her face drains of what little color is left in it. Good. She does remember. "They were simply punished for their disloyalty."

"Disloyalty? What of your disloyalty? Besides, you knew those people!" I hiss. "They were servants who'd waited on you for years."

Her eyes snap open. "What do you think I should have done? It's not as if I could have stopped him."

"But you did not even try!" Our angry gazes hold for a long moment.

"Neither did you."

Her words are like a kick to my gut. Afraid I will slap her, I shove to my feet, cross over to her wooden chest, and begin fumbling through her pots of powder, jars of cream, and crystal vials. "But *I* am not his favorite, the one voice he listens to. That role has belonged only to you for as long as I can remember." At last I find a linen cloth. I dampen it with water from the ewer, then return to her side and practically fling it onto her forehead.

She flinches, then glares at me. "Your tender ministrations may well kill me."

I sit down and busy myself with my skirt, afraid she will see just how close to the truth she has come. Our secrets sit heavy in the room, not only the ones that we share, but those that we keep from each other. Neither she nor Rieux is marqued, and I am plagued by this nearly as much as I am by d'Albret's lack of a marque.

When I speak again, I am able to keep my voice calm. "And what of the duchess? You have cared for her since she was in swaddling clothes. How could you let d'Albret spring such a trap on her?"

She closes her eyes to the truth and dismisses my words with a quick shake of her head. "He was only claiming what was promised him."

Her steadfast denial is like flint to tinder, and my temper flares again. "He was going to kidnap her, rape her, declare the marriage consummated, then perform the marriage service after the fact." Not for the first time, I wonder if he is as rough with Madame Dinan as he is with others, or if there is some softer emotion between them.

She lifts her small, pointed chin. "She betrayed him! Lied to him! She had been promised to him by her father. He was only doing what any man would when such promises are broken."

"I've always wondered what you tell yourself so you may sleep at night." Afraid that I will say something to break our precarious truce, I rise to my feet and head for the door.

"It is the truth!" The normally elegant and refined Dinan screeches at me like a fishwife. While getting under her skin is no small accomplishment, it does little to wash the bitterness of the day from my tongue.

It is no easy or pleasant thing to examine d'Albret for a marque. Ismae claims it is a way for the god to keep us humble, marquing men where we cannot easily see. I say it is the god's own perverted sense of humor, and if I ever come face to face with Him, I shall complain.

But after today's spectacular bit of treachery, d'Albret must be marqued for death at last. It is the one reason I allowed myself to be sent back, because the abbess promised he would be marqued and that I could be the one to kill him.

For once, luck is with me: the chambermaid is none other than Tilde, Odette's sister. Which means I have something with which to bargain. I find her in the kitchen, filling up jugs with hot water for his bath. When I tell her what I need, she looks at me with the frightened eyes of a cornered doe. "But if the count sees you . . ." she protests.

"He won't see me," I assure her. "Not unless you give me away by looking at my hiding place. Do not be so stupid as to do that, and we will both be fine."

She begins chewing her lip, which is already ragged from her constant worry. "And you will get Odette away from here? As soon as possible?"

"Yes. I will get her away tomorrow morning when the first delivery comes to the kitchens. She will be hidden in the cart as it leaves." I will smuggle the girl out even if Tilde and I do not reach an agreement. The child reminds me far too much of my own sisters, who, if not for my desperate machinations, would be here in this vipers' nest with me now.

It was the biggest argument I had with my father since the convent forced me to return to his household six months ago. Last autumn when he made ready to travel to Guérande to put his case before the meeting of the barons, he was planning on bringing all his children. He wanted them nearby, where he could use them for his own ends and needs. I argued long and hard that little Louise was too young—and ill—to make the trip. And that Charlotte was too close to young womanhood to be near so many soldiers. He ignored me and had their nurse administer them each a sound beating—simply to punish me—then ordered their things packed.

But I would do anything to keep my sisters from d'Albret's dark influences. Including poison them.

Not too much. While I am not immune to poisons as Ismae is, I did pay careful attention to Sister Serafina's poison lessons and used only enough to make both my sisters and their nurse too ill to travel.

I blamed it on the eel pie.

Little Odette is in every bit as much danger as my sisters but has none of the protection afforded them by virtue of their noble blood. So I will get her to safety regardless, although I do not tell Tilde that.

"Very well," Tilde says at last, her eyes taking in my borrowed servant's gown and headscarf. "You have certainly dressed the part."

I give her an encouraging smile when what I want to do is wring her skinny neck so she will quit talking and get on with it. That would not, however, reassure her.

She thrusts a copper jug at me. It is full of steaming water and so heavy I nearly drop it before I can settle my grip to the handles. Together we begin our climb up the back stairs to d'Albret's bedchamber. We meet no other servants on the way. Indeed, since d'Albret has taken over the palace, most of them stay out of sight as much as possible. They are nearly invisible, like enchanted servants in a hearth tale.

Once inside the room, I set my jug down next to the tub in front of the fire and look for a hiding place.

Two of the walls are covered in carved wooden paneling and two are covered in fine crimson and gold wall hangings. I make for the wall hangings, a spot just behind an ornately carved chest, which should hide my feet from view should they show beneath the curtains. "Remember, do not look over here, no matter what happens."

Tilde glances up, a new flare of alarm in her eyes. "What would happen, demoiselle? You said nothing would happen, that you just wanted—"

"I merely meant that no matter how nervous you get or what the baron does, do not look over here. It could mean both our deaths."

Her eyes widen and for a moment I think she will lose her nerve altogether. "For your sister's sake," I remind her, hoping to strengthen her resolve.

It works. She gives a firm nod and turns to the task of filling the tub. I slip into my hiding place behind the silk wall hangings and pray they will not also serve as my shroud.

The stone wall is cold against my back, and the curtains part just the slightest bit. If I bend my knee a little, I do not even need to touch the silk to be able to see into the room.

I have not been in place longer than a handful of moments before there is a noise at the door. Tilde freezes, then resumes pouring water from the ewer into the tub.

The chamber door bursts open and Count d'Albret strides in, followed by a handful of retainers, my half brothers Pierre and Julian among them. Although they share the same parents, they look nothing alike. Pierre takes after our father, with a thick build and coarse manner, while Julian favors their mother, with more refined looks and manner. D'Albret unbuckles his sword, and Bertrand de Lur steps forward to take it from him. "I want another score of men riding for Rennes tonight," d'Albret tells his captain. "I want them in the city as soon as possible, hiding among the citizens. I'll need reliable eyes and ears there if we are to retaliate against her treachery."

My pulse quickens.

"As you wish, my lord." De Lur takes the sword and lays it on one of the chests.

D'Albret shrugs his massive, bull-like shoulders, and my brother Pierre jumps forward to take his mantle before it can fall to the ground.

"I want them to report on the city's mood, the garrison, the provisions. I want to know if the city can withstand a siege, and for how long. They are to find out who is loyal to the duchess, who is loyal to the French, and whose loyalty is still for sale."

"Consider it done, my lord," de Lur says.

Pierre leans forward, his hooded eyes bright. "And what of your message to the duchess? When shall we send it?"

Like a striking snake, d'Albret reaches out and clouts him across the mouth. "Did I give you leave to speak of the matter, whelp?"

"No, my lord." Pierre dabs the blood from his split lip, looking resentful and sullen. I could almost feel sorry for him, but he has worked so hard to become just like d'Albret that I feel nothing but contempt.

The room grows quiet and I angle my eye to better see d'Albret. He is studying Tilde, who is concentrating very carefully on the steaming ewer of water she is pouring into the tub. "Leave me to my bath," d'Albret tells the others.

With a knowing glance or two in Tilde's direction, they quickly disperse.

I can see Tilde's neat linen veil tremble as she shakes with fear. D'Albret takes two strides toward her and comes fully into my view for the first time. He grabs her chin between his fingers and pulls her head up so he can look into her face. "You know better than to speak of what you hear in my chamber, do you not?"

She keeps her gaze averted. "I am sorry, my lord. You will have to speak up. My father boxed my ears so often I am fair hard of hearing."

Oh, clever girl! My estimation of Tilde grows, but this ruse will not be enough to save her.

D'Albret studies her for a long moment. "Just as well," he says, and Tilde cocks her head to the side as if straining to hear him. He studies her another few seconds before letting go of her chin.

D'Albret holds his arms out to his sides, a silent order to remove his shirt. When Tilde steps forward to lift it over his head, d'Albret's eyes roam up and down her slender body, and I see the exact moment his desire awakens. The rutting pig will bed her before he orders her death.

Now I will need to find a way to smuggle Tilde out of the palace as well as her little sister. Unless I have an opportunity to kill d'Albret before then.

Tilde removes his shirt and steps away.

D'Albret's chest is shaped like an enormous wine cask, his flesh the pallid whiteness of a fish, but instead of being covered in scales, it is covered with coarse black hair. I ignore my disgust and force myself to search his body. Mortain *must* have marqued him for death.

But nowhere among all that hair is the marque I seek. No smudge, no shadow, nothing that will allow me to kill this monster with Mortain's blessing. My hands grip the silken wall hangings, and I crush them in my fists. It would be too dangerous to attack him head-on. Perhaps Mortain intends for me to stab him in the back or pierce the base of his skull with a thin, needle-like blade.

D'Albret unlaces his breeches and steps out of them and into the tub. I stretch my neck to try to get a glimpse of his back, but I cannot see it from this angle.

As Tilde starts to move away, he reaches out and grabs her hand. She grows still, afraid to move. Slowly, with his eyes on her face, he pulls her hand down into the tub, into the water, his lips growing slack with anticipated pleasure.

Please, Mortain, no! I cannot watch this, else I will have to kill him, marque or no.

Like an unsettled flock of pigeons, every one of the nuns' warnings rushes through my head: killing without a marque is killing outside Mortain's grace and I will imperil my immortal soul. It will be sundered from me forever and forced to wander lost for all eternity.

But I cannot stand here and watch him rape her. Still uncertain of what I intend to do, I begin inching from my hiding place and reaching for my knives. A sharp knock at the door halts my step.

"Who is it?" d'Albret growls.

"Madame Dinan, my lord."

D'Albret drops Tilde's hand—is that her sigh of relief or my own?—then nods his head toward the door. The maid rushes to open it and let Madame Dinan in.

Her glance flicks in annoyance toward the younger, prettier serving girl. "Leave," she orders the girl. "I will attend the count."

Tilde does not wait for d'Albret to agree but slips silently from the room, proving once again that she has her wits about her.

When the two are alone, d'Albret rises from the tub, and I have a clear view of his back. The water sluices over the coarse black hair like a stream running over rocks, but there is no marque. Not even a smudge or shadow I can pretend is one.

Disappointment strikes me like a fist, and I feel sick. Not merely a sourness in my stomach, but a sickness of the heart. True despair. If this man is not marqued, then how can Mortain exist?

On the heels of that thought comes a more welcome realization. If Mortain does not exist, then how can there be any danger in stepping outside His grace?

But am I certain that He does not exist? Certain enough to stake my eternal soul on it?

Before I can decide, the chamber door bursts open and d'Albret's head snaps up. "Who's there?"

Marshal Rieux's voice holds a note of faint distaste. "I apologize for the inconvenience. But the scouts have returned from Ancenis."

"And it could not wait until morning?" d'Albret asks.

I am certain d'Albret will strike Rieux down where he stands for his gross insolence in interrupting, but he does not. Either Rieux was born under a lucky star or d'Albret has some need for the man and does not wish to destroy him just yet.

"No, it could not. What Captain Dunois told us is true. The French have taken Ancenis. We must send a show of force immediately to help defend it."

"Must we?" d'Albret asks, and there is another pause that sends a shard of ice deep into my gut.

"But of course!"

Through my sliver of curtain, I see a frown on Madame Dinan's face as she smooths her skirt over and over again, even though there is not a wrinkle in sight. D'Albret cocks his head. "Very well." He allows Dinan to help him into his chamber robe, then turns to Rieux.

"Your sword." D'Albret puts his hand out, and my heart starts to race. Now the fool has done it. He's annoyed d'Albret once too often.

Marshal Rieux hesitates. D'Albret puts a finger to his lips, as if sharing a secret. I cannot bear to watch, for while I do not care for Rieux, the man has at least tried to cling to the standards of honor. I avert my eyes, shifting my gaze to the left, away from the gap in the curtains through which I've been watching them all.

I remember the blood . . .

I want to put my hands over my ears like a child, but I am unwilling to let go of my knives.

There is a ring of steel as Rieux draws his sword, followed by a soft meaty thud as d'Albret takes it in his hand. A moment of silence, then a faint whistling as the blade arcs through the air. It is followed by a ripping sound as the silk curtain to my right is sliced in two. Surprised silence fills the room as the bottom half slowly puddles to the floor.

I stay as still as possible, huddled far to the left and praying I cannot be seen behind the remaining piece of curtain. My heart threatens to gallop out of my chest. So close. So very, very close.

"What is wrong, my lord?"

"I thought I heard something. Besides, I detest those hangings. See that they are removed by the time I return. Now, come, let us hear what these scouts have to say."

Then, so suddenly it nearly leaves me breathless, they all quit the room and I am left cowering behind the remaining drape staring at a tub full of cooling water. I close my eyes and shudder at how close I came to death.

At least it would have been quick.

I am still shaking as I make my way to the servants' quarters and begin searching among all the sleeping bodies on the floor. The room smells of cold nervous sweat and stale breath from so many people crowded together, although their sheer numbers help keep them warm. I pick my way through them, looking for Tilde, but there are so many young women wrapped in blankets and headscarves—and anything else they can find to keep warm—that it is an impossible task. Odette, then. But there are only a handful of children in here, and all of them are young boys—the pages the palace uses for fetching and carrying and sending messages. Which means Odette is not here.

Perhaps she is still in the chapel. *Please do not let me be too late,* I pray as I slip silently from the servants' quarters and hurry along the quiet stone passageways to look for them there.

The moment I step inside the chapel, I know I am not alone. Two pulses beat somewhere nearby. But that is not my only company. There is also an ice-cold pall that lies over the room. A restless fluttering reminiscent of moths moves silently across my skin. Ghosts. Drawn to the warmth of life like bees are drawn to nectar. Indeed, I do not even need to search for Odette and Tilde; the ghosts hover hungrily above their hiding place.

I hurry over and swat the ghosts away with my hand. Tilde is holding the sleeping Odette, and slowly, she looks up. Her face, pinched and white, goes slack with relief when she sees it is me. "I was afraid you wouldn't come," she whispers.

That she did not believe I would do as I'd promised stings, and I scowl at her. "I said I would, didn't I? I went to the servants' quarters first. Here. I will hold the girl while you get dressed."

Tilde frowns in puzzlement. "Why?"

I lay the bundle of men's clothing—purloined from the slaughtered servants, although I do not share that with her—on the pew and take the sleeping Odette from her arms. "You would not survive the night," I tell her, careful to keep my voice matter-of-fact. "Not now that you have heard d'Albret's plans. I must get you both out immediately."

Her face softens and her mouth wobbles and I fear she will break down in tears. "Hurry!" I hiss. "And you may well curse me before the night is through."

She slips out of her gown and pulls on the clothing I have brought. When she is done, we wake the sleeping Odette and coax her into the unfamiliar garments. They are far too big, and when I pull my knife to trim the breeches, both she and Tilde shrink back in fear.

"*Débile!*" I growl. "I have not come this far nor risked this much just to kill you. Stay still." Fear holding her in place, Odette stands while I saw at her pants until they are short enough that she will not trip on them.

"Be very still now," I warn her. Before she or Tilde can protest, I reach up, place the edge of my knife against her rich, curly locks, and slice them off.

"My hair!" she cries, one of her hands flying to her cropped head.

"Do not be silly," I scold her. "It is just hair and will grow back, but it will only get in your way tonight. You must make people think you are a boy. Which of the pages do you like the most?"

She wrinkles her nose. "None."

Good girl, I think. "Then which do you find the most annoying?"

"Patou," she says, without hesitation.

"Perfect. Pretend you are Patou. Do all the annoying things he does, walk as he does, spit as he does. All those things you must do tonight."

She looks at me warily. I lean forward. "It is a game. A trick you must play on the entire palace. To prove that a girl is better than a boy. Can you do that?"

She looks to Tilde, who nods, then turns back to me, and I am relieved to see that some of the fear has left her face. "Yes," she whispers, so soft and quiet no one could ever mistake her voice for a boy's.

I turn to Tilde. "Try to see that she does not speak. Her voice will give her away." Then I lift my knife. "I must do yours as well."

The serving girl does not falter but steps closer for me to reach. "I cannot ever repay you," she whispers.

"You have only to get free," I say as I cut her hair. "That is payment enough."

An hour later, they are safely tucked up on the seat of the night-soil cart. Odette protests loudly at first. "Bud id stinks!" she says, holding her nose.

I glance slyly at Tilde. "I warned you you might not thank me, but it is the only cart that leaves during the night and can get you into the city without question."

"It is fine," Tilde says through the scarf she has brought up to her face to cut the smell. We stare into each other's eyes for a beat, and the gratitude I see there warms me, makes me think there is some small sliver of good left inside me. I reach out and grab her hand. Squeeze it. "Be strong. Once inside the city, take yourself to the convent of Saint Brigantia. Tell them—tell them the abbess of Saint Mortain has asked that they grant you sanctuary."

Tilde's eyes widen at that, but before she can say anything, the night-soil man calls out, "You gonna gab all night or can I be about my business?"

"Hush—you got your payment," I remind him.

He spits off to the side. "Won't be worth nothing if I don't get out of here."

True enough.

As I watch them leave, I am filled with a nearly overpowering need to follow them. Follow them out of the stable yard, past the guard tower, and into the streets of the city, where I can lose myself among the crowds of people. I take one step, and another, then stop. If I go with them, d'Albret will send a full contingent after us. Tilde and Odette's chances of escape are much better without me.

Besides, I was sent here to do a job, and like that last knight who held off d'Albret's men this afternoon, I will not leave the field until it is done.

I have not been in bed but half a turn of a glass when the scratching at my door begins. It is soft at first, no more than the whispering of leaves in the wind or the creaking of branches against the wall. I hold still in my bed, listening more closely. There it is again. This time more distinct. My heart begins to pound, and I lift my head from the pillow.

Scritch, scritch, pause, *scritch, scritch, scritch.*

It is Julian, using the secret code we devised when we were children, a dozen lifetimes ago. But it is not a child's game he wants to play tonight. I burrow farther into the mattress and pull the covers up over my ears, then hear the muffled rattle as he lifts the latch. I hold very still and keep my breathing even, praying that he will close the door and move on, relieved when he does.

Even so, the scratching follows me into my dreams and turns them into nightmares.

Chapter Four

I AM AWAKENED IN THE morning when my two ladies in waiting come bursting into the room. Jamette de Lur leads the way, pausing barely long enough to keep the door open for Tephanie Blaine, who struggles with a tray.

"Did you hear?" Jamette asks.

She is a vain, silly girl given to drama and putting on airs and takes far too much pleasure in my fall from d'Albret's favor. "Good morning to you too," I drawl.

Reminded of her place, she flushes slightly, then dips a begrudging curtsy. "Good morning, my lady."

"What is this news you are screeching about?"

She is torn between denying that she was screeching and launching into her drama. The drama wins. "They rooted out a nest of traitors and rebels yesterday! If not for their quick action, we could all have been slaughtered in our beds."

So that is the story d'Albret and the others are putting out. There is a faint rattle as Tephanie sets the tray down on a table. "Also, a servant girl went missing during the night."

I throw off the covers and get to my feet. "My, the castle was busy while I slept! Surely this servant just snuck off to visit her lover?"

Tephanie looks at me with stricken eyes and I see that she is genuinely frightened. "They searched the castle high and low and found no signs of her."

Jamette tosses her head and hands me my chamber robe. "Some say she was in league with the traitors."

Débile! I should have seen that coming. I was so concerned with getting them away as soon as possible I didn't stop to consider the timing.

"I heard she was killed for seeing something she shouldn't have," Tephanie says as she gives me a cup of heated wine.

My head snaps up to study her more closely, but she does not appear to be insinuating anything. "Where did you hear that?"

She shrugs. "The servants were talking when I fetched your tray."

I say nothing and sip the wine, taking a moment to compose myself.

Jamette's eyes go wide. "Mayhap the ghosts got her."

I bite back a sigh. Must I give up sleeping altogether in order to stay abreast of what goes on in this castle? "What ghosts?" I ask.

"The ones in the old tower. It is well and truly haunted. Many have heard the ghosts moaning and wailing and making a terrible noise."

Tephanie crosses herself, then turns to me. "Here is your clean chemise, my lady."

I set down my wine and shrug out of my robe. Tephanie's cheeks pinken with embarrassment as she helps me into my shift. "My lady is growing thin," she murmurs. "You must try to eat more."

While I cannot help but wish she were less observant, I am inexplicably touched that she has noticed.

"It does not help your looks any that you insist on wearing all these dark colors," Jamette says, holding out a gown of patterned black brocade. "It makes you appear unnaturally pale." What she chafes at is that my complexion is fairer than hers.

"I'm afraid my time at the convent of Saint Brigantia has lessened my love of material luxuries," I tell her. Since rejoining d'Albret's household, I have worn nothing but somber colors—not because of some newfound piousness, but out of respect for all those d'Albret has murdered.

Tephanie hands me the silver chain from which my special crucifix hangs and helps to fasten it about my waist. The chain also holds nine glass rosary beads, one for each of the old saints and every one of them filled with poison. "If we hurry," she says, "we can attend mass this morning."

I glance up at her. "Do you *want* to attend mass?"

She shrugs. "It seems like a good day for it."

"Tephanie, my little mouse, what forgiveness must you pray for?" Her sins can only be those of a small child—the wanting of a sweet or a new gown. But she blushes in embarrassment, and I am pricked with guilt for having teased her. "Go," I tell her. "Attend your mass."

Her face falls. "You mean, alone?"

"*I* do not wish to pray for forgiveness."

"Although, Heavenly Father knows, you need it more than most," Jamette mutters. I pretend I do not hear her but add it to her long list of transgressions.

"Wait," I tell Tephanie. "You are right. With rebels and ghosts lurking in every corner, it is not safe to wander this castle's halls." They do not catch my irony, but the truth is, we have more to fear from those who claim to protect us than from any rebel or spirit.

I tug my skirt into place and then hurry to one of my trunks. I retrieve two of my smaller knives and turn back to the others.

Tephanie's eyes widen. "Where did you get those?" she asks.

"From my brothers, goose, where do you think? Here." I thrust one at her. "Carry it from the chain at your waist. You, too." I hand the second one to Jamette. "Now, hurry along or you will miss your mass," I tell Tephanie.

"But—"

"When you are done, come find us in the solar." Realizing she will never leave unless I order her to, I add, "You are dismissed."

After a moment's hesitation, she bobs a curtsy and then, still clutching her knife, hurries from the room.

When she is gone, I sit down so Jamette can dress my hair. In truth, I can do a better job myself, but it irks her to have to serve me, so I relish giving the task to her. It is almost not worth it, for she is intentionally ungentle and there are some days, like today, when I fear she will tug all the hair from my head. It makes me long for Annith and Ismae, their gentle hands and soothing ways. Not to mention their razor-sharp wits. My heart twists with longing, hot and bitter.

As I glance resentfully at Jamette's reflection in the mirror, I see she sports a new ring on her finger, fashioned of pearls and a ruby. A prize, no doubt, for carrying reports of my movements and actions back to my father. I cannot help but hate her for it; I already feel trapped and suffocated. Knowing that she relays my every move to him makes it nearly impossible to breathe.

After I have dressed and broken my fast, there is nothing for it but to join the other ladies in the solar. I dare not attempt any spying today, as my father and his men will no doubt be extra alert in the days to come. I must be content with what I accomplished yesterday, for I *did* accomplish much, I remind myself. I saved the duchess from d'Albret's trap and got Tilde and Odette to safety. There are many weeks when I am not granted any such victories.

With a resigned sigh, I grab my embroidery basket. At least I will have something entertaining to occupy my mind: plotting how best to kill the two marqued barons. Smiling, I open my chamber door and nearly bump into — "Julian!" I say, all the joy I have been feeling crumbling to dust. "What are you doing here so early?"

"I come to wish you a good morning, fair sister." He glances over at Jamette, who is making calf eyes at him. "We must speak privately for a moment, if you please."

Looking disappointed, she curtsies, and before I can think of an excuse to keep her near, she is gone. "What is it?" I ask, my face a picture of concern.

Julian's face is carefully blank. "Where were you last night?"

My heart thuds painfully against my ribs. "I was here in my room — where were you?"

He ignores my question. "Then why did you not answer when I knocked?"

"I took a sleeping draft for the vile headache I had."

Julian's face softens and he lifts his hand to tuck a strand of my hair in place. "I could have soothed away your headache, had I but known."

With all my secrets that he keeps hanging in the balance, I smile up at him and tap him playfully on the chest. "Then next time, knock louder."

When he smiles back, I know that he believes me. As he lifts my hand and places a lingering kiss upon it, I wonder — for the hundredth time — how on earth I let the convent talk me into returning to my family.

Chapter Five

AFTER A WEEK OF RAIN and being trapped inside the castle with d'Albret and his raging suspicions, we are all at our wits' ends. I even more so than the others, for I have two kills I am eager to make, which is nearly impossible with so many underfoot.

Since I have had nothing but time on my hands, I have considered my options carefully. Sister Arnette believed that arming me was her greatest challenge, since so few of Death's handmaidens have ever had to maintain such a deceptive role for so long. She gave me nearly a dozen knives, most of them long and thin and easily concealed. I have lost four of them along the way, having to leave them with their victims. I also have a thick gold bracelet that holds a garrote wire, but I have no crossbow or throwing rondelles, since they are too difficult to hide or explain away.

Since these barons are allies of my father, I must be subtle. If I leave a trail of murdered men behind me, d'Albret will turn his household upside down in search of the one responsible. A stabbing might be blamed on some soldierly quarrel or a thief in the night, but a garroting would never be. And two such incidents would make d'Albret suspicious and wary.

Although poison is my least favorite weapon, it is often the best choice when subtlety is required. Besides, with the plague having so recently come through Nantes, it will be easy enough to make it appear as if these men simply fell ill and died.

Getting the poison to them is more difficult than it should be. I cannot just slip it into their food, for they eat with the rest of the household, and as much as I dislike everyone here, I am not willing to poison them all. At least not yet.

I could place a candle filled with night whispers in each of their chambers, but there is a good chance some poor servant would light it for them and breathe its deadly fumes, and I have no wish to see more innocents die.

It might be possible to visit one of them bearing a flask of poisoned wine and promising seduction, but that would not work for them both. It would also be difficult to arrange, as Jamette sticks to me like a thorn in soft flesh. Julian, too, is watching me more closely than normal, ever since he found me up on the north tower.

Saint Arduinna's snare then, but I will have to be careful in choosing which of their personal items to poison—I must be sure that only the intended victims will touch them.

In the end, it is Julliers who provides an answer to my problem. He is fastidious about his hands and has more gloves than I have gowns. I find it easy enough to leave the great hall early one night, slip into both barons' rooms while they and their squires are at their dinners, and apply the poison to the insides of their hunting gloves. Still, it is a close thing, as I run into Jamette on my way back to the hall.

"Where have you been?" she asks.

"I went to the privy," I tell her shortly. "Shall I invite you to come with me next time?"

She wrinkles her nose and falls into step beside me. The small jar of poison is a heavy weight in my pocket, one I would rather have taken back to my room as soon as possible. Instead, with Jamette's discovering me, I have no choice but to return to the hall with the evidence of my crime still upon me.

Two days later, the rain finally lifts, and we are all eager to be out of the palace, which has begun to feel far too much like a prison. Julian, Pierre, and some of the barons, Julliers and Vienne among them, have arranged for a hunt, and it was not overly difficult to get myself and my ladies in waiting invited along. Of course, I do not need to be on the hunt in order for the poison to work, but I prefer to see a job through to its end.

Besides, I fear I shall go mad again if I do not get out of the castle, even for just a few hours.

The huntsman rides ahead, followed by the handlers and their dogs, who are churning and woofing and barking in their eagerness to be off the leash. I make certain to position myself near Julliers and Vienne but carefully avoid paying any attention to them lest someone should note my doing so.

Pierre had been hoping for a deer, but the huntsman was unable to find a trail. Which was perhaps good, since the ground is thick and muddy after more than a week of rain, and the horses could easily founder and risk breaking a leg if we were to chase deer. Instead, we will be hunting for small game, and so have brought our falcons.

My own sits on my wrist, her small leather hood with its bright red and blue feathers covering her eyes and keeping her calm amid the commotion. Julian gave her to me for my twelfth birthday. When I ran away to the convent, he watched over her for the full three years I was gone, as if knowing I'd be back. When I returned, she'd grown so used to him that at first she would go only to his wrist, not mine.

Just outside the city wall, my falcon grows agitated, turning her head from side to side and causing the tiny silver bells on her jesses to tinkle. We have reached the very place where the duchess's men met their deaths but a handful of days ago, and I wonder if the sensitive creature can feel the lingering presence of death. The heartbreaking bellow of the last knight as he went down echoes in my ears, unnerving me.

"Is everything all right?"

I look up to find Julian has nudged his mount closer to mine.

I shoot him a glance, careful to hide my agitation and fill my expression with annoyance. "Other than half our party being fools? Yes, except for that, everything is fine."

He smiles. "I am glad you decided to come. I should have expired of boredom otherwise. I might even have had to shoot one of the barons, just for entertainment. They would all be grateful if they knew that your presence has spared them such a fate."

His words strike a chord of unease. Is he fishing? Does he suspect that I am behind the scattered deaths in our party over the last few months? I twist my mouth in a cruel smile. "Do not feel you must resist shooting them on my account. I could do with some entertainment as well."

Julian laughs, a rich easy sound that does much to alleviate my concerns. "Watching Pierre seduce Baron Vienne's wife out from under his nose should be amusing enough."

I turn my gaze to Pierre. He is flirting outrageously with a buxom lady in vermilion velvet. I cannot help but wonder what she sees in him. He is thickly muscled and barrel-chested like our father, and he wears his black hair long and straight. His mouth is full and red, like a girl's.

There is no love lost between Pierre and me. When he was twelve years old, he wanted to prove that he was no mere boy but a man full grown, and did so by forcing my first kiss on me when I was but nine years of age.

I was so startled by the kiss, so taken aback and affronted at this violation of my person, that I retaliated in the only way I knew how: I kissed him back. I didn't simply return the kiss while his lips were already planted on my own. Instead, I waited until he was busy polishing our lord father's armor, sauntered up to him as I had seen Marie the upstairs maid do to one of the men-at-arms, grabbed his smooth cheeks in my hands, and smacked him soundly on his lips.

The scar that adorns his left eyebrow is from where I whacked him with our father's scabbard when he tried to force a second kiss.

But while I rarely have occasion to feel grateful to Pierre, today I do. If Pierre is courting Vienne's wife, any suspicion over her husband's death will fall on their shoulders rather than mine.

I turn to Julian with a sly smile. "How long will it take Baron Vienne to realize that Pierre is cuckolding him?"

Julian smiles back. "Not long, for Pierre will not truly enjoy himself until he can rub the baron's nose in it."

Since we are speaking of the baron, I allow my gaze to drift over to him and Julliers. I can feel the rapid beating of their hearts—as if two horses are galloping far in the distance, just beyond true hearing. Beads of sweat have begun to form on Julliers's brow, but Vienne shows no signs of distress. He is heavier than Julliers and so will no doubt need to absorb more poison before his symptoms begin in earnest.

Before either Julian or I can say anything further, the huntsman sounds his horn. It is time to hunt.

I remove my falcon's hood, and she fluffs her wings in readiness, her sharp, keen eye scanning the field. I launch her from my arm, painfully jealous of her freedom as she rises high in the sky, wheeling around once, twice, watching for her prey.

But I have prey of my own. Both the barons have grown ashen, and Julliers's left arm hangs useless at his side. If he is experiencing numbness in his limbs, it will not be long now.

Then the huntsman sounds his horn again, and the hounds are off the leash, the teaming swarm of them racing toward the underbrush to flush out the game. A frantic thudding of wings follows as the startled partridge take flight.

Like heavy stones thrown from a trebuchet, the falcons drop from the sky and plummet toward their prey. A series of soft thumps follow.

But one falcon — mine — is still moving; a lone rabbit has also been flushed from the brush. The poor creature's death squeal is harsh in the quiet of the forest, and every nerve in my body flares, for the noise made by a dying rabbit is shockingly similar to that produced by a dying man. As the falcon returns, I thrust out my arm and hold my breath, waiting to see whose wrist she will return to. When she lands on mine, I decide to take it as a fortuitous omen.

I glance once more at the two barons and wonder yet again why Mortain has marqued them for death but not d'Albret. Their sins and betrayals are small when weighed against his.

It would have me questioning Mortain's very existence if I did not so desperately need to believe in Him, for if He is not my father, then d'Albret is, and that I could not bear.

Flushed with the pleasure of our morning's hunt, we head back to the castle. Julliers has given his hawk to his groom to carry, and Vienne slumps drunkenly in his saddle. While I am glad that the poison is working, I feel a tinge of regret at not being able to use my knives. They offer a much quicker and cleaner end, and I have no appetite for the lingering deaths of soft, pampered barons.

Everyone is happy with the morning, except Jamette, whose little goshawk caught nothing but a vole. "It is a good thing we do not have to eat only what we catch," I tease her.

She glares at me, which makes me laugh out loud.

We are nearly to the city walls when I feel something watching me. It is not Julian, for Jamette is busy trying to draw him into conversation. Nor is it Pierre, who has taken full advantage of Vienne's poor health and is practically making love to his wife in plain sight of us all. I glance over my shoulder, but there is no one there.

I turn back in my saddle. Are the French troops close enough that they could have scouts nearby? Or did some of the Rennes garrison stay behind to keep an eye on d'Albret's movements?

Or perhaps it is no living thing I sense but the soul of one of those men who died so violently on the battlefield.

I glance over my shoulder once more. When I do, a crow flutters from a far tree to a closer one. His left wing is crooked, as if it had once been broken.

Merde.

I whip back around in my saddle. It is my very own crow. The one Sister Widona had rescued and kept in a cage when I first arrived. She used the frightened, wounded creature to draw me out of the morass my own mind had fallen into. Without that crow, I might be there still.

The convent has sent me a message. It has been four long months since I last heard from them, and I had nearly given up hope that I ever would again. But now. Now there is a message. My spirits soar just like the falcons did moments ago. Perhaps old Sister Vereda has Seen what I could not—d'Albret's death.

"You seem restless." Julian's voice yanks my mind from its daydreaming. The crow's timing could not be worse.

"Not at all," I say.

Ever jealous of the attention Julian pays me, Jamette sticks her long nose in. "Why is that crow following you?" she asks.

"You are deluded," I scoff. "He is not following me. I think he is after the vole you caught."

"No, no," she says, and my hand itches to slap her silly face. "It *is* following you. Look!"

The crow flutters another tree closer.

"*Tsk.* Does not the lowly crow realize he is far beneath my sister's notice? Here." Julian moves his hand toward his falcon's jesses. "I will dispatch the uncouth creature for you."

"No!" I say, too sharply.

He cocks an eyebrow at me, and I give him a cool smile. "What am I to do with a crow? Put it in a pie with Jamette's vole? Besides," I add in a bored voice, "it is wounded, or deranged. No healthy crow would hover this close to falcons. And see how it holds its wing? Leave it be. Or," I say, smiling in open challenge, "better yet, do try to catch it. That way I can beat you back to the castle."

With that challenge thrown down, I put my heels to my horse and fly forward. A split second later, the others follow.

I even let Julian win.

When we reach the castle, I hand my falcon to the waiting groom, then dismount. My gaze scans the horizon for the crow, half fearing he will land on my shoulder in front of everyone. I must think of a way to get the message without half the castle seeing.

Jamette lingers near the stable, still trying to flirt with Julian, and Tephanie is nowhere to be seen. Perhaps I can steal a few moments in my room alone and coax the wretched creature to the window long enough to remove the message he carries. Leaving the others to their own amusements, I quit the courtyard and enter the palace, then head for the stairs.

No one follows. My luck holds, and when I reach my chamber, it is empty. I head straight for the window and open the casement—but there is no sign of the crow. I wait a few more moments, willing him to find me, then huff out a sigh of frustration. Just as I am about to close the window, I hear a caw and see a flap of black wings. But too late. I can hear Jamette and Tephanie at the chamber door. I slam the window shut and close the thick velvet curtains.

"What are you doing?" Jamette asks as she comes into the room. "Now it is too dark in here."

I put my hand to my temple. "I have a headache," I say crossly.

A look of genuine concern appears on Tephanie's round face as she hurries over to my side. "Shall I fetch a tisane? Or lavender water?"

I *could* send them to fetch a tisane or hot wine, but that requires only one of them. Besides, Jamette will just linger in the hallway with her large ear stuck to the wall.

"You were fine but moments ago," she points out.

I spear Jamette with a vicious look. "Was I really, Jamette? Were you paying close enough attention to know that?"

She flushes at this reminder of just how poorly she has attended me. Then I make a decision. "I am going outside."

Jamette gapes at me. "But you have a headache!"

"Indeed I do. I believe it is your screeching voice and the vile perfume you favor, which is why I need fresh air."

Her mouth closes with a snap, and I feel the smallest tweak of conscience, for her scent is fine. And then I remember that she reports every move of mine to my father, and my regret evaporates.

Outside, the day has grown blustery, the wind proving that February is indeed the whirling month. Just like the leaves and twigs that dance in eddies across the courtyard, hope dances deep inside me. Perhaps d'Albret is marqued in such a way that I cannot see it but Sister Vereda with her seeress skills *can*. The thought of finally being able to move against him fills me with a dark joy. If I am at last able to kill him, the duchess and kingdom will be safe from his grasping ambition and brutal ways. Perhaps I can even arrange for my sisters to come finish their schooling at the convent. Not to train them in the killing arts, but because most of what the nuns teach us is much like the education that any noblewoman receives. Then my sisters would be safe even from Pierre and Julian. Although I do not think Julian would ever hurt them. At least not intentionally.

The gardens are deserted, since no one else is fool enough to venture out to this raw, barren spot. I take a slow breath and revel in the solitude. I am forever attended by someone — my ladies in waiting, my brothers, the various hangers-on of my father's court — and I crave solitude. That and freedom. I glance overhead and try to recapture that soaring feeling I had when my falcon launched from my wrist, but I cannot.

Instead, an irritable caw brings me back to earth as Monsieur Crow lands on a branch before me, then cocks his head, as if wondering why I have taken so long.

"You're a fine one to talk," I scold him, but he knows I do not mean it and hops close. As I move toward the branch, I see that the note is wrapped tightly around his ankle and covered with black wax so that someone would have to be very close in order to see he bore a message.

I slip my knife from its sheath, and the bird gives a caw of objection. "I have no other way to get it off, you silly creature." A quick snip and a slice, then wax crumbles and I am able to unwind the note from his leg. As I shove it into the knife sheath at my wrist, the crow looks to me for a reward. "I have nothing for you today — I am sorry. Now go. Quickly! Before you get us both killed." I flap my hands at him and he hops but one bush away. "Hsst!" I say, and with a caw of reproach, he launches into the sky and disappears over the castle wall.

"Talking to the crows, my lady?"

Bertrand de Lur's deep voice nearly causes me to jump. Instead, I use the startled movement to swing gracefully around and face him.

"That will earn you a reputation of witchcraft," he says.

I tilt my head and smile mockingly at him. "Do they not say that already?"

He inclines his head, conceding the point. "Even so, it is not safe for you to be out here alone, my lady." While his voice is rich and cultivated, there is something about the way he says *my lady* that makes the words feel like a slur. Or perhaps it just seems that way because his lust is so thick it reaches out and enfolds me like a mantle. How long has he felt this way?

"Where are your attendants?" he asks, his voice hard.

Even though I do not care for Jamette, I cannot surrender her to the threat I see lurking in his eyes. "I ordered them from my side. I have a headache and wanted fresh air."

He glances around at the secluded section of garden, his eyes missing nothing. "I would think my lady's beauty would attract a nightingale or a linnet, not a bedraggled crow." He steps closer then, and for the first time I grow wary. Does he think me such damaged goods that he can take liberties without fear of reprisal from my father?

"It is not safe to be alone out here, not with all the men-at-arms we have posted. Any one of them might come upon you and be moved to take advantage of your unattended solitude." He takes another step toward me.

Because I want to back away from him, I force myself to move forward until there is but a handbreadth between us. I gaze steadily into eyes. "Do you really think any of the men would be so foolish as to risk my father's wrath in such a way? Surely they would not wish to see their guts strung up from the castle walls?"

There is a long moment of silence, then finally he nods. "Your point is well taken, my lady. Come, I am to escort you to your lord father."

A cold trickle of fear slides into my belly. "Did my lord father say what he wished of me?" I hate myself for asking, for it shows my weakness, but I cannot help it. It is never wise to wander into d'Albret's lair unprepared.

"He did not share his purpose with me, no."

But he knows. I can see that knowledge in his eyes, and he looks for all the world as if he is gloating. I remember the convent's order concealed in my sheath and permit myself a small secret smile as he takes my arm and we begin walking back to the palace.

The trip to d'Albret's chambers lasts forever and puts me in mind of how a man approaching the gallows must feel. How long was de Lur watching me before he made his presence known? Did it appear to him as if I was just shooing away a crow, or feeding it, mayhap? Or did he see me take the message from the creature's leg?

And what of d'Albret? Has he found some reason to tie me to the duchess's escape? I was so careful. So very, very careful. I must continue to do everything in my power to assure him that I am committed to his cause so that he does not have his guard up when I am at last able to act. To force my mind away from its ceaseless worry, I anticipate all the ways I could kill d'Albret. It would be so satisfying to choke the life from him with a garrote around his fat neck. Or fillet his big white belly like a fish. But there is danger in those methods, for they require I get close to him, and he has uncanny strength and could possibly overpower me. Poison or a crossbow would be safest.

Too soon, we reach our destination, and Captain de Lur announces my arrival. Holding my head high and willing my heart to stop its wild, erratic beating, I step into the room.

Chapter Six

SUCH IS THE FORCE OF d'Albret's presence that he's managed to taint even the rich opulence of Duke Francis's elegant palace. Everything, from the frescoes on the walls to the carved stag heads bursting from the overmantels, looks morbid and faintly threatening.

I sink into a deep curtsy. "My lord father, how may I serve you?" Because showing too much humility and blind obedience would ring false, I raise my eyes and allow them to fill with just a hint of mockery as they meet his cold, flat gaze.

"My prodigal daughter has deigned to pay me a visit. Where was she?" d'Albret asks the captain, his eyes never leaving mine.

"In the garden, talking to a crow."

D'Albret arches one heavy black eyebrow, and I shrug as if mildly embarrassed. "My time at the convent of Saint Brigantia has given me an appreciation for wild things, my lord." For that is the lie the abbess and I concocted to explain my long absence from d'Albret's household: that I had retreated to the sisters of Brigantia for healing and training.

D'Albret snorts in disgust. "They have made you soft." He turns to one of the guards at the door. "Go see if you can find this crow and catch it. Perhaps I will feed it to her for her supper." A faint flutter of dismay moves in my breast, but hopefully the foolish bird will be long gone by now. If I am forced to eat my crow, of a surety I will spew it back up, and I will be certain to do so on d'Albret's fine cordwain boots. The thought of that gives me some small measure of courage, and I am able to meet his gaze with true amusement in my own.

The guard bows once, then departs. "Search her," d'Albret orders de Lur.

The captain glances uncertainly at d'Albret. At the count's nod, de Lur slowly smiles, then moves to stand in front of me. The smirking pig puts his hands on my shoulders and then draws them down my arms, feeling every inch of my skin beneath the fabric of my sleeves.

I refuse to give him the satisfaction of shuddering at his touch. Instead, I amuse myself by wondering if de Lur will try to stop me from fulfilling the convent's order to kill d'Albret. If he does, I may have to kill him as well.

When his hand connects with the sheath strapped to my left wrist, his eyebrows shoot up in surprise. "What is this?"

"'Tis but my knife, my lord. You would not expect a d'Albret to wander about unarmed?"

He starts to peel back my sleeve. "Careful," I warn him. "The edge is most sharp."

That gives him a moment's pause. While he is still trying to decide if I have threatened him, I reach for my knife. As my fingers close around the handle, I carefully slip the tiny, rolled note against my palm before unsheathing the blade.

He glances warily at the sharp edge, then stuffs two fingers into the leather sheath at my wrist and begins poking around. I cast an annoyed look at d'Albret. "Is it seemly for him to enjoy it this much?"

"I told you to search her, not make love to her," d'Albret says. "How would you like it if I did such to your daughter, eh?" The threat is unmistakable, and de Lur's movements become much more circumspect.

However, when he reaches my buttocks, he cannot resist giving my cheeks a faint pinch. That is when I realize I am still holding my knife, and it is all I can do not to plunge it into his gut. Instead, I move my hand as if to return the knife to its sheath, but I do not pull the blade back quite far enough. The point of it rakes across his cheek.

He swears and shoves me away as he puts his hand to his face.

"I *did* warn you that it was sharp."

His nostrils flare in fury, and he glances at d'Albret. "She carries nothing," he says, "but a small dagger and an even smaller heart."

I smile as if his words have pleased me greatly. D'Albret waves for him to step back. "You will be happy to know I have found a use for you at last, daughter."

My heart gives one slow beat of dread, for I know d'Albret believes women have but two purposes: to bear him sons and to slake his lust. With his own daughters, he begrudgingly allows a third: to be used as a bargaining piece in marriages that will increase his wealth and power.

It is the note from the convent that gives me the courage to lift my chin and smile sweetly at him. "I can think of nothing that would bring me greater pleasure, my lord, than to be of service to you."

"I have yet to discover who betrayed our plans to the duchess and gave her warning. I wish to watch the Nantes barons more closely. Perhaps one of them pretends loyalty to me and then reports all my plans to her. With this suspicion in mind, you will become intimately acquainted with Baron Mathurin."

I keep my face perfectly still. This is a new low, even for him—whoring his own daughter out for political gain. "The fat one with the double chins? I am not certain that we must become *intimate* in order for me to coax his secrets from him," I say lightly.

D'Albret leans forward, his black beard bristling. "You are refusing?"

"Of course not." My heart beats faster now, for I am well aware of what happens to those who refuse him.

D'Albret cocks his head to the side. "Do not tell me you have maidenly qualms, for we all know what a lie that is."

His words are like a slap to my face and send me reeling down a long, painful corridor of memories. Memories so terrifying that my vision darkens before my mind scrambles away from them. "I am merely pointing out that there are many methods available to extract the information you wish to have."

Satisfied with my answer, he leans back in his chair. "You will sit next to him at dinner."

Before he can give me further instructions, his steward arrives, escorting a road-weary and travel-stained courier. D'Albret waves his hand at the captain and me. "Leave us," he orders, and Captain de Lur escorts me from the room.

Despair and frustration threaten to rise up inside me, but I tamp them down. Even though d'Albret is all but announcing to his men and vassals that I am so sullied that I do not warrant his protection, I need not panic just yet. I place my hand over my wrist sheath, drawing comfort from what hides there, and hurry to my rooms.

I arrive at my chamber, where Tephanie and Jamette fuss and cluck and are horribly relieved to see me. Irrationally, I blame them for what has befallen me this afternoon. "Draw a bath, at once," I order curtly.

As they begin that task, I slip into the garderobe and remove the note from its hiding place. My hand trembles as I unroll the message, careful to hold it over the privy hole so that no traces of black wax can be found and used as evidence against me. I hope that these are the instructions I have longed for. Of course the note is in cipher. Holding back my impatience, I quickly count out the necessary sequence, but I have no ink or parchment, so it takes me far too long to decipher the message.

"My lady? Your bath is ready. Are you ill?"

"I am fine," I snap at Tephanie's worried question. "Except I cannot find privacy."

"I beg your pardon, my lady," she says meekly, and I turn back to the note.

> *Dearest daughter,*
>
> *We believe that Lord d'Albret has taken Baron de Waroch prisoner. The duchess has great need of the Beast of Waroch if she is to have any hope of raising an army against d'Albret or the French. We thereby order you to determine if he is indeed alive and, if so, to find a way to secure his release and see that he is brought to Rennes immediately.*
>
> *Abbess Etienne de Froissard*

Disbelief roils inside me, and my entire body turns hot, then cold, then hot again. I turn the note over, hoping I have missed something, then rework the code one more time. The message is the same. And it is not an order to kill d'Albret.

Anger rises up, so great it sears the breath from my lungs. She *promised* that I would be an instrument of divine vengeance—that d'Albret's retribution would be delivered at the hand of his own daughter.

That very promise kept me from laughing in the abbess's face when she told me of her intentions to send me back to his household. That promise had me redoubling my efforts to learn as many death skills as I could in my last weeks of training before I left the convent.

But more than that, her promise had given meaning to all that I have suffered and endured. Without that divine purpose to shape my life, I am nothing but a hapless victim. The anger inside surges through me once more, so dark and overwhelming I fear I will suffocate under its weight.

I will quit the convent. She cannot force me to stay here. Tucked far away on her little island, she will not even know I have left.

But d'Albret will.

And no place is safe from him, for his arm is long and he could snatch me up from anywhere in Brittany or France. No place is safe, except perhaps behind the walls of Rennes, and not even there if d'Albret decides to move on the city.

And so I must sit like a brainless coney. My future stretches out before me, grim and endless. I have been fooled by the convent and am now to be whored out by d'Albret as he weaves his malevolent snares for his enemies.

No. I clench my fists, crumpling the note and then casting it into the privy. *No.*

When I emerge from the garderobe, I ignore my attendants' worried glances and yank off my clothes before they can assist me. I spend the next hour scrubbing my father's and the abbess's filthy schemes from my skin.

I do not know how I will make it through dinner. I cannot help but wonder how many know of the role d'Albret has given me. Nor can I help but wonder whom he will assign me to next. That fool Marshal Rieux? The quiet and serious Rogier Blaine?

As soon as I step into the dining hall, d'Albret's gaze is upon me — as cold and dead as the meat on his plate. I keep my head held high and chatter inanely with Tephanie as I approach the dais, then curtsy. My smile is as brittle as glass — and as fragile. But lost in his own dark mood, he waves me toward Baron Mathurin.

As I make my way to the table, I wonder: How does one kill a monster such as d'Albret, someone with nearly inhuman strength and cunning? Can it even be done if the god of Death Himself does not will it?

How could I get near him? Get him to lower his guard? Especially when I cannot—*will* not—use seduction, one of my most effective weapons.

As I take my seat beside the baron, his eyes light up. "Fortune smiles upon me, demoiselle. To what do I owe the honor of your fair company?"

I want to shake him and warn him that it is not an honor but a deathwatch. Instead, I smile coyly at him. "It is I who am fortunate, my lord," I tell him, then lift my wine goblet and drain half of it. Hopefully his attention will remain so focused on my breasts that he will not notice I must drink myself under the table to endure his company.

"Have you recovered from today's hunt?" he asks.

The question nearly causes me to sputter. "Recovered, my lord?" It takes all my willpower to keep the scorn from my voice. "A hunt is not so very taxing as all that."

He shrugs. "It was for Barons Vienne and Julliers. They have excused themselves from dinner tonight and taken to their beds."

"Well, I am not as soft as they."

"Nor I," he says. "Indeed, the afternoon has got my blood stirred," he adds, and there is no mistaking his meaning. Well and good—I will not even have to try very hard to snare this dumb goose.

A trill of laughter pulls my attention to the other side of the table, where Jamette hangs on Julian like a flea on a hound. Feeling my gaze on him, Julian looks up, and our eyes meet. He gives me a mocking smile and lifts his goblet to me. Does he know? I wonder. Does he know what our father has asked me to do? He must suspect something, for he knows I have no love for puffed-up buffoons or jackanapes such as Mathurin.

Jamette notices he is no longer paying attention to her and follows his gaze. Her eyes narrow and it is then that I see she is wearing a new brooch, a gold sunburst with a ruby in its center, and I wonder which secret of mine she has shared to earn it.

Chapter Seven

I HAVE DECIDED I WILL keep my rendezvous with Mathurin. I will even play the part I have been given—up to a point. Then, when I've learned all that I can, I will put a stop to it. If he protests overmuch or thinks to force me to continue, so much the better, for then I can kill him in self-defense. I am in desperate need of killing *something*.

When I reach the appointed chamber, I stop long enough to tug the bodice of my gown lower and loosen my hair. The overly eager Baron Mathurin is already inside, his pulse beating so heavily with lust I can scarce hear myself think. "Did anyone see you?" he asks when I step inside the room.

"No," I assure him, then move closer, shaking my loose hair over my shoulder. He reaches out to capture one of the curls. "Like ebony-colored silk," he murmurs, rubbing it between his fingers.

His desire is a heady perfume, for I know precisely what to do with desire. I run a finger lightly along the front of his doublet, and his mouth parts, his breath hitching in his throat. Then I wrap my arms around him and begin playing with the hair at the nape of his neck. "I bet you say that to all your conquests."

He blinks in surprise, as if no one has ever accused him of having a string of conquests before. I lean up and begin nuzzling his great white jowl. "Do you know what put my lord father in such a foul mood tonight?" I ask. "He was in high spirits when I saw him this afternoon."

And even though the baron and I are alone, his eyes dart around the room before he answers. He is not quite as dumb as he appears. "He received word that the duchess was crowned today in Rennes."

Although this is good news for the duchess, I fear the crown will not save her from d'Albret's aggression. The only thing that will do that is a strong husband with an army of thousands to defend his claim. I wonder if the courier who brought this report yet lives, for my lord father does not believe in sparing the messenger. "Do you trust d'Albret to rule Brittany?" I ask, then shudder. "For he frightens me well enough with the power he has. I cannot imagine him in charge of the entire duchy."

As I utter these words, I can feel Mathurin's desire begin to shrivel, so I quickly change the subject to distract him. "We do not have much time before my attendants come looking for me."

This spurs him to action, and he unlaces his doublet, then his fine linen shirt below. When I see a dark shadow covering his chest, my heart soars. He is marqued! That makes everything so much simpler. I smile then, the first true smile that has touched my lips all day, and step closer, backing him up to the wall so I will not have to take the full weight of his body when I kill him.

But before I can do more than remove the knife hidden in my sleeve, he gasps, a puzzled, almost hurt look crossing his face.

"What? What is wrong?" I murmur, not wishing to break the mood.

He does not answer; instead, he reaches up to his chest as if it pains him, then blood appears on his lips. Sweet Mortain! Is he having a fit of some sort?

Like a hanged man cut down from a gibbet, he collapses, all his weight slumping onto me so that I nearly topple backwards. A great, dark flapping thing rises from him.

It is the part I hate most about killing, having to endure the forced intimacy of the victim's soul touching mine as it leaves their body. It is just as shocking and unwanted as my first kiss. I steel myself and allow the rush of images to wash over me: D'Albret's thick arm around the baron's shoulders, lulling him into a misplaced sense of security. A feeling of smugness, that I had chosen him rather than Julliers or Vienne. And hidden deepest of all, a twinge of conscience at having betrayed the young duchess, well buried under false assurances that d'Albret would make her a good husband.

Suddenly, the baron's lifeless body is thrust aside, and I come face to face with a tall, dark figure holding a sword that still drips with blood.

"Julian!" I whisper, shocked to my core.

He steps forward, his mouth set in hard lines, his face cast in shadow. "Have you forgotten, sister? You are *mine*."

His words chill me to the bone, and I fold my arms across my middle and grip my elbows to keep my hands from shaking.

"Only mine," he says softly, as if whispering a lover's endearment. "No one shall put his slobbering mouth or groping hands upon you." He looks down at the body and nudges it with his boot. "And certainly not this craven creature."

Now I understand the look he sent me at dinner. It was a promise of reprisal.

I step quickly and easily into the role I must play. Indeed, I am as skilled as any alchemist, but instead of turning lead into gold, I turn my fear into daring, and assuredly that is a far greater trick. The smile I give him is brittle with annoyance, and I toss my hair for full effect. "Is that what you thought was happening, Julian? Can you truly know me as well as you claim?"

The banked fury inside him cools somewhat. "Then why are you here?"

Has he not heard? I tilt my head. "Our father assigned me to use my feminine wiles to ascertain if Mathurin planned to betray him to the French."

A muscle in his jaw clenches. "And would you have gone through with it?"

In answer, I raise the knife that I hold in my hand.

His eyes burn intently into mine, as if he can scorch the truth from their depths. "Truly?"

I laugh. I cannot help it. "You think I *wished* to dally with that soft, thick goose? Julian, have a little faith. In my taste if not in me."

He drops his sword on the floor, steps over the body, and grabs my shoulders. My heart slams against my ribs as he spins me around and backs me against the wall. He leans in close. "Do you swear it?"

My heart beats too fast—he must not smell that fear. I take that fear and use it to stoke the fires of my anger. I push him—hard. "You are acting the fool. I swear it on God and all nine of His saints. Now let go, you're hurting me."

Like quicksilver, his mood shifts. He snatches my free hand and brings it to his mouth. "I should not have doubted you." His breath warm against my skin, he turns my hand over and presses his mouth to my wrist.

"No, you should not have." I tug at my hand, relieved when he lets it go. To be certain he does not grab it again, I begin re-coiling my hair into place. "How will I explain this to Father?"

Julian shifts his gaze to the dead Mathurin. "We shall say he was guilty, just as Father suspected, and you caught him in the act. You had no choice but to kill him before he got another message to the duchess."

"*Another* message?"

Julian's eyes are unreadable. "Of course—for you learned that it was he who warned the duchess of our failed trap."

Reluctantly, I admire how nimbly Julian has used this to our advantage. To *my* advantage, for once again, he has found a way to protect me from d'Albret's wrath. But this presents a new danger as well, for I must now assume Julian suspects it was I who issued that warning.

"I will take care of the body," he adds.

I arch a brow at him and sniff. "It is the least you owe me for your lack of faith in me."

He grabs my hands. "A kiss," he begs, "to prove that you are not angry with me."

I consider refusing, but I am a coward and dare not, not when he may know so many of my most dangerous secrets. Dread hammers through my veins as he leans down and places his mouth on mine. I allow my mind to drift away from my body, much like Mathurin's soul left his. It is the only way I can bear Julian's touch.

He is not my brother, he is not my brother.

That is another reason I cling so fiercely to my tattered belief in Mortain. If He is indeed my father, then Julian and I do not share so much as a drop of blood.

Julian sends me back to my room while he stays to clean up his mess. I move stiffly, like a puppet on a string, feeling as hollow and gutted as the fish we had for supper.

When I finally reach my chamber, it is empty except for a scullery maid, who is building up the fire for the night. She sees me and scurries away, afraid one glance from me will turn her into a toad, or that I will strike her for daring to breathe the same air as I.

Servants of my father have been punished for less.

I go immediately to the comfort of the bright yellow flames and stand as close to their warmth as I dare. My hands are trembling, my very bones shivering, and every fiber of my being is screaming for me to flee.

I think of the rush of Mathurin's soul as it left his body. I want—crave—that release for myself with a longing so deep, and sharp, it cuts like a blade. I remember standing atop the battlements and feeling a heady sense of freedom as the wind promised to carry me far, far away. Is that what souls feel when they are released from their earthly bodies?

Tephanie comes in just then, her big awkward feet shuffling along the floor. She curtsies hurriedly, then rushes to my side. "My lady! I am so sorry to have left you alone. I thought you were . . ." She waves her hand inelegantly.

I am too weary and heartsick to even pretend to snap at her. "See that it does not happen again," I say tiredly.

Her brow creases with worry. "Yes, my lady," she says. "Are you ill?"

"No, just tired."

"But you are shivering! Here, let me fetch you something hot to drink."

I allow her to fuss over me, and once she has handed me a goblet, she goes to turn down the coverlet on the bed and warm the sheets.

As she shuffles quietly about the room, I stand near the fireplace and gulp my wine, waiting for the trembling to pass. I wish, desperately, to take a bath, but it is far too late and would call too much attention to myself. Even so, between Mathurin's blood and Julian's kiss, I feel tainted beyond bearing.

"My lady?"

When I look up, Tephanie is holding out my chamber robe. "Shall I help you undress?"

"If you please."

Her hands are gentle as she helps me out of my clothes. Unlike Jamette, she knows how to keep silent, and I find the quiet of her company soothing. As she puts away my gown, I take the cup of wine over to my small jeweled casket and open it. After setting the goblet down,

I remove a small crystal vial from the box. It is a sleeping draft Sister Serafina gave me as a parting gift when I left the convent. She did not say so, but I could see she was unhappy with the abbess for sending me out so soon and knew I would need help if I were to sleep at all.

For a brief moment, I consider dumping the entire contents into my wine. If I drink all of it, I will never wake up. The thought of going to sleep and never having to deal with d'Albret or the abbess or Julian again is as seductive as a siren's song.

But what if Death rejects me once more? Then I will be forced to lie, weak and vulnerable, at the mercy of others while I recover. A most terrifying thought.

Besides, what if the knight truly is alive—what will become of him if I am dead? I slip two drops into my wine, return the vial to the box, and lock it.

Even more important, if I am dead, who will kill d'Albret? For he must die, marque or no.

Tephanie has finished warming the bed and comes to unpin my hair. She begins combing it out with a surprisingly light touch, given how clumsy and awkward she is. I close my eyes and let the gentle strokes calm some of the fear from me. Her ministrations remind me of how Ismae and Annith and I used to take turns combing and dressing one another's hair at the convent. Sweet Mortain, how I miss them.

Abruptly, I turn around. "You will sleep in here tonight," I tell her.

She stops what she is doing and looks at me in surprise. "My lady?"

I cannot tell her that I need her, that I wish her company, so instead I say, "I am not feeling well and may require someone to attend me during the night."

She looks stunned, but pleased. The ninny thinks this is some great honor, not the desperate act of a coward, and I do not disabuse her of that notion.

* * *

That night, when Julian comes scratching at my door, Tephanie gets up to see who it is. I do not hear what she says, as my head is groggy from Sister Serafina's potion, but her presence is enough to drive him away. She returns to the bed and crawls back under the covers. "Your brother wished to see how you were doing. He said you had a headache at dinner and he wanted to be sure it was gone."

"It is," I say, and scoot over so she may have the warmest spot. She deserves that much, at least, for chasing off the monsters.

Chapter Eight

WHEN I COME AWAKE IN the morning, my first thought is of the knight the abbess wishes me to free. His anguished bellow of defeat as he was struck down haunted my dreams.

Even at the convent, we had heard of the mighty Beast of Waroch and of how his ability to rally his countrymen—noblemen and peasant alike—to the duke's cause allowed us to win our past three battles.

As I listen to Tephanie's gentle snoring, I wonder why the fallen knight has so captured my imagination. Was it because he fought so valiantly against such overwhelming odds? Because of his dedication to his young duchess? Or simply because I looked into his eyes just before he died?

For he *is* dead. I saw him struck down with my own . . . ah, but Julian arrived just then. I never saw the knight's lifeless body. And it is said that men in the throes of battle lust can suffer much damage, yet live.

When I went to bed last night, I vowed to ignore the abbess's message. But now, now all I can think of is that noble knight rotting—or worse—in d'Albret's dungeon.

I place one of my cold feet on Tephanie and she stirs at last—the great slug. She blinks twice to clear the confusion from her eyes, then remembers where she is and with whom. "My lady! I beg your forgiveness. I have overslept."

"Did you know that you snore?" I say, amused at the bright spots of red that stain her cheeks.

She looks away. "I am sorry—you should have shoved me from the bed or awakened me in some fashion."

"I did not say it disturbed me, only that you did it."

She does not know what to say to this, so she leaps out of bed, curtsies, then hurries to fetch my chamber robe.

Just as she is about to help me into it, Jamette enters the room babbling like a brook. "Barons Vienne and Julliers were found dead in their chambers this morning—" Her mouth snaps shut when she finds us standing together in nothing but our shifts.

She blinks, her mouth opening then closing as she searches for something to say. Because she annoys me so very much, I reach out, place a finger under Tephanie's chin, and turn her head gently toward me. "Thank you, Tephanie," I say. "For everything." Tephanie's cheeks turn a dull red, and I almost laugh and spoil the effect I have so carefully created.

Poor Jamette cannot decide if she is shocked or jealous. "So, who are these barons whose chambers you visited last night?" I ask languorously.

"Not me," she snaps. "It was the servants who reported they died of the plague in their sleep."

"Could you bring the water? I'd like to wash now," I say with a sleepy yawn.

"Do you think we will catch it?" Tephanie asks. "The plague, I mean?"

The look Jamette sends Tephanie is so full of venom I am surprised the other girl does not wilt on the spot. She does look acutely embarrassed, however, and hurries away to finish dressing in the privacy of the garderobe.

Jamette's temper makes her careless, and she splashes water everywhere. "Watch what you are doing," I warn her. "Else I will have you clean it up with that sharp tongue of yours."

Our eyes meet, and I can see all the insults and accusations she wishes to hurl at me. Instead of saying them, she mutters to herself, "At least now I know why she ignores the few men who cast their attention her way."

I run my finger along Jamette's arm. "Do not tell me you are jealous, little one?" I have found an entirely new way to get under Jamette's skin and anticipate hours of fine sport.

She pulls her arm away. "Of course not!" She turns and moves across the room to the clothespress. "Which gown do you want today?"

"The dark gray satin with the black underskirt."

She helps me dress, but her movements are stiff, and she touches me as little as possible. When she laces up my bodice, she pulls so hard she nearly cracks my ribs.

I jerk away and grab her hand. "Careful. Your duties are to attend me, not cause me bodily damage."

She glares at me, and I can feel her temper humming in her veins. Tephanie chooses that moment to come stumbling back into the room, slipping her belt into place and affixing to it the small knife I gave her.

"Enough of this," I say. "I have in mind something more entertaining for us this morning." D'Albret and most of the garrison plan to go to Ancenis today to take back Marshal Rieux's holding from the French. Which means it is a perfect day for ferreting out secrets. "Where did you say the sounds of ghosts were coming from? I would like to hear them for myself."

For while ghosts do not make noise, prisoners do.

It turns out that the ghosts are rumored to haunt the old tower, the very place from which I watched the battle. It is also the most logical place to keep a prisoner, since it is well away from the living quarters and the high-traffic areas of the castle.

Neither of my attendants wishes to come face to face with ghosts and they both decide to wait for me in the chapel right next to the tower and pray for the newly dead barons. That suits my purposes perfectly, as I would much rather do my snooping away from their prying eyes.

The old tower was built nearly two hundred years ago. The stones are roughened with age, and the tower roof is in need of repair. I try the heavy wooden door and find it locked.

My heart quickens in excitement, for it was not locked when I was last here.

There is no guard posted so I peer through one of the arrow slits cut into the thick walls. The tower *is* haunted; I can feel the ghosts' chill presence seeping out from the window—but ghosts do not clank, or make any sound at all.

I glance over my shoulder at the courtyard. There are just enough servants and men-at-arms about that I do not dare pick the lock.

Ignoring the ghostly chill, I search for some sense of a heartbeat within, but try as hard as I might, my power to detect such things cannot penetrate twelve feet of thick stone. I climb the winding, external staircase to the catwalk, then stand on tiptoe to peer in through another arrow slit.

The small shaft of light barely touches the gloom. I do not see anyone. No guard, no prisoner, no signs of life.

But wait. Some faint hint of sound wafts up—as if from the bowels of the earth itself—followed by a groan. Or a whisper. Or mayhap it is the wind. But since it is all I have to go on, I call it moaning. And even though it is so very little, it heartens me. I will have to find a way to pick the lock or steal the key when my actions can be hidden by darkness. The task is still impossible—but if I must sit here and do nothing while waiting for orders that are not coming, I shall no doubt go mad. Again.

Besides, I would like to think I am capable of doing something other than killing and acting the whore.

When I return to the chapel to collect the others, I find Tephanie alone, kneeling before the nave. Under the crucifix at the front of the church are nine small niches, each holding an image of one of the nine old saints: Saint Mortain; Dea Matrona and her daughters, Amourna and Arduinna; Saint Mer; Saint Camulos; Saint Cissonius; and, one of my personal favorites, Saint Salonius, the patron saint of mistakes.

I briefly wonder if I should leave an offering for Mortain. Does He suspect that my belief is a shallow thing? A small, flimsy protection against the more terrifying idea that He does not exist at all? What would I ask of Him, anyway?

Deliverance. That is what I would pray for.

Dear Mortain, please deliver me from this dark nightmare from which I can find no escape.

And then I snort, startling poor Tephanie. I have uttered that very prayer for nearly six long months, and look what it has gotten me. No, the truth is, Mortain has forsaken me. Either that or He does not exist.

But if that is the case, then d'Albret is my father. It is more comforting to think that Mortain has forsaken me.

Chapter Nine

WITH ALL THE MEN OFF harrying the French at Ancenis, the ladies of d'Albret's household take dinner in the winter parlor instead of the great hall. It is a smaller room, and more intimate. And considerably warmer.

Madame Dinan takes great pride in her role as chatelaine, standing at the head of the table and waiting for everyone to arrive. That I am nearly late earns me a scowl of disapproval, but I pay no attention to that. Instead, my gaze falls on the thick ring of keys she wears at her waist.

D'Albret's keys.

I tear my eyes away before she can notice my interest and spend the rest of dinner gossiping with the other ladies. But throughout the entire meal, my thoughts keep returning to those keys and how very much easier it would be to conduct my search of the tower before d'Albret's return.

I wait a full hour for everyone to be abed. While I wait, I open my jeweled casket where I keep the few items I brought with me from the convent. Sister Serafina saw to it that I had a decent supply of poison, all of it artfully disguised. There is a crystal vial that contains what looks like the same belladonna that all the women use to make their eyes lustrous, but mine is far more potent. I have a small gold box filled with arsenic powder, and a jar of Saint Arduinna's snare disguised as a salve for burns. There is also a hairnet spun of gold and decorated with dozens of white pearls, each one filled with a poison called vengeance.

I remove a paper twist filled with the fine white powder Sister Serafina calls night whispers. A full packet is enough to kill a large man. Half of that will put a woman down. Only a pinch is required to assure that Madame Dinan sleeps through the night.

I tuck the small packet into the knife sheath I wear at my wrist, then hunt for the boots that the convent had made especially for me. They are of the softest leather and allow me to move as silently as a shadow. I leave the safety of my room and head for Madame Dinan's chamber.

Once, when I was ten years old, d'Albret became so enraged at his favorite hunting hound for not bringing down a twelve-point stag that he shot the creature with his hunting bow. After a brief yelp of pain, the loyal beast began dragging himself toward d'Albret, the arrow embedded in his hindquarters, whining softly in his throat and begging forgiveness. D'Albret finally relented and delivered a second shot that put him out of his misery.

With disgust, I realize that I am precisely like that hound: even when the convent has wounded me deeply, I still doggedly do the sisters' bidding.

No, I remind myself. I am doing this not for the convent, but for the knight. The man's loyalty and determination in the face of such overwhelming odds is the most noble thing I have ever seen. If he lives, he deserves a much better fate than the one he will find in d'Albret's dungeon.

When I reach Dinan's room, I pause and put my ear to the door, relieved to hear only one pulse beating inside.

The hinges are well oiled and make no noise as I open the door. Once inside, I creep across the floor to the bed and carefully ease the thick velvet curtains apart. When Madame Dinan does not so much as stir, I take the twist of paper from its hiding place, remove a pinch of the night whispers, and silently blow it at her face. Moving quickly so I do not breathe any of the deadly powder, I yank the bed curtains shut.

The next few moments drag by, as there is nothing to do but stand there and wait for the poison to take effect. Eventually her breathing grows deeper. When she begins to snore faintly, I know the powder has done its work.

Next I go to the windows and part the thick drapes to let in just enough moonlight to illuminate my search. Luckily, d'Albret's keys are not hidden but sit in plain sight on a small carved table near the bed. It would be quickest to take the entire ring, but I do not know what I shall find or how long I will be. Smarter to take only the key I need in case she wakes before I return.

Keeping the keys pressed against my palm so they do not rattle or clank, I search for the most likely one. Nearly all of the keys are shiny and new, like the palace itself, but there is one that is old and made of iron. It is larger than the others and coated in rust that looks like dark blood in the moonlight. Certain it is the key I seek, I remove it, then set the others back on the table. I return to the window, close the curtains so the room is once more in full darkness, and quit the chamber.

I move lightly, almost holding my breath, as I creep down the hallway and descend the stairs to the main floor. I do not allow myself a sigh of relief until I have reached the door that leads to the courtyard. Even then, I force myself to wait long, precious minutes so I can be certain no guards are patrolling at regular intervals. Only then do I step outside.

Silence fills the courtyard like a thick wine fills a cup, and the white stone of the palace walls glow eerily in the moonlight. I dart forward, skirting the large staircase and cursing all that whiteness that casts my dark figure in harsh relief. My blood thrums through my veins and every muscle in my body is taut with nerves. The urgent need for caution tingles on the back of my tongue, as if I have drunk some brew of bubbling silver.

But in the end, there is nothing to fear. Nearly all the soldiers have gone with d'Albret to Ancenis, and all the servants have been so thoroughly terrorized that there is little need for guards or sentries.

When I reach the tower door, there is a cold, dark fluttering sensation, as if I have disturbed a nest of unseen bats, but the flutterings are too big—and too cold—for something as alive as bats, and too silent for owls. Their cold seeps into me and the chill of them causes my hand to shake so much that it takes me three tries before I am able to fit the key into the lock.

The door hinges, which should creak with age and rust, are as silent as moth wings. I slip inside and shut the door behind me.

In the faint moonlight shining in through the arrow slit, the dark shadows flutter and float gently through the air. Those that are not huddling next to me are drifting downward. Down it is, then, for ghosts are ever attracted to the warmth and comfort of life.

The stairs descend in a tight circle, and I put my hands on the wall to guide me. It would not do to fall and break my neck. The stone is rougher here and wet with dampness from the nearby river, the steps crumbled slightly with age.

At the foot of the stairs is another locked door. *Merde!* I should have brought all of the keys with me! But no, this key fits the second door as well. My teeth threaten to chatter and I pretend it is the chill and not my fear as I turn the key and slowly open the door.

It is the smell that reaches me first. A rank mixture of mold and mildew, old blood and human filth. I brace myself for the worst, but I find only an antechamber. On the far side is yet another door, this one with a high window covered in narrow iron bars. Faint light flickers from within. Quiet as one of the ghosts who trail after me, I cross the small space.

When I reach the third door, I press myself against the wall so I cannot be seen through the bars. I wait for a dozen heartbeats, but no one comes.

Slowly, with my heart hammering against my ribs, I inch to the grille and peer inside.

A lone torch casts a faint light into the dark chamber, and shadows bounce and flicker against the stone wall. Someone is moving about and making strange formless noises to himself. In truth, it looks like a small gnome or dwarf from a hearth tale, but then I see it is simply a man who is gnarled and bent over. At first I think he is chortling and dancing, and then I realize that he is lame in one leg and that is merely how he shuffles across the chamber. And the chortling is chewing—he is gnawing on a stale crust of bread. Disgusted, I tear my eyes from him and survey the rest of the room. An ale pot, a chamber pot, a wooden ledge for sleeping and sitting. And another be-damned door sits in the far wall.

I pull away, back against the wall once more. Is that all that is keeping this knight imprisoned? Four locked doors—at least two of which have the same key—and a decrepit old man? *Is the prisoner even still alive?* I wonder, and then I scoff at the stupidity of my own question. Of course he is still alive, for they would not set a guard—not even one such as the little gargoyle in there—to watch over a corpse.

Unless they wanted to be certain no one found out he was dead.

Holding my breath, I let my senses explore the locked room. I feel the twisted little man's heart beating strong and steady. Coming from beyond the door, fainter and slower, is the beat of a second pulse. The knight is alive, at least for now.

Almost as if he feels my mind searching out his, the prisoner groans.

The little guard shuffles over to the prisoner's door and makes some guttural noise through the grille. The prisoner groans louder, and the sound is followed by the rattle of heavy chains. He is manacled, then, and his chains are the origin of the rumors of ghosts.

I stay and watch for a while longer, trying to get a feel for the guard's rhythm: when he sleeps, and how deeply, and if he ever leaves. But he does not. He pisses in a pot in the far corner. There is a small pile of stores against the east wall, a keg of ale. He pauses to grunt at the prisoner now and then, but whether it is an encouragement or a taunt, I cannot tell. When I have tarried as long as I dare, I inch away from the door. It would not do to grow careless now and kick a stone or shuffle my feet. As I begin making my way up the stairs, I decide it has been a decent enough night's work. I know where the knight is, that he is alive, and how he is guarded.

What I do not know is how I will get him out of there without getting us both killed in the process.

Chapter Ten

WHEN I RETURN TO MY chamber, instead of crawling into bed, I go to the table and take two fat white candles from their holders. I shove one on the end of the poker near the fireplace, then hold the poker next to the flames. It is tricky, as I do not want the candle to drip away, only to soften enough that I can mold and shape it. When I judge it ready, I pull it from the heat. Working quickly before it cools, I shove the tower key into the soft wax, pushing so that it makes a deep impression. I soften the second candle in the same way, then press it down on top of the first.

Once that is done, I use a knife to whittle away all the extra wax so that my mold is as small as possible. I toss the shavings into the fire and hide the wax casting in one of my velvet jewelry pouches.

It is a long, tense walk back to Madame Dinan's chamber, but as I go, a plan begins to form, as fragile and tenuous as a spider's web.

I have followed the convent and Mortain's wishes so far, and it has brought nothing but tragedy. Even worse, d'Albret is still alive and spewing his evil across the land. It is long past time for me to fulfill the role the abbess had planned for me, with or without her orders. I will kill him, marque or no.

But I will attempt to free the prisoner first. If, as I suspect, he is too wounded and broken to make the trip to Rennes, I will grant him a small mercy and put him out of his misery, for certainly that is what I would wish for if it were me.

I will not even make him beg.

In the morning, I convince Tephanie and Jamette that we must go into town. I cannot march up to a blacksmith and demand he make me a key without raising a host of questions. So instead, I tell my attendants that I must find a silversmith to repair one of my favorite belts. Jamette wants to know why, if it is one of my favorites, she has never seen it before. Tephanie comes to my rescue. "Because it is broken, you ninny!" She is as excited as a young child at the thought of an outing and begins chattering about the monkey one of the soldiers saw in town.

Even though impatience makes me want to hurry, because of Jamette and our escort of guards, I force myself to browse the stalls. I stop to rub some bright red satin between my fingers and admire the thick rich nap in a piece of green velvet. Smelling money, the shopkeepers cluster around us like flies on a drop of honey. I flirt and pretend I am seriously considering a bolt of blue damask. All the while, Jamette watches me far too closely, as if memorizing every move I make, every word that comes from my lips. I half expect her to pull a scrap of parchment from her sleeve and begin making notes, and I have no doubt she would, if she could write.

At last we come to the street of silversmiths, the faint sound of the rapid tapping of their hammers as distinct as a hailstorm. I pretend to shop for a silver bauble, but I am actually searching for a smith who looks stouthearted and trustworthy and not inclined to run tattling to the castle in the hopes of currying favor with the new lord. I find just such a man — or so I hope — at the third shop we visit.

The silversmith puts down his hammer as we approach and comes forward with a bow. He is of middle years with a stolid face and strong hands that are roughened with a lifetime of scars from the hot metals he works with and silver dust is worked into the creases of his skin. A woman who has been sweeping the workroom — his wife, no doubt — hurries to join him.

As the smith draws closer, he glances at the men behind us. His look of pleasant greeting turns into one of guarded suspicion as he recognizes the standard and colors of the house of d'Albret emblazoned on our escorts' tabards. His wife nudges him with her elbow and keeps her pleasant smile firmly in place.

"How may we serve you, my lady?" The smith's cold, distant voice is at odds with his words.

"I have a belt that has broken a link, but it is of gold. Do you work in gold?"

"I do," he says slowly, as if reluctant to admit such a thing if it will cause me to tarry at his shop.

The woman is less reluctant. "Gold is too valuable to put on display, my lady, but my husband's skill is equal to any smith's in the city." The sure, quiet pride with which she says this moves me in some way I cannot explain.

The smith, however, sends her an aggrieved look, and that is when I know he wishes we would go elsewhere. Which makes him imminently suitable for the job I have in mind. "May I see the work, then?" I ask.

"Certainly, my lady. Let me fetch a tray."

I hold up a hand. "Wait. I wish to see the work area before I decide. I will not leave my valuables in a pigsty."

The good wife bristles at this, but opens the half door to the workroom and curtsies.

"I will be right back," I tell the others.

The smith and I move to the farthest workbench, and the wife excuses herself to fetch a tray of her husband's best work. I hand the man my belt. As his practiced eye and sure hands move over the piece, probing it for weak links or breaks, I maneuver myself so that I am standing with my body blocking what we are doing. The smith frowns up at me. "There is nothing wrong with—"

"Shhh," I say quietly. I step closer to him, as if I am looking at something he is showing me. "That is not my true commission for you. I have a key that needs copying." I slip the velvet pouch out of the larger purse at my belt and hand the small blocks of wax to him. Keeping one eye on me, he opens the pouch to see the impressions of the key. "My lady, I am no blacksmith—"

I smile and say sharply, "Do you not think I can read the sign above your shop? This key is a gift for someone. Someone *special.*" I smile coyly so that his mind goes precisely where I want it to. He frowns in disapproval and opens his mouth to refuse, but I pull a second, smaller pouch from my purse. "I will make the job—and your silence—worth your while."

Just then, his wife comes back with a tray of finely worked gold belts, circlets, intricately carved cups, and paternosters. When she sees the bag, her face lights up. I hand her the pouch before the smith can refuse the job, knowing that once she closes her hand around those coins, she, like any good housewife, will not let them go.

"Oh, and one other thing," I say, as if just remembering.

The smith looks at me, clearly vexed and wishing I would take myself far away from him and his shop. "I will be back in three hours for the . . . belt."

"My lady!" he protests. "That is not nearly enough time."

"Ah, but you will make the time, will you not?" Our gazes meet.

"But of course, my lady. I will make the time."

We spend the rest of the day wandering around the shops of Nantes. Jamette buys a rose-colored ribbon and a gold-braided cord for her hair, a cord I cannot help but daydream of strangling her with. Tephanie looks at everything with hungry eyes, like a starved child, and I end up buying her a pretty comb for her hair. I assure myself it is only to make Jamette jealous.

Three hours later, the bells of Nantes cathedral call everyone to afternoon prayers. Even Jamette has worn out her penchant for shopping, and the guards' eyes are rolling back in their heads from boredom, so we return to the silversmith's.

He and his wife are waiting for us, and the look she gives me now is full of censure and reserve. The smith says nothing, no doubt counting the minutes until he can be rid of me. Once again, I am careful to stand with my body blocking the view of his workbench. "Is my belt ready?" I ask in a bright voice.

"Just as you asked, my lady." He gives me the small velvet pouch at the same time he gives me the belt. The pouch is still warm from the hot metal of the newly made key. As I take them from his hand, my fingers grasp his. I pause. "If you speak of this to anyone, my life — and yours — will not be worth the ashes in your hearth."

His eyes meet mine and then turn away. "And well I know it," he mutters. "For that is no bedroom key." He starts to pull his hand back, but I grip it tighter.

I do not know why, but I am filled with an urgent need to have this simple, honest man know that I am capable of decency. "Not everyone in the palace supports the baron." I let all my artifice fall away so he may see the truth behind my words.

He studies me carefully a moment, then nods once in understanding.

"Thank you." I give him a genuine smile this time and squeeze his hand. He blinks. "I will not jeopardize you or your family again, I swear it."

Relief washes over his face, and I slip the key into the purse at my waist and leave.

Chapter Eleven

D'ALBRET AND HIS MEN HAVE not yet returned from Ancenis when we retire for the evening. I wait for what feels like an eternity for Jamette and Tephanie to undress me and prepare me for bed. The fact that Jamette chatters like a nervous magpie does not help the time go by quicker. At long last, they finish their fussing and take their leave.

When I am finally alone, I go to my chest and look among my few poisons for one that is both swift and merciful, but I have none. Some are gentle but work slowly, and those that work quickly, cause too much pain and discomfort to be used for a merciful killing.

Instead, I remove my favorite knife and a sharpening stone, then go sit by the fire and begin sharpening the blade. I still do not know if the prisoner can sit a horse, or ride one, or if he is even conscious. If he is not, he will be of no use to the duchess. Not unless she can use his dead, martyred body to incite loyalists to take up arms.

He will not be marqued, but I no longer care about that.

It used to scare me, the idea of killing without a marque from Mortain to guide my hand, but now, stepping outside His grace holds no more fear for me. Especially since what little I know of that grace has been harsh. My biggest fear has always been that once I began killing at my own whim rather than Mortain's, I would become no better than d'Albret. But over the past few days, I have begun to wonder if being the daughter of Death is any different than being the daughter of a cruel, sadistic murderer. There is little enough difference that I can see, so better to make my own choice in this, the one I think will do the most good.

The nuns' warnings for the fate of my soul rise once more in my mind, but what the fool nuns did not realize is that my life is already a living hell, so trading one form for another is not so great a deterrent.

When a full hour has passed, I dress and collect the supplies I have selected. In addition to the night whispers and the newly sharpened knife, I arm myself with two other knives and a garrote bracelet as well as my lethal crucifix. If the knight must die tonight, then I will go immediately from the dungeon to d'Albret's chamber, where it will be easy enough to gain access with him gone. Once there, I will simply lie in wait for him. Even he must sleep sometime. And when he does, I'll make my move.

I will most likely not survive the attempt, but at least I will have tried, and surely that will prove that the darkness that lives in him does not live in me.

It is not the sort of escape I have prayed for, but it *is* an escape.

When I reach my door I pause just long enough to feel a faint throb of a heart beating steadily on the other side. Is it Jamette with her constant spying? Or some new guard my father has posted?

I quickly prepare a half a dozen lies and excuses, then open the door.

It is Tephanie. She is rolled up tightly in her cloak, like a sausage in its casing, sleeping outside my door.

I scowl down at the foolish girl, but while her presence is puzzling, she is easily enough dealt with if she discovers me. I close the door softly behind me, then step over her and make my way down the stairs to the main floor. Sensing no guard or sentry, I step out into the night.

The moon is nearly full and shines down onto the palace courtyard with the light of a thousand candles. My heart slams against my ribs as a shadow flies overhead, then swoops in among the trees in the outer court. An owl. It is only an owl, hunting for its dinner.

I wait a moment to be certain the movement has not caught any-one's attention, then skirt along the palace wall toward the old tower. I am filled with an unfamiliar calm. I know in my heart that what I am planning is the right thing to do. The sensation is as welcome as it is unfamiliar. This time, my hands are steady as I remove the key from the small pouch at my waist and then fit it to the lock.

There is a satisfying snick as it turns and I send a heartfelt thank-you to the cautious silversmith and his skill. As soon as I step inside, I am swarmed by the spirits of the tower, their icy presence chilling me to the bone.

Hugging the crumbling wall for support, I descend until I come to the second door. The key works here, too, and then I am standing in front of the final door. I move to the side, out of the line of the jailor's sight. I can hear him shuffling across the floor, muttering unintelligibly to himself.

When I am certain that he is not near the door, I slowly bring my face up to the grille and peer in. If I could get close enough to his ale pot, I could drop some of my own sleeping draft into it, but it is too far from the door. My only choice is to call him over and use the night whispers powder. With my hood pulled low he will not be able to recognize my face when he wakes up. I cannot help but wonder if I am truly doing him a favor by not killing him outright. There is a good chance d'Albret's wrath will fall on him if the prisoner is found dead, and the punishment will be swift and brutal.

Unless the prisoner is well enough to travel. Then all the jailor will have is a groggy head. At least until my next visit to break the knight out.

Just as I pull the twist of night whispers from my wrist sheath, there is the scrape of a boot on the stairs behind me. I glance around the antechamber, but there is no place to hide. I shove the packet back in its hiding place, grab the handle of my knife, and whirl around to face the stairs.

The tall, dark figure scowls in disbelief. "Sybella?"

Merde! It is no mere guard or sentry, but Julian. He takes three silent strides toward me and grabs my arm. "What are you doing here?" Behind the anger, I see true fear in his eyes.

"You're back." The joyful lilt in my voice is so convincing that even I almost believe it. I smile coquettishly. "How did you know where to find me?"

"I searched until I thought to check the one place you should not be." He gives my arm a little shake. "You cannot imagine the danger you have put yourself in."

"I could not sleep for the rattle and clank of the ghosts. Did you know this tower is haunted?"

"You could hear the sounds of haunting all the way from your chambers?" His eyes are wide with disbelief.

"Of course not." I glance out from under my lashes. "I came to the chapel to pray for your safe return. That's when I heard the rattling."

The harsh planes of his face relax slightly. "While I appreciate your prayers, you have put yourself in harm's way, prying where you should not."

"How was I to know my prayers would be answered so quickly?" I smile, as if with true gratitude. Then I grow serious once more. "*Ghosts,* Julian. Can you feel them?" I allow a shiver to rack my body—easy enough with the chill of all the unquiet dead clinging to me like a mantle and so much fear coursing through me. I make certain to put a sparkle of excitement in my eyes. "Ghosts of all the prisoners who have died here, unshriven." There is a faint rattle of chains just then, the first I have heard from the prisoner all night. I clutch at his arm. "There! Did you hear it? They could sneak into our rooms at night and suck the souls from our bodies." I cross myself for good measure.

He studies me for a long, silent moment, then seems to make a decision. "Here. Let me show you these ghosts." He lets go of my arm, then pounds once on the grilled door. As footsteps shuffle toward us, he glances down at me. "How did you get in?"

I blink, as if I do not understand his question. "I opened the door and walked in."

"Impossible," he hisses. A dark eye peers through the grille. He looks up so his face can be seen, then there is a rattling sound as the latch is lifted.

Interesting that the jailor opens the door so easily for my brother. Just how deeply is Julian in d'Albret's confidence? I had thought him peripherally involved in d'Albret's schemes, just enough to keep from drawing attention to himself, but now I must rethink that.

The door opens, and the strange little man makes a crooked bow. "That," I say, looking at the creature, "is no ghost, but a crippled old man. Or a gargoyle."

Julian shoots me an exasperated look, grabs my arm, and half drags me across the small room. I cover my nose with my hand. "And that is most definitely not an otherworldly stench," I say.

"Behold." Julian thrusts me toward a second door that also has a barred window at the top. "Your ghost." Julian takes a torch from the wall and shoves it through the bars.

"Sweet Jésu," I whisper. The man groans and tries to turn away from the bright flames. His face is beaten and misshapen and lumpy and crusted with blood. He is half naked, with naught but rags to cover him, and two great wounds in his left arm ooze darkly. I cannot believe this is the same creature who so valiantly fought off the duchess's attackers but a fortnight ago. D'Albret has taken yet another bright, noble thing and ruined it. "Who is he?" It is no great trick, putting revulsion and disgust in my voice, for the prisoner has been treated like the vilest of criminals, a violation of all decent standards for ransom. We would not treat our oldest hound this poorly.

"Just a prisoner from the battlefield. Now come. If anyone else learns that you have been here, I do not think even I can save you from our father's wrath." With that, Julian sets the torch back in the wall, then drags me from the dungeon.

Once outside the cell, I take in great gulps of the sweet, cold air. "Is our lord father planning to ransom him?"

"No."

"Why doesn't he just kill him, then, and be done with it?"

"I think there is some old history between the two of them, and our father has planned some special revenge. I believe he intends to use the man to send a message to the duchess."

I keep my voice light. "The man does not appear capable of getting a message across his cell, let alone to Rennes."

"You misunderstand me. The knight will be the message. When his hanged, drawn, and quartered body is delivered to the duchess, it will serve as a warning that even her strongest and most loyal men cannot stand against the d'Albret name."

The vileness of this plan makes my stomach roil. I smile and poke Julian playfully in the ribs. "My, but you are fully in our father's confidences now. Have you risen so very high in his favor?"

We have reached the top of the stairs. Julian ignores my question and turns to face me. "How did you get in, Sybella?" It is his most serious voice, the one he always uses when he worries we are in danger.

"The door was unlocked," I tell him. "Was it supposed to be otherwise? If so, you'd best check with the guards and see who was last on duty, for it was not when I came upon it. "

He still looks unconvinced. I step closer to him and ignore the sharp wave of revulsion that rises up from deep within me. I place my arms around his neck and rise up so that my lips touch his ear. "I am telling the truth, but you may search me if you like. It would make a very fine game." My heart is thundering so hard in my chest, it is a wonder he does not hear it. Afraid that he will, I do the only thing I can think of to distract him. I place my mouth on his.

His eyes widen in surprise, and then he wraps his arms around me, drawing me closer so that our hearts beat against each other and I can feel the entire length of his body against mine. He pulls away long enough to sigh my name.

He is not my brother, he is not my brother.

When he moves in to kiss me again, I step sharply back, rap him on the chest with my fist, and scowl. "Next time, do not leave me for so long," I say with a pout. If he thinks I am playing a game, he will play too. If he thinks I am rejecting him, he will turn on me. I wait, holding my breath, wondering which it will be.

When he blinks in mild surprise, I know the moment of danger has passed. "How did things go with Mathurin?" I ask to more fully distract him. "Was our father satisfied with the explanation you gave him?"

"Yes. He was pleased, in fact, that you acted so quickly to see to his interests." Julian almost smiles, for he knows how poorly that sits with me.

"And the others. Have they returned yet?"

"No. I rode on ahead. To hurry back to you." His voice holds an accusing note, and his eyes are but pools of darkness in this lightless place. I wonder if he is telling the truth or if he is more wrapped up in my father's games than I have guessed.

But no, not Julian. He is the only one in my entire family who hates our father as much as I do. But he has also changed in the three years I was away at the convent, and it worries me, for I do not know him as well as I once did.

Besides, he has betrayed me before. There is nothing to say he will not do so again.

Chapter Twelve

OUR TRIP BACK TO THE room is long and tense and we do not speak at all. I glance sideways at him, but his face is obscured by the shadows.

Has he bought my explanation? Has he guessed my true purpose in going to the dungeon? No, he cannot have, for even *I* was not sure of my true purpose. Although now that I have seen how weak and injured the prisoner is, I am even less certain he can be saved, let alone ride the twenty-six leagues to Rennes, where the duchess awaits him.

When we reach the residential wing of the palace, Julian nods to the newly posted sentry at the door. As we climb the stairs to the upper floor, my desperate kiss to divert Julian's suspicions lies thick in the air between us. I fear he has taken it as a bold invitation. What will he do once we reach my room?

We stop at my chamber door, and even though I know Julian is waiting for me to open it, I turn as if to bid him good night. "I am glad you are back safe and sound," I murmur.

He steps closer to me and leans forward to nuzzle at my hair. "You know I hate being parted from you. I came back as soon as I could."

I put my hands on his chest and play with the gold braid on his doublet to keep him from pressing closer.

It does not work. He ignores my hands between us and moves his lips from my hair and brings them down to my mouth. Despair fills me, and I scramble to think of some way to turn his own desire against him, but I cannot. Not now, when I am tired and chilled and the panicked dregs of discovery still run through my veins.

Then, praise Mortain, the door behind me opens and I nearly tumble backwards into the room. Julian's head comes up, black fury in his eyes. I whirl around to see who has interrupted us, wanting to get my body firmly in front of Julian until he can get his temper in check.

It is Tephanie. Dear, awkward, *sweet* Tephanie! Her gaze flickers briefly to Julian and then comes back to me and never wavers. "You asked me to wait for you, my lady."

"I did—thank you, Tephanie." My voice is calm, steady, and holds the faint note of scorn Julian would expect.

I glance at Julian as if to apologize for this overly dutiful servant. His temper has dissipated, and in its place is a faint mocking expression. "It is late, and I am sure your attendant would like some sleep before the night is over." He turns to Tephanie. "You may leave," he tells her.

Hidden behind my skirt, my hand reaches out and grabs her arm, an iron grip that holds her in place. She curtsies and murmurs, "It is no inconvenience, my lord, but a great honor to be able to serve my lady in any way she wishes."

I tilt my head at Julian. "Do you hear that, my lord brother? She is honored to serve me in any way she can."

He looks at me, then at Tephanie, and I see in his eyes the exact moment he concedes the battle. "I cannot argue with such devotion, then. I bid you both good night."

After Julian takes his leave, I stumble into my chamber and nearly sag to the floor. My knees weaken, my guts turn watery, and I cannot stop trembling.

"My lady?" Tephanie's simple face is clouded with worry. "Are you all right?"

"I am fine." Uncertain of my ability to school my features just yet, I do not look up.

Ignoring my words, she hurries to my side. I brace myself for her barrage of questions, but she surprises me by saying nothing. She simply takes one of my ice-cold hands in hers and begins chafing some warmth back into it.

Something about her touch, the simple, undemanding nature of it, makes me want to weep. Or perhaps it is still the aftereffects of my fright.

Once again, Julian has interfered, ruining my plans and destroying my hard-won resolve. Even worse, I suspect he is more fully in d'Albret's confidence than I had thought. How far will his loyalty go? Which is his greater desire—to keep me safe or to serve our father?

And the knight! Sweet Jésu, what they have planned for him! To be hanged, drawn, and quartered is the most hideous torture I can imagine. He will be hanged by the neck—but not so long that he actually dies. No, they will cut him down before he escapes into that sweet oblivion. Then they will slice him open and remove his entrails while he watches, finding endless ways to keep him conscious and alive as they do so. When that is done, they will throw him to the ground, secure each of his limbs to a horse, and send them all galloping off in different directions until he is ripped apart.

Fearing I will be sick, I force the image from my mind. Sensing my shivering, Tephanie leaves my side long enough to fetch my night shift, then quickly helps me undress by the fire. She slips the clean gown over my head, presses a cup of heated wine into my hands, and goes to warm the bed.

When she has finished, she curtsies, still not meeting my gaze. "Will that be all, my lady?"

I study her bowed head and flushed cheeks and wonder what makes her so loyal to me when all the others revel in my fall from favor. But loyal she is, and determined, too, with her stubborn insistence on serving me in the face of Julian's not insignificant displeasure. "Stay." I intend it as a command but fear it sounds more like a plea.

She blinks in surprise, then curtsies an acknowledgment. While she makes ready for bed, I crawl between the covers. Even the warmth from the heated bricks cannot remove the trembling from my limbs.

Is the prisoner cold in his dungeon? Or is he well past consciousness and too far gone to feel anything at all?

The bed dips as Tephanie crawls in. I give her a moment to settle, then scoot back toward her heat, as hungry as any ghost for her vital warmth.

Just as I finally stop shivering and begin my downward tumble into sleep, I feel a pair of soft, tender lips press against my hair. Or perhaps it is but a dream. Either way, it seems like a promise of absolution.

Chapter Thirteen

My father and the rest of his men are back in time for the midday meal. They have not taken the time to wash, and they reek of horses, sweat, and old blood, but that is not why my appetite evaporates at once. It is the sight of d'Albret in such high spirits, for he is only ever that cheerful when he is planning something truly heinous. As I take my place at the table, Julian sends me a look of warning— *Tread carefully.*

With Julian's discovery of me in the tower dungeon, all my fine plans have turned to ash. I cannot possibly break the Beast out now, or save him from the fate they have planned. They have probably doubled the guard on the tower. Plus, Julian will know precisely who is to blame.

Although, since I would likely not survive the attempt, I suppose that part does not matter overmuch. My fingers drift to the ring I wear on my right hand, the black cut-obsidian stone that hides a single dose of poison. One meant only for me.

With his eerie sense of timing, d'Albret turns his sharp gaze in my direction just then, his eyes dancing with a predatory gleam. "What have you been up to while I was away?"

It is all I can do not to look at Julian. Surely he hasn't spoken of my trip to the dungeon with d'Albret?

No, of course he hasn't, for if he had, d'Albret's beard would not be bristling with goodwill. I decide a humble approach is best, at least until

I know what this is about. "I entertained myself with the ladies of the castle and went into town to see what amusements it offered."

He takes a sip of wine, studying me the entire time, letting the silence—and my apprehension—build until I fear my nerves will snap. "I also had a belt that needed fixing," I tell him, not sure if this is a test to see if my explanation matches Jamette's.

"So?" he asks, gesturing with his goblet. "How did you find the city? Did they treat you well? Deserving of your station?"

His face is unreadable, and I cannot tell if I am walking into a trap or if he is actually curious. "The townspeople were circumspect, although the workmanship of the smiths was not what we are used to."

He nods, as if he expected nothing else. "And how was the mood of the town? They are always sullen when my soldiers ride through, but that is the way of townspeople toward soldiers. How they received you is a better indication of their true loyalties."

I think back to the smith and his reluctance to wait on us. Of the nervous glances of the pie seller and how the shopkeepers looked at us with suspicion. I shrug. "They were accommodating enough."

Jamette turns and looks at me in surprise. It is then that I see her new bauble—a round, pink pearl that dangles in the middle of her forehead from a delicate gold chain. "Did not the smith almost refuse to wait on you?" she says.

I cannot decide which I wish to rip out first—her loose tongue or her too observant eyes. I do not *think* she was close enough to the smith and me to make out the actual words between us. "I fear you are mistaken. He was merely unsure of whether he could have the job done in the time I required."

"Oh," she says, looking faintly sheepish.

I turn back to my father, wanting to make certain the smith will not fall into his disfavor. "He was courteous, if a bit provincial. And his wife was most obsequious."

"That is too bad," my father says.

Marshal Rieux looks at him in surprise. "Isn't that a good thing?"

My father grins, truly one of his most horrifying expressions. "I was looking forward to making an example of their lack of respect."

A chill scuttles down my spine and I try to think of something to divert his attention from the smith. I receive help from an unexpected quarter.

Pierre, who has had too much wine, raises his glass. "Instead, we should make an example of the duchess and ride on Rennes!" Baron Vienne's wife sits at his side, ignored and forgotten. She looks as if she has aged ten years over the past few days, whether because of her husband's recent death or Pierre's attentions, I cannot be sure.

Julian looks at him askance. "Except that they are too well supplied and can easily withstand a siege. We will be left standing on the battlefield looking like fools."

"Not with *our* might," Pierre slurs.

Julian pointedly waves away the page who is waiting to refill Pierre's goblet. "Might counts for nothing if we cannot get inside the city walls."

D'Albret's expression turns sly and he begins playing with the stem of his goblet. "Ah, but what if we *had* help from inside," he says, and my heart drops. Has the duchess not purged her council of all the traitors? There is no one left, by my reckoning. All of the traitors sit here at this table.

"Help?" Rieux says, clearly puzzled.

D'Albret draws out the moment, draining his wineglass and waiting for the steward to refill it before continuing. "I have sent men to infiltrate the ranks of the mercenaries Captain Dunois has hired to augment the duchess's troops. They have been ordered to ensure they are assigned to the vulnerable parts of the city—the gates, the bridges, the sewers; anyplace that could provide an entrance point.

"Once they are in position, we will have several chinks in her armor to use at our convenience. When the time is right, they will be able to open the city gate for us. Once our forces are inside, it will be easy enough to overpower her guardsmen and man the ramparts with our own. The duchess's sanctuary will quickly become her prison." He smiles, his teeth brilliantly white against the blackness of his beard.

It is clear that d'Albret's unbridled ambition will yield to nothing but death. The thought of his forces descending on Rennes and invading the city causes my stomach to shrivel into a sour knot.

Pierre raises his goblet in salute. "Is now the time to send her our message, my lord?"

D'Albret stills, and for one long moment, I fear he will hurl his goblet at Pierre. Instead, he smiles. "Tomorrow, whelp. We will send her our message tomorrow."

It appears the injured knight has just run out of time.

Chapter Fourteen

I LEAVE JULIAN SPRAWLED IN a chair by the fire. His head is thrown back, his mouth agape. He almost looks dead. Indeed, I thought—briefly—about killing him, but in the end, I could not. Not even after all he has done. We have survived too much together, been each other's allies when no one else would stand by us.

Besides, he is one of the few things that has ever loved me and survived.

He will feel groggy and ill from the overdose of sleeping draft I gave him, but it is no more than he deserves for coming to my chamber uninvited. Just the thought that I will never again have to endure his nightly scratching at my door is enough to lighten my step.

Once I have armed myself with every weapon I own—the knives, the daggers, and the garrotes—I slip from my room. Indeed, I feel like a traveling tinker with as many potions, weapons, and tools as I carry on me. I am lucky I do not clink my way down the stairs.

There are few enough options left to me, and there is no room for error. I will finally fulfill my wish to kill d'Albret—or at least, I will attempt to. If I fail—and there is a good chance I may—then it is even more important that the knight live, for he must escape the fate d'Albret has planned for him and get a warning to the duchess as soon as possible.

I am the only one in a position to stop d'Albret. And even my chances are slim, since my plan relies on a grievously injured knight and my own limited skill.

Nearly all the servants and men-at-arms in the palace are asleep as I make my way from my chamber to the courtyard. It did not come easily, and has taken every drop of poison in the pearls from the hairnet and glass beads on my crucifix chain. I slipped all of it into the men's dinner while the stew still bubbled in the pot hanging at the fire. Such a diluted dose will put the entire garrison to sleep, but only for a few hours. When they wake, they will feel as if they have been trampled by a herd of oxen, but at least they will be alive.

I would have loved to poison them all, for if they are loyal to my father, they do not have an innocent bone in their body. But killing so many men reeks too much of one of d'Albret's schemes. Instead, I satisfy myself with the knowledge of how much trouble they will be in when morning comes and the full impact of my night's activities becomes clear.

Only the guards on duty at the eastern gate will present trouble, for they have not had their suppers yet. I will have to deal with them in order to get the prisoner to the waiting cart.

The cart cost me dear, as the night-soil man was loath to lose the source of his livelihood. But when presented with enough jewelry, he finally agreed to empty the cart and drive its mysterious load out the east gate. Of course, I did not pay him with my own finery but with Jamette's. It was easy enough to slip into her room and take a handful of the baubles her betrayal of me had brought her.

As I draw closer and closer to the tower, the weight of secrets and careful movement, of illusions maintained and lies convincingly whispered, falls from my shoulders, leaving me so light I wonder that I do not float across the courtyard.

I reach the old tower and slip the key into the lock. My blood is moving so wildly through my veins that I hardly even notice the waiting spirits as they rush toward me, their chilling presence barely penetrating the heat of the moment.

At the foot of the stairs, I pause long enough to pull my hood close to shield my face from view, then nearly laugh at the gesture. After tonight, it does not matter any longer. Even so, old habits do not die easily, and I leave the hood in place.

I have thought long and hard on what to do with the jailor. I am surprisingly reluctant to kill him, for every kill I make without Mortain's blessing is but one more step to embracing the very evil I loathe in d'Albret. But I cannot risk his ruining my plans, for if the knight is too wounded to ride to Rennes, I will have no choice but to put him out of his misery, as undoubtedly he has suffered enough.

Besides, if I fail and d'Albret lives through the night, any punishment he bestows on the jailor will make the little man wish he had died. Looking at it that way, it is clear I will be doing him a favor by killing him.

When I peer through the grille I think perhaps some god is smiling on this venture after all, for the old jailor lies on the floor, sound asleep. If I can get to him without waking him, he should be easy enough to deal with.

I step quietly into the dungeon. There is no sound from the prisoner's cell, and the gargoyle does not stir. Perfect. I creep closer and lift my knife, ready to slit the man's throat. But before I can strike, the little demon leaps up and swings at me with his empty tankard.

I hiss and dodge the blow. The jailor grunts and then faces me, and any chance I had for surprise is gone.

"Surrender and be done with this," I tell him, careful to pitch my voice low. "You cannot stop me."

I lunge for him, but he twists away—how can one so clumsy and awkward move so quickly?—and throws himself in front of the cell door.

Keeping my eyes on his contorted little face, I change my plan. "I will not kill you. Just put you to sleep for a while. Just long enough to free the prisoner. You will have a goose egg on your head and can explain to the others how you were overpowered and were helpless to prevent the escape."

At the word *escape* the little man stills and cocks his head. He pauses for a long moment, then carefully steps away from the door and motions me toward it.

I frown. What trick is this?

The little man gestures at me to open the door while he nods and smiles. At least, I think it is a smile, for it is hard to tell in his creased, misshapen face. "You *want* me to free him?" I ask.

He nods vehemently, then takes another step back.

I cannot begin to fathom what his purpose is, but time is not standing still for me to figure it out. D'Albret will be on his way to visit Madame Dinan's chamber, if he is not already there, and that will afford me my greatest chance of catching him unawares. "Very well, come with me." I motion toward the cell. I will not risk his shutting me in with the prisoner, then crying for help. He nods happily but scuttles away like a spider.

Keeping one eye on him, I withdraw the key again and unlock the cell door. The ripe stench makes me blink but I ignore it and hurry over to the corner where the prisoner lies on the floor.

He is the size of a giant. Any hope I had of being able to drag him anywhere, let alone up a flight of stairs, evaporates. He does not stir at my approach, but neither did the little gargoyle, so I remain on my guard. When he still doesn't move after a few moments, I reach out and nudge him with the toe of my boot. Nothing.

At a sound behind me, I spin around, dagger at the ready. But it is only the gargoyle standing there, watching. I narrow my eyes. "Is he dead?"

An emphatic shake of the head, then the man places his hands against his own cheek as if sleeping. *Ah,* I think. "Can he walk?" I ask sharply.

The old man hesitates, then puts his hand out and wiggles it back and forth. A little. Maybe. My heart sinks. There is no way I can drag him. *Merde.* How will I ever get word to the duchess?

I kneel down next to the knight so I can see just how injured he is. A large cut bisects the left side of his face. I think, but cannot be certain, that it is an old scar rather than a fresh one. The rest of his face is battered, and old crusted blood still clings to it in places. It is also a strange yellow and green color. At first, I fear it is putrid flesh, then realize his entire face is one giant bruise. A great wound festers in his left leg, and another two in his left arm. I take a deep breath, then put my hand on his shoulder. "Hsst! Wake up. We must get moving."

He stirs, then groans, but that is all. Muttering a string of curses, I reach out and try again, this time grabbing his arm in a pincer-like grip and tugging on it. "Come on, you great ox. I cannot carry you out of here."

His massive head rolls to the side, then lifts a few inches from the floor. The eyes open and squint in my direction. I cannot tell if his vision is blurry from his head wound or if he cannot see me at all. I look over my shoulder at the jailor who is no jailor. "Get over here and help me."

He scuttles forward, hops onto the other side of the knight, and grabs his arm. With much grunting and urging and swearing, we manage to get the prisoner to a sitting position, but that is all. Despair begins to fill me, more chilling than the touch of the spirits hovering nearby. The man's injuries are inflamed and he himself is feverish. If I am able to get him out of here, I am not certain — not certain at all — that he will not die of blood fever on the way to Rennes. Even so, I must try. I nod to the gargoyle and we both stand, trying to pull the prisoner up with us, but it is no use. We might as well be attempting to move the dungeon itself.

I nearly weep with frustration. If I were more certain of my ability to kill d'Albret tonight, I could just put the prisoner out of his misery, but I am not. D'Albret is uncanny in his instinct for survival, and if I fail, someone must warn the duchess of his plans.

Besides, what sort of cruel god robs a man of a glorious death on the battlefield and leaves him to rot—or worse—in a dungeon? If I close my eyes, I can still see him on his magnificent horse before they brought him down; how valiantly he fought, never stopping, not even when the odds were overwhelming.

That's it! I must find a way to tap into his battle lust. The very thing that drives him to such unholy feats on the battlefield is the only thing that will get him out of here.

I glance over at the jailor, give him a nod of reassurance, then turn back to the injured man. "Get up," I hiss. "The duchess is in danger." His head snaps up. "If you do not get up right now, they will be upon her within minutes. Get up." I pull on his arm and he growls. "Will you cower here on the floor like a whimpering babe while your duchess is in peril?"

The jailor looks at me, horrified, shaking his head, for the beast is rising in our knight. Blood rushes into his face, and fire kindles in his eyes. "You would never have been chosen to protect the duchess if they'd known how weak you truly are," I whisper in his ear.

And then it happens: like a great wave rolling up from the ocean floor, the knight propels himself to his feet. He sways for an instant, regains his balance, then lets loose with a mighty roar and lunges in my direction.

I dance nimbly out of his reach. As soon as I leave his side, he nearly topples over onto his face, but the small gnome of a jailor wedges himself under the knight's arm and keeps him from falling.

Furious and befuddled, like a bull in a field, the prisoner swings his head from one of us to the other, not sure whom to attack first. "Come," I say before he can collect his wits. "The duchess is this way. If we hurry, we can get to her in time." And in truth, it is no lie I offer him.

The words act like a lance to his backside. He takes a step forward, then grunts as his face turns white with pain. As his leg gives way beneath him, I realize I have no choice but to help him again and hope he will not kill me on the spot. I return to his side and insert myself under his arm to prop him up. But he is huge and weighs twenty stone at least and nearly drags me to the ground with him. I brace my knees and my back, and between the jailor and me, we keep him upright. As he sags against us, I know we cannot carry him the entire way, but it is as if all the fight has seeped out of him. Already my own shoulders and arms grow numb from his weight. We will all die here like rats in a trap if we cannot get him moving.

Fear and anger lend urgency to my voice. "Would you let your duchess be taken while you rest your lazy bones and thick head? *Move!*"

With a deep-throated growl, the man lurches forward, a great shuffling step that brings us nearly to the door. I snag the lone torch from the wall with my free hand and pray that I will not set myself—or the prisoner—on fire. But we need it, as the stairs are in pitch-darkness and there is no way we can maneuver him up by feel alone. Indeed, as we stop at the first step, it is not clear than we can maneuver him up at all.

The gargoyle mutters and grunts and motions me to get in front. As I move around them and hold the torch so they may see where to place their feet, I see that the jailor has inserted himself under Beast's arm, a human crutch for the prisoner to lean on. His right leg is strong and he is able to climb the stair with it, even though his left arm hangs limp and useless at his side. He braces his right arm against the wall and hops up onto the next step, and the weight his arm does not take is supported by the jailor. The prisoner's face contorts with pain and I pray he will not faint before we reach the cart.

"Hurry," I whisper urgently. "They are circling her even now." The agony of not being able to reach his duchess is plain upon his face, and my heart aches for him, but I harden it. Softness will not serve either of us now.

He pauses, sweat beading upon his face, his lungs working like a blacksmith's bellows.

Only four more steps. "How will you kill them," I call out softly, "these men who have threatened your duchess?" He lunges forward another step. "With your bare hands, is my suggestion, so you may look into their bulging eyes as you drive the air from their lungs." From beneath the giant's arm, the little jailor squints up at me with faint horror, but I do not care, for we have gained another step and I can feel the cool night air upon my back. "Mayhap tear them limb from limb."

With a faint growl, he lunges up the last step. I put my hand out to stop them both, afraid Beast will barrel out the door and straight into a passing sentry.

But he leans against the wall and closes his eyes while the jailor pets at his arm.

I peek out into the courtyard. There is nothing there but darkness. "We must make for the east gate. There are only two sentries posted there, and once I have dispatched them, we will be able to get across the bridge unseen. A cart with horses waits there to carry you to the duchess." The gargoyle's eyes widen in surprise, then he smiles. At least, I think it's a smile. It looks far too much like a grimace for me to be certain.

"Can you do it?" I ask, hating that I must trust this mysterious jailor with such matters. "Can you get him to Rennes?"

He nods so hard I fear his neck will snap.

It is easier going outside. For one thing, there are no more stairs, and for another, there is a thick solid wall for the knight to lean against. We make slow, shuffling progress, the skin along my shoulders urging me to hurry, but we cannot. Indeed, it is a miracle we have come this far.

I glance once behind me. A light shines from one of the upper chambers. Good. D'Albret still lingers with Madame Dinan. I wonder whom he will have guarding the door tonight, for he always posts two sentries when he visits her chamber. I find myself hoping that one of them is Captain de Lur, as I would dearly love an excuse to kill him.

When we reach the end of the wall, I see the small gatehouse and the two guards there. They are not standing at attention but instead are speaking together in low voices. "Here." I thrust a small square of yellow and black fabric at the gargoyle. "You will need this to get out of the city. There are some supplies in the cart, and also some jewels that you can use to purchase what you need. Put the plague flag on the wagon and no one will stop and search you. Understand?"

When he nods his understanding, I motion for him to stay put until my signal, then creep forward.

The guards are grumbling that the others have not come to change the watch and are trying to decide whether they should stay here or go fetch the captain.

Clinging to the wall like a shadow, I move into position behind the first guard. I must kill him—I cannot risk them raising the alarm and I have no idea how long the sleeping draft will last or how deeply the others sleep.

I remind myself that these deaths are necessary. There is no way we can get the knight past the sentries, and if they are d'Albret's men, they are no doubt guilty of some terrible crime.

The weakest link in my plan is killing the first guard without alerting the second guard to my presence. Speed and stealth are my greatest weapons, for if the second guard sees me, there is a good chance he will call out a warning before I can silence him.

One thing at a time, I remind myself, then slip silently out of my hiding place. I take the cord from my waist and wrap it around my fists as I creep toward the first sentry, looping it once, twice, to be sure it will not slip. When I am directly behind him, I make my move. Sensing me, the guard starts to turn my way, but I step up, quickly slip the cord around his neck, and yank with all my might.

The man jerks in surprise, his weapon clattering to the ground as he scrabbles for the rope at his throat. I pull harder and drive my knee into his back for leverage, dodging his elbow as it tries to connect with my ribs.

But the clatter of his weapon has called the second guard's attention. His eyes widen when he sees me and his hand goes for his sword as he takes a step forward. I swear, for the first man is still struggling and taking far too long to die. I cannot even let go to reach one of my throwing knives and defend myself. The alerted sentry draws his sword and rushes toward me. I put the dying guard between us to afford myself some protection. There is a small thud, and the attacking guard stiffens in his track, then keels over like a felled tree. I glance up to see the gargoyle, a sling dangling from his right hand and a look of satisfaction on his twisted little face. Just then, my victim finally slumps into death. I do my best to block my mind to his soul as it slithers from his body, and I release the cord from his neck.

The jailor gives me a nod as if to say *You're welcome*—even though I have not said thank you—then motions for me to get moving, as if it is he who is leading this rescue.

I tamp down my irritation, and we both hurry back to where the knight leans against the wall. His eyes are closed, and his face is bleached white by his efforts to get this far. I cannot tell if his battle fever has left him or if it still simmers quietly in his veins. Pray Mortain the latter, else we will never get him across the bridge.

Even so, now that his mind is no longer clouded, it is the best time to give him my message. "Listen to me, for this is important. When you get to Rennes, you must get word to the duchess. D'Albret has men inside the city's walls, men who will open the gates to him when the time comes. Can you remember to tell her that?"

Merde! I cannot tell if he nods in agreement or if his head is simply lolling to the side. Frustrated, I turn to the gargoyle. "Did you get all that?" He nods and I sigh. It will have to do.

I adjust the massive arm around my shoulders, then begin the long torturous journey across the courtyard. At the bridge, the knight pulls his arm off me and uses the side of the bridge as a crutch. I do not argue with him but instead slip ahead to be sure the promised cart is there and to give the driver his instructions and the rest of the payment he was promised.

At first I do not see the wagon, and my heart jolts in dismay, for we cannot coax this man much farther. But when I look again, there it is, tucked deep in the shadows against the city wall, two decrepit-looking mules dozing in their harness. The driver, however, is missing. He must have decided that half the promised payment was better than the entire amount, for at least he'd live long enough to spend it.

I turn back to see the men's progress across the bridge, but they have paused midway. Do they not realize how closely we have shaved this? We do not have time to stop and admire the scenery. I glance back at the palace windows and see that the light is out in Madame Dinan's chamber, and renewed urgency fills me. I must get there soon, while he is still tangled in her sheets and distracted.

I rush back to the others. "Hurry! We need to get to the cart before we are seen. New sentries could arrive any moment."

The jailor looks up at me with his sad little face and shakes his head. He does not think his prisoner can take another step. I glare at him, wishing he would speak so he could be the one to cajole this knight forward. I had not thought it possible to hate myself more than I already did, but the vile things I have called this tortured knight have proven me wrong. "Wake up, you. How dare you sleep while your duchess is in danger?" His eyelids flicker, but that is all. True worry sets in and I must use the most cruel weapon in my arsenal. "They are closing in on her, those men. D'Albret's men. Do you know what they say about d'Albret? How he treats his women?"

The jailor motions to me — to my face. There is a softness in his gaze that I do not understand. He motions again and I put my hand up to my cheek. It is wet. I glare at him as I scrub the dampness away. "If you cannot be bothered to bestir yourself on her behalf, he will maul her with his rough, hairy hands, violate her flesh—"

With a roar that startles a bray from one of the waiting donkeys, the knight pushes himself from the wall and lurches forward. The little jailor tries to steer his lumbering charge to the cart, but the knight resists, instead lunging toward me. Startled, I look up and our eyes meet. His are a pale, silver blue, I realize, just before his fist connects with my jaw and everything goes black.

Chapter Fifteen

I SLOWLY BECOME AWARE THAT I am dreaming, for I feel as safe and snug as a babe in a cradle. Or perhaps a babe in a boat, bobbing in the sea.

A very bumpy sea, I amend, as a jarring thud rattles my entire body. I try to open my eyes, but it is as if they've been sewn shut. When I finally wrench them open, all I can see is a dark sky filled with fading stars.

Where in the names of the Nine Saints am I?

I try to think, shuffling back through my memories like a banker though stacks of coin. The knight. I was getting him to the cart and then . . . what? Filled with a trickle of foreboding, I struggle to sit up. The movement has my stomach roiling like a nest of eels. Just in time, I lean over the side and retch miserably.

When I have finished with that, the throbbing in my head lessens enough that I can begin to make sense of my surroundings. A strong smell of manure fills my nose, making me think of retching again, and I see a jaunty yellow flag flapping in the night breeze.

Frantic, I glance around. The knight lies still and lifeless beside me as we jolt and bump along the road. There are no houses, no shops, no city walls anywhere. There is nothing but gently rolling countryside and farmsteads as far as my eye can see.

I am in the be-damned cart! The knight . . . he hit me. Knocked me

out cold with his great ham-shaped fist and, for some reason, he—and
the jailor—have brought me with them.

No. *No!* I look around once again to try to get my bearings. How
long have I been out? Moments? Hours? More important, how far away
are we from Nantes? Perhaps it is not too late to go back.

But no matter how hard I squint and peer, I cannot see the walls of
the city. Which means all my plans—and my hard-won resolve—have
turned to ash. The giant ogre beside me has given Fortune's wheel such
a hard turn that it has spun out of my grasp entirely.

The prisoner next to me does not so much as stir at the vile oath
that flies from my mouth, but the jailor, who is driving, looks over his
shoulder and tips his cap. That cheerful gesture infuriates me further
and I scramble to my feet, ignoring the wave of nausea that follows. As
we hit a bump in the road, I nearly tumble out. Grabbing the back of
the bench, I clamber gracelessly into the front next to the jailor, then
wait for the dizziness to pass before I begin railing at him. "What have
you done?" I finally manage to get out. "I was not supposed to come
with you! You have ruined everything!"

The little gnome shrugs and points his thumb at the unconscious
knight.

I glance at the hulking form laid out in the wagon bed. How dare
he? What addlepated thought crossed his fevered brain and caused
him to bring me with them? I want to leap into the back of the cart
and pound my frustration out on his thick, misbegotten hide. Instead,
I curl my hands into fists, press my nails into my palms, and hope
the pain of it will clear my head. To have been denied my desire to
wreak vengeance upon d'Albret for so long, only to have it snatched
away when it is finally in my grasp, is nearly unbearable. It is all I can
do not to put my head back and roar out my fury at God and all His
saints.

Then suddenly, like a kettle boiled dry, my anger is gone and I am left feeling as empty and hollow as a drum. My one chance, the one I have waited months—no, years!—for, has been irrevocably lost. Never again will I be in such a position to exact vengeance on d'Albret.

Never again. The words rattle around in my head like two stones in a bucket.

But that also means I cannot go back—cannot be *sent* back—for even the cold-hearted abbess will recognize how impossible it would be for me to earn d'Albret's trust again.

Which means . . . I have escaped.

I try to think. In all my seventeen years, have I ever known any-thing—anyone—to escape d'Albret? Not his wives, nor his children, nor his enemies. Only the duchess, and she did so twice, once in Guérande and the second time almost a fortnight ago.

While it makes sense that the gods would bestir themselves for the duchess, I cannot believe they would bestir themselves for me. They never have before.

Escape. The word is as ripe and seductive as summer's first fruit, so much so that I must shy away from it and remind myself that hope is but the god's way of mocking us, nothing more.

I give myself a moment, then another, to compose myself, then turn to the jailor beside me. I pretend I have not stormed and railed and fumed for the last mile and ask calmly, "How is our charge?"

Relief crosses his wrinkled little face, and he gives an enthusiastic nod of his head. I glance over my shoulder, uncertain the knight's con-dition warrants such enthusiasm, but say nothing. With all my other options scuttled, it seems my best course of action is to get the knight to Rennes. Alive, if possible.

And with that thought comes a reminder. None of it will matter a whit if d'Albret finds us, for even now he is likely gathering forces for pursuit. Luckily, all of his soldiers will be groggy and ill for a few more hours yet, and I do not think he will ride out himself.

Somewhere in the distance, a rooster crows. Soon, sleepy farmers will stumble out of their cottages and begin tilling their fields. And see us. We cannot risk that. "We must find shelter," I tell the jailor.

He nods sagely, as if he has already thought of this.

"There *will* be pursuit," I warn him. "So our shelter needs to be well hidden from the road." What has taken us all night to travel could be covered in a matter of hours by one of my father's men on a swift strong horse.

The jailor nods again, points to a copse of trees in the distance, then steers the cart in that direction.

I study his crooked, lined face. Can I trust him? For the hundredth time I wonder at the strange relationship between the knight and his jailor. Does the Beast of Waroch command courage and loyalty even from those who guard him? For surely my father assigned only the most loyal of his men to tend to his valuable prisoner, and yet the jailor not only did not try to prevent our escape but joined us.

Hopefully, he has not risked so much and come so far only to betray us now.

Just as true dawn breaks, we come in sight of an old stone lodge. It is far from the main road—indeed, from any road at all, I realize as the cart bumps over a rock—and well secluded in a patch of woods. The gargoyle pulls the cart to a halt and waits just inside the trees. It is a small manor house built of gray stone and, by all appearances, deserted. There is no activity in the courtyard, no scratching chickens or bleating goats, and no smoke rises from the chimney. It is almost too much to hope for, that this hidden place is empty and waiting for us. Still not completely sure of the jailor's motives, I jerk my head toward the house. "Go see if anyone is inside."

His quick nod of compliance assures me somewhat that this is no trap. Still, someone must scout the place out to be certain it is clear.

Until the old man has proven himself to be fully trustworthy, he may as well be the one to do it.

As he looks around, I steer the cart to the back of the lodge and fret once more over my situation. *Should* I attempt to return to Nantes and finish my self-appointed task? Once I am committed to a purpose, it is no easy thing for me to walk away.

I could claim Beast abducted me.

Except they know how weak and wounded he was, and my involvement is the only explanation for the drugged guards. I fear my hand in this is plain to see.

Perhaps, a small voice inside me whispers, *Mortain has simply answered your prayers.* Can it not be as simple as that? But of course, nothing—nothing—has ever been simple.

Our shelter is one of the late duke's lesser lodges, the sort he would retreat to with a handful of his most trusted men or one of his least favorite mistresses. It is perfect for our purposes: sturdy and hidden from the casual passerby. Most important, I have never heard d'Albret or any of his men speak of it, which gives me some hope that they do not know it exists.

Just as the jailor comes scampering out, indicating that no one is home, the thick clouds overhead release their burden and it begins to rain. However, even wounded and ill and passed out, the knight is still a giant of a man. "We cannot carry him in," I tell the jailor.

He reaches out and shakes the knight, but not even his eyelids flicker in response. Concerned that he has died on the way here, I look to his chest, relieved when I see it rise and fall with his breathing. The jailor begins to shake him harder, but I stop him. I glance up at the rain falling from the sky, big fat drops that plop down onto my face. Cleaning the prisoner up will be a mighty chore involving buckets and buckets of water. "We will let the rain do some of the hard work for us. It is not a freezing rain — let it wash some of the prison grime from him before we take him inside."

The jailor scowls, as if this is some great insult or injury I have offered his master, but I ignore him, grab two of the bundles tucked up against the side of the cart, and head for the lodge. He can follow or not, it makes no difference to me.

While the jailor stays to cluck over the knight, I make a quick exploration of the lodge to see with my own eyes that no one is here. The back door opens directly into a large kitchen with a fireplace. There is a hall beyond, and three chambers on the second floor. They are all empty of any but the most basic furnishings, and nothing but cold ashes sit in the hearths.

Since getting the knight up the stairs is out of the question, we will have to set up a trestle table in the kitchen. I go to the door and see the jailor dripping by the side of the cart, as if his getting soaked will somehow lessen his prisoner's discomfort. I motion him over.

When he is close enough, I hand him a rough cloth to dry himself. "I need to set up a table in here, but I cannot move it myself."

Together with many grunts and muttered oaths we get the trestle in the kitchen and cover it with two old blankets we found. The effort has chased any remaining chill from my bones. "Let's go see if we can get him in here," I say with a sigh of resignation, for it will be as easy as trying to maneuver a greased ox.

Outside, the rain has not only cleansed some of the filth from the patient but roused him from his sleep. As the jailor and I peer down at him over the sides of the cart, he blinks up at us, the water spiking his thick lashes. When he sees me, his eyes cloud with confusion, and suddenly my anger rises up in me again, a white-hot fury that he has robbed me of my prize — the one thing that would have justified all I have endured the past six months. I lean down and get my face close to his. "I have been sent on the duchess's own orders to aid you, and how do you repay me? By ruining all my carefully laid plans."

His eyes widen in surprise. "From now on, until I get you safely to Rennes, you will do exactly as I say and no more, do you understand? Else I will leave you here to rot in the rain."

"What did I ruin?" His voice is rough, like a shower of rocks tumbling downhill.

"Plans that I worked six long months to put in place. Why? Why did you do it?" I ask.

"Do what?"

I reach up and touch my tender jaw. "Take me with you."

He shakes his head, as if trying to clear it. "The last thing I remember is an insistent, soul-searing voice spewing venom and lies."

"That was me," I say curtly.

"You?" He looks thoroughly nonplussed, as if he cannot reconcile that voice with what he sees before him.

"Yes, you great lummox. It was the only way I could get you moving up the stairs and into the cart."

"You *tried* to bring the battle lust upon me? Have you feathers for brains?"

"No one had a better idea on how to get you out of that dungeon. I simply used the tools at hand."

"You're lucky you only got a clout to the jaw." He squints up at me again, as if trying to make sense of something in his mind. "Besides, you looked afraid," he mutters.

I gape at him. "Now who has feathers for brains? I had a mission—there was no fear involved." But that is a lie. I was terrified, and I hate that he saw it.

Chapter Sixteen

PALE AS A CORPSE AND breathing heavily, the knight eases onto the trestle table, then the jailor helps him lie down. He closes his eyes, and it is clear that even this small amount of activity has cost him much. *Merde.* It is just as well I am not returning to Nantes because this man will need every ounce of my paltry healing skills—and a bit of the gods' own luck—in order to make it to Rennes. If he dies on the road, then I will have well and truly nothing for all my work and sacrifice. I snag a bucket from a hook on the wall and thrust it at the jailor. "Here. We'll need water to finish washing him. And fetch the two bundles left in the cart."

Without questioning me, he takes the bucket and heads back outside into the rain. I take a tinderbox from one of the bundles I brought in and move to the fireplace to start a fire. The clouds overhead will likely mask any smoke that manages to clear the treetops. Even so, I build only a small fire, just enough to heat some water for the poultices I must make up for the knight's wounds.

When the jailor returns, he sets the two bundles next to the others, then busies himself pouring water from the bucket into a battered old tin pot. I thrust a wad of cloth in his hand. "Finish washing him so that I may tend his injuries. Cut away his garments if you have to." Again the jailor does what I ask, and I begin to relax somewhat.

For the next little bit, we work in companionable silence, the jailor washing the prisoner, the prisoner gathering the strength to ask all the questions I can feel swirling in his head, and myself mixing the powdered elm bark and mustard with the boiling water and praying the damage to his body is not too far beyond my skill.

When my preparations are done, I slowly rise. It is time to see just how dire his situation is.

The man's feet jut over the edge of the table, and his face, still ashen beneath the black and green bruises, is as cheerfully ugly as any I have ever seen. His cheeks are pockmarked, and a long scar puckers one side of his face. His nose has been broken—more than once—and he has a notch in one ear. None of which will improve once the swelling and bruising go down.

His body is as thick as a boar's, with bulging ropes of muscle and sinew. If a sculptor wanted to bring brute strength to life, he would carve a body such as this. Nearly all of it is covered in some sort of scars, the red, angry recent ones mingling with the silvery white of the older.

In spite of myself, I am fascinated—perhaps even impressed—by the damage this one man has sustained.

And survived.

I step closer, and, of its own volition, my hand reaches out to him, my fingers skimming oh so lightly across his battered, ravaged flesh. "How is it you are still alive?" I wonder.

"I am nearly impossible to kill." The deep rumble of his voice fills the room to the rafters. My gaze snaps up to his face; I had not realized I'd spoken aloud. His eyes, though filled with pain, are fiercely intelligent and put me in mind of a wolf's, with their eerie light coloring.

"Ah," I say, "that is good to know. Now I need not worry quite so much while I tend to your wounds."

His eyebrows shoot up. "You?" Those fierce blue eyes rake up and down my entire body, not with prurient interest but in detached assessment.

I make a great show of looking around the empty kitchen. "You have someone else in mind? Your jailor, perhaps? Surely if he were able, he would have tended to them already."

I thrust my hand out at the jailor, who has been watching our exchange with nervous eyes, and wiggle my fingers. After a moment's uncertainty, he hands me the cloth, and, in spite of my threat of roughness, I begin gently cleaning the patient's face, removing yet another layer of grime. It does not help his appearance any, but I am relieved to see there are no serious cuts or breaks under the dirt.

I turn my attention to the long gash that runs along the meat of his forearm. It does not go to the bone, nor were any tendons or ligaments severed, but it will need a deep cleaning, which will not be pleasant for either of us. The two puncture wounds from the arrows in his left shoulder are infected and inflamed. Covering my fingers with the cloth, I press gently against them, searching for any remaining shards of wood or iron. The patient sucks in his breath sharply, but that is all.

"No splinters, then, so those will be easily enough dealt with. And the arrows appear to have missed any vital ligaments."

He nods, but says nothing.

There is more bruising and swelling along his middle. I reach out and gently press. He gasps, then grabs my hand with his good one, surprising me, for the gentleness of his touch is incongruent with his size and bulk. "You do not need to prod and poke at my ribs for me to tell you they're broken."

"Very well. There is nothing left to do but examine your leg, and that is the one injury that frightens me the most."

The jailor was too lazy—or modest—to remove the man's riding breeches, so I take the small knife from the chain at my waist and quickly cut away the sodden, filthy leather. As I reach to pull it aside, he swats my hand aside. Puzzled, I look up to find his cheeks pink and cannot help but smile. The Beast of Waroch is embarrassed. "Pish," I tell him. "It is nothing I have not seen before." His eyes widen in surprise, but I reach out and pull the leather from his thigh.

The jailor gasps—in shock, perhaps?—and I suck in my breath. "That bad?" the knight says.

The entire thigh is red and swollen and hot to the touch. Foul stuff oozes from the wound itself, and streaks of red have begun to work their way up and down the leg. I glance up to find a faint grin on his face and, not for the first time, wonder if all he has endured has caused him to lose his wits. I turn my gaze back to the cut. "It *is* bad," I agree. "Fortunately for you, I am not a surgeon, so I cannot cut it off were I so inclined."

"Nor would I let you."

"I am not sure you are in a condition to stop me," I mutter, then hold up my hand before he can begin arguing. "I will not cut it off, but what I must do will not be enjoyable either."

Beast studies me. "Who are you that you know so much about caring for battle injuries? I have yet to meet a noblewoman who tends wounds like a field physician."

To give myself some time to think, I return to the fire and fetch the hot brew from the bubbling pot. *What do I tell the man?* I wonder as I begin spooning the herbs and mud into the linen cloths I have prepared. *I am d'Albret's daughter, you oaf, and you have just ensured he will follow us to the ends of the earth.* But I find I am unwilling to trumpet my true identity. Indeed, I wish to leave it far, far behind me, bury it like a corpse, and never speak of it again. Besides, if he learns who I am, he will never trust me to get him to safety. Still, I must tell him something.

I think back to the first time I saw him, down in the field with the duchess and her party. "I am a friend of Ismae's."

"Ismae!" He tries to prop himself up on one elbow, then winces and eases back down on the table. "How do you know Ismae?"

I can feel his eyes upon me, assessing, weighing, but I concentrate very carefully on folding the square of soft linen around the boiled herbs. "We trained at the same convent."

There is a moment of silence during which I think he will let the matter drop, but no. "If you are an assassin trained, why are you here tending me?"

Unable to help it, I twist my mouth into a bitter smile as I return to his side. "It is a question I have asked myself many times, you can be certain. My orders were to ensure you got safely to Rennes so that you could further serve the duchess." I look up and meet his gaze. "So that part of my taunting was true."

We stare into each other's eyes for a long moment, before the knight gives a small nod—of understanding or forgiveness, I am not certain. "Well then." He smiles, an utterly charming and devastating grin that makes me want to smile back at him. Instead, I lay the hot poultice on his thigh.

He sucks in his breath so hard I fear he has swallowed his tongue. His face grows red from the heat and the pain and the effort to not cry out. "I thought you said you were not here to kill me," he finally says with a gasp.

"I am sorry," I say. "It is the only way to draw out the poison so you will not die of blood fever."

"Just warn me next time."

"Very well, I am putting one on your shoulder now."

He gasps out again, but it is not as forceful as before. Good. The wound is less tender, then, and will hopefully be that much quicker to heal. I glance back up at him to see how he is doing. "You should, by all rights, be dead from these wounds."

A brief flash of white teeth. "A gift from Saint Camulos. We heal quickly."

As the poultices draw the foul humors from his body, I turn my attention to his arm. "This must be cleaned," I warn him. "Vigorously."

My patient grimaces. "Do what you must so that I may have full use of the arm."

The next hour is not a pleasant one. I lay a wet cloth on the cut to soften it, then replace the poultices with fresh ones. "Would you like some wine or spirits to ease the pain?" I ask, but he gives a sharp shake of his head.

When the scab is soft enough I take a cloth and begin gently sponging away the dirt and grime and old mud that cakes the wound.

"You never said how you know so much about treating injuries," the knight says.

I glance up at him in annoyance. "Why have you not yet passed out from the pain?"

"I welcome pain; it lets me know I am alive."

While I cannot help but admire his spirit, I remind myself that it is wasted effort to like someone who will likely die of his wounds anyway. "You are as mad as your reputation suggests."

He grins. "You have heard of me?"

I roll my eyes. "I have heard of a madman who dons battle fever like most men don armor and charges out into the field killing nigh unto hundreds of souls."

He settles more comfortably onto the blanket. "You *have* heard of me," he says, the satisfaction thick in his voice. "Ow!"

"My pardon, but the gravel and mud is ground in deep." I work in blessed silence for a while, marveling that a man so ugly can have such a charming grin. Annoyed that I am thinking of such things, I get up to fetch a knife. The wound is infected and will need to be drained.

"You still have not told me how you come to know so much about treating injuries."

"You talk too much. Lie still and try to heal quickly, will you?" I say, returning to his side with the knife. "We have a long way to go and your condition will slow us down considerably. Indeed, we will likely be captured if you do not get better soon."

The Beast of Waroch scowls, and I can feel the jailor studying me. I wonder how much he has pieced together from my visit to the dungeon with Julian. "Perhaps you are hiding something?"

Only the truth of who I am. "No, I just prefer to work in silence. However, since you insist—I was trained at the convent in small medicines such as this."

Disbelief is plain on his face. "This is no small medicine."

I lay the finely honed blade of my knife along the oozing scab. It parts easily, like a flower opening before the sun. "My brothers were knights as well. They often had injuries such as these that needed to be treated."

"By their sister?" he asks between clenched teeth.

"We were close." Also, my father did not keep a physician on staff, and my brothers were too embarrassed to seek out the surgeon of the men-at-arms for the beatings and lashing my father bestowed upon them. "However, now that I have answered your question—"

He snorts. "That was no answer."

"—you must answer one of mine." He looks at me cautiously. "Who is your pet gargoyle and how is Count d'Albret's own jailor more loyal to you than to the count? For not only did he allow you to escape—he helped me."

Of a sudden, all lightness and good humor disappears from Beast's face. "Perhaps he did not wish to stay behind and accept d'Albret's punishment."

"Perhaps not," I say, disappointed, for I know that is not the reason, or at least, it is only one part of it.

"What do you know of d'Albret?" Beast asks.

"More than I care to," I mutter as I place another poultice on his arm to draw out the infection.

"You do well to fear him. Even for someone with your skills, it is not safe to be near the man."

I fight the urge to laugh in his face for daring to warn *me* of the dangers d'Albret presents. "You need not worry. I know all about Count d'Albret. Stories circulated throughout his hall faster than the annual plague. Indeed, it was one of the old women's favorite pastimes, terrorizing us with the tale of d'Albret's first wife. Have you heard it?" I glance up, my eyes wide and innocent.

He gives a curt shake of his head.

"Oh, la, everyone knows the story of his first wife. Indeed, it has become legend, one told by beleaguered husbands and tired matrons when they wished their wives or young charges to be more pliant. 'Did I ever tell you the story of Count d'Albret's first wife, Jeanne?' they would ask. 'She thought to escape her wifely duties and fled to her family home, where she begged sanctuary with her brother. Well, her fool brother should have known better than to come between a man and his wife, but he had a soft heart and agreed to harbor her against the cruelty she claimed of her own husband.

"'But that d'Albret,' they'd say, often with admiration in their voice, 'he let no man take what was rightfully his and certainly not some baron from Morbihan. He rode with a full battalion of men straight to the baron's holding, where he burst through the gates and slaughtered every one of the men-at-arms as they scrambled for their weapons. He rode his horse right into the main hall and killed the baron at his table, and then d'Albret struck down his own wife even as she begged for mercy.'"

As I tell the story, I feel those earlier tendrils of hope begin to wither. What was I thinking? There can be no escape from d'Albret. All I have done is delay the inevitable.

"To be certain his point was made," I continue, "d'Albret killed the baron's wife and two young sons and the newborn babe she nursed at her breast." My heart twists painfully at the thought of that babe. "Wives usually did what their husbands asked of them after that tale was told." I look up to see that Beast's face is hard as stone. "So yes, I do know what d'Albret is capable of."

I remove the poultice, relieved to see the swelling has already gone down. Next, I reach for the flask of spirits. "This will sting a bit," I tell him. It is a lie, for it will burn like fire, but I cannot talk to this man anymore. I know from long experience that hope is but a taunt from the gods, and I hate that somehow this man causes me to feel it.

Beast opens his mouth to speak just as I tilt the flask. "My sister was his sixth wife —" The spirits hit his raw flesh and he rears up on the table, roaring in pain, before finally blacking out.

Chapter Seventeen

SHOCKED, I STARE DOWN AT the unconscious giant before me. His sister was d'Albret's wife? How can that be? What crazed, tangled web have the gods woven around us?

I study the lumpy, bruised face, searching for signs of Alyse, d'Albret's sixth wife. She spoke of having a brother, but it is hard to imagine them springing from the same womb.

Knowing I will not be able to sleep with Beast's admission plaguing me like the biting flies of high summer, I tell the gargoyle that I will take the first watch. Even though this hunting lodge is well hidden, we dare not lower our guard.

He does not argue and curls up near the dying fire and falls asleep with an ease I cannot help but envy. Only then, when no one can see, do I let myself think of Alyse.

Her hair was the reddish blond of a fox kit's fur, and her face covered in freckles that my brothers claimed were the pox but that I thought were merely homely. She was always bringing flowers into the house, not just from our formal garden, but from the meadows as well. Even budding branches from the fruit trees in our orchard, which made the servants think she was daft.

Even more exhilarating, she brought smiles and laughter. It was as if the sun had finally emerged from the clouds in our household, or at least at first. My older brothers took cruel delight in tormenting and teasing her. And Julian, well, I think he begrudged her my affection, for every minute I spent with her was one I did not spend with him. And even with all of that, she was kind to me up until the end.

That Beast is her brother . . . well, clearly the gods are having a rich jape at my expense.

Or . . . the thought comes to me slowly . . . perhaps they are giving me a chance to balance the scales of justice. For if I am able to save this man from d'Albret's dungeons and deliver him safely to Rennes, I will have paid back some small part of the debt I owe his family.

Desperate to distract myself from the truth I have just learned, I push away from the sleeping knight and pick up the filthy discarded clothing and the dirty rags. We will have to bury these. Or perhaps I will send the gargoyle out to burn them. If he could set the fire at a great enough distance, it might even direct d'Albret's search away from us.

When I have tidied as best I can, I take a sharpening stone from one of the bundles and move outside. The rain has stopped, which will make it easier to listen for approaching horses. I remove one of my knives from its sheath and draw the stone along its edge. The faint scraping sound is as calming as a lullaby to my frayed nerves. Like a scavenger eager to pick over carrion, my reeling mind keeps returning to the one thing I do not want to think about. Truly, the gods have outdone themselves this time, for there are few people in this world I owe a greater debt to than Alyse. There are fewer people my family has wronged more horribly.

Is it possible I have been given a chance to right those wrongs?

Not that it matters, for getting Beast to Rennes alive and whole and without being found by d'Albret's scouts is not any easier simply because he is Alyse's brother.

It is, however, that much more vital that I do so, for more than the kingdom's future hangs in the balance—my one small chance at redemption does as well.

When I run out of chores to keep me outside, it is time to return to the kitchen. There is much to be done—new poultices to be prepared, bandages to be cut, fires to be tended. Those tasks do not care one whit for the newfound shyness I feel toward Beast. Will he bring up the subject of his sister when he awakens? And if he does, how can I keep all the questions I have from spilling out?

Inside, I see that Beast's eyes are open and he is staring at the ceiling above him. "You are still alive," I say. "That is more than I dared hope for."

He turns his head to me. "I told you I was hard to kill."

"You did warn me, yes." I can feel his eyes on me as I busy myself with putting more water on to boil. Does he even remember that he spoke of Alyse? And what would a simple assassin wish to know of that connection? Nothing, most likely. "Is that why you were not slain on the battlefield?" I ask. "Some gift of Saint Camulos? Or was it because d'Albret had other plans for you?"

"Saint Camulos does not protect us from death." Beast's voice is dry. "Nor did the men realize whom they had unhorsed. However, once d'Albret saw who I was, let us just say he is not one to let such an opportunity go to waste." He is quiet for a moment, then speaks again. "Do you know what they had planned for me?"

Unable to help myself, I look up and meet his gaze. "I do."

He nods. "Then you understand the debt I owe you."

Uncomfortable with the gratitude I see in his eyes, I look back to the pot of water. "Do not be so very grateful. If I had not been able to get your lumbering carcass up those stairs, I would have killed you myself and saved d'Albret the trouble."

"Then I would have owed you an even greater debt, for not everyone recognizes the mercy in a quick, clean death." He pauses then, studying me. "How would you have done it?"

His question surprises me. "You mean how would I have killed you?"

"Yes. Do you have a favorite method for such things?"

Since he knows I am an assassin, there is no need to be coy. "I prefer a garrote. I like the intimacy it allows me when I whisper reminders of vengeance in their ears as they die. But in your case, I had sharpened my favorite knife especially for the occasion."

His brows quirk up. "Why no garrote for me?"

I look pointedly at his thick neck, bulging with muscle and sinew. "I do not have one big enough," I mutter. "Besides, yours was to be a merciful death. A knife is quicker and less painful." If I thought my confession would shock him into putting some distance between us, I was sorely mistaken, for the great lummox laughs.

Frustrated by this kindness—one I do not deserve—I set the new poultice on his thigh, and his laughter quickly turns to grunts of pain.

Shortly after that, I gently nudge the gargoyle awake, for if I do not get some rest soon, I fear I will grab Beast by his shoulders and force him to answer all the questions crowding their way onto my tongue. It would not take him long to figure out my connection to d'Albret if I were to do that.

The jailor springs nimbly to his feet, checks once on his prisoner—now his patient—then goes to sit by the door. I stretch out by the fire and pray I will not dream of Alyse. Indeed, I do not wish to dream at all.

* * *

I come awake with a start, surprised that I have slept. It is nearly dark outside, and the ashes are cold in the hearth. I have slept almost all day. As I sit up, it occurs to me that it is too quiet. Is that what woke me? And then I hear it. The faint jingle of a harness and the soft whinny of a horse.

Panic surges in my breast and I leap to my feet. The gargoyle lurks in the doorway, peering out into the yard. With one hand he holds up three fingers, and in the other he holds his slingshot and a fat round rock the size of a quail's egg.

There is a rustle as Beast stirs. I hurry over to him, desperate to keep him quiet. He opens his eyes, but when he sees me put my fingers to my lips, he gives a curt nod, then motions me closer. "Give me a weapon," he whispers hoarsely.

"You are too sick to fight," I whisper back.

He grabs my arm, his eyes burning with determination. "I will not go back there alive." A moment of complete understanding passes between us. I nod, then retrieve one of the knives strapped to my ankle and hand it to him. When he takes it, his hand wraps briefly around mine and gives it a firm squeeze. "How many?" he asks.

"Three," I tell him. "With horses."

His eyes light up and he smiles. "Horses?"

I hurry back to the door and peer out. The men have reached the courtyard and I can hear their voices. "I still say we should just make for Nantes. We'll be there shortly after dark."

"Empty-handed," another one points out. "And I don't relish being the one to tell d'Albret that they got clean away and we've nothing to report."

The little jailor sends me a sly look.

"Hell, we don't even know what we're searching for. The girl? The prisoner? How far could either one of them have gotten?"

"I say we should just keep riding and not return," one of them mutters darkly. "Who knows where his wrath will fall."

As the men dismount, I chafe at the convent's theology. It is not nearly well enough suited to the real world for my liking. I am allowed to kill in self-defense, but is the danger these men present enough to qualify as self-defense? For all that I have decided I no longer care what the convent or Mortain thinks, their teachings are not as easy to discard as an old gown.

But these are d'Albret's men, not innocents. And if I do not kill them, Beast will not reach Rennes. Which means their deaths are necessary for me to follow the convent's most recent orders. If Mortain does not like it, He can take it up with the abbess herself.

"See to the horses," the leader says, taking his saddlebags from his mount. "I'll go start a fire."

"Don't drink all the wine!"

The leader's grin flashes white in the gloaming. The others dismount and head for the stables. The gargoyle and I exchange a glance. Our presence will be known once they see the mules and cart. A minute later, a shout goes up, and one of the men sticks his head out of the stable door. The captain pauses.

"Someone's here," he calls out.

The captain nods. "We will tell them we need lodgings for the night." His hand goes to his sword hilt. "And we will discourage them from arguing the point."

I catch the gargoyle's eye and hold up my garrote, letting him know that I will take the captain. He nods his understanding and points to the stable. He will take the first one to come out. The third one is up for grabs—whoever gets to him first. My knife would be quicker, but in the dusk I cannot be certain of a kill strike, and I do not want to risk his calling out a warning.

I wrap the ends of the garrote firmly around my hands and wait. The captain approaches, calling out a greeting. "Hello? You in there. We have need of your hospitality."

When there is no answer, his hand drifts away from his sword. As he draws closer, a still calm descends over me. When he is within arm's length, I step quickly from the shadows, wrap the wire around his neck, jam my knee into his kidneys, and pray for strength. My movements are so quick and sure there is not even a whisper or a gurgle. But the man is strong and he flails against me, trying to grab his sword. I lean my body weight into him and jam his hand against the stone wall of the lodge.

The second man emerges from the stable. His eyes widen as he sees his captain and I locked in our deadly embrace. Before he can reach for his sword, there is a soft *thwack* as the gargoyle's stone splits his forehead.

But the third guard must have heard something for he comes out of the stable with his crossbow cocked and loaded. I maneuver the struggling captain around so his body can shield mine, then brace myself for the violent bite of the crossbow bolt. There is a faint whisper of sound instead, as if a swift bird has just darted by, then a knife — my own knife — is jutting from the man's throat.

I look over to find Beast hanging out the window. He is pale as milk and leaning heavily against the sill, but he sends me a grin. "I'll take the chestnut gelding," he says, just before his eyes roll up and he crashes to the floor.

Merde. I hope he has not ripped out the stitches.

Once we are back inside, the jailor starts to scuttle over to the fallen Beast. I tell him to leave him be, then grab a blanket from the trestle bed and cover the passed-out giant. Except for the paleness of his face, he looks as if he is sleeping peacefully. I cannot decide if I want to kick him or thank him. It will be impossible to keep him alive if he does not have a care for his wounded body.

I look up to find the little gargoyle watching me, his head cocked as if he is puzzling something out. "Go fetch your master some new clothes from the fallen men," I tell him. "And weapons. Collect all the weapons they carry. We will have need of them soon enough."

The little man's face lights up and he heads outside. "And check their saddlebags for any provisions!" I call after him. I packed only enough for two, and for only three days. I fear we will need twice that much to reach Rennes now. If Ismae were here, she would say that Blessed Mortain had delivered a solution into our waiting hands, but I say I have just grown adept at snatching providence from the jaws of disaster.

I return to the hearth to stoke the fire back to life so that I may prepare yet another batch of poultices. As much as they pain Beast, they are no fun for me, either. My hands are red and raw from the heat and the mud. At least they will not look like a noblewoman's much longer.

The little man returns carrying a pile of clothing, and I sort through the pickings, looking for the ones that will come the closest to fitting Beast. The soldier that took the knife in the throat is the biggest by far, but now there are bloodstains on his jerkin. Even so, we use the bulk of his clothes, and I remove a jerkin from the next largest soldier. The rest I will use for bandages.

"We will take their horses with us when we leave," I tell the gargoyle. "Then we can change out the pulling team on the cart, which should allow us to make better time."

"I will not be hauled around like a bushel of turnips to market." Beast's deep voice rumbles from behind us. "I will ride one of the horses."

Slowly, I turn around. "You're awake."

"Aye."

All my questions about Alyse crowd their way to my tongue and nearly leap out of my mouth. Instead, I ask, "How do you plan to stay in the saddle when you cannot even look out the window without fainting? It is a full twenty leagues between here and Rennes."

"I did not faint. And being carried in that cart is like being bumped along the road in a sack full of rocks. I will arrive in Rennes with my bones ground to dust. Lash me onto one of the horses instead. That way, even if I lose consciousness, I will not fall off."

And that is when I finally see a faint resemblance between him and his sister: in the stubborn set of his jaw. "You are not even well enough to sit up, much less ride a horse for the next several days."

"I am better," he says obstinately, this time reminding me far too much of my sister Louise when she had lung fever and did not want to miss the Christmas festivities. "See?" He moves his injured arm more freely than before. I kneel next to him—to inspect his wounds more closely, I tell myself. But even as I put the back of my hand to his forehead, my eyes search his, looking for echoes of Alyse. Her lashes were not so dark or thick, but her eyes were very nearly as light a blue. "You still have a fever," I tell him.

"But it does not burn as hot."

"True." Next, I inspect his arm. The redness and infection have gone down by half. "But your other injuries. Your ribs—"

"You will bind my ribs tightly so they will not move. I can ride with only one hand on the reins."

I look up into his cold blue eyes that are not cold at all. "And what of your lance wound?" I reach for the blanket so I may look at it.

The wound is still red, the flesh angry and swollen and oozing. "It will hurt like the very devil," he concedes, "but the pain will help keep me alert."

The man is truly mad, possessed by battle fever even when there is no battle. "Everything I know of blood poisoning says the patient must rest in order to be strong enough to fight off the infection."

"Put another sack of mud on it," he says, as if that will make this scheme more reasonable.

"I plan to," I say, annoyed that the person I risked so much to rescue is now ordering me around as if I were a serving wench.

He leans closer, pressing his case. "You know I am right. We will move at a slug's pace in a cart and be an easy target for any pursuers. Or random bandits and outlaws, for that matter."

And of course, he *is* right. I glance behind me at the door to the courtyard, where the three men-at-arms lay dead, a chill moving across my shoulders at how very close d'Albret came to discovering us. "Very well," I concede. D'Albret has cast his net, and if we do not get moving, he will find us.

We spend the next hour making our plans. We will sleep one more night here, then leave as soon as it is light enough to see. I make another small fire in the hearth and set the mud and herbs for another poultice to boiling. When the mixture is nearly hot enough to blister skin, I fill a linen square with the mud and herbs, wrapping it as quickly as possible so the heat does not escape, nearly burning my fingers in the process.

As I move away from the hearth, the jailor comes in from the yard, where he has collected every weapon d'Albret's men carried. He sets them down next to Beast, then moves to take a turn at the dwindling embers in an attempt to prepare something for our empty bellies.

Beast hisses as I lay a poultice on his shoulder. "Lie still," I tell him.

"I am," he says between clenched teeth, then hisses again as I place the second poultice on his festering leg wound.

He glares at me. "You needn't enjoy this so much."

I send him a scathing glance. "You are deranged if you think I am enjoying being trapped in an abandoned hut with an ogre and a gargoyle as my only companions." I turn away from him to collect the linen strips I made from the soldier's unused shirts, surprised to realize I *am* enjoying this. There are no vipers slithering about underfoot nor nightmares lurking in the shadows.

When I turn back to him, I make sure none of my thoughts show on my face. "Can you sit up so I can bind your ribs?" If he cannot sit, best we know it now so we can alter our plans. He grunts an assent, the muscles in his abdomen shifting and rippling like waves as he pulls himself into a sitting position. His eyes close for a moment.

"Are you going to faint again?" I hurry around to block his fall so he will not crash to the ground. Although like as not he would just take me to the floor with him.

"No," he grunts.

I wait a minute to be sure he isn't fooling himself, then go back and pick up the linen strip and begin wrapping it around his torso. Even after being locked away for more than a fortnight, he is as thick as a tree trunk.

"For a woman with a sharp tongue, you have surprisingly gentle hands," he says.

"I think your injuries have caused you to lose the feeling in your body, for while I am many things, none of them are gentle."

He says nothing but watches me, as if trying to peer past my skin and my bone to my very soul. Under his scrutiny, my movements grow clumsy. "Here," I say shortly. "Hold that in place." I turn and fetch another piece of linen.

"Did these brothers of yours suffer broken ribs often?" he asks.

"Once or twice," I mutter, busying myself with the second strip. "They were clumsy lads and constantly falling from their horses." I do not meet his gaze, for of course they were not. Pierre's ribs were broken when, at twelve years of age, he was unseated from his horse by a blow from a lance in tourney practice. My father kicked him until he rose to his feet and remounted his horse. He suffered far more from my father's kicks than from the fall.

And Julian—ah, Julian. His ribs were broken while trying to protect me from my father's wrath.

"What's wrong?" Beast asks softly.

"Nothing," I tell him, pulling the bandage so tight that he grunts in protest. "I only worry about how we will get you back on your horse if you fall off."

Beast says nothing more until the gargoyle motions to us that our supper is ready. I secure the last bandage and hand Beast the bowl of what appears to be gruel with something unsavory-looking floating in it. "So," I say, taking my own bowl. "Your man cannot tend wounds, nor even wash your face properly, nor is he a cook. What, precisely, is he to you?" I ask.

Beast ignores me and shovels the gruel in as fast as he can. If his appetite has returned in full, that is a good sign. Or perhaps he is merely afraid that if it grows cool it will be inedible. Certainly that is my fear.

When he is done, he sets the bowl down and turns his steady gaze to me. "Yannic was once my squire. When my sister left for d'Albret's household, I ordered him to accompany her and send me regular reports on her well-being."

I gape at him, then turn to stare at Yannic. I am certain I never saw him in our household, although that would not be so unusual. My father has hundreds of servants and thousands of vassals, many of whom I have never met. "Could he speak then?" I am afraid I already know the answer.

"Aye," Beast says grimly. "And write, too."

I glance down at Yannic's right hand to see that the top half of each of his three middle fingers has been removed so he cannot hold a quill.

Unwilling to look either of them in the eye, I pretend I am busy fishing for a piece of sausage in my bowl.

Did d'Albret remember this connection between his prisoner and his sixth wife's attendant and use it as one rubs salt into a wound? Or was Yannic the only one available who lacked the power of speech and so made an ideal jailor? One could never be certain with d'Albret. "Does that mean Yannic would not mind if we asked him to pile the dead soldiers into the cart and set fire to them? It would be better to leave no signs of our stay."

The two men exchange a dark look, then Beast answers. "No, he would not mind a bit."

"Good, because we should not waste an opportunity to lead our pursuers well away from us. The smoke from such a large fire should get their attention, and the dead bodies will make them question just how many are in our party. If Yannic can drive the cart a mile or two east of here, the fire will also lead them in the wrong direction."

Beast grins. "If you ever tire of being Mortain's handmaiden, I am certain Saint Camulos would be more than happy to accept your service."

I roll my eyes at the mere idea of such a thing, but his words please me, all the same.

Chapter Eighteen

WE TRY TO GET AN early start the next day, but between the little gnome of a jailor, the wounded giant, and—what role do I assign myself? The charioteer?—we are like a mummers' farce. At last we get the horses ready and the gear packed and—most difficult of all—the lumbering, crippled Beast onto his saddle. I am exhausted before we even leave the yard, but when we finally do, I breathe a sigh of relief.

In spite of what Beast claims, he is far from well enough to travel. We should stay at the hunting lodge another day or two to allow him more time to recover, but we dare not. While the lodge is well off the main road and not widely known, I have no doubt more of d'Albret's men will find it soon enough. Luckily, I do not think it will be the first place they look, for they will assume we want to put more distance between ourselves and our pursuers. And they are right. The back of my neck tingles with foreboding.

Brisk winds have blown the rain clouds away, and the sky above is clear and blue. All that clear sky makes a perfect backdrop for the thin trickle of smoke that rises from the smoldering remains of the night-soil cart and its inhabitants nearly a mile away.

Please Mortain, let it buy us some time.

But in case it does not, we are each armed with weapons scavenged from d'Albret's men. With Yannic's help, Beast has altered a scabbard so he may wear the sword on his back within easy reach. I, too, have a sword, but it is strapped to my saddle next to the crossbow that hangs there. Beast has also purloined the woodcutter's ax from its place near the lodge's woodpile. It hangs from the left side of his saddle near his injured arm. Although how he expects to wield it, I do not know.

We ride out in silence. Beast is wisely conserving his energy, and I have far too much to think about to waste time in idle conversation. If all goes well, we should be there in four days. *If* the fever does not consume Beast's weakened body, and *if* he can stay in the saddle, and *if* d'Albret's riders do not find us.

My mind keeps running over what I know of the countryside, trying to think of the best route for us to take. The area around the hunting lodge is sparse woodland, which serves us well enough, but eventually we will come to fields or a road or, worst of all, a town. How many men will d'Albret have sent out, and where will they focus their search?

And how long can Beast stay in the saddle? Already his head nods and he looks to be dozing. Or perhaps he has fainted again. I nudge my horse over to him to check, surprised when his head snaps up, his eyes focused on the trees in front of us. "Do you hear that?"

I tilt my head. "What?"

We continue forward, but more slowly. "That," he says, his head cocked to the side. "Raised voices."

I stare at him in disbelief, for my own hearing is as sharp as anyone's and I have not heard a peep. "Mayhap it is simply ringing in your ears from your injuries."

He gives a sharp shake of his head and urges his horse forward.

"Wait!" I make a grab for his reins but miss. "In order to avoid trouble," I remind him, "we move away from the noise, not toward it."

His head swings around and he pins me with the full force of his intense gaze. "What if those are more of d'Albret's men? Will we have some innocent pay for our freedom?"

"Of course not," I snap. "But I am not used to this idea that your god allows you to kill at your own whim."

Beast's eyes narrow in that way he has that sees past my skin into my very bones. "My god allows me to save the innocent," he says. "Does yours not?"

I am ashamed to admit that my god does not allow any such thing. "There are no innocents where Death is concerned," I tell him, then move into the lead. We continue our approach, easing our horses forward until we have a clear view of where the noise came from. It is a mill house, its wheel turning briskly in a stream made fat by the recent rains. It is as peaceful-looking as a painting. "See? It was nothing. We can continue on our way with no one the wiser."

Just as Beast nods in agreement, a man steps out of the mill and hurries toward us. When he is half a bowshot away, he stops. "The mill is closed today," he calls out. "Broken, and needing repair."

"Something is not right," Beast says quietly. "The man is whey-faced, and sweat beads his brow."

"My job is to get you to Rennes in one piece, not to stop and offer assistance to every peasant in need we come across. Perhaps he has simply been working hard this morning? Besides, once you dismount, I am not sure we can get you back on that horse." But something *isn't* right. The man's heart is beating at a frantic pace.

"For one, he is a miller, not a peasant. And two" — Beast gives me a grin as infectious as the plague — "I can kill without getting off my horse."

Easing my own horse forward with small, unthreatening steps, I allow myself to draw closer. "We have no need of the mill," I call out to him. "We are just passing through and thought to refill our water skins."

The miller wrings his hands. "This is not a good place for that. The bank is too steep. There is a much shallower access just a short way up the road."

I nudge my horse to take another step, then another, and that is when I feel four more heartbeats nearby. One of those is lighter than the others but racing as wildly as the miller's.

"Ah, but we are thirsty now." I swing out of my saddle and onto the ground. "And the sound of all that sweet water so close by is like torture to our dry throats." I keep my voice and movements light as I turn and remove one of the water skins from my saddle. While my body is blocking my movements, I also load and cock the crossbow, poke an extra bolt through the fabric of my gown, then unhitch the bow. I give Beast a pointed look, and he nods. Hiding the crossbow in my skirts, I turn around and head toward the miller.

He hurries forward, nearly dancing in distress. "No, no. You must not—"

I put one hand to my stomach as if I am ill and stumble into him. "Who is it they have?" I whisper. "Your wife? Your daughter?"

His eyes widen in fright, and he crosses himself, then nods.

"All will be well," I tell him, and hope that it is not a lie. There! A glint of steel from the barn door. Another from the branches of the tree in the yard. "The barn!" I shout to Beast as I pull my crossbow out and aim for the man in the tree. I hear his grunt as the bolt finds him. Before his body hits the ground, I slap the second bolt in place. A girl screams and darts from the mill into the yard, followed by a soldier. He raises his crossbow in my direction, but mine is already trained on him, and my bolt catches him in the chest before he can release his own. The girl screams again as he tumbles to the ground, nearly taking her down with him. The man from the tree is not moving, and there is no heartbeat coming from the barn, so Beast's aim must have been as good as mine. Just to be certain, I draw a knife before hurrying to the girl and the fallen soldier.

Beast steers his horse to the miller. "Peace," he says. "We will not harm you. We merely wanted to stop trouble in its tracks."

The miller's relief is tempered with wariness and he begins talking fast, proclaiming his own innocence, telling how these soldiers, these thugs, showed up at their door and began beating and questioning them. "They had just gone into the mill to cut open all the sacks of grain when they heard you coming."

It would, I admit, be a good place to hide. I let Beast deal with the outraged man and turn to the daughter. Her blouse is torn and she is breathing fast, too fast, as if she has run some great distance, and I can still feel her heart beating frantically in her breast, like a small, frightened bird. "Did they harm you?" I ask quietly.

She looks at me, her eyes wild with barely checked terror, then shakes her head no.

But I know it for a lie, even if she does not. Those men have destroyed her sense of safety for months—possibly years—to come. Unable to stop myself, I reach out and grip her shoulder. "It was not your fault," I whisper fiercely. "You and your father did nothing to deserve this except be in the wrong place at the wrong time. It was not a punishment from God nor any of His saints—it was simply brutish thugs who happened upon you."

Something in her frightened eyes shifts slightly, and I can see her grasp my words like a drowning man grabs a rope. I nod, then turn to retrieve my crossbow bolts.

We do not tarry long. Between Yannic and the miller and myself, we hoist the three dead bodies back onto their horses, and take the horses with us when we go.

"We will have to veer farther west if we wish to avoid d'Albret's men," I tell Beast as we ride away.

Beast nods in agreement, then grins. "I've never met a lady who enjoys her work as much as I enjoy mine."

"My work?"

"Killing. Assassin-ing."

"What are you implying?"

He looks puzzled at the anger in my voice. "That you are very good at what you do. It was a compliment, nothing more."

Of course, *he* would mean it as a compliment. "Just how many other lady assassins have you met?"

"Other than you? Only Ismae. And she seemed to approach her duty with more earnestness than true joy, whereas you come alive with a knife in your hand."

Hotly uncomfortable with his assessment, I fall silent.

Do I enjoy killing? Is it the act itself that brings me joy? Or do I embrace the sense of higher purpose it gives me?

Or do I simply enjoy having something at which I excel, as there are few enough skills that I possess?

However, if I do enjoy killing, how does that make me any different from d'Albret?

It is only Mortain—His guidance and blessing that separates us. And I have rejected that.

But Beast kills as well, efficiently and expertly, and does not seem tainted by the same darkness that colors d'Albret and myself. I have never seen anyone kill so cheerfully or eagerly, and yet he is light of heart. "How did you come to serve your god?" I ask, breaking a long silence.

Beast grows quiet, grim even. Just when I have decided that he is not going to answer, he speaks. "It is said that when a man rapes a woman while the battle lust is still upon him, any child that results belongs to Saint Camulos. I was such a babe. My lady mother was assaulted by a soldier while her own husband was off fighting against King Charles."

"And yet she loved you and raised you as any of her other children?" I ask, somewhat in awe of her charitable nature.

Beast snorts out a laugh. "Saints, no! She tried to drown me twice and smother me once before I was one year old." He falls silent. "It was Alyse who saved me, usually toddling in at just the right moment."

"You remember that far back?"

"No, my lady mother was wont to throw it in my face at every opportunity. She was afraid of explaining my presence to her lord husband, but in the end, he never returned — he was killed on the fields of Gascony, pierced through with a lance.

"By then, I was nearly two years old, and little Alyse had grown fond of me. She rarely left my side in those years. I think she was afraid of what would happen to me if she did." He grows quiet for a long moment before speaking again. "I owe Alyse my very life, and I failed her."

I dare to ask the question that has been haunting me since I learned that Alyse was his sister. "Why did your mother wish for the marriage? Why did d'Albret, for that matter?"

"D'Albret pressed for the marriage because part of Alyse's dower lands abutted one of his lesser holdings that he wished to expand. And she was young and healthy and able to bear him many sons. Or so our lady mother promised him."

And thus sealed her daughter's death warrant when Alyse could not. What sort of woman promises such things?

"I did not want her to marry him," he says softly. "I did not trust him, or the fact that five wives had preceded Alyse. But our lady mother was blinded by his title and wealth, and Alyse herself was always eager to keep our mother happy." His voice trails off, and the silence that follows is so filled with sorrow, I cannot bring myself to break it.

Leaving Beast to his painful memories, I turn my thoughts to our travels. How far west will we need to go to avoid d'Albret's men? And when should we release the horses with the dead soldiers? I fear we are still too close to the miller and his daughter, and I would not wish the dead to be found anywhere near them.

Even though we cannot see it through the trees, we are drawing near a large stream that, by the sound of it, has swollen to the size of a river with the recent rains. The raging water rushing over the rocks is nearly deafening and I must shout for Beast to hear me. "We must look for a place to cross."

He nods and we turn our horses in that direction, skirting the thicket until the trees finally thin and we are able to gain passage onto the bank of the stream.

Where soldiers wearing d'Albret's colors are watering their horses.

Chapter Nineteen

THERE ARE TWELVE MEN ALTOGETHER. Two kneel at the water's edge, filling their water skins. Another is watering three of the horses, and a fourth is taking a piss by a tree. That is the only thing that saves us with such uneven numbers: that half of them have dismounted and are taking their leisure. That and Beast's quick reflexes.

Before I have fully registered my surprise, Beast draws his sword and charges into the startled group of men before they can react. He aims straight for the three closest riders. The bank explodes in activity as soldiers scramble for their weapons.

As Beast rides into the fray, my body reacts without conscious thought. I drop my reins and pull my knives from my wrists. The first one strikes one of the mounted soldiers closest to me, catching him in the throat. My second knife takes the next mounted soldier in the eye so that he is thrown backwards just as his horse leaps forward. Some days, like today, my aim and timing is so true it takes my breath away and I feel certain Mortain's hand guides my own.

As I reach for my crossbow, Beast gives a battle yell that fair curdles my blood. His sword arcs through the air, decapitating one soldier and then slicing a second man near in two on its backstroke. Before Beast can regroup, a third raises his sword, then reels in surprise when a stone from Yannic's slingshot punches through his teeth, giving Beast time to finish him off.

My crossbow loaded and cocked, I turn to the riders by the stream and pick one off. Two others go for their own crossbows, but not fast enough. The bolt catches one and sends him stumbling into the second man, which gives me time to grab another of my knives and throw it, the silver blade whipping fast and sure across the distance to sink into his eye socket and send him reeling into the stream.

I use the time that buys me to reload my crossbow, but one of the mounted men breaks away from Beast and wheels in my direction before I can get it cocked. I drop the bow and pull the sword from its scabbard, getting it between me and my attacker. "Lady Sybel—" It is only when he hesitates long enough for me to get past his guard and cut off the rest of his words that I realize they have been ordered to take me alive.

Which gives me some small advantage, for I do not care if I kill them. Indeed, I pray that I will.

One of the remaining men is reloading his crossbow, which is aimed right for me. I am out of knives, and Beast is too far away to help. He shouts, drawing the man's attention, and then I watch open-mouthed as Beast hurls his sword toward him.

I hold my breath as it spins through the air. The hilt catches the soldier full in the face, stunning rather than killing him. But it is enough to give the charging Beast time—he draws his ax, surges forward, and delivers a sickening blow to the soldier's head. Yannic finishes off the last two of them with well-slung rocks.

The stream's bank is awash in departing souls, shocking in their chillness, as if winter had suddenly returned. Some rush upward, eager to flee the carnage, even though it can no longer harm them. Others hover, like desolate children, lost, adrift, not sure they understand what has just happened.

It sickens me that I somehow manage to feel sympathy for them. To chase the unwelcome feelings away, I whirl around to rail at Beast.

"What in the names of the Nine Saints was that? *Throwing* your sword? Is that some special trick of Saint Camulos?"

He grins, and I am startled by how feral he looks, all gleaming white teeth and pale eyes in a blood-splattered face. Indeed, I do not believe he is quite human in that moment. "It slowed him down, didn't it?"

"By mere chance," I point out. It was the most foolish, jape-fisted bit of buffoonery I have ever seen, and I am impressed in spite of that.

A short while later, as I stare down at the bodies of the six men I have just killed, I cannot help but wonder: *Do* I love killing? Of a certainty, I love the way my body and weapons move as one; I revel in the knowledge of where to strike for maximum impact. And of a certainty, I am good at it.

But so is Beast. He is perhaps even better at it than I am, and yet for all that, he feels as bright and golden as a lion who roars in the face of his enemies and stalks them in broad daylight.

Whereas I — I am a dark panther, slinking unseen among the shadows, silent and deadly.

But we are both great cats, are we not? And do not even bright things cast a shadow? "Were they waiting for the men at the miller's?" I ask. "Or are they a separate party of scouts altogether?"

"A separate party, I think. See?" Beast points to a series of hoof prints in the muddy bank where the men had just crossed the stream. "They were on their way back."

My heart sinks. "Which means they have all the western routes covered. We will have to head due east and approach Rennes from that direction."

We risk riding into the arms of the French, but at least they will simply kill us and not try to take us back to d'Albret. If the truth be told, I'd rather take my chances with the French.

* * *

By the time we stop for the night, Beast is gray with exhaustion and fatigue and hardly able to do more than grunt. As we make camp, it is hard to know which is the greater threat: d'Albret and his be-damned scouts or the blood fever coursing through Beast's veins. In the end, I decide we must risk a small fire for the poultices, but by the time they are ready, Beast is fast asleep. He does not so much as stir when I place them on his wounds. As I stare down at his still, ugly face, I find myself praying that I will not be left with nothing but his limp, dead body to bring before the duchess.

By some miracle or stubbornness of constitution, Beast is better in the morning. Even so, I insist we travel at an easy pace, well away from the roads. When we stop for a midday break, I almost decide to make camp for the night then and there so Beast can rest, for he is exhausted again, and fresh blood flows from the injury at his thigh. He waves my concerns aside. "It is a good thing, for it will wash the foul humors from the wound." He insists we keep going, as the farther we get from our pursuers, the better.

Shortly afterward, we draw near the main road to Rennes. Apprehension fills me, for I am certain d'Albret will have it watched, but we must get across. Besides, even d'Albret does not have enough soldiers to man the entire road. Our hope is to find an unguarded section.

We lurk awhile, watching the travelers from our hiding spot in the trees. A farmer carrying hens by a pole across his shoulders goes by, followed by a tinker who clanks and clatters along. Neither of them tarry or linger or appear to be dawdling, so I doubt they are spies. A short while later, a sweat-stained courier races by on a lathered horse, and we can only wonder what news he carries, and to whom.

Since he is not followed—or accosted—we deem it safe to cross. We put our heels to our horses and hurry to the other side before anyone else comes along. Beast catches my eye and flashes me a grin, the first I have seen today, then leads us into the brush and spindly trees on the east side of the road, where we turn north.

I glance over to see how he is faring only to find him watching me. "What?" I ask, uneasy under the weight of that gaze—the man has a way of looking at me as if he can see beneath all the layers of my deception. It is most unsettling.

"One of the soldiers recognized you," he says.

Merde! With all that was going on, how could he have heard that? "Of course he recognized me," I scoff, as if he has hay for brains. "I have been in d'Albret's household for some time. How else do you think I was in a position to rescue you?"

Is it just my imagination or does his face clear somewhat? He frowns as if trying to work out some puzzle. "How did the convent secure you a position in d'Albret's entourage? By all accounts, he is more suspecting and distrustful than most."

"The abbess has many political connections among the noble families of Brittany." I use my most haughty voice in the hopes that it will deter further questions.

It does not look as if it will, for Beast opens his mouth once more, then—praise Mortain!—pauses and cocks his head to the side, an alert look on his face.

"Now what?" I ask.

Beast holds his hand up for us to halt. As I rein in my mount, I hear it: it is not the sound of fighting, exactly, but shouting and men's voices. "Oh, no," I whisper at him. "We are not playing at rescue again. You barely have enough strength today to stay in the saddle."

Ignoring me, he gives some silent command to his horse, who moves forward, winding along a path among the trees and drawing closer to the sounds. Hoping to forestall him, I follow, while Yannic hangs back with the pack animals.

There are five men with horses stopped in front of a farmhouse. Two sit upon their destriers with great, white fluffy bundles in front of them. It takes me a moment to recognize the bundles as sheep. Two of the others are trying frantically to corner a goose, which is doing its best to evade them, honking in irritation all the while. It would be almost comical except for the farmer and his wife standing in the yard held at spear point by the fifth man.

"French," Beast spits out.

"They do not appear to be harming the farmer or his wife."

"No, just raiding their food stores to feed their own troops." He turns to me and smiles. "We will stop them."

I stare at him in disbelief. "No, we won't. We cannot pick a fight with every soldier we see between Nantes and Rennes!"

"We cannot just leave these poor people to be bullied by our enemies. Besides"—he shoots his maniacal grin my way—"that will be five French soldiers I will not have to kill later."

"We cannot risk something happening to you over *foodstuffs*," I hiss back.

At an impasse, we stare at each other. Then his horse lifts its leg and steps forward, breaking a small branch under its hoof. A loud crack echoes through the air, and the shouting stops. "Who's there?" a voice calls out.

I glare at Beast. "You did that on purpose."

He scowls in mock annoyance. "It was the horse. But now that our presence is known, we have no choice." He removes the crossbow from its hook on the saddle and pulls three quarrels from the quiver.

I resign myself to our fate and decide to get it over with as quickly as possible. "I must get closer. When I am in place, I will hoot like an owl."

Now it is Beast's turn to frown. "I am not sure that is safe."

I roll my eyes as I dismount. "You are not my nursemaid. Remember, *I* am rescuing *you.*" I loop the reins around a nearby branch and begin to move quietly through the trees toward the house.

The leader is ordering one of the goose-chasing men to go in search of the noise they just heard. The woman is wringing her hands and crying about her new down pillow, but I block all of that out as I pick my spot next to a tree that is partially covered by a thick shrub. I pull out my knives and take careful aim at the soldier closest to the farmer and the one most likely to harm him. As I hoot like an owl, I send the first knife flying.

With knives, the two best choices for a kill shot at this distance are the throat or the eye. My aim is perfect and the knife catches him in the throat. The farmwife is made of sturdier stuff than the miller's daughter, for she does not scream, simply jumps out of the way of the splatter of blood.

My second knife and Beast's three crossbow bolts make quick work of the rest of them. When they are all dead, the three of us emerge from the trees. The farmer and his wife approach us, their greeting effusive. "Praise be to Matrona! She has sent you to deliver us from certain disaster."

"Well, you were not in *mortal* danger," I point out.

The farmwife bristles at this. "Not in mortal danger? What is starving to death, then, if not mortal danger?"

The farmer glances uneasily at the road. "Do you think more of them are coming?"

Beast follows his gaze. "Not immediately, no. But we'd best get the horses and bodies out of sight."

"*You* will do no such thing." I angle my horse to block his. When he starts to argue, I urge my horse closer and lower my voice. "If you do not have a care for yourself, then at least give a thought to what the duchess and my abbess will do to me if I arrive with nothing but your lifeless body."

An odd, pained expression crosses his face and I think that at last he understands my peril, if not his. "Besides, it will take all of us working together to get you off that horse and laid down somewhere where I can tend your wounds."

The farmwife's hand flies to her cheek. "Was he injured?"

"'Tis an old injury, but a bad one. Is there somewhere we can settle him?"

The farmwife nods. I leave Yannic and the farmer to help Beast from his horse and let the farmwife lead me into the house. As I enter, I look around in surprise, for outside, the farm seemed to me somewhat poor and rundown. Inside, the house is anything but. The farmwife meets my eye. "'Tis not by accident. Living so close to the border, and with so many wars and skirmishes over the years, we have learned to conceal our prosperity. When we are lucky enough to have it."

She stops at a small storeroom, takes a key from the ring around her waist, and unlocks the door. Two boys spill out, wearing fierce glowers. "Next time let us stay and fight," one of them says. He is on the cusp of true manhood, all gangly limbs, clumsy feet, and too-large nose.

"Mind your manners and greet our guest."

For the first time, both of them notice me. Even though I wear three days' travel grime instead of my finest jewels, their gaping admiration does wonders for my spirits.

The farmwife clucks her tongue. "Go on now, go help your father and the others get rid of the bodies."

"Bodies?" They perk up, then clatter out of the house.

"My husband is old and no threat to the soldiers, but I could not trust these hotheads not to do something foolish." The farmwife rolls her eyes, but it does not disguise the pride she feels in her sons.

The farmhouse has a large kitchen and a great room with a long table and benches. While looking for a spot for Beast to rest, I also try to note any exits. We may need to leave suddenly, for there is no guarantee the French will not send others to check on their comrades. And if the French can stumble upon this place, so can d'Albret and his men.

Besides the front door, the three windows with wooden shutters are the only way in and out. And certainly there is no place big enough to conceal Beast.

I nod to the area in front of the hearth. "That will work. The fire will keep him warm and allow me to mix the poultices I need for his leg."

Her face creases in concern. "How bad is it?"

I meet her intelligent brown-eyed gaze. "Bad enough. If I had any surgeon's skills, I would consider removing it, but luckily for him, I do not. A prayer or two on his behalf would not go amiss."

She nods. "This whole family shall pray for him," she says, and I know I can consider it as good as done.

Chapter Twenty

THE FAMILY IS SO GRATEFUL for our intervention, and so wonder-struck at being saved by the mighty Beast of Waroch himself, that once the floodgates of their gratitude have opened, it is impossible to stop it. They insist on slaughtering the goose so they may reward him with a feast fit for a hero of the realm. ("May as well start working on that pillow now," the farmwife points out.) Since we are all of us in need of a decent night's rest and would not begrudge a good meal, we accept their kind offer.

Amid much muttering and grumbling, Beast is assisted inside and made to lie down where I can tend him. It chafes him sorely to have to rest while other men take care of the remains of the French soldiers. "Leave it be," I tell him. "Anyone can hide those bodies or dispose of them, but only you can help the duchess, and she will have my hide if I do not deliver you as safe and sound as possible."

Fortunately for me, he is so exhausted that once he is laid out flat and the poultice is placed on his leg, he falls asleep. The bruises have faded away by now, and nearly all the facial swelling has gone down. He is still as big and ugly as an ogre.

"Won't win a prize at the fair, will he?"

I glance up to find the farmwife standing right behind me, staring down at Beast. "He has other skills," I tell her sharply.

"Eh, don't be biting my head off. I didn't say he wasn't worth his weight in gold. Besides, I wager he's very skilled with his blade." The faint leer in her voice makes her meaning plain enough, as well as her assumptions on what sort of relationship Beast and I have.

My even sharper retort is interrupted by a great clatter as her two sons come bursting inside, brandishing the weapons they've stripped from the soldiers. "Papa says we might as well profit from the stinking Frenchmen," the younger one says, nearly decapitating his brother with a sword that is almost as long as he is.

"Profit, yes; do bodily injury to your brother, no. Go on now, put those away."

The boys scramble up the ladder to their rooms, and I start to follow the farmwife as she heads to the kitchen to begin preparing the meal, but she quickly shoos me away. "Those were your knives that pierced two of the brutes. What kind of thanks would it be if I made you cook? Here." She thrusts a bucket of water at me, then takes a kettle from the hob and adds it to the bucket. "Go have yourself a wash. I'm sure it'll feel good after being on the road."

I should be insulted, but I am too grateful to have the opportunity to get clean. I take the bucket of water and go upstairs to the loft so I may take advantage of this unexpected bounty.

The dinner is as satisfying as any feast I have ever eaten. Not only is the goose cooked perfectly, crisp skin and juicy succulent meat, but there is a thick, hearty stew of mutton, leeks, and cabbage, dark brown bread and new cheese, thin red wine and pear cider, as well as baked apples with cream.

The dinner has the air of a party, with the farmer and his wife — Guion and Bette — full of the good cheer that follows a near miss. Even Yannic smiles and nods happily — although perhaps that is simply because his belly is finally full. The farmer's sons dither between awed hero worship that they are dining with the Beast of Waroch and clumsy attempts to impress him. Or at the very least, to shame the other.

"Anton squealed when the soldiers first arrived," Jacques says.

Flushing, Anton elbows him hard in the ribs. "Did not. My voice cracked is all."

Jacques snickers. "From the force of the squeal."

"Well, at least I didn't try to use a ham as a weapon. Besides"—he raises his arm and brandishes his purloined dagger—"next time I will be armed and the French will not get off so easily."

"I do not know that lying dead amid the cow dung in your barn could be called getting off easily," I point out. Much to my surprise, everyone laughs.

"True enough," Guion says, raising his cup. Then he sobers. "What is happening with the French, Sir Waroch? Are we at war with them again?"

"It is not good," Beast says. "Half the duchess's council has left her side. Marshal Rieux has joined with Count d'Albret, and they hold Nantes against her.

"The French have been looking for any excuse to invade our kingdom and have crossed our borders to pursue that goal." He turns to me. "Have they taken any cities other than Ancenis?"

"Not that I've heard. Nor has d'Albret given up on his plan to force the duchess to marry him." I turn back to Bette and Guion. "She only narrowly escaped a trap the baron laid for her, thanks in large part to Sir Waroch. That's how he came by his injuries."

The farmer and his wife raise their cups to him, which makes him duck his head in embarrassment.

The farmer's face creases in worry. "So those are our only choices now? To be ruled by the French or by Count d'Albret?"

Bette shudders. "I'll take the French, I think," she says, then drains her cup. Interesting that the dark tales of d'Albret have traveled this far.

"We will know more once we reach Rennes," I say. "The duchess is there with her advisors and they are no doubt forming a plan even as we speak."

"And I," Beast says, "I will be rousing the good people of Brittany to her cause. As soon as I can ride out in earnest," he adds with a grumble.

Young Anton, his face alight with thoughts of valor, raises his knife. "I will fight for the duchess," he says.

It is all I can do not to sigh. Beast does not even have to ask — peasants are already promising to follow him.

"It may come to that, lad, and if so, the duchess will be glad of your support. Yours, too," he tells Jacques.

Both boys turn to look at their mother, who is torn between pride that they are willing to fight and dismay that they are old enough to do so. The farmer takes one look at his wife's face and says, "Enough of this grim talk, eh? Surely a man such as you has a story to entertain us with?"

We spend the rest of the dinner telling stories. Beast has more than a few lively tales of campaigns and skirmishes that cause Anton's and Jacques's eyes to glow with promises of glory. It is easy to see that they imagine themselves in his role.

When all the dishes have been picked clean and everyone is stuffed, it is time for the last round of evening chores before bed. Yannic has fallen asleep at the table, so we simply lay him out on the bench to sleep for the night. The clatter of plates and crockery do not cause him to so much as stir.

I find I am surprisingly reluctant to end this evening. I have eaten finer dinners, supped in far more elegant surroundings, and been entertained by far wittier companions. And yet, there is a simple warmth and joy here that is headier than the strongest wine I have ever drunk. Two years ago I would have mocked their simple life. Now I envy it.

"Here, I'll take those," Bette says. "You go tend your man and his injuries."

I want to protest that he is not my man, but instead I thank her and go fix one last round of poultices while Anton and Jacques help Beast back to his place by the fire.

By the time the poultices are ready, everyone else has gone up the stairs to their beds. One of the boys murmurs some last taunt to his brother, which is followed by an *oof* after the offended party throws something at him.

"Do that again," Beast says.

I look up, confused. "What?"

"Smile. I have never seen you smile before."

"You are daft. Of course I smile." Uncomfortable under that gaze, I turn and begin removing the bandage from his leg.

"How long were you hidden in d'Albret's household?"

My heart thuds painfully. Has he figured out who I am? "Why do you wish to know?" I ask, stalling.

He looks away and plucks at the bandage on his arm. "I was wondering if you might have been there when Alyse was still alive."

And just like that, I am completely undone. His words pierce my heart and erode the last of my defenses against him. I put the poultice on his leg and stare at it as if it is the most fascinating thing in the world.

"You knew of d'Albret's other wives," he hurries to point out. "I thought perhaps you knew of Alyse as well."

Stick as close to truth as possible — that is what we learn at the convent about crafting lies. "Yes," I say, and hope my reluctance does not come through in my voice. "I knew her, but not well."

"Tell me of her." He stares at me intently, as if he would pluck the answers he seeks from my skin.

I look away, my gaze scanning the room, the fire, anything but his ravaged face. What do I tell him of Alyse? That she grew thin with nerves and fright? That the calm, serene woman turned into one who would jump when she was touched and who startled at loud noises?

That Julian and Pierre teased her cruelly because of it, making every loud noise they could think of, sneaking up behind her in the dark empty corridors? That she ate little in the last months before her death?

Or do I tell him of the few stolen happy moments she found? Our trip to pick blackberries, their plump sweetness bursting in our mouths so that the juice would trickle down our chins and make us laugh? Or how the minnows nibbled at our toes when we dipped our feet in the brook?

"She was kind and pious," I finally say. "Always remembering to honor God and His saints. Bluebells were her favorite flower, and there was an entire meadow of them behind the keep one spring. The taste of honey made her nose stuffy."

Beast smiles, a heartbreakingly wistful thing. "I remember that," he says softly.

Of course he knows that. I rack my brain for something to comfort him. "She was strong of spirit and laughed a lot." At least at first, and that was what caused me to lower my guard and befriend her, in spite of all my vows to never grow close to any of d'Albret's wives again.

A deep silence grows in the room, fed by our separate memories.

"I came back for her."

"What?" I ask, certain that I have not heard him correctly.

"I came back for her." Beast repeats the words casually, as if coming back for her were the most natural thing in the world.

But it is not. For despite all the wives d'Albret has ill used, and all the vassals and innocents he has wronged, no one—*no one*—has ventured forth to speak for any of them or to claim justice on their behalf.

My world is so completely upturned by this revelation that it takes me a full minute to find my voice. A thousand questions fill my mind, but none of them are anything a daughter of Mortain would be hungry to know. "What happened?" I finally ask, careful to keep my voice neutral and my eyes on the new bandage I am preparing.

"When three of my letters to her went unanswered, I knew something was wrong, so I obtained a leave of absence and came looking for her.

"When I arrived in Tonquédec, I was refused entrance. And when I thought to linger, I was encouraged to be on my way by a party of twelve armed soldiers." His hand drifts up to the scar that bisects the left side of his face. "They sought to improve my appearance somewhat."

"But they let you live?"

Beast cuts a scornful glance at me. "There was no *letting* about it. I fought my way free."

"Against twelve of d'Albret's men?"

He shrugs, then winces as his shoulder pains him. "It did not take long for the battle fever to come over me." He flashes a grin that is two parts death and one part humor. "I killed eight of them, leaving four to limp back and explain the disaster to d'Albret." Then the grin fades, and the depth of pain and despair I see in his face takes my breath away. "As soon as we've secured the duchess's crown against the French, I will pay another visit to d'Albret and call him to account."

I decide that it is a very good thing I did not tell him that Alyse died trying to help me.

Chapter Twenty-One

IN THE MORNING, WE MAKE ready to leave. Anton and Jacques are desperate to saddle up the dead Frenchmen's horses, grab their new weapons, and follow us to Rennes, but we refuse their offer. There are at least twelve more leagues between here and Rennes, all of them crawling with d'Albret's scouts. We will need the gods' own luck to get there. Which means it is too dangerous for them to travel with us. "Better to meet us in Rennes in a fortnight," Beast tells them.

So they content themselves with the plan they cooked up over breakfast. Guion, Anton, and Jacques saddle up the French soldiers' horses and hoist the dead men across the animals' backs. They take a tabard Yannic stripped from a d'Albret scout and tie it around one of the dead soldier's arms. "Maybe that will prod the French to tangle with d'Albret's men and buy you a little time," Guion says.

It is a pleasant thought, but in my experience, the gods are not nearly that accommodating.

Then Guion and the two boys lead their grisly retinue south, while Beast, Yannic, and I head north. Our path to Rennes will be like trying to thread a needle, weaving our way through d'Albret's men to the west, and Châteaubriant to the east with all its ties to the Dinan family and therefore to d'Albret. Not to mention the added spice of French sorties scattered throughout. But we have no choice. We must keep moving, especially if we do not want to risk d'Albret's stumbling upon this innocent family.

Well, perhaps not so innocent now, after their encounter with the French.

I feel as if the huntsman's snare is closing in around us, and it has me fair twitching in my saddle. Since I do not wish to spook my horse, I force myself to stillness, an art I have mastered during my long years with d'Albret.

I glance over at Beast. He is still pale, and it seems as if he does not sit as tall in the saddle as he once did. No matter how strong a man he is, he is only human. Or at least, mostly human. It is a wonder he has made it this long, and I can only hope his strength holds until we reach Rennes. Guion told us of a small abbey run by the brothers of Saint Cissonius where we can take shelter for the night.

Unless d'Albret has thought to post guards at all such places.

Hopefully they will have medical supplies as well, for my own stores of healing herbs are running dangerously low. And while Beast's fever has gotten no worse, neither has it gotten any better. For once, he is being smart and not wasting his dwindling energy. Or at least, not at the moment. Who knows what he will do if we come across some lost goat or wandering child?

I came back for her. The memory of his words still echoes in my head. It makes no sense that five simple words should shift everything so sharply, but they do. It is as if I have woken up in a world as different from yesterday as spring is from winter. It is the difference between a world with hope and one without. I wish to crawl back into my younger self and hand her this knowledge, this small spark of light, and see how it would shift her perceptions of the darkness all around her. Or would it have been more cruel, that glimmer of hope causing her to look for a rescue that never came?

The farther we get from Nantes, the more I am plagued by doubts. While this taste of freedom is as sweet as I dreamed it would be, I cannot help but wonder about the cost. For so long, I was convinced it was my destiny to kill d'Albret. As relieved as I am to be gone from him, I fear I have shirked my fated duty.

But there was no other choice, I remind myself. To have ridden boldly back into his arms after drugging the entire garrison and freeing Beast would only have ensured my slow and painful death.

I also cannot help but worry about the convent and my role there. It was the one place I felt safe from d'Albret, hundreds of leagues away on an island inhabited by assassins. But I have gone against their teachings, their rules, defied Mortain's will and replaced it with my own. If they cast me out, what then?

Just before noon, the goat track we have been following opens up onto a small meadow. On the far side of the meadow lies the main road, and on the other side of that is the forest. It will be slower going, but d'Albret's soldiers cannot scour every inch of forest between here and Rennes. With luck, we can avoid being seen.

As we draw closer to the road, I hear the sound of an approaching party. I pause to listen for the distant hoofbeats. More than a few. And they are riding hard. No merchant party, then, nor casual travelers.

The timing could not be worse. I glance behind us, but we have crossed over half the meadow and the shelter of the trees is too far away.

"We must get across the road. Quickly!" I order the others.

The whiff of danger has stirred Beast from his dozing and he spurs his horse forward to the road and the thick screen of trees and low branches on the other side of it. Yannic bounces along behind him like a sack of the miller's grain, and I bring up the rear, nipping at their heels, urging them to move faster.

We are in luck, for there is a sharp bend in the road, and while the jingle of harnesses and the rattle of weapons grows louder, the party is still out of sight. Which means they cannot see us either. We hit the road at a full gallop and cross it in a few swift strides. Beast reaches the cover of the trees first, then Yannic. Just as my horse leaves the road, a shout goes up from behind. We've been spotted.

"Faster!" I shout to the others, but the forest is a tangle of fallen limbs and gnarled roots, forcing us to slow down. Beast falls back to ride beside me. "Return to the road and keep riding. Yannic and I will lead them away."

"You're daft!" I shout, ducking a low-hanging branch. "I'll not leave a wounded man and a cripple to stand alone against so many."

"Now you're being daft. Did you see how many there were?"

"Twenty. Maybe more. Here!" We have reached a small clearing with a ring of tall, jagged ancient stones, some of them high and wide enough to hide us from sight. At least until we are ready to make our stand.

Beast's mouth is set in grim lines as he nods Yannic toward one of the stones. His jaw is clenched—at first I think he is in pain, and then I realize he is furious. "Go!" He puts the full force of command in his low, urgent voice. "I'll hold them off."

I look at him in disbelief. "Your fever has eaten your brain if you think I'll leave now."

He leans out of his saddle as if to grab me, then stops as his ribs bite him. "This is no fight."

"I know." I steer my horse toward one of the stones. The sword is not my favorite weapon, but its longer reach will be of greater value here. Once I take out a few with my throwing knives—

"No!" Beast makes a grab for my reins, but he misses and nearly falls off his horse. "I will not stand by and watch you struck down before me." His eyes burn—with anger, I think, until I see that he is also afraid. Afraid for me.

His concern inflames my own temper, for I do not deserve such consideration, and certainly not from him. I will not abandon Alyse's brother like I abandoned her. "And I will not stand idly by and watch you die a second time," I tell him.

Then d'Albret's men are hard upon us. Resigned, Beast draws the sword from his back with his right hand while his left closes around the handle of the ax. "I will not let them take you alive."

Of all the things he could have said, that is the one thing that comforts me the most. "Nor I you," I say around a strange lump that has formed in my throat.

Then he smiles his great big maniacal grin just as our pursuers burst out of the trees, their horses' hooves churning up the forest floor.

Yannic makes the first move, launching one of his rocks with his customary skill and striking one of the foremost men on the temple. I raise the crossbow and take the leader between the eyes. While he is still reeling from the force of the bolt, I drop the bow and reach for my throwing knives. Beast keeps the rock wall at his back and stands in his stirrups to swing at the four horsemen who engulf him.

Even as my first three knives hit their targets, I know there are too many. I reach for the sword strapped to my saddle, but before I can free it, one of the men charges me. I throw myself to the left as he swings, and misses. Before he can swing again, there is a loud *thwap,* and he slumps forward on his horse. I send a silent *Thank you* to Yannic, until I see the arrow in the man's back. Yannic does not have a bow.

I have no time to look for the archer as I struggle to free my sword from its scabbard. A half a dozen men have Beast pinned against one of the stones. His sword arm flashes quick and bright, but his left arm is barely able to move the ax. I spur my horse toward him, lunging forward with the sword. It is an awkward, clumsy thrust but it does its job.

Except that the soldier's horse jerks away, taking the dying man and my sword with it. *Merde.* I pull my last two daggers from my wrists. I glance at Beast. Should I save them for us or use them to attack? Before

I can decide, arrows rain down from the trees, shocking me into stillness. Even as I ready myself for their sharp bite, five of d'Albret's men wheel around to meet this new attack, and a second volley is let loose. Suddenly, the small clearing is alive with movement as the trees and the forest floor itself comes to life, spitting out creatures of the old legends. Or demons spawned in hell. They are dark of skin and misshapen. One has a leather nose, another's arm seems to be made of wood, and a third appears to have had half his face melted away. Whatever their infirmities, they finish off the rest of d'Albret's men with ruthless efficiency, pulling the men from their horses and dispatching them with wicked little blades or quick twists of their necks. Within the span of a dozen heartbeats, all of d'Albret's soldiers are dead, and we are surrounded.

Chapter Twenty-Two

BEAST RAISES HIS DROOPING SWORD, but a curt command from the man with the leather nose stays his hand. He tilts his head up to the branches above us. I follow his gaze and see a dozen archers hidden there, arrows trained upon us. We all eye one another warily.

The leather-nosed man steps forward. He is small and wiry and wears a dark tunic and a leather jerkin over patched breeches. As he moves out of the shadows, I see that he is not as dark-skinned as I had first thought—he is coated with grime. No, not grime. Dust. Or ash, mayhap. As he draws closer still, I see a single acorn hanging from a leather cord around his neck, and then I know. These are the mysterious charbonnerie, the charcoal-burners who live deep in the forests and are rumored to serve the Dark Mother.

With no more noise than a breeze rustling through the leaves, the rest of the charbonnerie emerge from their hiding places. There are twenty of them, counting the archers in the trees. I glance over at Beast. We cannot fight our way out of this one.

With an effort, Beast straightens in his saddle. "We mean you no harm. By right of Saint Cissonius and the grace of Dea Matrona, we wish only to pass the night in the forest." It is a bold gambit, and a smart one, for while the Dark Matrona is not accepted by the Church, the Nine are her brethren gods, and invoking their blessing cannot hurt.

One of them, a thin fellow with a chin and nose as sharp as blades, spits into the leaves. "Why do you not spend the night at an inn, like most city dwellers?"

"Because there are those who wish us ill, as you just saw." As Beast speaks, another of the charcoal-burners—a young, gangly fellow who is all elbows and knees—sidles up next to the leader and whispers something in his ear. The leader nods, his gaze sharpening. "Who are you?"

"I am Benebic of Waroch."

The man who had murmured in the leader's ear nods in satisfaction, and whispers of *the Beast* go up around the charcoal-burners. Beast's exploits have made him famous even among the outcasts.

"And who is it the mighty Beast wishes to avoid?"

"The French," Beast says. "And those who would support them. At least until I can heal and meet them in a fair fight."

I hold my breath. The charcoal-burners hate the French as much as most Bretons do, and I can only hope that having a common enemy will give us common cause. One of the older men, the one with a wooden arm, nudges a body with his foot. "These men aren't French."

"No, they're not. But they are traitors to the duchess and wished to detain us." Then Beast grins one of his savaage grins. "There is plenty of room for you in the war against the French, if you so desire. I would be honored to have such skilled fighters on my side."

There is a long pause, which makes me think the charbonnerie receive few such invitations.

"What is in it for us?" the sharp-faced man asks, but the leader motions for him to be silent.

Beast smiles. "The pleasure of beating the French." To him, any fight is its own excuse.

The leader reaches up and scratches his leather nose, suggesting it is a recent replacement. "You can spend the night in the forest, but under our watch. Come. Follow us." He motions to the others, and a half a dozen of them fall in around us.

They are eerily silent as they guide us deeper into the forest, and our horses' hooves are muffled by the thick layer of decaying leaves on the ground. The gangly youth cannot keep his eyes off me, and when I catch him staring, he blushes to the roots of his hair.

The trees here are ancient, tall and thick and gnarled like old men bent with age. Even though there are hours of daylight left, little sun gets through the thick tangle of foliage overhead.

At last we reach a large clearing ringed by a half a dozen mounds of earth, each one as big as a small house. Smoke burbles from holes in the mounds, which are tended by nearby men. Interspersed among the mounds are small tents made of stripped branches and stretched hides. Cooking fires are watched over by drably dressed women, while dark, gritty children play close by. When we enter the clearing, everyone stops what they are doing and turns to look at us. The youngest child—a girl—sidles up to her mother and slips her fingers into her mouth.

The leader—Erwan is his name—grunts and points to a section of the clearing far away from the earthen mounds. "Make your camp there."

All of them watch as Yannic and I dismount, secure our horses, then turn to help Beast off of his.

His breath comes in quick, shallow gasps. "Did you take a new injury?" I ask quietly.

"No." His grunt is followed by a short bellow of pain. By the time we have him off his horse, the entire camp knows of his condition. Yannic and I are able to steer him but a few feet before he comes to a complete stop. "I think this is a good place to make camp," he says, then grabs for a nearby tree so he will not crash to the ground.

"Not sure that one is going to live through the night," the wooden-armed man mumbles, and I glare at him.

The gangly fellow catches my eyes. "Oh, don't mind Graelon, miss. That's just his way." He glances mischievously at the old man, then leans in closer to me. "He was like that before the fire got his arm." The youth's charm is infectious.

"I'm Winnog, my lady. At your service."

"As if she'd have you," someone mutters.

Ignoring the mutterer, I give Winnog my brightest smile. "Thank you." As I turn back to Beast's side, it is all I can do not to clap my hands at the onlookers and cry, *Shoo!* But they would no doubt consider that a rude repayment of their hospitality, meager as it is.

I sense a movement behind me and feel the beating of a lone heart. Still untrusting of these charbonnerie, I whirl around, hand going to the knife concealed in my crucifix.

The woman I see pauses and casts her eyes down in a gesture of submission. She is dressed in a dark gown, and, like the rest of the women, her hair is wrapped tightly in a coif of some kind. She carries a small sack. "For his wound," she says. "It will help."

After a moment, I take the sack from her and peer inside. "What is it?" I ask.

"Ground oak bark to keep infection from setting in. And ashes of burned snakeskin to hasten the healing."

"What is your name?" I ask.

She glances up at me, then down again. "Malina."

"Thank you," I say, and mean it. For I am running out of ideas on how to keep Beast's wounds from overtaking him before we make it to Rennes.

"Do you need help?" she asks shyly.

While I am certain Beast will hate having his weakness seen by others, it seems prudent to accept any help they offer, an attempt to forge some tenuous bond between us. "Yes, thank you. Do you have any hot water?" She nods, then slips away to fetch it. While she is gone, I quickly sniff the oak bark and the ashes, then put a dab to my tongue to be certain it will do no harm.

"It was not in jest that I invited them to fight with us." Beast's voice rumbles up at me. "Did you see how ferocious they were? How unexpected their tactics?" He is as excited as a squire with his first sword. "They could prove valuable allies."

"If they do not stab us in the back," I mutter. "Are they not known to be clannish and untrustworthy?"

Beast considers a moment. "Clannish, yes, but that is not the same as being unworthy of trust."

Malina returns just then, bringing a halt to our conversation. She and I tend Beast's wounds while he lies back and pretends he is dozing, but his jaw clenches as we work on him. By the time we are done, supper is ready, and, much to my surprise, we are invited to partake of it. It seems we are to be treated as guests rather than prisoners, then. Wishing to capitalize on this, I take one of the cheeses and the two roast chickens that Bette gave us to contribute to the meal.

The charbonneries' eyes widen with pleasure and the unexpected bounty, and when I sit down to eat, I can see why. Dinner is some sort of mash—acorn, I think. As I take a bite, I cannot help but remember how I called the convent's food pig slop and how Sister Thomine threatened to force it down my gullet.

A lump forms in my throat, one that has nothing to do with the mash and everything to do with a sense of deep homesickness, for as much as I rebelled against the convent, it was the safest place I have ever lived. I miss Ismae and Annith more than I ever thought possible.

Yannic shovels his gruel into his silent gob steadily, and, beside me, Beast eats with great gusto. "You like it?" I ask softly.

"No. But I do not wish to insult their hospitality." Since these words are delivered with a pointed look to my own barely touched portion, I turn my attention to eating it while it is still warm.

When dinner is over, the charbonnerie linger around the fire. A few murmur among themselves, but most of them simply stare at us. One of the boys brings out a small wooden flute and begins piping a soft, haunting melody. Erwan leans back against a rock, folds his arms, and studies us in the flickering light. "Tell us of this war with the French," he says.

Beast takes a sip of whatever spirit it is they have given us. Fermented dew collected from the trees, most likely. "Our young duchess is besieged from within and without. Upon the duchess's father's death, the French tried to declare her their ward. Of course, she laughed in their long-nosed faces." He takes another swig. "But they do not give up, those French. They know that she is young and untried, and as yet unwed. They see our country as ripe for the plucking and are looking for any chance to do just that."

Erwan appears unmoved. "What is in it for us if we fight?"

"Freedom from French rule," Beast says simply. But it is clear these cautious men will need more to convince them than that.

"Your way of life," I add, drawing their eyes to me. "We Bretons at least respect your right to the wildwood. The French will not, and they will claim all the forests and the wood in it as their own. You will be forced to pay dearly for what you now have for free."

Erwan studies us in silence a moment longer, then barks out a harsh laugh and leans forward to put his arms on his knees. "Freedom, you say? Freedom to scavenge in the forest, reviled by all? Freedom to sell our wares to people who would like to pretend that we do not exist and that their charcoal is left on their doorsteps by some korrigan of hearth tales?"

Beast meets his gaze, unblinking. "The French will not honor your right to the old ways, your right of woodage and coppings. In France, men must pay hard coin for such rights; they do not come to them by birth. And while yours is not an easy life, it was always my understanding that you chose it, chose to follow your god into this exile."

The other men shift restlessly on their seats and Erwan looks away from Beast to stare deep into the flames. "*Choice.* That is a funny word. Our father's father's father chose for us, did he not? And how long must we live with that choice?" He turns and looks to the pile of sprawling children asleep under their blankets. "And how long must they?" he asks, his voice softening.

"What would you wish different?" I ask.

He looks surprised by the question, but before he can answer, Malina does. "To not have people whisper when we walk by; to not have them make the sign against evil when they think we are not looking; to not be chased from villages or markets when all we wish to do is buy combs for our daughters' hair or new wheels for our carts." She looks at me, defiant, her head held high.

"Respect," I say. "You want respect and to not be reviled."

Our eyes meet in a moment of perfect understanding, then she nods. "Exactly so."

"Perhaps if the people saw you take up the duchess's—and the country's—cause, they would regard you in a different light," Beast suggests.

"Most likely not," the dour Graelon says. "And we'll have lost our lives for nothing."

"Every action has some measure of risk," Beast points out. "You could lose good men simply by doing nothing." He gestures to those gathered around the fire, with their missing limbs and ruined faces, injuries received while tending the charcoal pits.

"Tell me of the Dark Matrona," I say softly, giving the truth of Beast's words time to simmer and do its work. "For I have heard very little of Her."

172

Erwan snorts. "That is because the Church does not accept Her."

Malina takes up the story. "It is said that when Dea Matrona and the rest of the Nine are not strong enough to answer your prayers, it is time to turn to the Dark Mother, for She is a fierce and loving god who especially favors the fallen, the scarred, the wounded, and the castoffs.

"She rules over those places where life rises up out of darkness and decay. The first green shoot in a forest devastated by fire, the pile of dead ash that holds a single red ember, the small creatures that are born in the midden heap.

"Which is why the Church did not invite Her into its fold. The priests saw Her as competition for their Christ and His promise of resurrection."

Malina reaches up and fondles the acorn at her neck. "The darkest hours of night, just before dawn, belong to Her. The moment when all hope is lost, and yet you dare to hope one more time. That is the power of the Dark Matrona.

"It is She who gave us the gift of coal. Back when we were simple forest dwellers, we grew careless with our fires, and the entire forest went up in flames. For days it burned, killing every tree, every bush, every shrub and blade of grass, until nothing but ash and dust remained. Or so we thought.

"But hidden in those ashes were pieces of wood that had only partially burned and still held the heat of the flames. That charcoal was Her gift to lead us to a new livelihood."

Malina looks from the flames and meets my eyes. "So of course, we honor Her still, She who provided in our hour of need and gave us hope when it was all but lost."

In the silence that follows her tale, all that can be heard is the crackle and snap of the burning logs in the fire pit. I cannot say why, but I am moved by this idea that hope—that life—can spring from darkness and decay. It is not something I've considered before. "What if this is another chance She is holding before you?" I ask.

Malina blinks in surprise.

"You have given up hope of gaining respect or fellowship, and yet here we are, offering you just such a chance."

Beast leans forward. "We can do little to sway the Church, but the people *can* be swayed, and they often embrace things the Church wishes they would not. And so I ask you: Will you join us?"

Their gazes hold across the fire—Beast's challenging, yet inviting. Erwan's doubting and full of questions. Before either of them speaks, Malina says, "Let us consult with Brother Oak."

There is a murmur of consensus among the charbonnerie, then an ancient man creaks to his feet and draws near the fire. His gnarled, trembling hands untie a pouch at his waist and he extracts a big, misshapen brown lump. At first I think it is an enormous dark mushroom, but when he draws closer to the fire, I can see it is an oak gall.

The old man places it carefully on one of the rocks that circle the fire, then removes a small ax that hangs from his waist. He closes his eyes and holds the ax over the fire, his lips murmuring in some old language I do not understand. The rest of the charbonnerie murmur with him. When they stop their murmuring, the old man takes the ax and, with surprising strength, brings it down to break open the oak gall. Because I am close, I can see a small white grub wiggling in the wreckage. After a moment, the grub spreads its wings—no grub, then—and flies.

The old man looks up to the waiting charbonnerie. "The Dark Mother says we fight."

And so it is settled.

We ride out at dawn's light, accompanied by a full cadre of charbonnerie. As luck would have it, they have a load of charcoal to bring to a blacksmith in Rennes. I have disguised myself as one of their women, and Beast sits in the back of one of the carts and plays the simpleton. Yannic fits right in.

Not even d'Albret, with all his suspicion and distrust, would think to look for us here.

Chapter Twenty-Three

FOR ALL HIS EARLIER PROTESTS that he would be pummeled to pulp if he rode in a wagon, Beast sleeps the entire way to Rennes laid out in the back of one of the charbonnerie's three carts. Twice d'Albret's scouts pass us on the road, and both times they scarcely glance at the charbonnerie, let alone think to look for us among them. And best of all, by the time we come in sight of the city walls, Beast is better, whether due to all the rest or to the herbs Malina provided, I am not sure.

The cathedral bells are ringing out the call to late-afternoon prayers as we approach the city gate. Although I do not know all of d'Albret's men by sight, I study the sentries and everyone in the crowd at the city gates. I ignore the slouching of the peasant and the confident stride of the city guard; I stare past the clothes they wear and study their faces, for if I can don a disguise, so can they.

I cannot believe we have done the impossible. Not only have we escaped d'Albret, but we have evaded recapture as well, and that is hard to wrap my mind around.

Beast point-blank refuses to be hauled into the city with a load of charcoal, so we pause long enough to get him up on a horse. A hum of urgency buzzes in my head like a swarm of gnats, and there is an itching between my shoulder blades that is nearly unbearable. Four men and much grunting later, the great lummox is astride his mount. Soon, I promise myself. Soon he will no longer be my responsibility but someone else's—someone far more capable than I. The thought does not cheer me as much as it once did.

As our small group makes ready to approach the gates, I try not to fidget. We are heavily covered in black dust from the charcoal-burners and their wares, which aids our disguise somewhat, but nothing can disguise Beast's size or bearing. "Slouch a bit," I tell him.

He looks at me quizzically, but honors my request, bringing his shoulders forward and bowing his spine so that he slumps in his saddle. "Why?" he asks.

"You are difficult to hide, and the longer we keep your arrival secret, the better. It would be wise to prevent d'Albret and his forces from knowing we are in Rennes for as long as possible."

And then we are at the gatehouse. Erwan informs the soldiers of his charcoal deliveries and is waved through. One of the soldiers eyes Beast warily, but the truth is, between the knight's time on the road and his stay in the dungeon, not to mention the grievous injuries he still bears, it is not difficult for him to look like a giant simpleton.

I breathe a hearty sigh of relief once we are inside the city. Indeed, every one of my muscles seems to unclench now that there are twelve-foot-thick walls, twenty leagues, and an entire city garrison between us and d'Albret.

Much like my own mood, the city's borders on jubilant, drunk on its own importance of being the duchess's place of refuge, just as I am nearly drunk with the thrill of completing my mission. But there is caution here as well, in the way the people going about their business glance at newcomers, assessing.

We stay with the charcoal-burners as long as possible, passing by the tannery conducting its foul-smelling business down by the river, then turning up the street that leads to the section of town where the smiths can be found. They consume enough coal in their furnaces to keep the charbonnerie in pottage for the entire winter. We bid the charbonnerie goodbye, and Beast promises to send word when he has spoken to the duchess and her advisors of his plan to use the charcoal-burners against the French.

As he and I begin making our way toward the nicer part of town, I unwind the distinctive charbonnerie coif from my head and comb my fingers through my hair, then take the shawl from my shoulders. I use a clean corner of it to wipe the charcoal dust from my face so I am no longer one of the despised charbonnerie but merely a comely—if grubby—serving maid.

By the time we reach the palace, dusk is falling, and the sentries are just lighting the torches. It is not like Guérande, where people came and went as they pleased. The guards at the door speak with everyone who wishes to enter. "That's new," Beast says.

"At least someone has an eye toward the duchess's safety." It is one more barrier between d'Albret's spies and the duchess, and it will give them pause if they must stop and present themselves. "However, the guards will likely not grant us an audience with the duchess when we look like this, at least not without a full explanation of who we are, and I do not wish to announce your arrival to these men."

Beast pauses in wiping the charcoal dust from his face. "You don't trust them?"

"It is more accurate to say that I don't trust anyone. I wonder if Ismae is still assigned to the duchess. Perhaps I can get a message to her."

Beast glances at the sentries. "I am not sure they would grant you an audience with Ismae even if she is here."

I grimace, for he is most likely correct.

Beast thinks a moment, then reaches into some hidden pouch tucked on his person and removes something. "Here." He hands me a small brooch—the silver oak leaves of Saint Camulos. "Ismae should recognize this, and if she does not, Captain Dunois will. As will the guards. They will honor any who carries this symbol."

Holding the brooch tightly in my hand, I dismount, leaving him and Yannic to stay with the horses. I approach the palace and wait for the guard to finish questioning a burgher who is there to meet with the chancellor and complain about the most recent round of taxes. After the burgher has been told the chancellor has much more important business at hand—such as keeping the city from being attacked by the French—he is sent on his way, and then I am facing the sentry. He scowls at my poor clothing and the grime I am covered in. Even so, I tilt my head and give him my most fetching smile. He blinks, and his scowl softens. "What do you want?" he asks. "If you're looking for scullery work, you must go around to the kitchens."

I glance at the handful of pages lingering just inside the door. "I wish to get a message to one of the duchess's attendants."

The second sentry saunters over. "What business could you have with one of the duchess's ladies in waiting?" he asks, as if the mere idea is some great jest.

I decide that a little mystery will aid my cause. "Ismae Rienne is no mere lady in waiting," I tell him. "Give her this and bid her come as quickly as she can."

I do not know if it is the mention of Ismae or the sight of Beast's silver oak leaves that catches the guard's attention. Whichever it is, he takes the brooch, hands it to a page, and murmurs some instructions. When the boy scampers off, I saunter over to wait by the wall, trying to look important but harmless—a surprisingly difficult combination. After a few moments, the sentry decides I won't dash in on my own, so relaxes his guard somewhat.

I rest my head against the stone and allow the sense of jubilation to flow through me. Beast is still alive and we are as safe here as anywhere in the entire kingdom. With the abbess tucked away at the convent on the other side of the country, she will not know that I have arrived in Rennes until she receives a message. She cannot send me on a new assignment. At least not for a while. That gives me some time to work out what I would like to do next. Suddenly, the world looms large, full of possibilities and freedom.

And no one—*no one*—here in Rennes knows my true identity, so my secrets will be safe.

At the faint murmur of approaching voices, I carefully tuck my moment of triumph away and inch toward the causeway.

"No, you cannot kill him. He is the duchess's own cousin," a man's voice points out wryly.

"All the more reason not to trust him," a woman says.

It is Ismae, and the joy and relief I feel at hearing her voice is nearly overwhelming.

"If something should happen to the duchess," she continues, "he stands to inherit the kingdom. Besides, he has been a guest of the French regent for the last year. How do we know where his true allegiance lies?"

"He was a prisoner!" The man's exasperation is nearly palpable.

When Ismae speaks again, she sounds aggrieved. "Why did you not stay with the council? The message was for me, not you." Unable to stop myself, I smile. For it is such a very Ismae-like thing to say.

"Because the message was the sigil of Saint Camulos, whom I serve, not you."

Then she and the gentleman emerge from the entryway and hurry toward the sentry. "Where did you get this?" the nobleman demands. He is tall, with dark hair and the well-muscled grace of a soldier.

The guard points to me. The man's head snaps around and I am speared by a gray gaze that is as cold and hard as the stone at my back.

He takes a step in my direction. "Who are you?" he asks in a low, angry voice.

Before I can answer, Ismae shoves him aside. "The message was for *me*, Duval. Oh! Sybella!" Then she throws herself at me and I am encased in a fierce hug. I hug her back, surprised at how very much I want to weep into her shoulder. She is alive. And she is here. For a long moment, that is enough, and I simply savor the feel of her familiar arms about me.

She pulls away to eye me carefully. "Is it really you?"

I smile, although I can tell it is a lopsided effort. "In the flesh."

"The oak leaves?" The nobleman's impatience rolls off him in waves as he clenches the silver brooch in his hand. Duval, Ismae called him, which means he is the bastard brother of the duchess.

"I have brought you something," I tell them. "There." I nod to where Beast and Yannic wait on their horses.

Duval's face lights up just as Ismae's did when she saw me, but before he can hurry to him, I grab his arm. "He is gravely injured. Once you get him off that horse, you will need men and a litter to move him. And you must do it quietly. I bring much news and none of it good."

Duval frowns his understanding and gives the guards an order to send for help — and to keep quiet about it — then rushes off to greet his friend.

"You did it!" Ismae whispers fiercely. "You got him free. I knew you could."

I stare at her. "You knew of my orders?"

She grabs my hands. "It was my idea! The only way I could think of to get you out of there. Every time I saw you in Guérande, I feared for your safety and your sanity. Now here you are, and that haunted, mad glint is gone from your eyes."

I do not know whether to kiss her for getting me out of d'Albret's household or slap her for all the trouble her idea has caused me. In any case, her words ring true. I no longer feel as if I dance along the edge of madness.

Ismae puts her arm though mine, and we begin walking toward the others. "I will never forgive the reverend mother for assigning you to d'Albret. She might as well have sent you into the Underworld itself."

A faint wave of panic threatens, then recedes. Ismae does not know—has never known—my true identity, for all that we are like sisters. I am saved from further conversation when I hear Beast bellow, "Saint's teeth! You're *alive*? How is that possible?"

It is Duval who answers. "By the same batch of miracles that has you astride that horse, you great ox."

Then Ismae and I must jump aside as a half a dozen men come trotting by bearing an empty litter. Ismae points them toward Duval and Beast. "Come," I say. I let go of her arm and hurry after the litter. "I must give them instructions as to Beast's care."

Over Beast's loud protestations that he is fine, I warn Duval that, in addition to having a fever, Beast cannot put any weight on his leg.

Duval and the men have a quick conference among themselves. "We will take him to the convent run by the sisters of Saint Brigantia. If anyone can tend his injuries, it will be them." He shoots me a look that lets me know he will be wanting answers soon, then he directs his men to help Beast.

But it is no easy thing to remove an injured twenty-stone man from his horse, and it cannot be done without some jostling and bumping. Beast grits his teeth, and his face turns white as he mutters something about being tossed around like a sack of onions. Then one of the men loses his grip, and the horse startles, slamming Beast's wounded leg between its flank and the helping guard, and Beast faints.

I sigh. "I fear that has become a new habit of his," I murmur to the others. "Although it is probably for the better." I motion for Yannic to dismount so he and I can show the damn-fool soldiers how to get Beast off the horse without killing him.

* * *

It is clear that Duval is torn between concern for his friend and his duty to his sister. In the end, I assure him that Yannic is as able as any of us to see to Beast's care, so he gives stern instructions to the men on what to tell the sisters of Saint Brigantia, with promises that he will be there shortly. Then he turns to me. "Come now. We would hear your accounting of what has happened."

"But of course, my lord." Indeed, I cannot wait to discharge what I know. It is as if I have been carrying a hot ember deep inside my body that is slowly turning my insides to ash. It will be no hardship to be rid of that burden.

Ismae loops her arm through mine as we follow Duval to the palace door. "Where is he taking us?" I ask under my breath.

"To the duchess's chamber, where she is holding council with her advisors."

"At this hour?"

Ismae grows sober. "At all hours, I'm afraid."

"Are they trustworthy, these advisors of hers?" I have not been impressed with the steadfastness of her guardians Marshal Rieux and Madame Dinan.

She grimaces. "Yes, that is why it is such a small group."

As Duval leads us through the maze of palace halls and corridors, I allow myself to adjust to the cacophony of the beating hearts and hammering pulses. It is as if a hundred minstrels have all decided to bang their drums at the same time.

I also study the faces of the people I pass—servants, retainers, even the pages—trying to get a sense of their characters.

Duval leads us to a small chamber guarded by two sentries, who step forward to open the door to admit us. The duchess stands at a large table flanked by three men who stare at the map in front of her. One is dressed in travel-stained clothes and it is clear he has only just arrived. The second man is dressed in bishop's robes and hovers near the duchess like a fat scarlet toad. The third is slender and serious, his brow wrinkled in thought. With relief, I realize I recognize none of her advisors, which means they will not recognize me.

It is the first time I have seen the duchess up close. She is young, and short, with fine skin and a high noble brow. Even though she is but thirteen years of age, there is something regal about her that commands respect. At the sound of our entry, they all look up, questions in their eyes.

Duval's smile transforms his face. "Beast is here. In Rennes."

The duchess clasps her hands together as if in prayer and closes her eyes, joy lighting her young face. "Praise God," she says.

"I rather think we should be praising Mortain," Duval says dryly, "as it is His hand that guided him here." He motions in my direction, and all eyes turn to me.

"Then you and your saint have my most sincere thanks and profoundest gratitude," she says.

I sink into a deep curtsy. "It was my pleasure, Your Grace. However, I bring you not just your noble knight but vital information concerning Count d'Albret and his plans."

"You mean the man is not content to steal my city out from under me and sit on it like a brooding hen?"

"No, Your Grace. Even now he has put into motion a number of plans, any one of which could bear rich fruit."

The thickset bear of a man on the duchess's right gestures with his hand. "By all means, share with us these plans."

"Count d'Albret, Marshal Rieux, and Madame Dinan hold the city against you, and while there are many who remain loyal to Your Grace, Count d'Albret does his best to make it . . . difficult for them to remain so."

"Wait, wait. Start at the beginning. How were they able to take the city from the attendants and retainers who were still in residence there?"

Before I can answer, there is a rustling behind me, a sound that reminds me of a snake slithering in dry grass. In that moment, I recognize why I am uneasy: I sense eight pulses but see only seven bodies before me.

Slowly, as if I am in a dream, I turn around and see the abbess of Saint Mortain standing behind me. She skulks in the far corner, like a spider, which is why I did not see her when I first came in. Her blue eyes study me coldly, and my heart plummets like a stone.

I have not escaped my past; it has been waiting for me here all along.

Chapter Twenty-Four

"GREETINGS, DAUGHTER." WHILE HER WORDS are friendly enough, her voice is cool, and the kiss of welcome she gives me is as cold and impersonal as Death Himself. "Excellent work. We are pleased that you were able to perform your tasks so admirably."

I curtsy deeply, my eyes watching her warily. Ismae and Annith always got along well with the abbess, and genuine fondness seemed to exist among them. Indeed, Annith was treated like a court favorite much of the time, and Ismae always saw the woman as her savior, as if it were the abbess's own hand that had lifted her up from her drab life as a peasant.

The abbess and I had a different sort of relationship. One built on mutual dislike and distrust, brought together only by our shared needs: mine for a sanctuary, hers for a finely honed weapon she could let loose as Mortain willed. I trust her as much as I do a viper.

She motions for me to rise, then she turns to the others in the room. "I would remind you that Sybella has traveled far and at great discomfort and risk. No doubt she would like to make herself presentable before she tells the rest of her tale."

At her words, I am suddenly aware of just how filthy and travel-stained I must appear, as if I am some grub that has scuttled out from under a rock.

The duchess is quick to apologize for her lack of hospitality and insists I take the time to refresh myself before reporting to the council. I had been so concerned with sharing my news that I had given no thought to my appearance until the abbess pointed it out. The evil cow. She likely did it on purpose, to throw me off balance.

My unease increases when the abbess insists on escorting me to my chamber herself. Ismae sends me a nervous glance as I curtsy to the duchess and then follow the reverend mother from the room.

As we walk, she says nothing except to order a servant to fetch things for a bath and make the room ready. She holds her head high, her posture rigidly straight as she glides down the hall. I do not know if her silence is because she fears being overheard or if it is yet another way to unnerve me.

We reach a chamber with a cheerful fire. A tub has been placed in front of it, and two maids are emptying kettles of hot water into the bath. The abbess quickly dismisses them. Once we are alone, she turns to face me, her beautiful face contorted with anger. "What are you doing here, Sybella?" she hisses. "You were only to free him, not personally escort him to Rennes."

I toss my head in the face of her anger, both to give myself strength and to annoy her. "And how would he have gotten here, with me practically having to carry him from the dungeons? It was only after days of my tending his wounds that he was even able to stay on a horse — and then only when he was tied on."

The abbess's nostrils flare in irritation, for as much as she longs to, she cannot argue with my logic. She shoves her hands in her sleeves and begins pacing. "But now we have no one in Nantes."

"It does not matter, Reverend Mother, for none of the traitors was marqued. Not Marshal Rieux, not Madame Dinan, and not d'Albret." I watch her carefully to see if she recognizes that her promise to me — that I would be able to kill d'Albret — was broken.

She does not. "There is still great value in having you there. Some-one will need to keep the duchess informed."

And suddenly I am furious. Furious that she does not even care that she lured me back to hell on earth with a false promise and that for a span of time, death was more inviting to me than the life I was forced to live—the life *she* had forced me to live, using lies and a lure she knew I would find irresistible.

I take a step toward her, my hands clenched into fists so that I will not slap her. "Great value? Great value? For whom? And at what cost? You promised me I could kill him. Promised me Mortain had marqued him and was waiting for me—not any of His handmaidens, but *me*—to go back there and kill him. You lied to me."

She tilts her wimpled head and studies me. "Something as paltry as a lack of Mortain's permission would not stop the Sybella I know. Perhaps in the end, your ties to d'Albret are stronger than your ties to Mortain. You have, after all, known him and served him far longer."

Her words strike all the air from my lungs and I am so shocked by a sense of violation that I cannot dredge up anything to say and am left gaping at her like a fish.

She gives me a scornful glance. "Make yourself presentable so you can report to the duchess," she says, then lifts her skirts and sweeps out of the room.

As I stand in the empty room, the abbess's words echo in my head and take up residence like a nest of maggots in a rotting corpse. I feel small and tainted, as if I should not be in this room, this palace, this city. I start to rub my arms, then stop, for my skin feels flayed raw by her accusation.

Then, praise God and all His saints, the anger comes, a sweet hot rush of fury that burns the pain I am feeling to ash. I have done what I was told to do, what I promised I would do. I have risked much and ventured back into my worst nightmares, all because I believed the abbess—believed that even though she did not like me, her service to Mortain would ensure that she would be truthful with me, see me as a useful tool, if nothing else. But clearly I have been duped and have allowed myself to be the worst kind of pawn.

Even worse, I wasn't able to accomplish the one thing that would have made it all worthwhile—killing d'Albret.

Anger surges through my body, so powerful that I shake with it. I glance around the chamber, desperate for something to break, to throw, to *destroy*, just as the abbess has destroyed me. But there is nothing. No mirror nor crystal, only the candles, which would start a fire if I threw them, and while I am angry, I am not angry enough to bring down the very castle that holds us.

Which is something, I guess.

Instead, I cross to the bed, grab a handful of the thick, burgundy damask curtains, wad them up in my fist, then shove the wad into my mouth and scream. The relief of all the anger and fury leaving my body is so sweet that I do it again, and again. Only then do I let the crushed, wrinkled fabric fall from my hand, and I turn back to the room, somewhat calmer.

I will leave this place, leave Mortain's service. I have warned the duchess of d'Albret's plans. Once I have told them all that I know about his intent to infiltrate their defenses, my duty is done. And my duty to Mortain? I snort like one of Guion's pigs. Look what my service to Him has gotten me so far.

Heartened by this decision, I reach behind and begin to unlace my gown, thrilled to be able to step out of its grubby drabness. I walk naked to the tub and am pleased to find the water scented with lavender and rosemary. The duchess, at least, is not stingy with her hospitality. Slowly, and with a great sigh of contentment, I lower myself into the water.

The heavy curtains are drawn against the cold winter winds, and the room is lit only by the fire burning in the hearth and a brace of beeswax candles. As I sit there, I imagine all of my anger being drawn from me and let it flow out of me into the warm scented water, for I will not be able to make effective plans if my vision is clouded by my own anger. I lean forward and dunk my entire head so that I may wash it, too. Who knows what vermin I have picked up over the last few days' travels?

Just when I pull my head back up and am rubbing the drips out of my eyes, there is a soft knock at the door. "Sybella?"

At the sound of Ismae's voice, I call, "Come in."

The door opens, then closes as Ismae hurries into the room. "I've brought you some clean clothes," she says, pointedly not looking at me naked in the bathtub.

Her familiar modesty cheers me, and I lean back and place my arms along the sides of the tub, fully exposing my breasts, just to fluster her. However, she knows me too well and simply rolls her eyes at me. "Would you like me to wash your hair for you?"

I find that I would, surprised at how much I missed the kind, gentle touch of friendship. Because I want it so much, I only shrug. "If you wish." I do not think she is fooled, for she plucks an empty ewer from one of the tables and moves behind me.

We are both silent as the warm water sluices down my head and falls across my back. "I have been so very worried about you," she whispers. "Annith checked the crows daily for word of your whereabouts and safety, but there was nothing. And no matter how many doors she listened at, she could not catch a whiff of where you'd been sent or what your assignment was. When you didn't come back for months, we began to fear the worst."

"And now you know. I was sent to d'Albret."

Behind me, I feel a shudder run through Ismae's body. "I do not understand how the abbess could ask that of anyone."

For a moment, a brief, reckless moment, I consider telling Ismae the truth—that it was my own family I was sent back to—but I am not sure I am willing to risk it, not even with her.

"I must write to Annith. She will be so relieved to hear you are safe. She's checked every message that's come to the convent since you left, desperate for news of you. Better still, once you are rested enough, you should write her yourself."

"I will," I say, halfheartedly, for the plain truth is, I am jealous of Annith, safe and snug behind the convent's walls. I have never envied her special place in the convent's heart more than I do now. "Has she been sent out yet, or is she still waiting in vain for her first assignment?"

Ismae hands me a linen towel with which to dry myself. "How did you guess that all this time, they never intended to let her set foot out of the convent? I received a message from her just after you left for Nantes." She takes a step closer to me. "Sybella, they mean to make her the convent's new seeress. Sister Vereda is ill, and they want Annith to take her place."

Is that why there was no order to kill d'Albret? Not only could I not see it, but neither could Sister Vereda? "At least she will be safe," I say, thinking of how often I longed to be back behind those thick, cloistered walls.

"Safe?" Ismae asks sharply. "Or suffocated? If memory serves, you could hardly bear being held behind those walls for three years, let alone the rest of your life."

I wince at the memory and cannot help but marvel at how hard I worked to escape the convent when I first arrived. I remember Nantes, d'Albret slaying those loyal servants, the look of terror in Tilde's eyes, and the scratching at my own door. "More fool I," I say quietly.

As she helps me into a clean gown, the look on Ismae's face softens. "Assigned to d'Albret's household, you have faced more horrors than any of us. But truly, Sybella, I do not think you understand how hard it is to be left behind, to feel as if you will never be given a chance to prove yourself or make a contribution. Especially for one such as Annith, who has trained for this her entire life."

"She would not survive a fortnight outside those walls," I say, my voice harsh.

Ismae sends me a disappointed look. "She will never know now, will she?"

Since I do not have the heart to argue with her, I change the subject. "What is between you and Duval?"

She makes herself very busy pouring us each a goblet of wine. "What makes you think there is something between us?"

"The way you look at each other. That and the fact that you listened to him when he told you you could not kill whomever you were talking about. So, do you love him?"

Ismae nearly drops the goblet she is handing me. "Sybella!"

"You *are* in love." I take the goblet and sip the wine, trying to decide what I think about that.

"What makes you say such a thing?" she asks.

"You are blushing, for one."

She fiddles with the stem of her goblet. "Mayhap I am embarrassed you would ask such forward questions."

"Oh, do not be such a stick-in-the-mud. Besides, remember who taught you how to kiss. Duval has much to thank me for."

Unable to restrain herself, Ismae picks up the wet towel and throws it at me. "It is complicated," she says.

For some reason, I think of Beast. I swirl the wine in my goblet. "It always is," I say, then drain the cup.

"He's asked me to be his wife."

This surprises me, but it also makes me like the man more. "Are you not still married to the pig farmer?"

"No. It was never consummated, and the reverend mother had it annulled the second year I was at the convent."

"What did you tell him?"

"That I would think about it. For, while I love him, and will do so always, it is very hard to give anyone that kind of power over me again."

"What did the reverend mother say?"

Ismae wrinkles her nose and refills her goblet. "It is just one of the reasons I have fallen so far out of her favor."

"You? But next to Annith, you were her favorite."

"No." Ismae gives a firm shake of her head. "It was not I who was her favorite, but the blind, adoring acolyte that she loved."

And that is when I know just how fully Ismae has changed.

Before we can talk further, there is a knock at the door. Ismae answers it, and a whispered, urgent conversation takes place before she closes the door and turns back to me. "The council meeting will not be resumed until tomorrow. The duchess's sister has taken a turn for the worse, and the duchess wishes me to mix a sleeping draft for her."

I arch an eyebrow. "You are a poisons mistress, not some healer for hire."

Ismae gives me a sad smile. "It is a dance with Death, nevertheless."

Chapter Twenty-Five

SINCE I AM DRESSED IN one of Ismae's habits, the guard at the palace door salutes respectfully and makes no move to prevent my leaving. I step out into the cold night air and head toward a bridge that is lit by a sparse row of torches whose light is reflected in the dark water below.

It also leads to the convent where Beast is being held. I need to assure myself that I did not bring him all this way only to have him expire while in the sisters of Saint Brigantia's care.

I reach the main gate at the convent and find it closed. Just to the right of the gate is a large bundle of what looks like rags. It takes me a moment to realize it is a sleeping Yannic, as loyal as the most faithful of hounds and no doubt banned from the convent for being a reasonably healthy man. Only ill or wounded men are allowed through those doors. I consider ringing the summons bell and announcing my presence to the entire convent, then reject the idea. What if they will not let me in? Or worse, what if they ask why I am here? For a moment, uncertainty grips me. Surely Beast has no need of me. Not now, when he is surrounded by the most skilled healers in our land.

I pause. Why am I here?

He is safe. And will soon be in a position to help the duchess. My role in his life is done. I saved him from d'Albret, the way I could not save Alyse. That should be enough.

So why do I feel this need to linger? Why this reluctance to part?

If I were anyone else feeling this, I would name it love, but I — I am far too smart to ever give away my heart again. Especially when to do so is as good as a death sentence for those I care about.

The old, familiar swirl of panic tries to surface. Instead of fighting it, I try to open myself to it, to let it come.

I remember the screaming. And the blood.

And that is as far as I get before the memory dissolves into pain.

Frustrated, I turn and follow the high walls surrounding the nunnery, looking for a low section or a back gate with a lock I can pick.

That is when I spy the lone branch. It is thin, too thin to bear a man's weight, which is most likely why the nuns have not cut it down. But it is not too thin for me.

I toss my cloak over my shoulder, then look for a sturdy burl I can use as a foothold. It is a long stretch to the next branch, which hovers just out of my reach, so I must shimmy up the trunk, most likely ruining Ismae's habit.

Since it belongs to the convent, I do not mind overmuch.

My hand closes around the branch, and victory surges through me as I pull myself up. The limb creaks and bows, but does not break. Lying flat to distribute my weight evenly, I begin inching across, hoping the limb will not snap and send me plummeting to the ground, breaking my neck. Mortain cannot have brought me this far for such an ignoble end.

At last the wall is below me. I swing my feet down onto it and let go of the branch, which springs back up. I stop to survey my surroundings. This convent is laid out much like the convent of Saint Mortain. I can make out the long low building that is the nuns' dormitory, and the larger refectory. And, of course, the chapel itself. But where would they keep the sick and wounded?

A building set aside from the others has a faint light coming from one of the windows. That is as likely a place to begin my search as any.

Perhaps a lone candle or oil lamp burns so the nuns can oversee their sleeping patients.

I lower myself from the wall into a garden filled with greenery. My boots crush the plants, releasing the pungent odor of herbs — the ones the sisters of Brigantia use for the famous healing potions and tinctures.

The very same ones we at the convent of Saint Mortain use to mix our equally infamous poisons.

I make my way to the path, trying to crush as few of the plants as possible, then follow the flat, round paving stones to what I hope is the infirmary. Near the door, I stop and press myself up against the building, using the shadows to conceal my presence. I close my eyes and try to feel how many are in the building.

I immediately sense a strong, booming pulse and nearly smile at how easily recognizable Beast is. There are other pulses that are thin and weak — patients', perhaps. The second slow and steady pulse is most likely that of the sister who tends them.

It is my hope that I can slip in undetected, see how Beast fares, then simply slip out again. My plan is foiled, however, by the old nun who sits near the door quietly mixing something with her mortar and pestle. I am certain I make no noise and equally certain that the thick pool of shadows near the wall conceals my presence. But something alerts her, for she starts and looks up. Since there is no point in pretending, I step away from the wall, prepared to explain why I am here.

Her eyes widen as she takes in the habit I wear, and the hand gripping the pestle turns white. "Who?" she whispers. "Who have you come for?"

I cannot decide which annoys me most, her fear or her assumption that I have been sent to kill one of her patients. "No one, old woman. I merely come to see how the one called Beast fares. I escorted him here from Nantes and would like to see with my own eyes that I did not do so only for him to perish in your care."

She bristles, her fear forgotten. "Of course he will not perish in our care." Her face softens. "Are you the one named Alyse? For he calls that name in his sleep."

"No, that is his beloved sister, dead these past three years." The depth of my disappointment that it is not my name he calls takes me completely by surprise.

"Ah," the old nun says sympathetically, as if she somehow knows what I am feeling. "Then perhaps you are Sybella. That is the name he asks for when he is awake."

A flutter of joy quickens my pulse. I scowl so that she will not see it.

"However, he is asleep now," she continues. "Indeed, we had to give him a tincture of opium and valerian in order to calm him. He was most insistent that he could walk out of here and be of use to the duchess, even though his body said otherwise and he could barely keep his eyes open, let alone sit up."

"I will not wake him," I promise. "I only wish to assure myself that he is well."

The nun nods her permission, and I start to move away, but she stops me. "By the way, whoever tended his wounds on the road did an excellent job. The man owes that person not only his life, but also his leg."

Her words please me far more than they should, this knowledge that my hands can heal as well as kill, and it takes every ounce of self-control I have to keep my pleasure hidden. I turn and begin making my way to where Beast lies.

One-third of the beds here in the infirmary are occupied, mostly with the elderly and frail. It is eerily still. No fretting or moaning or frail cries for help. Perhaps she has sedated them all.

It is easy enough to pick out Beast's hulking form, even when it is draped in white linen bedsheets, for he is easily twice the size of any other patient here. I am pleased to see the beds on either side of him are empty. That should afford me some small measure of privacy.

He lies as still as if he had been carved from marble, the high color he normally boasts leached from his face by the dim light and fatigue. His face is made even uglier by the harsh planes and shadows revealed by the flickering light from the few oil lamps in the room. His eyelashes—thick and spiky as they rest against his cheeks—are possibly the only beautiful things about him.

I marvel at this man who carried me away from my waking nightmare, determined that I not fall victim to d'Albret's terrible retribution. Even after I had done nothing but spew vile accusations at him to light his temper, he would not leave me behind. What does he see when he looks at me? A harridan? A shrew? Some spoiled noblewoman playing at helping her country?

I glance back toward the attending nun and see that she has dimmed the oil lamp and now lies on her cot, resting until one of her patients needs her. With no one to see, I plunk myself down on the floor and lean back against the bed frame. It is quiet. So quiet. I can hear the breath move in and out of Beast's lungs, hear the blood move through his veins, hear his pulse, strong and steady and alive. Slowly, some of the terror of d'Albret's pursuit begins to seep out of me. Beast stirs in his sleep just then, his good hand slipping out from under his covers to hang over the side of the bed.

I stare at his hand, its thick, blunt fingers and multitude of scars and nicks. Unable to resist, I slide toward it, wondering what that hand would feel like resting on my shoulder.

"I knew that you would miss me."

It is only a lifetime of training that keeps me from leaping to my feet at the sound of Beast's voice. I snort to mask the small noise of surprise that escapes my throat. "I did not miss you. Merely wanted to be sure my effort in getting you here wasn't wasted."

"They drugged me," he says with mild outrage.

"Because you were too stupid to lie still and let your body heal."

"You didn't drug me," he points out.

"Because I had to get your maggoty carcass from one end of the country to the other. Once we arrived, trust me, I would have drugged you too."

"Humph." We are both quiet a moment, and then he asks, "What of the duchess?"

"She will no doubt come visit you herself. As will Duval and the entire small council, most like."

He shifts uneasily and plucks at the covers on his bed. "I do not wish to receive them like this. Trussed up like a babe in swaddling."

"To them you are a hero, and they wish to thank you for your sacrifice."

He makes another rude noise.

"Are you certain you are not an ox in disguise?" I ask.

In answer, he just grunts again. "I am surprised they have not sent you off to rescue some other fool knight while I slept."

"Not yet."

"If they are not careful, soon they will have men locking themselves in dungeons so that you can rescue them."

"Then they shall undoubtedly perish, for I would not go through *that* again."

"Where is Yannic?"

"Camped just outside the convent walls. Except for patients, no men are allowed inside." I wait to see what his next question will be, then hear a faint rumble from his chest. He has fallen asleep. I allow myself a tiny smile, for if he is well enough to spar with me, then he is well enough to live. I settle myself more comfortably on the floor and promise I will stay only a few more moments.

* * *

I awake some time later from a dreamless sleep. As I blink, I see that the flames in the lamps are sputtering as the oil grows dangerously low. Not quite morning yet. I feel the heavy weight of Beast's hand still on my shoulder, then slowly inch myself out from under it, not wanting to wake him.

Not wanting him to know precisely where and how I spent the night.

I pause outside the convent and turn toward the city gate. I could leave now. I could simply walk down this street to the city gate, go across the bridge, and be gone from this place forever. No more abbess. No more threats of d'Albret.

But the stark truth is, I have nowhere to go. No home to return to, no kin to offer me shelter, and the convent will no doubt be closed to me now.

I could work as a tavern maid—if they would hire me. In troubled times such as these, people are reluctant to trust strangers.

I could even seek out Erwan and throw my lot in with the charcoal-burners. Or return to Bette and marry one of her sweet, eager sons. I could control either of them well enough.

Except they have sworn to fight at Beast's side in the coming war.

The grim reality of my situation nearly makes me laugh. I am beautiful and educated and have all manner of useful—and deadly—skills, but all of that together is worth less than a bucket of slops.

I pull my cloak close around me against the chill breeze and continue across the bridge. As I draw near the gatehouse, I quickly rearrange my weapons, making sure that the dagger at my waist is clear and visible and that my wrist sheaths peek out from under my sleeves. Better that they think I was out on an assignment for Mortain than suspect I spent the night curled at the feet of the Beast like a mournful dog.

The guard on duty nods, his eyes taking in my habit and my weapons, and waves me through. The convents of the old saints seem to receive proper respect here in Rennes.

I reach my chambers and am relieved to find them empty. Too tired to remove my gown, I simply loosen the laces, climb into bed, and draw the bed curtains closed to block out the morning light. I pray that no one will have need of me for the next few hours, for I will be useless until I can get some sleep.

Chapter Twenty-Six

A SHORT TIME LATER, I am awakened by a knock on the door. A little serving maid enters, carrying fresh water for washing and the news that I am expected to attend the duchess's council meeting.

That summons prods me from my bed and into my clothes like few other requests could, for the truth is, I am sorely anxious to discharge all I know and be rid of it.

When a second knock sounds at the door, I hurry to open it and find both Ismae and Lord Duval waiting outside. I cannot decide whether to be flattered or worried at the nature of this escort, but Ismae gives me a warm greeting, and Duval's eyes are friendly enough, which eases my mind somewhat.

Duval bows formally to me. "We would like to hear a full report of all that transpired in Nantes, if you can bear to tell it."

"But of course, my lord," I say, then step into the hall. Ismae gives me a reassuring wink.

Duval leads us to a more formal chamber than the one I was in last night. The two sentries nod in greeting when they see him, and step forward to open the door.

Even though I have bathed and now wear clean clothes, I still feel dirty in some way I cannot name, as if the taint of being a d'Albret will never leave. The maps have been put away, and instead there are flagons of wine set upon the table, as well as fine silver goblets.

My eyes are drawn immediately to a corner of the room near the head of the council table. Beast is here. They have brought him over on a litter and have rigged some sort of chair and stool for him so he can sit with his leg elevated. He is none too pleased about it and keeps trying to stand up. "I should not be sitting in the presence of the duchess," he grumbles.

The nun in the blue habit of Saint Brigantia patiently points out that all the other councilors and advisors do.

"But I am a mere knight, not a councilor."

"Well," the duchess herself says, putting the matter to rest, "you are now. I appoint you, Sir Benebic Waroch, to my high council so you may advise me on how best to win this war. What say you?"

The look of surprise on his face is near comical. "I humbly accept, Your Grace." He moves to stand and bow, but the nun pushes him back in the chair.

The duchess turns to me. "I trust you are more comfortable now," she says kindly.

"Yes, Your Grace. Thank you for your consideration."

"It is the least I can do for one who has served me so well." She motions to Duval, who shows me to a chair of my own and hands me a goblet of wine. I take it, glad to have something to hold, and glance uneasily at the others in the rooms, some of whose names I do not even know.

Catching the drift of my thoughts, Duval says, "Perhaps some introductions are in order." His mouth quirks charmingly. "The abbess and Beast you already know. This is Chancellor Montauban, who fought at my father's side in many battles. Jean de Chalon, the duchess's cousin, just recently released from his arrest by the French regent. Captain Dunois, whom I believe you saw carry the duchess to safety on his horse, and the bishop of Rennes, who placed the crown of office on her head with his own hands. The rest, I believe, are known to you. So now we would hear of d'Albret's plans, my lady."

I take a deep breath. "D'Albret has not given up his plan to marry the duchess, and will do so by force, if necessary."

Captain Dunois snorts. "He made that clear when he sprung the trap outside Nantes. He cannot think we are foolish enough to give him a second chance to trick us."

His dismissal pricks at me, but Ismae rushes in. "It was Sybella who warned us of that trap," she gently points out.

Out of the corner of my eye, I see the abbess's eyebrows lift in surprise.

Captain Dunois bows his head to me. "Then it seems we owe you more thanks, my lady, for you saved us all from certain disaster. But surely she is safe from him now."

I shake my head. "No. She is not. For that is not the end of it. Even now, he makes plans to march on Rennes."

A moment of silence fills the room, and then Captain Dunois scowls. "He would not be so foolish."

"Not to mention that it is impossible," Chancellor Montauban points out. "The walls are twelve feet thick, more than enough protection against any attack he could bring."

I lean forward. "Provided the attack come from within."

Another stunned silence fills the room. I have their full attention now. "Count d'Albret is not only ruthless, but cunning as well. He has already begun sending small groups of his own men to infiltrate the city. Then, when he is ready, he will march on Rennes and send the word for them to open the gates and allow his troops to break the siege."

"But knowing this, we can stop him. We have over eight thousand troops stationed here in Rennes, more than a match for a handful of his," Dunois says.

"Are you certain? Do you know every one of your men by sight, Captain? Is it not within those very numbers than many of d'Albret's saboteurs can hide unnoticed?"

The captain clenches his jaw but says nothing, so I continue. "I do not think you understand the true nature of his ruthlessness. He will show no mercy. The war he will wage is intended to sap the courage from men's hearts. He will take no prisoners, grant no quarter, collect no ransom."

"That goes against all rules of war and honorable conduct, demoiselle, and is a most grave accusation," Chancellor Montauban says. "I assume you have good reason to make it."

Disappointment as bitter as acid rises in my gut. Why did I think they would believe me?

"She does." It is the duchess who has spoken, and all in the room turn to look at her. "Do not forget, this man tried to entrap me when we parleyed in good faith with Marshal Rieux. That is not the mark of a man who respects the rules of engagement. Further, he did try to accost me in the halls of Guérande—would have succeeded if Ismae had not stopped him."

This shocks nearly everyone in the room—everyone except Ismae, Duval, and Beast.

"Are you certain you did not misunderstand his intention, Your Grace?" the bishop asks, and I want to slap his soft, white jowls.

"I am certain," she says shortly.

While everyone is reeling from this revelation, I decide to try a new approach. "May I tell you of how they took Nantes?" I ask, my voice deceptively sweet.

"By all means, demoiselle," Captain Dunois says. "I would very much like to hear it."

"Very well." I take a fortifying sip of the wine, then begin. "With Marshal Rieux at the head of our column, we were welcomed by the city with open arms. At first they thought the duchess had returned, and while they were disappointed she was not among the party, they did not understand the full treachery that was taking place.

"Once d'Albret and Rieux gained the castle, they bolted the doors and gave the retainers a choice. At the point of a sword. They could renounce the duchess and live. That was their only choice."

I stare into the flames burning in the fireplace. "Lords Roscoff and Vitre died that night. Lords Mathurin, Julliers, Vienne, and Blaine renounced the duchess and swore loyalty to d'Albret and Marshal Rieux." I glance up and meet the duchess's stricken eyes. "Your humbler servants were more loyal, Your Grace. A full half of them lost their lives that day.

"When a contingent of burghers arrived from the city demanding to know what was going on, troops were sent into town to rape their wives and daughters, thus ensuring their cooperation. It did not take long for d'Albret to exert his will and his own special brand of terror over the entire city."

The duchess has gone white as a corpse. When she lifts her hand to her temple, I see that it is trembling. "My poor people," she whispers. "All those deaths are on my conscience."

"No," snaps Duval. "They are on d'Albret's conscience, not yours."

Jean de Chalon speaks for the first time. "Such ruthlessness can be a great asset when it is wielded for one's own side. Given his ruthlessness and how much the French fear an alliance between you and the count, perhaps that alliance is your best hope for keeping the duchy independent."

The duchess appears to shrink in on herself, looking smaller and younger. "How wrong is it of me to expect my people to suffer so that I will not have to? I cannot let such violence and death spill over into the entire kingdom just so I can avoid an unpleasant marriage."

"No!" Duval, Beast, and I all shout at once. There is a moment of awkward silence and I stare at my hands while Duval continues. "You will not marry that brute."

"You are speaking as a loving brother, Duval, not as a clear-eyed councilor," the bishop points out. "Perhaps that is our best course of action."

I want to grab all these men by the shoulders, shake them until their teeth rattle, then ask them how they can be so cursedly *blind*. A rumbling begins building deep inside me, outrage that these men would so willingly consign this girl to a man such as d'Albret. It is just as it ever was: men of power are unwilling to believe anything ill of their own kind.

Suddenly, the weight of my own secrets nearly chokes me. If ever there was a reason to break the long years of silence, this is it—to prevent this innocent girl from becoming one of d'Albret's newest victims. To prevent such a monster from becoming ruler of the entire kingdom.

I am so desperate for them to understand the evil nature of this man that I do the unthinkable: I open my mouth and spill the secrets that I have kept for years. "Have you ever asked yourselves what became of the count's wives?" My throat tightens, as if my body is refusing to utter the words it has kept guarded and locked all this time. The knowledge I share will also raise questions, questions I'd rather not answer in front of Beast. But I cannot keep my secrets if the cost is the young woman before me.

"D'Albret is not just ruthless in battle and merciless in victory. He is a true monster." I must reach deep for the next words, for they are buried far beneath the surface of daily thought. Indeed, some of the memories remain locked away even from me. "D'Albret murdered all six of his former wives. Surely you would not consign your own duchess to such a fate."

In the long moment of silence that follows, the shock of what I have just done runs through my body. I am hot, then cold, then hot again. I half believe that d'Albret will somehow know what I have said, and I must remind myself that he is twenty leagues away.

By the grim look on Duval's face, I see that he at least believes me.

But not the others. Their faces are full of incredulity. Chancellor Montauban speaks. "It could be that his actions have been misinterpreted or misunderstood and these are but disgruntled rumors started by those who have suffered defeat at d'Albret's hands."

When I answer, my voice is colder than the winter sea. "I am an assassin trained, my lord Chancellor. Not a simpering maid who quails at talk of war." I consider having them ask Beast, for he will verify the truth of what I say, but it is not my secret to tell. I risk a glance at him and see that he is staring down at his clenched fists.

"I believe what she says is true," he says at last. "The count no doubt intends grave personal harm to the duchess—if not immediately, then soon after they are wed."

Dunois rises to his feet and begins to pace. "It is hard for me to believe such despicable accusations of a man who has guarded my back and fought bravely at my side. He has always fought with honor."

Chalon nods in agreement. "What you are accusing him of goes against every code of honor and chivalry we hold dear."

"That *you* hold dear, not d'Albret," I point out. "Besides, are you so very certain of his honor in battle? Have you never questioned why he and his troops arrived too late at the battle of Saint-Aubin-du-Cormier? Because that was not an accident, I assure you."

"I knew it!" Duval mutters under his breath. The duchess reaches out and places a small hand on his arm to calm him. Or perhaps she is clutching him for support. I cannot be certain.

But it is the bishop whom I have offended the most with my accusations. "If this is true, why have we not heard of it? Why should we believe you? Do you have any proof? In the name of Christ, girl, his brother is a cardinal!"

I glance briefly at the abbess then. "I have long been in his household and know far too well the nature of the man."

The bishop presses. "Then why have you not come forward sooner?"

A wave of helplessness and futility washes over me, but before I can begin a new round of arguments, the abbess's cool voice falls into the room like grace. "Gentlemen, you may rest assured that Lady Sybella has spoken the truth."

I am both surprised and grateful at this unexpected defense. Just as relief begins to unfurl inside me, she addresses them all again.

"Sybella is d'Albret's own daughter and knows whereof she speaks."

Chapter Twenty-Seven

I AM SO STUNNED THAT I can barely breathe. I could not be more surprised—or stricken—if the abbess had reached out and ripped the skin from my bones.

I would certainly feel just as raw and exposed. Indeed, it is all I can do to keep from leaping to my feet and running from the room as every eye turns on me. Is that a new glint of caution I see in Captain Dunois's gaze? A faint look of revulsion in Chancellor Montauban's? The bishop merely looks outraged, as if someone has disordered his carefully constructed world simply to spite him. Chalon's face is also interesting, for it is a carefully shuttered mask, and it is clear his interest has sharpened.

But it is Beast's gaze that feels the most like a blow.

Don't look, don't look, don't look. If I do not look, I will not have to see the disgust and loathing that now rises from him like steam from a boiling kettle.

And Ismae. What is she feeling right now? For I have known her the longest and have never breathed a word of my lineage. I stare straight ahead and tap my foot, as if I am bored.

The first to speak is Ismae. "Excuse me, Reverend Mother, but is Sybella not Mortain's daughter, rather than d'Albret's?"

It is all I can do to keep from leaping from my chair and hugging her.

"But of course, child. She was sired by Mortain, which is how she comes to serve the convent. But she was raised by d'Albret in his household for the first fourteen years of her life. For a certainty, d'Albret considers her his daughter."

Duval shifts in his chair and sends the abbess an unreadable look. That is when I realize he does not trust her. "I would think the more important question would be whose daughter Sybella considers herself to be. My lady?"

I look up and meet his kind gray eyes. He is giving me a chance to answer this accusation, and I begin to understand why Ismae is so fond of him. "The happiest moment of my life was when I learned I had not been sired by d'Albret, my lord. For as dark as Mortain is, He is a beacon of holy light compared to the baron. So yes, I consider myself Mortain's daughter."

Beast shifts in his chair, and every particle of my being screams at me not to be such a coward and *look* at him. But still I do not, certain that what I will see will break even my hard, shriveled heart.

"Then the matter is settled," the duchess says. "And it seems to me that if what the lady Sybella says is even remotely feasible, then we have nothing to lose by including that possibility in our plans. Much as when we expect an attack from the north, we still arrange for a strategy in the south, should we be proven wrong."

Captain Dunois strokes his chin and slowly nods his assent. "That seems wise to me."

"It cannot hurt," the chancellor concedes.

But the bishop is still reluctant. "I fear it will draw our energy and resources away from more dire needs."

"Even so," the duchess says. "We will act as if every word she says is true." She turns from the bishop to me. "Tell me, demoiselle, do you have any suggestions for us to consider?"

"We have secured a betrothal agreement with the Holy Roman emperor," Duval adds. "We could make that public if you think that will deter d'Albret at all. But if we announce it, the French will use it as an excuse to launch a full attack."

I shake my head. "I fear that news would only make d'Albret move more quickly—to prevent the marriage—rather than stay his hand. But I do agree that the duchess will only be safe once she is married. You must find a way to make the marriage happen now."

Duval smiles wryly. "That will be difficult with the Holy Roman emperor off fighting in Hungary."

Without troops, without a strong husband by her side, she is lost.

"Demoiselle."

At the duchess's gentle voice, I raise my head to meet her gaze. "You look utterly exhausted and we would command that you go find rest so we may speak again tomorrow. Thank you again for the great service you have done on our behalf."

I stand and sink into a curtsy. "It was an honor, Your Grace." And to my surprise, I find the words are true. I relish having something to lay before her besides more deaths. Even if that something now stares at me with hot, furious eyes.

With the meeting adjourned, I follow the abbess out into the hall, my jaw clenched tightly. When we are out of earshot of the others, I surprise both of us by reaching out and grabbing her arm. She stops immediately and looks down at my fingers resting on her sleeve. Even though my heart is pounding at my own daring, I wait a beat before removing my hand. When I do, the abbess lifts her cool blue gaze to my face and raises her eyebrows.

"Why?" I ask. "Why did you tell them who I am?"

She frowns slightly. "So they would know to believe you."

I study her closely. Is it that simple? Was she only trying to support my claim? "While it is true that their knowing my lineage chased away their doubts, I cannot help but think you could simply have confirmed my statements without revealing my true identity." Without revealing that I come from a family renowned for its cruelty and depravity — never mind that I have now just betrayed that same family, which is all many will see in my actions.

She moves her hand in an impatient gesture. "It does not matter that they know. Indeed, it is good for them to realize what powerful tools the convent has at its disposal and how long its reach is." She gives a curt nod, then removes herself from the hall, and I am left standing there, a lamb sacrificed for the elevation of the convent.

Without thinking, I head toward the castle door. I have no desire to go to my chamber and wait for Ismae to search me out, with a hurt and puzzled look in her eyes.

The cool night air does little to soothe my fury. My entire body itches with rage, as if it will burst out of my skin. I do the only thing I can think of, which is begin walking. Away from the palace, away from the abbess, away from Beast, whom my secrets have betrayed. Even with my talent for breaking things, I am astounded at the speed with which I have destroyed this budding friendship.

He knows. He *knows* I am the daughter of the man who killed his beloved sister. He knows that I have hardly opened my mouth without lying to him. Even now, he is likely going over every question he has ever asked and remembering all the lies I have told him.

He knows I have been shaped in the same dark stuff, with as little redemptive value. It would have been easier if I had been branded a whore or cast out as a leper.

My breath catches in my throat, and I press the heels of my hands against my eyes. It feels as if I've ruined one of the few things that has ever truly mattered.

At first, I was simply unwilling to admit to anyone — especially a prisoner d'Albret had treated so poorly — that I was a d'Albret. Then later, when I learned of Beast's connection to the family, nothing on earth could have compelled me to tell him the truth of who I was.

What else *could* I have told him but lies? The first time he asked we were but half a league from Nantes with no reason to trust each other. How would I have gotten him to safety?

My one true opportunity came at Guion's farm, when Beast asked me to tell him of his sister. But while I am strong enough to kill a man in cold blood, play Julian's razor-edged games, and rebel against the abbess, I was not strong enough to kill that mysterious, tender *something* that had sprung up between us in that moment.

And that weakness has cost me everything with Beast.

No. There could never have been anything between us. I was given a chance to tilt the scales of justice—just a bit—and that was all. As nice as it was to have someone view me in a flattering light, I was never worthy of his true regard. And now, now he will know that the person he saw when he looked at me was not real.

As if some small part of me seeks to cool my temper, my feet carry me through the darkened streets of the city toward the river. I storm past the elegant stone and timber houses, past the town square, to where the streets are smaller and the houses lean together like drunken soldiers. The streets are busier here, as the scum of the city goes about its business under the cover of night. Small bands of beggars, dividing the day's spoils; drunken soldiers avoiding the night watch; thieves lurking in the shadows, waiting to take advantage of those too weak or drunk to notice the silent removal of their valuables.

The taverns here do a brisk business, and voices spill out onto the streets. There is a wild, frantic energy in this part of town that fits my mood perfectly. I raise my head and dare any of the dangers lurking in the shadows to try to match its skill against mine. I even slow my steps so that I appear hesitant, fearful—but it does not draw anyone. Perhaps those who prey on others can sense my desire to prey on them.

Frustrated, I continue all the way to the river, where the very dregs of the city lurk. As I stand on the bridge and look into the dark water, the truth I've been running from for days rises up like a rotten log from the bottom of a pond. It was not just Beast's good opinion or respect that I craved, but his affection. The shriveled, withered bit of gristle that lives where my heart used to be has managed to fall in love with him.

The pain and humiliation of that is like a fist to my gut. I grip the stone railing of the bridge and stare down at the river. How deep is it? I wonder. I know how to swim, but my gown and cloak are heavy and would drag me to the bottom in no time.

"My lady."

Annoyed at the intrusion, I snap my head up.

A drunken soldier saunters toward me. Here is the release I seek. He is a hard-faced fellow, a mercenary, I think, for his jerkin is of boiled leather, and neither his cloak nor his brooch bear any insignia. He is wine soaked enough to be friendly, but not so much that he is impaired. I turn to face him.

"Is my lady lost?" he asks. "For this is no part of town for someone as fair as yourself to be wandering."

"Do you think I am not safe?"

"No, I think you are at grave risk, my lady. There are any number of louts and ruffians who would take advantage of you."

"But not you."

He smiles then, a wolfish grin. "I have only your pleasure in mind."

"Indeed?" At first, I am not sure if I want to fight him or bed him, but when he places his large, gloved hand on my arm to pull me close and I smell his sour wine breath, I realize it is not his lust I hunger for, but his blood. I want to bury my fury and betrayal in his thick, meaty neck and watch his blood spurt back at me in a red-hot rage that will meet my own.

I could even call it an offering to Mortain. Or the Dark Matrona.

Whichever god will listen to my prayers and deliver me from this nightmare I inhabit.

He leans in to kiss me but gives a yelp of surprise when he nearly kisses the tip of my knife instead. He grows still and watches me carefully. I feel his pulse beating in his throat, can see his artery throbbing with the blood that flows through it. Slowly I move my knife nearer. I am tempted—so sorely tempted—but he has done nothing wrong and bears no marque. He has not invaded our country, nor does he serve d'Albret. He has not even tried to harm an innocent, for I am no innocent. Of all the lines I have been willing to cross in my life, this is not one of them.

Just as the point of my knife touches the tender skin at his throat, a scream rings out. At first, I think someone has seen me and cried a warning, but the scream is followed by the sound of blows. My heart quickens at the thought of a true fight, and I content myself with simply nicking the chin of the fellow in front of me.

One fat red drop of blood wells up, then falls to the filthy cobbles beneath our feet. "Be gone from here," I tell him.

Anger flashes in his eyes, and for one moment I think he will reach for his sword. "Be careful of the games you play, my lady," he says. "Not all will be as forgiving as I."

I say nothing. When he turns and walks back the way he came, I hurry in the direction of the scream.

It came from downriver, near one of the stone bridges. As I draw closer, the sounds of a struggle reach my ears, and grip my knife more firmly. Cautious now, I move forward. In the shadow of a bridge's stone footings, two soldiers struggle with a man and a woman. The man's thin mouth is split and swollen, and his long, sharp nose is bloody. The woman is backed up against the bridge, and one of the soldiers is unlacing his breeches.

It takes but a second for me to recognize that the victims are char-bonnerie, which only serves to stoke my fury. Moving on quiet feet, I creep closer. Something feels familiar about the two soldiers, and when the one restraining the man turns to watch his friend, I feel a jolt of recognition. It is Berthelot the Monk, so called because he never touches a woman. Which means the second man must be Gallmau the Wolf, named thus because he cannot leave them alone. Both are d'Albret's men, and I feel in my bones it cannot be an accident that I have found them.

Killing two of d'Albret's own will do much to lessen the pain of my breaking heart.

Gallmau is still leering at the woman and taking his time, so I decide to strike Berthelot first. Clinging to the shadows, I move around the bridge's piling until I am behind the monk. It will be tricky, cutting his throat while he holds the charbonnerie, but the charbonnerie can take a quick dunk in the river to wash away the blood if he must.

Faster than a striking snake, I step forward, grab the man's hair and yank his head back, then run my knife across his throat, cutting his vocal cords as well as the main arteries. As Berthelot falls to the ground, the charbonnerie stumbles back, managing to pull his arms free just in time so that he does not go down as well. I feel him glance at me, feel the moment that he recognizes me, but I am transfixed by the marque I see on Berthelot's forehead. I smile then, and turn to Gallmau, who is so engrossed in his lustful activities he has no idea that death is reaching for him. When I am close enough to embrace him, the woman looks over his shoulder and sees me, and her eyes widen. I hold my finger to my lips, then shove my knife into the base of Gallmau's skull. In truth, this is not the best knife for this sort of job. A thinner knife would slip more easily between the bones of his neck, but I am able to make this work. And keep the blood from ruining the woman's dress.

To the girl's credit, she bites back her scream as Gallmau collapses into her arms, and then she shoves the body away so that he falls onto the ground. I peer down, happier than I can say when I see a second marque appear, for that must mean I have not stepped so far outside Mortain's grace that He no longer reveals His will to me.

I wipe my blade on Gallmau's cloak, then return it to its sheath and stand up. "Are you all right?" I recognize the thin, dark-haired man as Lazare, the angriest of the charbonnerie. I doubt that this incident has improved his temper any.

"I should have been the one to kill the pigs," he spits out.

"You can be the one to kill them next time," I assure him, and then I ask the woman if she is all right. She shakily nods her head. I turn back to Lazare. "Go, wash the blood off in the river before anyone sees. If you come across any other soldiers or the night watch, simply tell them you had too much wine and fell in."

He stares at me a long moment. Unspoken things move in his eyes. Rage at being preyed on, discomfort at being saved by a mere woman, frustration that he was not the one to avenge their honor. But there is gratitude as well, even if it is begrudging. He gives me a terse nod and does as I instruct. While he is cleaning himself, I ask the woman, "What happened?"

"We were returning from one last delivery, as Erwan wanted to leave at first light, when these two attacked us. They took our money and were going to . . . going to . . . and when Lazare tried to stop them, they beat him. Thank you, my lady. Thank you for arriving just when you did. The Dark Mother was looking out for us."

"Or Mortain," I say. "For that is the god I serve, and it was He who led me here to these two."

The excitement of the hunt has begun to leave and I realize I am tired. So very, very tired. Even so, I take the time to kneel beside the bodies, search for whatever coin they have on them, and give what I find to the woman. "Now go. Collect Lazare and get yourselves back to the others."

Once I see them on their way, I begin the long walk back to the palace, empty and hollow, nothing but a burned-out ember now that my rage has passed.

Chapter Twenty-Eight

WHEN I REACH MY CHAMBER door, I can feel someone waiting inside. A spurt of panic shoots through me. Is it Beast wanting to confront me? Furious that I even care, I draw a blade from my wrist and open the door.

It is only Ismae, slumped in a chair by the dying fire, and I cannot tell if it is relief or disappointment I feel. At the faint snick of the door closing behind me, she stirs, then blinks awake. "Sybella!" She comes to her feet and takes two steps toward me. "Where have you been?"

I cannot tell her I have been moping over a broken heart when I have worked so hard to convince her I do not have a heart at all, so instead I cock an eyebrow at her. "Are you going to rail at me for not having told you sooner?"

"No! I'm not surprised the abbess bade you to hold your tongue." The love and compassion I see on Ismae's face nearly undoes me.

"It was not the abbess," I say. The truth begins bubbling out of me like vile humors from a wound. "She never forbade me to tell you. I just . . . could not bring myself to do so. Especially once you'd met d'Albret in Guérande."

Ismae crosses the distance between us and takes one of my hands in each of her own and gives them a squeeze. I cannot tell if it is meant to show reassurance or exasperation. Mayhap both. "We all have our secrets. And our scars. Annith told me that my first morning at the convent. I have not told you everything about my past either."

"You haven't?"

Ismae shakes her head, and I study her to see if this is but a ploy to comfort me.

"I know you were married, and that your father beat you."

She winces slightly. "Both of those are true, but there is more to my story. I never told you of the poison my mother sought from the herbwitch in order to expel me from her womb. Nor of the long, ugly scar along my back where it burned my flesh. I never spoke of my sister, who feared me, or the village boys who taunted me and called me cruel names. Like you, I was so glad to have escaped, I had no wish to speak of them and taint my new life at the convent with those memories."

And just like that, she has granted me absolution, declared my crimes against our friendship no crimes at all. I have no words that will let her know how much this means to me. Instead, I smile. "What sort of taunts did they hurl at you?"

Ismae wrinkles her nose and lets go of my hands. "None that I care to repeat."

"So, then," I say, changing the subject, "why are you here waiting for me?"

"I was afraid for you."

"Afraid? What did you fear?"

She shrugs, embarrassed. "That the abbess had sent you somewhere again. That you had run away. The possibilities seemed endless as I sat here all night."

Something in my heart softens. "You've waited for me all night?"

"Once I was here, it seemed pointless to leave until I knew what had become of you." She turns and grabs a poker to stir up the embers in the hearth. "Where have you been?"

"I needed to get out of the palace, away from the abbess and all her manipulations."

"It does not help that you are exhausted. Here. Come to bed. You need to sleep. Knowing you, you have not slept more than six hours in the last six days."

That she has guessed so accurately makes me smile. "Even so, I will not be able to sleep. Not here, not now."

"Yes, you will. That is another reason I came to your room. To bring you a sleeping draft."

I feel tears prick at my eyes—*merde,* but I am becoming some soft, weepy thing! So she will not see, I turn my back and motion for her to help unlace me. "But what of the duchess? Do you not need to attend her?"

"Not for a few hours yet."

Some of the tension leaves me and I allow Ismae to help me undress, as if I am a small child, after which she puts me into the bed and draws up the covers. I wait while she pours the sleeping draft into a goblet, then drain it. Our eyes meet. I do not even know how to begin to thank her. And because it is Ismae, she simply smiles and says, "You're welcome."

I smile back, then study her while she finishes putting away my things. Once we begin going on assignments for the convent, we are forbidden to talk about them with others. But Ismae is no longer as beholden to the convent as she was, and I am half starved to hear about her experiences so I can see if she has the same doubts and questions I do. I begin plucking at a loose thread on the bedcovers. "Tell me," I say casually, "do you know if the Tears of Mortain wear off?"

She stops smoothing the gown she is holding. "I do not know. Mine haven't."

"So you still see the marque?"

"I have been able to see the marque since I was a child. I just didn't know what it was."

"Then why did they even give the Tears to you?"

"It heightened my other senses. I was suddenly able to — this will sound mad — feel people's life sparks. I am more aware of their living, breathing bodies, even if I cannot see them."

"That is a gift *I* have had since I was a child," I tell her. And more than once did it save me. I realize how useless Ismae's gift of seeing marques would have been in my circumstances; I had no need to spot the dying, but every need to avoid the living, which sensing their pulses allowed me to do. "I suppose you let that blind old woman nearly put your eyes out with her wicked crystal stopper?"

"Didn't you?"

"No, I took it from her and did it myself."

Ismae gapes in shock. For a moment it is as if the old Ismae, the one who worshiped everything about the convent and followed every rule, is back. Then she laughs. "Oh, Sybella! I would have loved to be a spider on the wall and seen *that*."

"She was most affronted."

"Why did you want to know if the Tears wear off?" she asks gently.

I take a deep breath. "Because there have been men who I know are guilty of treachery — for I have seen it with my own eyes — and yet they are not marqued." I look up and meet her gaze. "If Mortain grants mercy to d'Albret and Marshal Rieux, then I find it hard to want to serve Him." I did not mean to confess that to her, but the words spill out of me.

She studies me a moment, then comes to kneel beside my bed. "Sybella," she says, her eyes shining with some mysterious light. "I have met Mortain face to face, and the abbess, maybe even the convent, is wrong about so very many things."

I stare at her dumbly, and my heart begins to race. "You have seen Him? He is real?" I ask.

"I have, and He is more kind and merciful than you can imagine. And He has given us such gifts!" She looks at her hands. "Not only am I immune to poison's effects, but I can use my own skin to draw it from others."

"Truly?"

There is not a whiff of hesitation or doubt. "Yes."

I turn my face toward the wall and pretend I am snuggling into sleep so she will not see the hunger in my eyes. "Tell me," I whisper. "Tell me of this father of ours."

"Gladly." She pauses, as if she must collect her thoughts. When she speaks again, it is as if her voice is filled with light. "There is so much kindness in Him. And mercy. All the judgment and retribution we have been trained to expect of Him was not there. In His presence, I felt whole and complete in a way I have never felt before."

There is such certainty in her voice that I find myself filled with envy.

"We are not just His handmaidens, spawned to do His bidding. He loves us," she says.

The idea is so foreign to me that I snort.

"He does! For He is trapped in the realm of Death, and it gives Him great joy to know that we who were born of His seed are able to embrace life."

"If that is so, then why has He consigned us to lurk in the shadows and cloak ourselves in His darkness?"

She does not answer right away. I sneak a look over my shoulder and see that she is frowning at the window, as if she seeks the answer to this question there. "I believe those are not His wishes, but the convent's."

Those words are like a shower of winter hail down my back. I sit up and turn to look at her. "What do you mean?"

"I mean"—she chooses her words as if picking her way across a stream—"that I believe the convent misunderstands both Mortain and His wishes for us. Whether through ignorance or intent, I do not know."

The magnitude of this makes my heart clutch in my chest. "Explain," I say, shoving my hair out of my eyes so I may use every sense I possess to try to understand this huge revelation she has just shared.

"First, He does not insist we act with vengeance or judgment in our hearts. To Him, bringing Death is an act of great mercy and grace, for without it all people would be forced to struggle on in frail and broken bodies, riddled with pain, weakened. That is why He has given us the misericorde."

"The what?"

Ismae looks at me, puzzled. "You do not have one?"

"I have never even heard of such a thing."

Ismae reaches into the folds of her skirt and withdraws an ancient-looking knife, its handle of bone with chased silver. "It is an instrument of mercy," she says softly. "Just one nick causes the soul to leave the body, quick and sure and painless. But I do not understand why the abbess did not give you one."

"It could be she knew no one in d'Albret's household was deserving of mercy." Of a certainty, she knew I would not be interested in dispensing it.

She puts that aside for now. "But Sybella, what I learned is that He does not love us *because* of the acts we perform in His name—He loves us because we are *His*. What we choose to do or not do, how we choose to serve Him or not serve Him, will never alter that love."

"He told you this?"

"Not in words such as you and I speak, but I felt it. I felt this grace and love of His surround and engulf me like a river, and it stripped the ignorance from my eyes."

"Much like the Tears of Mortain allow us to see His will better."

"Precisely like that. Only a hundredfold more."

I reach out and grab her arm. "So have we been wrong all this time? Committing murder by striking when we see His marque?"

"Not wrong, exactly," she says slowly. "But I would say instead it is not *required* of us. Those who are to meet Death bear a marque, whether they are to die by our hands or by some other means."

"How do you know this?" Have I been killing men all this time, thinking I was doing His will when I was actually following some dark impulse of my own?

"After we were attacked at Nantes, I returned to the field to search for survivors among the fallen."

"There were none," I say tightly. "D'Albret does not leave survivors."

"No, but each of the dying soldiers bore some form of the marque. And the men I saw marqued when I was a child—none was killed by another's hand. I believe the marque appears when a man's death is in sight, and that includes a death at our hands. The mistake I think the convent has made is about the nature of those marques. They are merely *reflections* of what will happen, not *commands* to act."

"Does the abbess know this?"

"I do not know," Ismae says slowly. "I cannot tell. Although she was most angry when I suggested such an idea to her. Now sleep. Morning will come soon enough." She comes over to the bed, leans down, and presses a kiss on my brow. "Everything I have told you about Mortain is true. Do not doubt it." And then she is gone, and I am left with my entire world turned upside down.

Chapter Twenty-Nine

Even with the draft Ismae prepared, my sleep is fitful and restless. I am too consumed with reciting all that she has just told me, my mind scrambling to recast the world—and my role in it.

I am not certain I believe her, for Ismae was always wont to see Mortain and the convent in the best possible light. Even so, it has given my mind much to gnaw on.

When I wake, my head is so thick and woolly that it takes a moment for me to realize that someone is knocking. I fight my way out of the tangle of covers, get to my feet, and stumble to the door. I open it an inch and peek out. A liveried page awaits. To his credit, his eyes drift to my disheveled appearance only once before returning to my face and staying there. "The duchess cordially invites you to join her at your earliest convenience in her solar, demoiselle."

"Very well. Tell her I will be there shortly."

The lad gives a sprightly bow. Before he can scamper off, I ask him to send a maidservant to attend me.

The summons has chased the last cobwebs of sleep from my mind as I worry what the duchess wishes of me. Will she ban me from her court, now that she knows of my heritage? Or will she try to draw more of my secrets from me?

And if so, what will I tell her? For she, more than anyone, has a full right to know both the doings of her most traitorous subject and the nature of this man some would have her marry.

Whatever she wishes, it will most likely be just she and her ladies in waiting in the solar, so I will not have to face Beast just yet. While Ismae was most forgiving, my family has not harmed her or those she loved in any way. Beast's betrayal at my hand goes much deeper than a secret not shared between childhood friends.

By the time the maid arrives, I have already washed with the water remaining in the ewer, the coldness of it helping to restore my wits. I slip into the second of the gowns Ismae has lent me, a stark, simple black silk with severe lines. I settle my heavy garnet and gold crucifix on the thick chain around my waist and consider myself ready. At least, as ready as I'll ever be.

The maid herself leads me to the duchess's solar, which is two floors up from my own chamber. She murmurs my name to the sentry on duty, who nods and opens the door, announcing me.

"Come in!" the duchess's young voice calls out. Cautiously, I step into the room, blinking at all the golden sunlight spilling in through the mullioned windows.

The duchess is sitting near a couch, surrounded by three ladies in waiting. As they eye me furtively, I cannot help but wonder if news of my parentage has traveled to their delicate ears. Or is the council treating it as a secret to be guarded?

A young girl, no more than ten years of age, reclines on the couch, looking fragile and wan.

"Lady Sybella!" The duchess waves her hand at me. I step farther into the room, pleased that she has not used my last name. As I sink into a deep curtsy, I comfort myself that she has most likely not brought me here to censure me in front of her younger sister.

"Come. Sit with us." She pats the empty chair between herself and the couch, and I realize that this summons is an invitation. An open declaration of acceptance, and I am humbled by this great kindness she is showing me.

"But of course, Your Grace."

I ignore the glances of her ladies and cross to the chair the duchess indicates. As I sit down, the duchess gives me another smile. "I had thought to invite you to stitch with us, then realized you probably did not think to pack your embroidery silks when you left Nantes."

I smile at her gentle joke. "No, Your Grace. I did not."

One of the ladies leans forward, her brow creased. "How did you find Nantes, my lady?"

The duchess looks at her attendant and shakes her head with a glance in the young girl's direction. The woman nods in understanding.

"It is as magnificent as ever, a true testament to the house of Montfort," I say, and the duchess relaxes slightly.

"Demoiselle, I do not think you have met my sister before. Isabeau, dear, this is the Lady Sybella, a great ally of ours."

Her words cause a blush to rise to my cheeks—I, who never blush—and I turn to properly greet her sister. The child's skin looks nearly translucent, and her large eyes peer out of her pale, drawn face. And her heart—ah, her heart is beating slowly, weakly, as if it may give up at any moment. She reminds me wholly of my younger sister Louise, who also battles fragile health. Once again I am grateful that both my sisters are tucked away in one of our father's most remote holdings, far from his political scheming and influence.

Not welcoming all the painful memories that the young princess stirs, I harden my heart against her, but in the end, she is so small and weak and charming, I cannot keep myself from liking her. Her embroidery sits forgotten in her lap, and she plucks at her bodice, as if she finds it difficult to breathe. To distract her, I beg a length of scarlet embroidery silk from the duchess, then busy my fingers.

My action immediately catches Isabeau's attention. "What are you doing, my lady?" She pokes her nose forward to see better.

"I am making a cat's cradle, a puzzle of thread." A few more twists of my fingers and the red thread is shaped like a trestle bridge. The princess's face brightens and her mouth forms a small O of delight.

"Take your hands and pinch where the threads cross on each side," I tell her.

She glances at the duchess, who nods her head in permission, then reaches out with two slim fingers and hesitatingly pinches the crossed threads. "Ready now?" I ask.

She glances up at me, then back down at the threads. She nods. "Pinch hard," I say, "pull your hands out to the side, then bring them slowly back in and under my own."

Biting her lip in concentration, Isabeau does as I instruct. It is clumsy and awkward, but when she is finished, she has transferred the cat's cradle to her own small hands, and her face flushes with triumph and delight.

"Oh, well done," murmurs the duchess.

I smile at Isabeau, who smiles back. She is no longer plucking at her bodice, and her heart is beating a little more steadily. Thus it was with Louise as well. Her own illness made her anxious, which in turn made her feel worse. It comes over me with the force of a blacksmith's hammer that I may very well never see Louise or Charlotte again. Not after betraying d'Albret.

"Demoiselle?" the duchess asks, leaning forward with her brows pinched in concern. "Are you all right?"

"Yes, Your Grace. Just trying to remember another trick with the string." I force all thoughts of my sisters back into the small, cramped box deep in my heart, bind it once again with chains, and lock it tight.

I spend the next hour teaching Isabeau how to do the trick while the duchess talks softly with her ladies. Unobserved, I try to note each of them and take her measure. How long has the duchess known them? How loyal to her are they? I do not recognize any of them from Guérande, which suggests they have been culled from Rennes's noble families. Let us hope they are more loyal than her other attendants and retainers have been.

They in turn watch me, their glances like small, biting insects. I cannot tell if it is mere curiosity or if there is knowledge and censure in their gaze.

When it is time for dinner, the ladies put away their embroidery. Isabeau is being allowed to attend tonight, for the duchess has agreed to a performance by minstrels that she thinks her young sister will enjoy.

We leave the solar, and the duchess has one of the other ladies escort Isabeau while she herself walks next to me. Her steps slow somewhat, and I must alter my pace so I do not run ahead and leave her trailing behind. When no one is close enough to hear, she leans toward me slightly. "Demoiselle, I want you to know that I thank you for your sacrifice, for to go against your family, no matter how justified, is no easy thing. I also want you to know that I do not doubt a single word you have told us. Indeed, it aligns precisely with what my lord brother and I have long felt. I am only sorry that you have had to learn this knowledge firsthand." With that, she squeezes my arm gently, then turns the talk to the minstrels and what she has heard of their talents. I hear nothing she says; I am too busy holding tight this small nugget of trust she has granted me.

While the great hall in Rennes is smaller than that of Nantes, it is every bit as opulent. The rich carved paneling is decorated heavily with thick, brilliant tapestries, and the room is alight with the glow of scores of candles. The mingled scent of rose, civet, cloves, and ambergris hangs heavy in the air, and I feel the beating of a dozen hearts. It is, in every sense of the word, an assault upon my senses. Even worse, everyone in the room is infected with high spirits, and the guests' jubilant manner makes me uneasy. It is unwise for them to be so very happy, for the gods will feel the need to humble us.

The first thing I do is look for Beast, but the ugly oaf is not here. My entire body sags in relief, for I did not look forward to an entire evening spent trying to ignore his wrath. Not to mention I'm fairly certain his continuing fury would blister my skin.

The rest of the council is here, however. The abbess and the bishop have their heads together, whispering. As if feeling my gaze, the abbess glances up and gives me a cool nod. I dip a curtsy but do not go to her.

The earnest Captain Dunois is deep in conversation with the chancellor, his heavy, furrowed brow making him look even more like a bear. Wanting to test his reaction to me now that he knows who I am, I drift closer.

When he sees me, he nods a distracted greeting. Or perhaps it is a cool greeting, like the abbess's, a way to discourage my approach. I do not know him well enough to say. While I do not know Chancellor Montauban any better, there is no mistaking the distaste in his gaze. He makes no effort to hide it.

As I turn away from them, I see a small, hunched figure hovering just outside the doorway. It is Yannic, whom Beast has no doubt sent to spy on my movements.

Furious, I turn and search the hall, looking for someone I can attach myself to and prove that I am not moping over him. Nor am I the pariah he no doubts wishes me to be.

The duchess's cousin Jean de Chalon is but a few paces from me. When our eyes meet, he smiles, which surprises me somewhat, as the last time we were together he appeared most distant and guarded. But he is handsome and titled and will make a good story for Yannic to carry back to his master. I smile at Chalon, a smile filled with more mystery than sparkle, for he is not a man to be lured with simple wiles.

He draws closer and bows. "You look lonely, demoiselle."

"Ah, not lonely, my lord. Simply discerning in the company I keep."

"A lady after my own heart, then." He snags a goblet of wine from a passing page and hands it to me. As I take it, I let my fingers brush against his, and I feel his pulse flare with interest.

I pray that Yannic is watching all this, for it is far too much effort if he is not.

Chalon eyes me hungrily, and he is not an unattractive man. Tall, lithely muscled, and with a graceful arrogance that one expects from a prince. But looking at him, flirting with him, I feel . . . nothing. It is cruel of me to use him this way, for I do not desire his affection, simply his attention, and that only long enough to make an impression on Yannic. I murmur inanities a moment longer, then check to be certain Beast's little squire is watching. But he is gone, and at last I can bring this game to a close, for Chalon is too smooth and tame and far too pretty a creature to hold my interest.

The only other pleasure to be had from the evening is watching young Isabeau and her sweet, uncomplicated joy in the music. Her hands are clasped, her eyes bright. But as I watch her, I am again reminded of Louise and Charlotte and how very much I miss them. I have not seen them in nearly a year, not since my terror over their safety forced me to thrust them from my heart, from my mind.

Isabeau is a painful reminder of everything I have had to give up, all that I have lost. Even though the room is full of people, I feel suddenly surrounded by a moat of loneliness. I cast about, looking for Ismae, the one friend I have in this accursed place, but she has left the duchess's side and is grabbing a quiet moment with Duval. And while I do not begrudge her the love she has found, I am also filled with envy, for I know such a chance is lost to me.

Chapter Thirty

THE NEXT MORNING I AM summoned to yet another council meeting, which makes me uneasy, for the only business the council has with me is to grill me further on my time in d'Albret's household. Not to mention I am still filled with dread at having to see Beast. I would rather do anything else than face the accusations in his eyes: suffer one of the abbess's tongue lashings, play one of Julian's sordid games, even subject myself to one of d'Albret's punishments. But although I am many things, a coward is not one of them. My heart beating wildly in my chest, I square my shoulders, lift my chin, and enter the room with my head held high. Leaping from the barbicans back in Nantes would have taken less courage.

Beast's face is calm, and a polite smile hovers on his lips, but his eyes burn with the light blue of a fire's hottest flame, and the look he gives me has all the force of a physical blow. I smile vaguely at him, then turn to the others.

It is the same advisors as before. They even sit in the same places, except for the abbess, who is now seated at the table rather than lurking in the corner of the room.

"And here is Lady Sybella." The duchess's voice is warm and welcoming and gives me some small measure of courage as I take my seat.

"I'm afraid the latest news is dire," Duval says. "The French are on the march. They have taken Guingamp and Moncontour."

The duchess grips the arms of her chair, her fingers turning white. "And the casualties?"

"From all I can determine, the French did not meet with much organized resistance. The local burghers, worried about the town, quickly handed it over, and the small pockets of protest were easily dealt with."

The duchess stares unseeing into the distance. "They are so close!" she says. "What of the English troops? Are they close as well?"

"More bad news, I'm afraid." Duval's voice is grim. "A series of storms off the coast of Morlaix has kept the English ships from landing. Those six thousand troops will be delayed."

"How long will it take the British troops to arrive in Rennes once they have reached the coast?"

"At least a week, Your Grace."

"Is there any sign the French will attack before then?"

Duval answers with a shrug. "It is hard to say. They seem to be holding just inside our border and are sending out sorties and small scouting parties, nothing more. Except for their attack on Ancenis and the occasional pillaging for food, there have been no reports of fighting."

Captain Dunois taps his finger on his chin. "What are they waiting for? I wonder."

"For us to break the Treaty of Verger, is all I can surmise," Duval says. "We have had much acrimony between the French regent and our own politics, but we have honored the dictates of the treaty. At least openly," he adds with a rakish grin.

"Do you think they know of our negotiations with the Holy Roman emperor?" The duchess's brow is furrowed with concern.

Duval considers. "Suspect it, yes. But do they *know?* I do not think that they do. If they had actual knowledge of the betrothal agreement, they would have used that to justify an attack by now."

"True enough," Captain Dunois agrees. "I suppose it is too much to hope for that if Count d'Albret decides to march on Rennes, he will run into the French and they will eliminate each other."

Duval gives a rueful smile. "Would that we were so lucky." He pauses to look at his hands, then meets his sister's gaze full on. "It is said that bad news arrives in threes, Your Grace." Looking as if he could happily commit murder, Duval delivers the final blow. "We have received a letter from Count d'Albret."

All eyes in the room turn to me. I ignore the sharp sting of their regard and concentrate wholly on Duval and the duchess, as if we are having a private conversation. "Does he know Beast is here?" I ask.

"Not that he indicates. The purpose of the letter was to ask that the duchess reconsider honoring their marriage agreement, else he will be forced to do something she will not like."

"Besiege the city," I whisper.

Duval nods. "He does not come out and say so, but that is my assumption as well."

The duchess, who has gone pale at this news, visibly gathers herself. "What of the Holy Roman emperor? Has he received word of how dire our plight?"

"He has. He will send two auxiliaries to aid us." Duval's voice is drier than high summer.

"Two auxiliaries?" Captain Dunois says. "Is he serious? So few, and not even professional soldiers?"

"I'm afraid so. He is also suggesting that we perform the marriage ceremony by proxy in order to get the thing done."

Jean de Chalon shifts uneasily in his chair; it is his overlord they are speaking of, and perhaps he feels his loyalties are being stretched thin. "I am sure he is doing all that he can. He is much besieged by his war with Hungary."

Duval does not deign to answer this. The duchess's mouth tightens in disapproval, but she does not contradict her cousin, although I feel certain she wishes to. "Does a marriage by proxy even count in the eyes of the Church?" she asks the bishop.

"Yes, it can, if done properly."

"But we still won't have his troops to defend the alliance," Captain Dunois points out.

"What of mercenaries? How difficult would it be to get companies of mercenaries here?"

"Not too difficult." Duval's voice is gentle, as if he wishes to take the sting from the words that now follow. "What presents a problem, Your Grace, is that we have no money to pay them."

She looks at him blankly for a moment. "None?" she whispers, then looks to her chancellor.

He confirms Duval's assessment. "I'm afraid not, Your Grace. The duchy's coffers were greatly strained by the wars with the French over the last two years. The treasury is empty."

The duchess rises from her chair and begins pacing in front of the fire. She is very nearly out of options, and she must know it. "What of my family's jewels? The silver plate? The crown—"

The bishop gasps in horror. "Not your crown, Your Grace!"

"Will that bring enough coin to pay them?"

"Your Grace! Some of your jewelry has been in your family for generations," Chalon says. I cannot help but wonder if he is keeping track of what he would inherit if anything were to happen to the duchess.

"Jewels can be replaced, my cousin. Independence, once lost, cannot."

The room is silent as the company digests her words, then Beast leans forward to speak for the first time. "There are some who would fight at our side for free," he tells them.

"Who?" Captain Dunois and Chancellor Montauban ask at the same time.

"The charbonnerie."

"This is no time for jests," the chancellor says with reproach.

Beast meets his eyes levelly. "I am not jesting. Furthermore, they have already agreed to fight by our side."

"They are nothing but outcasts, ruffians who must scrabble in the forest to get by. Do they even know how to hold a sword?" Montauban asks.

"They do not fight by conventional tactics, but with the art of ambush and surprise."

Chancellor Montauban opens his mouth to argue some more, but Duval interrupts him. "I do not think we are in a position to turn down any offers," he says. "Beast and I will talk of this later."

The abbess of Saint Mortain breaks the awkward silence that follows. "What of d'Albret's men?" It is only years of practice that keeps me from flinching at her words, for while she directs her question to Captain Dunois, I know in my bones it is intended for me. "Have you been able to locate any of the saboteurs?" she asks.

The captain shakes his head. "No, there are so many men-at-arms in the city, all from such scattered parts of the country, and not all are known to me. I have begun to put word out to the garrison commanders to be wary, but there are over eight thousand men-at-arms, and two dozen places where they could help d'Albret's main force breach our defenses. It will take time."

Once again, I can feel the immense weight of Beast's gaze upon me. I do not know if it is that gaze, the abbess's veiled barbs, or my desire to erase some of d'Albret's taint from myself, but before thinking it through, I speak. "I could identify them."

All eyes turn toward me. One gaze in particular feels sharper than broken glass. "You?" the abbess asks.

"Who better?"

The duchess leans forward, her eyes serious. "You do not need to do this. You have already put yourself in far too much danger."

"My sister is right. Besides, in practical terms, if they saw you, it might tip our hand," Duval says.

I nod my head in agreement. "But they do not need to see me in order for me to identify them. It is no hard thing to don a disguise."

Beast speaks for the first time, his voice rumbling into the small room. "I am not certain that is advisable," he says.

My head snaps up. His dissent is like a kick to my gut, for while I know he is angry with me, I had not realized his newfound distrust would run this deep. "I do not see how we have a choice if we wish to gain the upper hand in this."

"There is always a choice." Beast turns from me and addresses the others. "I think this is a bad idea."

"Do you not think I am capable, my lord?"

His hands grip the arms of his chair so hard that it is a wonder the wood does not splinter. "I know full well you are most capable, my lady. What I do not know is whether the costs would be worth the risks."

"And what risks would those be, my lord?" My words drip with honeyed sweetness that is as false as it is polite.

He says nothing, but he glowers at me from across the table. The loathing he shows toward me is every bit as painful as I feared. "If you do not trust me—"

"Of course he trusts you, my lady! If not for you, he would still be rotting in some dungeon, or worse."

"I am so glad that someone remembers," I mutter. I take a steadying breath, and when I speak again, my voice is calm. "If you do not trust me, or are too worried about the *risks,* the captain can send whatever men he likes to accompany me. Indeed, the plan will only work if he does, for a man can stay close to the traitors and mark their movements, while I cannot." Beast and I hold each other's gazes for a long moment.

Captain Dunois begins stroking his chin again, a sure sign he is deep

HIS FAIR ASSASSIN

in thought. "I do not see how it could do any harm. And while I hate to ask this of you, it *is* unnerving knowing his agents are lurking about in the city, waiting for orders from him. We could start with the free companies and hangers-on. That would be the easiest place for someone to slip in unremarked."

"I concur, Captain. It is decided, then. How shall we do it?" We spend the better part of an hour hammering out a plan. The entire time, I can feel the abbess watching me. Her displeasure puzzles me somewhat, for have I not done the very thing she wishes, showing how helpful the convent can be in such times? But it may be that only she is allowed to offer such help.

By the time we finally have our plan in place, Beast is pale, whether from his injuries or his fury, I cannot tell. As we rise to leave, the abbess takes two steps toward me, her lips pressed into a flat line. Before she can say anything, the duchess calls out. "Lady Sybella?"

"Yes, Your Grace?"

"Will you attend upon me this afternoon? I have some things I would speak with you on."

My heart skips lightly at this reprieve she has granted me. "But of course, Your Grace." Without glancing back at the abbess, I follow the duchess out of the room.

Chapter Thirty-One

"Methinks your abbess was not pleased with the service you offered us in the meeting."

"She did seem most unhappy. Forgive me if I overstepped, Your Grace. I only wished to help in some way. It is my family, after all, that is plaguing you so."

Much to my surprise, the duchess stops walking and grabs my wrist. "No," she says fiercely. "I do not hold you responsible for Count d'Albret's actions. If I held you responsible for those, then would I not be responsible for what he has done in my name?"

I stare mutely, as I have no answer to give her.

"Tell me," she whispers, her hands twisting together in a knot. "Tell me of those who died at Nantes. Tell me so that I may honor their memory and the sacrifice that they made."

In that moment, my budding admiration coalesces into respect. She accepts not only the power and privilege of ruling, but also the painful responsibility.

"The nobles went first. Your seneschal, Jean Blanchet, tried to organize a true defense of the ducal palace, but he was betrayed by Sir Ives Mathurin. Sir Robert Drouet fell in that battle, as well as two dozen men whose names I do not know. The townspeople were confused. They were inclined to trust Marshal Rieux when he said that he spoke on your behalf. It was not until the nobles moved against him that the townspeople realized their error, but it was too late, for they had opened the gate to the city and allowed them in. D'Albret had his troops harry and terrorize the burghers first, in order to weaken any resolve they might have held and to squelch any desire to rise up against him. It worked.

"The servants were the most loyal. They had known and served you since you were a babe. Allixis Baron, your comptroller; Guillaume Moulner, the silversmith; Jehane le Troisne, the apothecary; Pierre the porter; Thomas the doorkeeper; a laundress; a full dozen archers of the guard; your master of the pantry; the cook; two cupbearers; and a full half of the palace guard. They all died with your name on their lips and honor in their hearts."

Her eyes are bright with tears and I am struck again that she is but thirteen years old. Younger than I was when I first arrived at the convent.

No, I was never that young.

I say the only thing I can think of to comfort her, and in the end, it is not much comfort at all. "The traitors Julliers, Vienne, and Mathurin are dead, Your Grace. They have paid the ultimate price for their crimes."

She looks up, her eyes gleaming fiercely. "Good," she says. "If Mortain would bid you kill all the traitors in such a way, I would be most pleased."

She thinks I killed them all at Mortain's command. I do not explain that one was done in by my own twisted brother's jealousy.

The abbess suggests I masquerade as a whore to look for the saboteurs, but Captain Dunois, for all his gruffness, has a chivalrous heart. He will not hear of it. He suggests I disguise myself as a laundress instead and points out, reasonably enough, that a laundress has an equally legitimate excuse for mingling with the soldiers. Besides, many of them traffic in both laundry and favors, so if needs must, I can play the whore in a pinch.

The abbess counts it one more mark against me that Captain Dunois opposes her plan, but it was not my doing.

I lean in close to the silvered mirror and apply small, thin strokes of charcoal to my eyebrows, making them thick and shapeless. Next I take an even smaller piece and create lines of fatigue on my face, after which I put a faint smudge of coal dust under my eyes so I will look exhausted from my toil. I finish the transformation with a smear of black wax on my teeth. In truth, I cannot wait to be someone else for a while, even a poor, drab laundress. Someone who does not leave pain and betrayal and heartache in her wake. Of course, the opportunity to thwart d'Albret is equally welcome.

I take a handful of ashes from the fire and rub them into my hair, making it a shade or two lighter and much coarser-looking. It was my hands that presented the biggest challenge, for even with my recent work with the poultices, they were smoother and softer than a laundress's should be. To correct that, I soaked them in a strong lye soap solution for nearly two hours. Now they are red and raw and chapped, and they sting accordingly. I am most pleased with my disguise.

"No one will ever recognize you," Ismae says from where she sits on the bed.

"That is the point," I say wryly.

"Even so, the transformation is more thorough that anyone could have hoped." She rises and brings me the linen coif for my hair. It is old and worn out, but far too clean, so I make her dirty it in ashes from the hearth. When that is done, she places it on my head and helps me tuck my hair up under it. "There." She steps away to see the full effect. Worry creases her brow. "You will be careful, won't you?"

"I have nearly a half a dozen blades under my washerwoman gown."

Two strapped at my waist, one on each thigh, and yet another hidden along my back. I feel nearly naked without knives at my wrist, but soldiers can be a grabby lot and I cannot risk them discovering thick, solid steel. "I am ready," I tell her.

She takes a step toward me, hands clasped in front of her. "Have a care for yourself," she pleads.

Touched by her concern, for she is one of the few who genuinely care about me, I give her a quick hug. "I will be, but remember, these are but d'Albret's men, not d'Albret himself. They will be no match for me."

Somewhat reassured, she smiles. "Very well, then. Let us go find Captain Dunois."

We find the captain waiting for me in the main hallway. Duval and the abbess are with him. I am torn between pride at showing the abbess how well I can do this task and not wishing to expose myself or my talents to any more of her plots and intrigues.

"Sweet Jésu," the good captain mutters. "I would never have recognized you."

Dunois had wanted to escort me on the search himself, but it would have called far too much attention to my presence. Instead, he has handed the assignment off to the commander of Rennes, Michault Thabor, and a few of his most trusted men.

I place perhaps less trust in them than he does, but it is the best we can do under the circumstances.

And then it is time to go. My heart beats with anticipation, and the thrill of a new adventure tingles through my limbs. Feeling saucy, I turn to the abbess. "Will you not invoke Mortain's blessings on our venture, Reverend Mother?" While I ask it of her out of spite, I realize I *would* like His blessing, for all that He and I are at odds with each other right now.

Her nostrils flare in irritation, but she bows her head and places a hand on my coifed hair. "May Mortain guide you and keep you in His dark embrace," she intones, then removes her hand quickly. Even so, I feel somewhat calmer, as if Mortain has somehow heard her in spite of her ill grace.

We leave the palace through the servants' quarters, but since it is late and most are abed, our passing goes unnoticed.

Outside, a disreputable-looking donkey awaits with two baskets, one on either side. They are even filled with laundry.

Commander Thabor speaks to me in a low voice. "We have identified all the vulnerable spots in the city: the gate towers, the sally ports, the bridges, the cistern, and the gates along the river."

"Excellent. What of the patrols?"

"We have doubled the watch along the city walls and increased the number of patrols at their base."

"Where do you suggest we begin?" I ask.

"The east gate, then we will work our way around to the other gates."

"Very well. Lead on."

Thabor nods and walks purposefully ahead while his men scatter out so that it will not appear as if we are together. It would not do for me to be seen with them, for what business would the captain of the city guard have with a laundress? I know it is supposed to give me comfort, being followed by the guards, but it makes the skin between my shoulders twitch, which I force myself to ignore.

The city streets are quiet, as all smart or respectable citizens closed their doors and shutters and took to their beds long ago. As we move through streets full of houses leaning drunkenly against one another, the clop-clopping of the donkeys' hooves echoes off the cobblestones and sounds loud to my ears. However, if people hear us, they just snuggle deeper in their beds or ensure their doors are latched.

The buildings become smaller and seedier as we move farther away from the palace area. Meager shops and small taverns are interspersed among these smaller houses, and the streets are louder. At last we reach the military road that runs along the city wall. No one but soldiers should be on this road at this time of night. We pass three small watchtowers before we finally come to the east gatehouse. Commander Thabor walks past as if hurrying on some business of his own, but he will find some shadow in which to wait for me.

Still leading the donkey, I walk up to the gatehouse and halt just outside the door. The sound of murmuring voices reaches me, as the men on watch amuse themselves by telling stories. I hoist one of the baskets from the donkey's back, settle it on my hip, then head for the door. The guard on duty watches my approach with lazy eyes. "What do you want?" he asks.

"I am looking for Pierre de Foix." It is the name of a soldier who has taken ill with the flux and is even now abed in the infirmary. He will most definitely not be on duty.

"He is not here, so you may be on your way."

My eyes snap with irritation—I do not even have to pretend—and I swat the basket of laundry in annoyance. "He owes me four sous for his laundry. I do not do this backbreaking work out of pity." I take a step closer to him, narrowing my eyes in suspicion. "Ah, perhaps that is it. Perhaps Pierre has lost all his money dicing. How do I know you are not hiding him, eh? I think he has spent all his money on gambling and will not pay me for my honest work."

"Honest work," the guard scoffs.

Like a fishwife, I am merciless. "He told me he was to be on duty this night at this post. Why would he lie to me unless he was trying to cheat me? I will report him to your captain."

Before I can continue, the guard reaches out, grabs my free arm, and pulls me close. "Do not call me a liar, wench, else I will have to punish you. Here. Look." With that he pushes me through the gatehouse door and holds me there. "See with your own eyes that the man you seek is not here, then be gone."

Praying that Thabor's men will remain in their positions and not do something foolish, I quickly glance at the small group of men. There are five of them, and none are familiar to me. A sixth man turns from the small brazier in the room and grabs his crotch in a rude gesture. "I have something you can wash for me, eh?"

For a brief moment, everything inside me stills. The hair on the man's head is as brown as a walnut, but his beard is red, and I recognize him as Reynaud, one of my father's men. Quickly, I toss my head and turn for the door so that he will not be able to see my face. "I do not do small pieces, only large," I call over my shoulder. That sets the room to guffawing, and I use the opportunity to step beyond the sentry's reach and back into the night where the cover of darkness will further obscure my features. "He is probably hiding somewhere," I mutter with ill grace.

The sentry puts a hand to his sword, but I move quickly away. As I do, I see two dark shapes—my guards—step back into the shadows.

I return to the donkey—grumbling just loud enough that the posted guard can hear me—and replace the basket on the donkey's back. It is not until we have moved into the next street that Commander Thabor appears at my side. "What happened there? Why did he grab you?"

"He thought I was calling him a liar. Which I was," I say with a smile. "But he let me in to see, so it was worth it."

"Have a care," he growls at me, "as I am personally responsible for your safety."

"Reynaud. I do not know if that is the name he is using here in Rennes, but one of d'Albret's men is on guard in that gatehouse. The one with the brown hair and the red beard." Thabor assigns one of his men to stay behind and attach himself to him, then we move on. I am thrilled with this first victory, and the night suddenly holds much promise.

The water tower has a smaller garrison inside. Only four soldiers this time, one of whom offers to buy Pierre's abandoned laundry, but none of them are d'Albret's men.

And thus the night goes, with me moving from one gatehouse to the next. Some with a dozen men, others with only four. But none of them with any more potential saboteurs. Bleak discouragement fills me, for if there is one man, I know in my bones there must be others. And I need to find them so we will not feel like sitting ducks waiting for d'Albret to spring his accursed trap.

We have patrolled only the towers on the east side of the city, but already the sky has begun to lighten. My disguise will not hold in broad daylight. With reluctance, I allow Commander Thabor to turn us around so we may begin heading back to the palace. "Do not look so discouraged," he tells me. "We found one. We will find the others."

"Yes, but I would prefer to find them sooner rather than later." Just then a man bursts out of a nearby door, startling my donkey and causing the soldiers to reach for their swords. But it is just a drunken stone-worker, stumbling his way home. I stop. But of course. "I wish to go inside," I tell Thabor. "For if the men I seek are not on duty, they will most likely be found in a tavern or wine shop."

"Those were not my orders," he says tightly.

"Your orders were to accompany me while I flushed out the traitors in our midst. I am not asking your permission, Commander, but telling you what I intend to do." Our gazes hold for a long tense moment, and I cannot help but remember how easily Beast accepted the risks I took. Despair raises its dark head and I let the pain of it fuel my impatience. "Well?"

Finally, he nods. "But one of us will accompany you."

I long to argue, but I am running out of time. "Very well. You." I point to the one named Venois. "Come here. You will be my companion for the night." He glances at his commander, who nods his assent, then comes to stand before me. I reach up and loosen the lacings at his throat. Even as the protest starts to form on his lips, I tousle his hair, then tug his sword belt so that it hangs askew. "You have been on a drunken revel with me through the taverns of Rennes tonight. You must look the part."

He glances at his commander again, and the mute appeal in his gaze makes me want to slap him. Does he not realize how many men have begged me for just such an opportunity as he is being handed? I grab his arm, tuck it into mine, and begin steering us sloppily toward the tavern door.

The tavern is nearly empty at this hour; only the dregs of its customers remain. Three men slump on tables, barely holding themselves up as they sip the last of the wine from their cups. Another man sits in a corner fondling a serving maid, who is dozing in his lap. A half dozen men squat by the light of the dying fire, dicing.

I take all this in as I lean heavily on Venois and stumble us both toward a bench. Venois is stiff, and I can only hope anyone sober enough to notice will assume it is his military bearing rather than unease. A harsh shout goes up among the dicing men, and I softly jab him in the ribs. "Slouch a bit," I whisper out of the side of my mouth. "And shuffle your feet, then call loudly for wine."

He does as I command, and an annoyed-looking serving maid nods in our direction. I gently steer Venois to a seat where I can better see the dicing men. I do not recognize any of the men at the tables, and while I do not know all of d'Albret's men by sight, there is a certain sameness of manner that they possess—an ill-tempered, belligerent way of looking at the world—and none of those men have it.

The dicing men are my last hope to make something of the evening. I wait for the serving maid to set our wine down before us, then take a big gulp. It is watered and sour and it is all I can do not to spit it out. Instead, I force myself to swallow, then lean toward Venois. "Do you dice?"

The soldier shrugs, then downs half his wine. "Upon occasion. But mostly, I try not to."

I wait half a beat, but he does not volunteer. Just as I open my mouth to tell him he must join the men in front of the fire, another shout goes up among them, this time accompanied by the ring of steel.

A quarrel has broken out, and my heart soars when I recognize Huon le Grande, who is nearly as large as d'Albret himself and possibly just as unpleasant. The man waving his sword at the other two, the one with the wispy beard and a large nose and only three fingers on his left hand, is Ypres. Next to him is Gilot, short and squat and mean as a wounded badger. I nearly laugh with pleasure that they are too stupid to avoid drawing attention to themselves.

I drape myself over Venois and pretend I am nuzzling his ear. "Three of the dicers are the men we seek."

That seems to perk him up somewhat, and he plays his part with more gusto, if not more skill, as I point out which of the men are d'Albret's.

But the night is nearly over, and the tavern keeper's a large, hard-fisted man who kicks all of d'Albret's men out before they can ruin his establishment. He kicks the rest of us out too, just for good measure. I am in infinite danger as I stumble out the tavern door practically on d'Albret's men's heels, but my disguise holds, and their gazes are bleary with drink. Venois keeps one firm hand on my elbow and the other on his own sword, giving the rowdy men no chance for an advantage. It is with a light heart that I describe them to Thabor and then watch as three of the captain's men slink off into the darkness to keep watch over the saboteurs.

Chapter Thirty-Two

HAVING FOUND A WAY TO turn my d'Albret heritage to a good purpose, I am riding high on the thrill of the night's success, for there is no one else in the entire city that could ferret out these men. Only me.

It is hard to trust that Captain Dunois's and Commander Thabor's men will watch these traitors closely now that they've been identified, but I cannot post myself in the garrison alongside them, so I have no choice.

I reach my chamber and am surprised but pleased to find Ismae waiting for me. I am less thrilled to see that the abbess is also waiting, her proud profile limned in light from the chamber's hearth. As I come fully into the room, her head turns, like a hawk that has sighted prey. "Well?" she asks sharply.

I refuse to let her rob me of this night's victory. "Good evening to you too, Reverend Mother."

Her nostrils flare, but she ignores my gibe. "How did it go?"

"Very well. We found four of d'Albret's men. Commander Thabor put a guard on each of them so that they will be closely followed and watched, their every movement reported, but none the wiser that we are on to them."

The abbess nods her head but does not give me the word of praise that I crave, and it galls me mightily that I crave it. Instead, she says,

"Best get some sleep so you will have your wits about you at tomorrow's council meeting."

Not trusting my voice, I dip my head and curtsy. Sensing the irony in my gesture, she sniffs then strides out of the room, closing the door behind her. When Ismae and I are alone, she turns to me with a look of mixed annoyance and amusement on her face. "Why must you taunt her so?"

"Me? It is she who taunts me. Not even a word of praise or thanks does she send my way."

Ismae frowns and shakes her head. "It is true that she has always withheld any such praise or commendation of you. I wonder why."

"Because she is a sow at heart?" I suggest, lifting my hands to take the dirty linen coif from my head.

Ismae's mouth twitches in humor. "That must be it. Here. Let me help you." She hurries to my side and removes the headdress, then unlaces the gown. As I step out of the rough homespun dress, I am surprised to hear myself say, "Truly, Ismae. Why does the abbess hate me?" My voice sounds young and vulnerable to my ears, so I laugh mockingly. "It has always been so and I have yet to understand it." We clashed at the convent, but I had simply thought that was because I was her most difficult pupil and tried her patience. However, here in Rennes, after I had carried out so many of my duties in accordance with her exact wishes and still received no recognition, I realized it must be more than that.

Ismae shakes her head. "I do not know. Annith tried and tried to see if she could learn what lies at the heart of the abbess's dislike, but to no avail. Whatever the reason was, it was not written down on anything Annith could find."

"It is probably in that accursed little book she carries with her always."

"It is probably not even written down, merely some dislike that has nothing to do with anything but her own prejudices."

"Have you heard from Annith? Is there any news of her or Sister Vereda?" It is a most hideous time for the convent's seeress to take ill, leaving only a reluctant, untried seeress to guide us through these treacherous times.

"Yes! I received a letter from her this morning." Ismae takes a step closer to me and lowers her voice. "Sybella, she is planning to escape from the convent."

"Escape?" I echo, not sure I've heard correctly. The Annith I know would never consider something so rebellious. But more than that, I do not think it is safe for her to be alone outside the convent walls.

"Escape." Ismae nods firmly. "She has decided she would rather leave than be locked up in the convent for the rest of her life."

"They will go after her, you know. They will not just let her leave when they have invested so much in her training. Plus, who will they get to take her place? The next oldest novitiate is eleven-year-old Aveline."

Ismae cocks her head, reminding me very much of Annith in that moment. "With all the skills they have given her, she should be able to evade them easily enough. Remember, most of the nuns have not been outside the convent in years."

"True enough. But where will she go? And who will see Mortain's wishes and report them to us?"

Ismae opens her mouth, then closes it. "I had not thought about that," she admits. "It is possible she will join us here in Rennes and serve among the duchess's court."

"And run smack into the abbess herself?"

Ismae scowls. "I wish the reverend mother would go back to the convent already. I am tired of living under her critical gaze."

"You do not have to tell *me* how tiresome she is."

Ismae smiles, but there is little humor in it. "No, I do not. Now, come, let me wash the ashes out of your hair, else you'll ruin the linens."

I spend the next two nights scouring the city with Thabor's men, searching in every nook and cranny to find each and every one of d'Albret's saboteurs. I find seventeen in all, and each one of them is now closely watched and guarded by Commander Thabor's men.

My nighttime activities have the added benefit of keeping me away from Beast and the abbess's politics, for I must sleep during the day in order to perform this task that is so critical to the city's — to the duchess's — safety.

There is also great pleasure in being viewed as the hero of the quest — a role with which I am wholly unfamiliar.

On the third morning, my sauciness toward the abbess is repaid with a summons to her chamber that comes far too early. I stumble out of bed, bleary-eyed and thick-headed, and make myself ready as quickly as I can.

When I am washed and dressed and certain that no hair is out of place, I make my way to her chamber. Outside her door, I pause to take a deep breath and smooth my gown. I remind myself that I am not a green novitiate in the convent being called into the office for some minor innocent rebellion.

For they *were* innocent rebellions, I recognize that now. I had been plucked from my home — however dark and oppressive it was, it was the only place I'd known for fourteen years — and plopped down on an isolated rocky island that I feared was the destination of the mysterious Night Rowers, rumored ferrymen to the Underworld itself. I was in a frenzy with near madness.

That realization — that I was damaged and broken when I first met her and deserving of her sympathy, rather than her harsh judgment—fills me with a righteous anger that is completely strange to me. I raise my hand and knock on the door.

"Come in," the abbess calls out.

I lift my chin, plant a mocking smile on my lips, then enter the room.

The abbess is retrieving a note from a crow that has just arrived. She does not look up as I enter or acknowledge my presence in any way. It is a tactic I remember well from the convent, one calculated to increase the visitor's unease. However, her small torments are nothing compared to all I have been through in the last several months, and my mocking smile turns into one of genuine amusement.

Instead of waiting patiently—or nervously—I cross to the lone window that overlooks the inner courtyard. I do not particularly care what is out there; I know only that I do not want her to think her games have intimidated me. I glance over my shoulder in time to see her eyebrow twitch in annoyance—just once—as she continues to read the note. My objective achieved, I go back to looking out the window.

Seconds later there is an impatient rustle of paper, then the abbess speaks. "Sybella."

Slowly I turn around and face her, the bright light coming in from the window behind me forcing her to blink. "Yes, Reverend Mother?"

"Come over here so I do not have to put a crick in my neck to speak to you."

"But of course." I cross the room and stand before her as she settles the crow on one of the two empty perches behind the desk.

"It is good that your thoughts have turned toward protecting the duchess. That speaks well of your training."

Not of me. Never of me. Only of the training that she and the convent are responsible for.

"Which is why I have called you here. I wish to discuss your next assignment."

My heart skips a beat. "I had not realized I was finished with this one yet."

She turns from the crow she's been tending and looks me square in the eye. "You must return to Nantes. To d'Albret's household."

For a moment, I am not certain I have heard her correctly. Then, foolishly, I say the first thing that comes to my mind. "Surely you jest."

Her face tightens in anger. "I do not jest. We must learn more details of d'Albret's plans, and you are best suited to the task."

"You realize that my ability to pose as his docile prodigal daughter disappeared the same time his prisoner did?"

"Something you did not receive orders to do," she points out.

"Something I was unable to avoid," I remind her, barely able to hold on to my temper. "In any case, d'Albret will never allow me back into his household. And certainly not in a position of trust where I might overhear important information. He will most likely kill me on sight." It would not be a quick or pleasant death, of that I am certain.

"Of course you will not go back as yourself. You have proven to be a master of disguises. We will dress you as a servant, which will give you an excuse for lingering at doors."

I long to shake her by her slender shoulders and then slap her cold, calm face. "Have you heard nothing I've said? D'Albret watches everyone and has others watch them as well. He has already killed over half the servants at the palace simply because he suspected they were loyal to the duchess. He would never let an unknown servant into his household."

The abbess inhales sharply, her nostrils flaring. That she is so visibly annoyed gives me hope that she is taking my words to heart.

She shoves her hands into her sleeves and crosses to look out the window. I stay where I am and try to mask the fact that I am seething inside.

"Very well, then," she says. "I will send you back with but one purpose: to get close enough to kill d'Albret."

Sweet Mortain. Does she truly think I will fall for that twice? "While I have longed to do that very thing, Reverend Mother, does it not go against every precept you have ever taught me? For he is not marqued. Unless"—I pause as a thought occurs to me—"has Annith seen it?"

The abbess's lips thin, and she removes her hands from her sleeves. For a moment, I think she will strike me. "What do you know of Annith? Have you been corresponding with her while in Nantes? That was strictly forbidden."

I am so surprised by this outburst that I do not even think to say anything but the truth. "No, Reverend Mother! I have not spoken with her—even by note—since I left the convent."

Slowly, with visible difficulty, the abbess reins in her temper and turns back to the window.

"How can d'Albret not be marqued after all that he has done?" she asks, as if Annith's name was never mentioned. "Perhaps you simply cannot see it. Or perhaps you have not looked hard enough. Perhaps your fear has made you weak and overcautious."

Anger spurts through me and I fight hard to tamp it back down. It will not do to lose my temper in front of her. "He is not marqued. Believe me, I checked often. I saw him in all his naked glory just two days before I left Nantes."

"It seems to me there is a good chance it has appeared since then," she says stubbornly.

That is when I realize she will not take no for an answer. She is doing everything in her power to force me back into the little box of her making. The moment has come in which I must choose between the convent's little box, or stepping fully away from everything I have ever known. I try one last approach. "If I do as you ask, I might be able to get into the palace, and I might even get to d'Albret himself, but I will never get out alive. Those loyal to him will see to that."

Even as I speak the words, I can see in her eyes that she already knows this. That is when it hits me: all I have ever been to her is a tool, a tool so damaged that she does not mind if it gets utterly destroyed.

"We are all asked to make sacrifices in our service to Mortain. And you in particular have wished for death ever since you first arrived at the convent. Perhaps this is Mortain's way of answering your prayers."

Her words pierce my heart like sharp black thorns, and the familiar darkness and despair threatens to overwhelm me. Has she ever been so willing to sacrifice any other novitiate for Mortain's cause? No, for *her* cause, for this is about bringing glory and recognition to the convent—to her.

But, I realize, there is a freedom in having so many of my secrets exposed—it gives her far less power over me. "Perhaps I am no longer fit for Mortain's service, Reverend Mother, for I will not go back."

Her head rears as if I have slapped her. Odd that as little as she thinks of me, she did not see this defiance coming. Her pulse beats angrily in her neck, and she turns again to stare out the window. Already I am feeling lighter, wondering just where I will go and who I will be once I am free of both the convent and d'Albret.

She draws a deep breath, then turns back to face me. I do not understand the faint gloat of victory I see in her eyes. Until she speaks. "Very well. Then I will send Ismae."

Sweet Jésu, not Ismae! D'Albret's anger that Ismae thwarted his attack on the duchess in the hallway at Guérande still burns hot and bright.

D'Albret does not know of my hand in that or I would not still be alive. "You cannot send Ismae." I keep my voice calm and unconcerned, as if I am merely pointing out a flaw in her plan rather than trying to save the life of my best friend. "For one, d'Albret has seen her. Her face is permanently etched in his mind after she foiled his plans in Guérande. The man is unearthly in his ability to see through disguises and subterfuge."

The abbess is not fooled by my calm demeanor. She has well and truly snared me in her trap and knows it. "We have many ways of creating a disguise. We can cut her hair, change its color, stain her skin. We can have her looking old and haggard in a matter of hours."

"D'Albret would never allow anyone into his presence, even a servant, who offended his eye so greatly."

Even if they did not recognize her and kill her outright, they would use her most poorly, simply for the sport of it. "I still think he would recognize her. And do not forget, many of his retainers have seen her at Duval's side. If by some small chance d'Albret himself were to miss her, one of his retainers would be all too eager to point her out to him, to gain favor."

The abbess folds her hands and rests her chin upon her fingers. "Ah, that is too bad, for it would be a most excellent solution." Her words chill me, for I do not expect a capitulation so soon. However, her next words turn the blood in my veins to ice. "Perhaps it is time to send Annith on her first mission. D'Albret has never seen her; no one outside the convent has ever seen her, and she is our most highly skilled novitiate ever."

She may as well send a lamb into a wolves' den, for while Annith's skill is great, she is also wholly good and could not even begin to guess what tricks and deceit they would use upon her. Is the abbess so ruthless that she would consign Ismae or Annith to certain death? She must be bluffing.

She must.

But am I certain enough to stake my friends' lives on it?

A cool calmness settles over me, and I meet the abbess's impersonal gaze. "That will not be necessary, Reverend Mother. I will go."

Her face relaxes slightly. "Excellent. I am pleased to see you know where your duty lies."

"When do I leave?"

"Within the next day or two. I will know more after this afternoon's council meeting."

Chapter Thirty-Three

DIZZY AND NUMB, I STUMBLE toward my chamber, desperate for solitude.

It appears all roads lead to d'Albret in the end. Whether I run at him in anger or run away from him in fear, the road will always curve back to him.

Why did I think I could escape? When I first realized I would need to travel with Beast, I knew there was no escape, merely a postponement of the inevitable. But then, once here, I was stupid enough to let hope slip in, even knowing it was merely the gods mocking me.

I had forgotten a lifetime of hard-won lessons in a matter of days.

Clearly I am fated to meet my death at d'Albret's hands. The real question is, will he meet his at mine?

For that is all that is left to me: to strike quick and sure and true and make utterly certain he dies before me.

Or is it? What would happen if I simply walked away? Surely Duval could protect Ismae. My thoughts are interrupted by a knock on the chamber door. Afraid Ismae has heard of my meeting with the abbess, I hurry to open it, dismayed to find Beast glowering in the hall, arm still raised to knock.

Every word I have ever known flees my head and I stare open-mouthed. He is no longer tinged with gray or green, and his hair has been trimmed. He leans on a cane, but other than that, he appears to have gotten here under his own power.

He lowers his arm. "So you *are* here. I thought you might be hiding from me."

Even though I have been doing precisely that for the past week, I scoff. "Why should I hide from you?"

His eyebrows lower ominously, and the look he gives me nearly singes the hair from my head. "I have sent Yannic every night to fetch you so that we may talk. Why have you avoided him?"

That is why he had the little gargoyle following me? I shrug. "I thought you didn't trust me to identify d'Albret's men and sent him to check up on me. You made your objections clear enough in the council meeting."

With visible effort, he unclenches his teeth. "I was objecting because it was too dangerous."

"Oh? Then you are not angry with me for being d'Albret's daughter?" I do not know what madness compels me to toss salt in the wounds I have made, but I cannot stop myself.

"I thought you established that you were Mortain's daughter?"

"Yes, well, that is a mere technicality, as the abbess made clear in that same meeting."

He shakes his great head. "I do not trust that woman, not wholly. Nor should you."

That he is right does nothing to warm me to him.

His face softens then, and his eyes lose their angry light. "Sybella, we must talk."

It is the softness that has me catching my breath, for not in any of my dreams did I imagine I would see him look that way at me. But *merde,* I cannot afford his sympathy or understanding. Not now, for it will crumble all my resolve faster than I can muster it. "What is there to say? I am the daughter of the man who killed your sister, and, what's worse, I lied to you about it again and again."

"Stop it," he growls. "There is far more to it than that."

His seeing that fills me with great joy, which I ruthlessly tamp down. "What I *know* is that I was supposed to stay and kill d'Albret that night, and you stopped me. You ruined the plans I had made and forced me to leave the city with my task undone, and now I must return to finish it." Saying the words aloud causes my throat to constrict so that I must pause a moment before continuing. "It would have been so much easier then, before I knew——" I stop again, unsure what I mean to say.

The fierce glower is back on his face and he takes a step into the room. "What do you mean, you are returning? On whose orders?"

"The convent's, for, like you, I am sworn to serve my god, and that is where He wishes me to go." But even as I say this, I know it is the abbess who wishes me to face d'Albret. I do not know if Mortain is in agreement with her or not. Perhaps this is my punishment for turning my back on Him and the teachings of the convent.

Before we can argue further, a page approaches. He glances from Beast to me, then back to Beast again, unsure as to what is going on. "Do you have a message for one of us?" I prompt.

He clears his throat. "Yes, my lady. Both you and Sir Waroch are requested to attend the council meeting in the duchess's chambers. I am to escort you there now."

"But of course," I say, for this interruption suits me perfectly. I do not wish to be having this conversation at all. "Lead the way." I step out of my room, forcing Beast to back up so that I do not shut his nose in the door, then I turn and let the page lead me down the hall. I hear the thump of Beast's cane as he follows.

* * *

We are the last to arrive in the council chambers. Seeing us enter the room, the abbess narrows her eyes in disapproval, and I do not know if it is for me alone or because Beast and I are together. Duval motions us to take seats as he continues speaking.

". . . have taken Lady Sybella's counsel to heart and have moved up the marriage between Anne and the Holy Roman emperor. It will be taking place this afternoon, by proxy. Hopefully the marriage will afford the duchess some measure of protection, especially since I have received reports that d'Albret and his forces are preparing to leave Nantes and march on Rennes. They may even have left by now, as the last message was hours old."

Even though I have been expecting the announcement, it sends a spasm of fear down my spine. He will sniff me out just as he did when I was but eight years old and hiding one of the mongrel pups his favorite hunting bitch had given birth to.

Except I will not be here. I will be heading straight for him. Under his own nose may be the one place he might not think to look for me.

Captain Dunois is the next to speak. "Thanks to the Lady Sybella, we have rooted out what we hope to be the last of the saboteurs, so d'Albret will receive no aid once he arrives."

How can he be so certain? I wonder. We have found seventeen men, but what if there are more? What if I missed some?

"What of the Spanish troops?" the duchess asks, her face drawn and shadowed. "Will they be here before d'Albret?"

"They arrived early this morning, Your Grace," Captain Dunois says. "My second in command is seeing to their quartering."

While that is good news, we all know that the one thousand Spanish troops is nearly insignificant against d'Albret's numbers.

"And the free companies?"

"They have been contracted, Your Grace," the chancellor tells her. "They should be here in a fortnight."

Not soon enough.

The duchess turns back to Captain Dunois. "Has the weather cleared enough to let the British troops land?" Those six thousand troops are our one hope of breaking d'Albret's siege of the city.

Dunois and Duval exchange a grim look. "We have just received word, Your Grace," he says gently. "The French have taken Morlaix." A gasp of distress goes up around the room.

"But the English troops!"

"Precisely. They will have to fight their way through the French to reach us—"

"Or be slaughtered where they stand," Captain Dunois finishes.

There is quiet while we all ponder this latest disaster. It is as if a noose is being tightened around our poor kingdom's neck. Duval bites back an oath and stands to pace.

Beast, who has been sitting like a simmering pot for the past few moments, finally speaks. "I will leave tomorrow and make all due haste to Morlaix, taking the charbonnerie with me." He looks at each of the councilors in turn, as if daring any of them to object.

Chancellor Montauban frowns. "You cannot take on a thousand French troops with a handful of charcoal-burners," he says, and I cannot help but wonder if he truly knows Beast at all.

"No, but we can provide a painful diversion that will allow the British a chance to land."

"It *is* possible," Duval says, sounding hopeful for the first time in days.

"As we travel, I will raise the countryside against these intruders who would pluck our very land out from under our noses. Perhaps some of them can join us in Morlaix."

"I still say we cannot put our trust in the charbonnerie," Chancellor Montauban says. "They are too unpredictable, too rebellious. I fear they will run when we need them the most."

Beast's eyes when they meet the chancellor's are as frigid as ice on a pond. "They have given their word, Chancellor. And I, for one, am inclined to believe it."

"But they are not well versed in the art of warfare," Chalon points out. "We do not have time to train them for battle."

Beast leans forward. "That is the beauty of the charbonnerie. They do not fight with conventional tactics. Rather, they use stealth, cunning, and surprise. Deception and ambush are their most effective weapons."

"But there is no honor in that," Chalon protests.

"There is no honor in defeat either," Duval points out. "I cannot help but wonder if d'Albret's move is timed to coincide with this latest French attack. Did he know our aid from the English would be delayed, and is that why he marches now?"

"We will know soon enough." The abbess speaks into the quiet room. "The Lady Sybella will be returning to her post with d'Albret's household, so we will have access to his plans, hopefully before he acts on them."

The duchess turns to me with stricken eyes, and Ismae's face goes white as snow. "But it is no longer safe for her there! He must know—or at least suspect—that she aided Beast in his escape."

"It is not a question of safety, Your Grace, but of how we can best serve you, and, through you, Mortain."

"Your loyal and dedicated service is duly noted, Reverend Mother." The wry note in Duval's voice reassures me that he does not wholly trust her either.

There is a long moment of silence, then the duchess speaks again. "I fear I must agree with Beast and the chamberlain, my lords," she says.

"We have few options available to us. I believe we will give these char-bonnerie a chance to prove themselves."

I will not be the only one riding to a likely death on the mor-row—Beast will be as well.

Chapter Thirty-Four

WHEN THE MEETING FINALLY BREAKS up, I rise to my feet and make my way to the door. I can feel Ismae watching me, begging me to turn and look at her, but I do not. I cannot. Not now. Beast, too, is boring holes in my back with the intensity of his stare, but I ignore him as well. What I need most right now is the privacy and sanctity of my bedchamber.

I reach my room and bolt the door behind me, vowing to open it for no one.

Think. I must think.

This latest news makes walking away infinitely more possible.

The reverend mother would not know for days. Weeks, even. And by then, d'Albret will either have won or been defeated, the direction of the war and our country determined. Duval would protect Ismae and keep her from being sent in my place when the abbess learns that I did not go. And at that point it will be too late for Annith to be of any use.

It is a good plan. A solid plan. Just thinking about it causes the tightness in my chest to ease somewhat.

I begin packing. I will take only those things that will make the reverend mother believe my deception, so only those items a camp follower would own. The laundress gown, and my weapons, of course. All my knives, but not the fancy garrote bracelets, as they are too fine for a mere camp follower to possess. Besides, I can strangle a man just as easily using his own belt.

As I carefully pack the knives I will carry, I marvel at how my desire to kill d'Albret once shaped my life and gave it meaning. But that was before . . . before what? When did my heart turn away from its willingness to die if need be in order to kill d'Albret?

Perhaps once I escaped, once I was no longer in his orbit or infected with the bleak despair that enveloped me while I was in his household. Or mayhap my short time away from him has reminded me that there are things worth living for. There are good people in this world, in this duchy. Those who mean to do all they can to stop d'Albret. Living inside his walls, it was all too easy to forget that.

There is the thrill of a fast horse, and the sun and wind in your face. The rare—and all the more precious for it—moments of laughter to be had. The excitement of seeing Mortain's marque and knowing the hunt is about to begin. The look in someone's eye when he truly sees you—not just your face and hair, but the very essence of your soul.

It is a raw and uncomfortable realization that Beast is partly behind this newfound will to live. Not *for* him, but because he reminded me of what life has to offer. He lives life so joyously—it is impossible not to want that joy for oneself.

My fingers drift to the ring I wear on my right hand, my last resort should my situation ever become unbearable.

Suddenly, my lungs cannot take in enough air and my head grows light. No matter how I wish it to be different, in spite of all our efforts, in spite of every saboteur I have rooted out, I still fear in my heart that d'Albret will win in the end. That he will seize the city and bring it to its knees.

And everyone in it.

Oh, they will fight. All of Anne's nobles and advisors and men-at-arms will do their best to protect her. And they will die trying, for d'Albret's ability to inflict death is unsurpassed.

I can see it unfold so clearly in my mind's eye.

He will fight his way to Anne personally, his long sword slicing through her guard as if they were soft cheese. It is possible my brothers will be at his side, attempting once again to earn his favor.

Ismae and Duval will guard the duchess with their lives—and that is precisely what it will cost them. Once they have paid with those, d'Albret will turn his vengeance upon Anne.

He might not hurt her at first. He will most likely hold Isabeau as hostage, knowing only too well that is where Anne's heart lies.

I stare down at the small bundle on my bed. What if I were able to stop him, but didn't? What will my freedom have cost in blood? Will not the very things I hope to live for be lost?

In that moment, I know that I must do as I have been ordered. Not for the abbess, or the convent, or even Mortain.

But for those I have grown to love.

It is late when I leave my chamber to seek out Ismae, but there is still much activity about as the palace prepares for Beast's departure and the coming siege. Ismae is not in her bedchamber so I head to Duval's apartments within the palace. It is the only place I can think to look, short of the abbess's chambers or the duchess's. It appears I am in luck, for when I reach his door, I sense two pulses beating within. I knock softly.

Duval opens the door. A brief flash of surprise crosses his face when he sees that it is me. "My lady?"

I give him a wry smile. "I have actually come in search of Ismae," I tell him.

It is hard to be sure in this dim light, but I think a faint tinge of pink spreads across his cheeks. You would think he and Ismae but thirteen years old and experiencing their first bout of puppy love. "She is here." He opens the door to let me in, then bows. "I will leave you to speak in private."

"No." I reach out and grab his arm. "You need to hear what I must say."

"Very well." He turns and leads me into his chamber, where I find Ismae curled up in front of the fire, sipping a goblet of wine.

When she sees me, she sets the wine down and leaps to her feet. "Sybella! Where have you been? None of the pages we sent could find you."

With a guilty start, I remember the series of knocks on my chamber door. "I was packing."

"You are going?" she whispers.

Unable to speak, I nod.

She takes a step closer. "It is not right," she says fiercely. "It must be someone else's turn. I will go."

Duval looks at her in alarm. "No one will go. We do not need the information at the cost of your lives."

"I am not here to whine about my fate. I am here to extract a promise from you." I slip the ring from my finger and hold it out to Duval. "Give this to your lady sister. Make her wear it. Should your last line of defense fail, it will be her best way out."

Duval stares down at the ring. "I cannot do what you suggest."

I grab his hand, shove the ring into it, then close his fingers around it. "You *must*. Trust me. Death will be preferable to d'Albret getting his hands on your sister. He has had far too long to plan all the ways he can break and humiliate her and bring her as much pain as he thinks she's brought him. Whatever else happens, you must not let him get his hands on her. Her death will be long and unpleasant."

He looks faintly sick but accepts the ring. "Do you promise?" I ask.

271

He looks into my eyes. Whatever he sees there convinces him. "I promise."

Something inside my chest relaxes somewhat. "Thank you."

"No—thank you. And for what horrors you have suffered, and what further horrors you will be subjected to, I am genuinely sorry. Know that my sister, that all of us hold this sacrifice of yours close to our hearts."

His words bring tears to my eyes, but I blink them away and get down to business. "Ismae, I came to see if I could borrow your rondelles."

"My offer was a serious one. I wish to go in your place."

"I know you do." I reach out and take her hands in mine. "Which is why you are so very dear to me. But you have duties you must see to here. I fully expect you and Duval to be the last ones standing between the duchess and d'Albret should the city not hold."

She throws her arms around me and I savor the feel of her holding me close, treasuring me. Then I pull away. "Now. About those weapons . . ."

After some discussion, Ismae gives me her rondelles and half of her poison supply. Now all I must do is wait until daybreak to be on my way. As I leave Duval's chamber, the urge to seek out Beast is nearly overwhelming. I promise myself I will face him in the morning, and I will tell him everything. Once I have made my confession to him, I can meet death with a clean conscience.

Before the sun has cleared the horizon I am dressed and heading toward the stable. It is not lost on me that of all the things in my life I have dreaded, telling Beast this simple truth is one of the most terrifying.

I find him in the stables, supervising the preparation of the mounts. Instead of using the thick staff they have given him as an aid to walking, he is waving it around, pointing and ordering the others with it. Yannic is with him, and more charbonnerie than I can count. My heart beats so loud I am surprised they do not all turn and stare at the sound, but they are so absorbed in their work that they do not even see me at first.

I try to call out to Beast, but I open my mouth and no words come. I must have made some small sound, however, for Beast turns around, his eyes widening in surprise at the sight of me, and he limps his way over to where I stand.

"I was hoping you'd come to see us off, else I'd have to come looking for you."

That heartens me, that he planned to say goodbye.

"I have something I would talk to you of in private."

Beast raises his eyebrows and follows me out into the stable yard. Afraid I will lose my nerve, I look down at my hands, which are clutched together so tightly that my fingers have turned white. I relax my grip. "There is something I must explain to you. I have meant to tell you many times, but there was never a good moment."

He does not so much as flinch, although his eyes become as unreadable as polished steel.

"At first I did not tell you because I was afraid you would not trust me, and I needed your trust so I could get you to Rennes safely. I had hoped that once we were here, no one would have to know my identity. It is not something I am proud of. But that did not—"

"Sybella?"

"Yes?"

"Please know if there were any other way to accomplish this, I would use it."

"Accomplish what?" I ask, puzzled.

The look in his eyes is tender, and he moves closer so that I wonder if he plans to kiss me. Then his hand flashes, sure and quick, and the world grows black.

Chapter Thirty-Five

THE NEXT THING I KNOW, all the devils of hell are hammering at my jaw, just under my chin, but I do not care nearly as much as I might, for I feel safe. I appear to be in a cave. A warm cave of stone that completely surrounds me, pressing firmly into my back, sheltering me.

I hear a soft whicker—a horse?—then a man's low voice. "You didn't tell us we could bring a bit of skirt along."

A second voice. "It's not a bit o' skirt, dolt. The captain would never bestir himself for a trollop."

"Well, what is she, then?"

"Damned if I know."

"Enough," a familiar voice growls.

A throat clears. "If you don't mind my asking, what's wrong with her, Captain?" The tone is much more respectful now.

There is a pause, and then the cave wall behind my back rumbles. "She fainted."

I wrench my eyes open, then clamp them shut as harsh bright sunlight pierces my brain and a wave of nausea washes over me. Slowly, my mind sharpens enough to understand that I am not in a cave but clamped between thick, strong arms. The firmness at my back is not a wall of stone, but an armored breastplate. We are moving with a gentle rolling gait.

I struggle to sit up, but the arms are like a vise and hold me firm.

"Shhh," the familiar voice says. "Do not flail about so, you'll spook the horse."

Beast.

The bastard has done it again!

The world spins as I try to sit up and put as much distance between us as possible, which is not so very much when we are sharing a saddle. Furious, I jam my elbow down into his thigh, pleased when he grunts in pain. "If you *ever* do that to me again, I will kill you. I mean it." And while I do mean it, the words do not sound nearly as threatening as they should.

The other horsemen draw away, giving us the illusion of privacy, for I've no doubt that their ears are all straining to hear every word.

There is another rumble from his chest and I cannot tell if it is words or laughter, and my head aches too much to turn around to see. Besides, even though anger and annoyance rumble in my gut like bad fish, I bask in the strength of these arms, relieved to have them between me and the rest of the world. Between me and d'Albret.

Merde! "Where are we?"

"On the road to Morlaix."

The jolt of alarm and dismay brings a fresh wave of nausea, but I grit my teeth and ignore it as I try to clamber down from the horse. Beast's arms tighten painfully. "Are you mad?" he says. "Hold still else you'll fall."

"I have someplace I must be."

He says nothing, but his arms tighten even more until I can scarcely draw breath. It would be easy—so easy—to surrender to the strength in those arms. Because I want to do just that, scornful laughter erupts from my throat. "My father will not pay a ransom for me, nor the abbess, if that is what you hope to gain."

When he speaks, there is an odd note in his voice. "Is that what you think I want? Ransom?"

"Why else would you abduct me? Ransom or vengeance are the only reasons I can think of."

"I didn't abduct you; I rescued you!" He sounds affronted by my lack of appreciation.

"I did not ask to be rescued!"

His gauntleted hand reaches out and oh so gently turns my face toward his. "Sybella." My name sounds lovely and musical on his tongue. "I will not let you go back to d'Albret."

The tenderness in his eyes undoes me. It is stupid, I tell myself. It means nothing. He rescues everyone he passes on the road.

But my false heart will not listen. Just like he came back for his sister, he has come for me.

Fearing he will see the naked longing of my heart, I turn my face away from his and search for the outrage I felt only moments before, but it is a mere echo of what it once was.

"I must go back," I say, as much to convince myself as him. "If I do not, the abbess will send Ismae, or perhaps even Annith, who has never even left the convent before. Neither will stand a chance against d'Albret." I was so ready to accept my fate — this time for the right reasons. Out of love, rather than vengeance. And once again this . . . man, this . . . *mountain* . . . has destroyed my hard-won resolve with a careless flick of his wrist. And even though none of the desperate reasons that compelled me to commit to that course of action have changed, I fear I will not be able to rekindle my determination.

"The abbess is no fool. Ruthless, perhaps, and unscrupulous, but no fool. She will not send one of her prized handmaidens to certain death. She is using them both to threaten you."

"I am not willing to risk my friends' lives on that," I say quietly. "Besides, what if it is my fate, my destiny, to stop d'Albret, and I do not?"

He is silent a long moment, his cheerfulness disappearing like last winter's snow. "Can we ever know our own destiny?" he asks. "I believed it was mine to rescue Alyse, but I failed, so clearly it was not. It is possible our fates cannot be known until we are cold in the ground, our lives over."

Even though I fear he is right, I am not willing to give up. "What if your mission in Morlaix fails?"

"We will just have to be certain it does not."

"It is a foolish commander who puts all his hope for victory in one basket."

"Sybella. You cannot stop him. Not alone."

His words are so seductive, I fear I will have to place my hands over my ears to keep them from tempting me. "But I must," I whisper.

"Ah, but you have no choice, for you have been kidnapped by someone far stronger than you and there is no escape. Best set your mind to that and be done with it. Besides, I have collected your belongings, so the abbess will think you have left for Nantes, just as you were scheduled to do."

I cannot help but admire his thoroughness, and some small part of me hopes it might work. To be free of not just d'Albret but the abbess as well? So must Amourna have felt the first time she was allowed to leave hell.

Beast places his big hand on my head and pushes it toward his chest. "Sleep now," he says. "Else I will have to clout you again."

Annoyingly, I do what he tells me. I assure myself it is only because I wanted to do it anyway.

When next I open my eyes, the horse has stopped moving, and the sun is angled low in the sky. We are halting for the night.

I blink as Winnog gangles over toward us and Beast prepares to hand me down from the saddle. At Winnog's approach, the horse prances and paws the air until Beast does something with his heels and mutters a command, and then the horse stills long enough for me to slip from the saddle into the charbonnerie's waiting hands. "What is wrong with your horse?" I ask once I am safely on the ground.

"That is no natural horse, my lady," Winnog mutters, "but some foul creature straight from the Underworld itself."

Beast flashes one of his lunatic grins then steers the creature to the edge of camp where the horses are being tethered.

"My lady? Do you need to rest?" Winnog asks, and I realize I am still clutching his arm.

I let go immediately. "No, thank you. I prefer to stretch my legs."

He bobs his head. "Then, if you'll excuse me, I'll go help with the horses."

I stand for a moment, watching the swarm of activity as the party rein in their horses and begin to dismount. A dozen men from the duchess's army are on fine coursers and stallions, and they jostle for position, trying to steer around an equal number of charbonnerie on their sturdy rouncies and ponies. None of them appears willing to give way before the others, and within minutes it is a chaotic jumble of cursing men and prancing horseflesh. *Merde.* If this is the sort of cooperation Beast can look forward to, he was beyond stupid to keep me from being the contingency plan. We will be lucky to even reach Morlaix, let alone run off the French so the British troops can land.

A slow realization creeps over me. Rennes is only a day's ride away, and d'Albret himself will not arrive until late tomorrow at the earliest. If I leave now, I can be there in plenty of time to slip unnoticed into the throng of camp followers that are sure to travel with him.

I glance around the clearing. Yannic is wrestling Beast's demonic horse to a tether. Beast himself has already fetched his maps and is rolling them out in order to discuss tactics and strategies with his commanders. The charbonnerie are busy casting sullen glances at the sol-

diers, and the soldiers are busy making their disdain for the charbonnerie plain as day.

No one is watching me. The resolve I feared lost for good rises once
more.

I begin sauntering toward the line of horses. As I draw closer, there
is a whisper of movement from the trees, and a half a dozen bodies
emerge. I freeze, as do the soldiers, their hands going to their swords until Erwan tells them to hold. It is only the charbonnerie women, come
to cook for the camp.

During the confusion that the new arrivals bring, I choose a dappled
gray gelding tethered the farthest from camp and quickly put his great
girth between me and the others, hoping he will hide me somewhat.

I reach out to pet the creature's silky nose and let him smell me,
as if I am merely saying hello. As I do, I glance around, looking for
saddle and tack. I will need a bridle if I am to steer this creature back to
Rennes. A saddle would be nice, although I can ride without one if need
be. "I'll be right back," I whisper to the gray, but before I have taken two
steps, a hand closes around my arm. A big hand as hard as iron. "Must
I hobble you as Yannic has hobbled the horses?"

Damn him. Will the infernal oaf just tend to his business so I can
tend to mine? I huff out a breath of annoyance, but there is some relief
as well. Furious at myself for being relieved, I pull my arm out of Beast's
grip. "No. You do not need to hobble me; you need only to let me go so
I may complete my assignment."

His normally open face is hard and ruthless. It is the first time I have
seen his ferocity focused on me, and I force myself to smile so he will
not see how unnerving it is.

"We have discussed this already. You are staying here. Camulos
knows this mission can use your skills."

"There must be a contingency plan in case this half-cooked scheme does not bear fruit. And as much as I loathe the abbess and do not trust her, she is correct in that the more opportunities we have to strike at d'Albret, the better our chances of success."

He reaches out with his other hand and grabs my shoulder. "I will not let you put yourself in that much danger." For the briefest of seconds, the anger gives way to a look of stark despair, and then it is gone.

His grip on my arms loosens, and slowly, he leans toward me. My own temper forgotten, I hold very, very still. "If you hit me again, I *will* kill you," I whisper.

"It is not hitting I have in mind." And then his hands move up to cradle my head, making me feel small and fragile—no, not fragile, but cherished. As if I am some precious treasure.

As he leans in closer, I do not move—I do not so much as breathe. I watch his lips as they draw nearer to mine, marveling at the shape of them, how there is the tiniest of dimples in the left corner of his mouth, so small you would not see it unless you were close enough to—his lips find mine. Warm, and softer than they've any right to be. I am awash in sensations that have nothing to do with relief or fury. I simply want. I want him, his strength, his honor, and his be-damned lightness of heart. I want to drink all those things up like honeyed wine from a goblet and have them fill me.

Unable to resist, I close my eyes and lean into him and let myself imagine that something between us is possible.

But it is not, not with all the secrets that exist between us still.

Slowly, with regret leaking through every pore in my body, I pull away. His eyes open, and they are filled with warmth. "How can you not be angry with me?" I whisper. "I deceived you repeatedly; nearly every word that passed through my lips was a lie." I am desperate to put some sort of barrier between us or I fear I will throw myself at him like some simpering maid.

He heaves a great sigh, then steps away to lean on a nearby tree and take the weight off his bad leg. "At first, I was. Furious at being deceived and lied to. And by a d'Albret. It seemed as if the gods themselves were mocking me. Intending to stoke that anger, I went over everything you had said, everything you had done. And while your words may have lied, your actions never did. I have seen you in the harshest of circumstances, escorting a wounded man across the countryside while dodging enemy soldiers and hostile scouts with little thought to your own comfort or safety. You gave more thought to the miller's daughter and the charbonnerie's plight than your own well-being. And you killed d'Albret's own men with a smile on your face and joy in your heart."

I gape at him, unable to speak, as he lays out this new Sybella I hardly recognize.

He runs his hand over his head. "Once I got past being angry, I was outraged that you hadn't trusted me enough to tell me the truth. But since I reacted precisely as you had feared, clearly I did not warrant that trust." He grows serious once more. "But Sybella, I have seen you when there are hard choices before you, not these false choices of memory, and every time, you have chosen well. Chosen the path that helps the most people and hurts others the least. And that is why I bear you no grudge."

Unable to help myself, I put my hand to his cheek, needing to be certain he is real and not some vision my overwrought brain has concocted. His skin is warm, and his whiskers rough beneath my fingers. "How did your heart grow so very big?" I ask.

A flash of something—pain and perhaps a touch of bitterness—shines briefly in his eyes, then is gone. "Because I have had no one to share it with since Alyse left."

A shout goes up just then, followed by a ring of steel. A woman screams.

Beast pushes away from the tree and hurries back to the clearing as fast as his injured leg will allow. I lift my skirts and follow.

There is a fight brewing near one of the cook fires. Two charbonnerie women stand warily. I recognize Malina, but not the younger one. Erwan, Lazare, and Graelon have planted themselves in front of the women, like a shield. Facing them all are two of Beast's soldiers, one with a shaved head, cold eyes, and a drawn sword. "God's teeth," Beast mutters as he limps forward. "What is going on?"

The soldier with the drawn sword never takes his eyes from the charbonnerie. "These men have insulted us by drawing their knives. I am only urging them to use their weapons." His chest is thrust forward, like an angry rooster's.

"We offered insult? It was you who slandered our wives and sisters by trying to drag them off to the bushes to slake your lust."

The second soldier—Sir de Brosse—gives a lazy shrug. "Thought she was a camp follower. Didn't mean any harm."

Beast reaches out and thwacks him across the back of his very thick skull. "Keep your dagger sheathed, you idiot. There are no camp followers here."

De Brosse's eyes slide in my direction, and Beast takes a step closer. "That is the Lady Sybella. She serves Mortain, and unless you wish to be gutted like a fish, I suggest you show her—and all the women in this camp—the utmost respect."

De Brosse grins sheepishly and bows an apology first in my direction, and then toward the charbonnerie women.

"Gaultier!" Beast snaps at the other soldier. "Put your sword away and see to the setting up of the tents."

The man's eyes linger on the charbonnerie until Beast grabs him by the scruff of the neck and shakes him. "My apologies. Sir Gaultier is hot-tempered, and Sir de Brosse has a weakness for women. It will not happen again. Not if they wish to remain in my command."

Once Beast has escorted his errant soldiers away, there is an awkward silence. "Go on," Erwan shouts to the onlookers. "You all have work to do. Get to it."

I retreat to one of the trees and sit down at the base of its trunk to think, still unable to decide what I should do: stay, or return to Rennes and make my way to d'Albret.

I cannot help worrying that I have not earned this boon. But I am only human and not sure I can turn away from such a gift. Besides, if it were my destiny to bring down d'Albret, would I not have already done so in those long months in his household? Why should now be any different?

I long ago ceased believing that prayers did any good, but now it feels as if they have been answered. As if the hand of Mortain Himself has reached into my life, plucked me from my nightmares, and placed me where I most wish to be: at Beast's side.

I decide to accept this gift the gods have offered me.

In the distance, a wolf howls. Let it come, I think. Beast will most likely simply howl back, and the creature will either turn tail and run or fall into line behind him, like the rest of us have.

Chapter Thirty-Six

THE RISING SUN HAS NOT yet shown its face when we get on the road, but at least it is no longer full dark. Even so, we walk the horses until the sun breaks over the horizon, then Beast gives the command to gallop, the urgency of our mission pressing at our backs.

Beast himself rides up and down the line, being sure to greet each man warmly or share some private joke with him. As he does, the men sit up straighter or square their shoulders, their hearts feeding on that encouragement as much as their bodies feed upon bread.

I think of my father, my brothers, and how they command men. They use fear and cruelty to whip them forward and bend them to their will. But Beast leads not only by example but by making the men hungry to see themselves as Beast sees them.

Just as I am hungry to believe I am the person he sees when he looks at me.

I am terrified of whatever is springing up between us.

Of just how badly I want it.

My own feelings for him began well before we reached Rennes, when he first told me he went back for his sister. But my belief that he wouldn't—couldn't—care for me in return created a moat of safety around my heart, and I had nothing to fear because the entire situation was impossible.

But now—now I look in his eyes and I see that he believes it is possible. Surely that is only because he does not truly know me. There are still things—momentous things—that I have kept from him. And while Beast is strong and his heart generous, I am not certain he is strong enough to love me and all my secrets.

I cannot decide if I should bury the rest of those secrets so deeply that they will never resurface or throw them in his face like a gauntlet. Better he hate me now rather than later when I have grown used to his love.

But haven't the gods already proved how futile it is for me to try to keep my past hidden? Which leaves me with one clear choice—one that has me wishing I had decided to obey the abbess and make for d'Albret's camp.

"Why so grim, my lady?"

I glance up, surprised to see Beast riding next to me. How can someone so large move so quietly? I open my mouth to ask him that very question but surprise myself by asking a different one. "Do you know that I have killed more than thirty men?"

His eyebrows shoot up, whether at my confession or the number of kills, I cannot say. "And of those, only sixteen were sanctioned by Mortain."

When he says nothing, I add somewhat impatiently, "I do not kill simply because Mortain ordains it, but because I enjoy it."

"So I have seen," he says. "I, too, take great pleasure in my work." He looks around us. "Is there someone here you wish to kill?"

Uncertain if he is teasing or serious, I resist the urge to reach across the space between us and punch him. Clearly, to a man who is rumored to have killed hundreds upon hundreds in battle, my puny body count does not hold much sway. Perhaps something that he has had less personal experience with. "I am wicked and carnal and have slept with lots of men. Possibly even dozens." Although in truth, it is only five.

Beast does not look at me but instead surveys the line of horses and carts stretched out behind us. "You hold yourself too lightly, my lady, for I cannot think of even a single man who deserves such a gift as you claim you have given."

His words prick at something achingly tender, something I don't wish to acknowledge, so I snort in derision. "What do you know of such things? I am likely one of the few maids who have not run from your ugly face."

He turns back to look at me, amusement sparkling in his eyes like sunlight on water. "True enough, my lady." Then he is gone, riding down the length of our party to make sure there are no stragglers, and I am left with the conviction that an avalanche would be easier to dissuade than that man.

Toward late afternoon, we reach a small forested area—a secluded place the charbonnerie scouts have picked out for us. The soldiers do not like it and grumble, for it is a dark, primordial tangle of trees and underbrush. Indeed, the trees here are so very large, their roots have burst from the ground and run along the surface, like the ancient bones of the earth itself. Although I cannot say why, I feel at ease in this place, as if the presence of Dea Matrona is strong. No. Not Dea Matrona, but the Dark Mother. For even though I do not worship Her, I can feel Her presence in the rich loam and leaf mold beneath our feet, and in the quiet rotting of the fallen logs. Perhaps that is what makes the soldiers uneasy.

Our party has grown throughout our journey, as if Beast is some mad piper whose tune calls eager young men who wish to fight at his side. In addition to the men-at-arms and original charbonnerie, we have been joined by a dozen more of the charcoal-burners, two blacksmiths, a handful of woodcutters and crofters, and three burly farmers' sons. One of whom is Jacques, Guion and Bette's elder son.

Soon, the clearing is full of the bustle and industry of nearly fifty people making camp ready for the coming night. I feel twitchy in my own skin, as if the very sap that runs through the trees is now running through my veins, bringing me alive after a cold, hard winter.

Wishing for something to do, I offer to help Malina prepare dinner, but she shoos me away. "You are a lady, and an assassin besides. You do not belong with the soup pot."

I turn and survey the camp. Some of the charbonnerie are busily erecting rough tents in the clearing; others are collecting water from a nearby stream so that the tired horses may drink. The soldiers have gone off hunting for our dinner, and even the greenlings have been sent to gather firewood. Since I refuse to sit idly by while others do the work, I snag one of the slings for gathering wood and head into the trees.

Moving among the trees calms me. In that quiet and stillness, I find myself content, a feeling I barely recognize. I like this life—the days full of hard riding and the evenings filled with chores and necessities, with little time left for idle pleasures or twisted games.

Mayhap I can simply ride at Beast's side as he travels throughout the kingdom raising an army to the duchess's cause. That thought has me smiling, for it is a fanciful notion that I would not dare indulge in were I not out here alone with no one to see it.

But am I alone? Voices and some strange cracking noises reach my ears. I move forward cautiously, careful not to step on any dried leaves or twigs that might give me away.

I come upon a clearing and find it is only the boys from the camp who have paused in their wood collecting. They have taken two branches and are playing at sword fighting. They are strong boys, but their movements are clumsy and unskilled. The charbonnerie are right to call them greenlings. I start to smile at their antics, but instead a cold chill slithers down my spine. This is no game we play, and I suddenly despair of our chances—not only of success, but of survival.

I step from between the trees. "Fools!" I scold. "You are not beating the straw from mattresses!"

The boys freeze, their faces filled with both embarrassment and defiance. "What do you know of such things?" the woodcutter's boy asks sullenly. "My lady," he adds as an afterthought.

"More than you, it would seem. You do not whack each other as if chaffing wheat. There is a rhythm of thrust and parry, attack and counterattack that you must know else you'll be gutted like pigs."

Resentment flares in the young woodcutter's eyes. I have pricked their male pride, and rubbed their noses in their lack of privilege, for of course they have had no opportunity to even witness sword fights, let alone practice at them. "There is not time in the three days before we reach Morlaix to teach you the art of sword fighting. That takes years. Add to that that there are no extra swords to be had, and you are wasting your time."

"What would you have us do? Collect wood?" One of the blacksmith's boys kicks at a branch at his feet in disgust.

"No," I say, stepping closer. "I would have you learn a few quick, deadly ways to kill a man so that you can be of service to the duchess in this mission."

The greenlings' faces are mixtures of suspicion and hope. "And who will take the time to teach us these skills? My lady."

I smile. "I will." I reach for my wrists and pull my knives from their sheaths. The boys' interest quickens, except for the blacksmith's son, who is still skeptical.

"What can we learn of fighting from a maid?" he asks the others, and looks of doubt appear on their faces. Two of them actually snicker. I want to take their fat heads in my hands and knock them together like empty jugs.

Jacques speaks up. "That is no mere maid, you fool. Did you not hear the commander yesterday? She serves Mortain." He lowers his voice. "She is an assassin."

The blacksmith boy blinks. "Is this true?"

In answer, I take one of the knives and throw it. He has time only to gape in surprise before his cloak is firmly pinned to the tree behind him, right above his shoulder. "It is true," I tell him.

Without further discussion, I turn to Jacques. "You will partner with me. The rest of you, pair up according to your size." With a sheepish glance at the others, Jacques shuffles across the forest floor to stand in front of me, hands hanging limply at his sides.

I remove the two knives I carry in my boots and hand them to two other boys. "Just like an assassin, your greatest strength will be your stealth and cunning. And speed. You will need to get in quickly, strike, then move away before anyone has even realized you are there. That means in addition to what I teach you here tonight, you must begin to learn to move quietly. Right now, you sound like a herd of oxen galumphing through the forest. Pretend you are sneaking up on some-body if you must, but learn to move without making noise."

"There is no honor in that," one of the woodcutters snorts.

Quicker than he can blink, I step inside his guard, whip his belt from his waist, and twist it around his throat, just tight enough to get his attention. "There is no honor in throwing your life away either. Not when the duchess needs every man in her kingdom if we are to win the coming war."

The boy swallows audibly, then nods in understanding. I step away and hand him back his belt. "Besides, if what you say is true, then those who serve Mortain have no honor, and I am certain that is not an ac-cusation you care to make."

They quickly shake their heads. "Now, the quickest and quietest way to kill a man is by slitting his throat, just here." I run my finger across my own. "This is not only an excellent killing blow but also a way to silence him so he cannot call out and alert others." I step into the lessons I was taught at the convent as easily as I step into a new gown. "Here. Put your fingers at your own throat. Feel the hollow at the base of it. The spot you want to strike is three fingers up from that." I watch as they all grope at their own throats. "Good. Now I will show you the striking motion from behind."

"On me?" Jacques asks, his voice cracking.

"Yes," I say, hiding a smile. "But I will use the knife handle, not the blade."

I spend the next hour teaching the greenlings some of my most basic and crudest skills. How to slit a throat; where to strike from behind so that a single blow will kill a man; where best to place your body when garroting someone so his thrashing will not dislodge your hold. We do not spend nearly as long as I'd like, but our wood is needed to feed the fires if we are to eat. They are all still awkward and clumsy with the movements, but now they have some small skills they can use.

That night, when we finally sit down to eat, I feel as if I have earned my supper.

When the meal is done and the fire burning low, I go in search of my bedroll. Someone—Yannic, I presume—has laid it out carefully between two of the great tree roots so that I am cradled between them. Near stumbling with exhaustion, I reach down to lift the blanket, then blink in surprise at the small clutch of pink flowers that have been laid on my pillow.

It appears that my sins are forgiven. At least, the ones Beast knows about.

Chapter Thirty-Seven

LATER, WHEN EVERYONE HAS RETIRED for the night, a large, hulking shape steps away from the dying fire and moves in my direction. "You look like a babe in a cradle," Beast says.

I glance to the root on either side of me and decide I like his comparison. "Dea Matrona is holding me close." I am certain I can feel the roots pulsing as they draw nourishment from the earth.

Being careful of his injured leg, he uses the tree to ease his way down to the ground beside me. "Have you finished confessing all your darkest sins to me?"

I am glad he can accept my earlier confessions with such a light heart, and clearly the gods are handing me this perfect moment for sharing the rest. I am grateful for the darkness that cloaks us, casting everything in shadow, muting life itself somehow. "Sadly, no." I take a deep breath. "I would warn you that you are courting the very woman responsible for your sister's death."

A moment passes, then another, and still he says nothing. I peer through the darkness, trying to see his face, looking for some sign that my confession has addled his wits or left him speechless with revulsion. "Did you not hear me?"

"Yes." The word comes slowly, as if he must haul it up from some deep well. "But I also know you are quick to paint yourself in the darkest light possible. How old were you?"

"Fourteen," I whisper.

"Was it your own hand that dealt the killing blow?"

"No."

Beast nods thoughtfully. "Can you tell me how a lone fourteen-year-old maid could stop one such as d'Albret?"

"I could have told *someone,*" I say in anguish.

"Who?" Beast says fiercely. "Who could you have told who would have had the means and the power to stay his hand? His soldiers, who were sworn to serve him? His vassals or his retainers, who had sworn similar oaths? No one could cross a dangerous, powerful lord such as d'Albret at the say-so of a mere child."

"But—"

"All those things you did—or didn't do—were a matter of survival. Telling anyone would only have exposed you as knowing the full scope of what went on in d'Albret's household and endangered you even further."

"It is not just that," I say. "I was unkind and laughed when my brothers teased Alyse or played cruel jokes on her. I would laugh as loudly as they did."

Beast's jaw clenches, and it is clear that I have finally managed to make him see the extent of my cruelty.

"And what would have happened if you hadn't?"

"Alyse would have had a true friend, someone to stand by her instead of someone who ran at the slightest threat."

He leans across the distance between us, getting as close to my face as he can. "If you had not laughed at the cruelty, you would have become the next target." He holds up a hand, stopping my flow of words. "Do not forget, I have seen you dreaming and know how much darkness haunts you. I am also fair certain that very little of it is yours. I say again, all those things you did—or didn't do—were a matter of survival."

We stare at each other for a long, hot moment, then my temper flares. "Why do you not have the good sense to see that I am not deserving of such forgiveness?"

He laughs—a harsh, humorless sound. "The god I serve is near as dark as yours, my lady. I am not one to pass judgment on anyone."

As I stare into his eyes, I see the faint echo of the horrors of the battle lust he has endured, and understanding dawns. He truly knows some of the darkness I struggle with.

We sit in the deepening night for some time. His face is mostly dark angles and planes, with only the faintest glow of the fire reaching this far away. "I would like you to tell me how my sister died," he says at last.

Even though he has every right to know this, my heart starts to race and it feels as if a great hand has wrapped itself around my chest. But Sweet Mortain, it is the very least of what I owe him. I close my eyes and try to grasp the memory, but it is as if a thick door bars my entrance, and when I struggle to open it, pain shoots through my brow and my heart beats so frantically I fear it will shred itself against my rib cage.

I remember the screaming. And the blood.

And then there is nothing but a black mawing pit that threatens to swallow me whole.

"I cannot," I whisper.

Something in his face shifts, and his disappointment in me is palpable. "No, no," I rush to explain. "I am not refusing or playing coy. I truly cannot remember. Not fully. There are just bits and pieces, and when I try too hard to force the memory, only blackness comes."

"Is there anything you do remember?"

"I remember screaming. And blood. And someone slapping me. That is when I realized the screaming was mine." The giant hand around my chest squeezes all the air from my lungs. Black spots begin to dance before my eyes. "And that is all."

He stares at me a long moment and I would give years of my life to be able to see his face clearly, to know what he is thinking. Through the darkness, his big warm hand tenderly takes hold of mine, and I want to weep at the understanding in his touch.

The road to Morlaix takes us uncomfortably close to my family's home. It sits but a few leagues to the north, and simply knowing how close it is makes my whole body twitch with unease. Beast says nothing, but I see his gaze drift in that direction a time or two and cannot help but wonder what he is feeling. Luckily, it begins to rain, soft fat drops that quickly turn into a torrential downpour, forcing our minds to other things. We cannot afford to stop, however, so we continue on. While no one complains, it is only the charbonnerie who do not seem to mind. By midmorning, the forest floor is muddy, and our progress is reduced to a slow slog. But as long as we can keep moving forward, we do. We must. Even now, d'Albret is likely camped in front of Rennes and giving the signal to his saboteurs. Please Mortain, let us have gotten all of them. And if not, let us hope Duval and Dunois are on their guard.

When the second horse flounders in the mud and it takes us an hour to dig out one cart's wheels, Beast decides we must wait out the storm and sends scouts ahead to find us shelter.

A short while later, they return. "There is a cave a mile or so north of here," Lazare tells him. "It is large and can hold all of us and the horses as well."

De Brosse's horse shifts uneasily on its feet. "It is an old cave, my lord. With strange markings and old altars. I am not sure the Nine would appreciate us trespassing."

I laugh—mostly so they will not hear my teeth chattering with the cold. "Between us we serve Death, War, and the Dark Mother. Whom do you think we must fear?"

De Brosse ducks his head sheepishly, and Beast gives the command to head for the cave. I almost hope it is a mouth that opens directly to hell, for of a certainty, we could use the heat.

Chapter Thirty-Eight

EVEN AS HALF THE PARTY is still filing into the cave, the charbonnerie have torches lit and get to work building fires. The cave is indeed enormous. We could easily fit twice our company inside.

There is much stomping of feet, groans of relief, and creaking of leather and harness as fifty mounted men dismount and jostle to create room for themselves and their horses.

Once I have dismounted and handed my horse to Yannic, I pace the perimeter of the cave, trying to get blood flowing in my limbs. I would also like to know in whose abode we will pass the night. The charbonnerie call this place the Dark Mother's womb, and it may well be, but other gods have been worshiped here, and more recently.

There is an old altar at the very back. The torches hardly cast any light that far, but I can see the faint outline of small bones, some offering made long ago. Old drawings flicker on the cave walls: a spear, a hunting horn, and an arrow. It is not until I see the woman riding the giant boar that I am certain we have stumbled into one of Arduinna's lairs, where she and her hunting party would rest from their hunts.

Thus reassured, I return to the front of the cave, where the rest of the party stands, torn between getting comfortable and bolting.

It is the youngest of the men, the sons of farmers and woodcutters and blacksmiths, who are the most unsettled. The charbonnerie have no fear of this place, and the men-at-arms are too disciplined to show such fear, even though I can smell it on them as surely as I can smell their sweat. But the green boys stand huddled together, looking about with wide eyes, their shivers equal parts cold and fear.

"Arduinna," I announce. "The cave belongs to Saint Arduinna. Not Mortain, nor Camulos, nor even the Dark Mother"—I send a quelling glance at Graelon, who looks to correct me—"but the goddess of love. There is nothing to fear." Although that is assuredly a lie, for love terrifies me more than death or battle, but these youths do not need to know that. Indeed, Samson snickers then, and his gaze goes to Gisla, who is helping Malina set up pots for boiling. Now, that is what we need. The goddess of lust moving in all these men with but half a dozen women among them.

"Come," I say sharply. "Grab your weapons and move to the back where there is room to spread out."

Samson, Jacques, and the others gape at me. "Here?"

"Do you think your skills are so great that you may set aside your practice?"

"But there's no room."

"Oh, but there is. Now, follow me, unless you are afraid. Samson, Bruno, bring the torches."

Of course, none will admit to such fear, and certainly not in front of me, so I lead the group deeper into the cave and have the boys secure the torches.

I place myself at the very back of the cave, for even though it is clearly one of Arduinna's, I can feel Mortain's cold breath upon my neck. I do not know why His presence should be so strong here, and I would not have the boys turn their backs to Him.

After much grumbling and complaining, the boys finally take their positions. "Begin," I order, and their arms, clumsy with cold, start moving through the exercises we have been practicing. Within half an hour, the cold is forgotten, along with their fear, and they are concentrated on besting their opponents.

My focus on the greenlings is so great as I try to keep them from accidentally killing one another that it takes me a while to realize we have drawn a crowd. Easily a dozen of Beast's soldiers have gathered round and are watching the boys with narrowed eyes and folded arms.

"My money's on the smith's boy," de Brosse says. "The one with the long hair."

"I'll take that wager. I think the boy with the ax will win the bout."

There is a rustle of purses and jingle of coin as bets are made. Their casual betting raises my hackles; this is no game. The boys' lives likely depend on what they learn here. Besides, the greenlings do not need the distraction of being surrounded by true soldiers.

Or so I think until I see how the greenlings take the soldiers' attention to heart. There—Samson has finally started taking the practice seriously, his face creased in concentration. Jacques, too, is no longer so worried about hurting his opponent and finally manages to wrestle him into position so that he can get the leather cord around his neck.

Cheers go up, and Jacques smiles shyly. Then Claude sneaks up from behind him and gets his knife handle around his neck. Another jingle of coin changes hands. I cannot decide if I am amused or annoyed that the soldiers' opinions seems to carry more weight than mine. "Again," I say. "And this time, Claude, try not to laugh as you slit your opponent's throat."

Dinner that night is a cheerful affair. Half of the soldiers' purses are heavier from their wagers, and the greenlings' sense of pride has grown in equal amounts. Even the charbonnerie seem to have relaxed some.

As men leave the fires to lie down on the cave floor, Beast comes to find me. I have selected a spot for my bedroll toward the back, still wishing to place myself between that faint chill of death that is haunting me and the others.

"We reach Morlaix tomorrow," he says, easing down onto the ground.

I try to ignore the heat coming off his body, try to pretend he is not close enough for me to touch and that my fingers do not yearn to do just that. "I know."

Beast reaches across the small space and takes my hand in his. It is a big hand, and hard, the entire palm filled with calluses and scars. "It was well done, you training the greenlings."

"I know." My answer startles a laugh out of him, but it is true—I do know that it was a good thing.

He shakes his head. "I fear I have lost my touch for commanding men. It is an assassin who has finally managed to bring them all together, not me."

"Now you go too far and mock me. I do not have any knack for bringing men together."

He threads his fingers through mine, then slowly brings my hand up to his lips and kisses it. "I would never mock you. I speak only the truth."

It is the most comforting thing I have ever felt, that hand on mine, the quiet steadfastness it promises. That he offers me this after all the secrets I have told him humbles me. I want, more than anything, to keep that hand in mine and never let it go.

Chapter Thirty-Nine

NEAR NOON ON THE FOURTH day of our journey, we come in sight of Morlaix. We do not approach the town directly but stay on the far side of the river, where we can just make out the ramparts of the walled city.

Beast turns our party northward. The farther north we go, the more the land changes. The rich fields and forests turn scrubbier with tall rippling grasses, and the sharp tang of salt is in the air. In the distance I can hear the steady crashing of the waves as they throw themselves upon the rocky shore.

Beast directs the main portion of the party to set up camp in the thicket of trees that we can just see off to the east. He orders two of his men and two of the charbonnerie to accompany him, along with myself. We follow a trail that is naught but a deer track and find ourselves winding our way to the coast. When the rocky shore comes into sight, I see an old stone abbey and beside it one of the even more ancient standing stones. I glance at Beast. "Saint Mer?"

Beast nods. "The abbess of Saint Mer has been keeping Duval informed. She and her acolytes have been in communication with the British ships, and have been keeping track of the French movements in the area as well."

I tamp down a little flutter of — not fear — apprehension. Saint Mer is a watery old hag of a goddess, with a tangle of seaweed for Her hair and bones formed of driftwood. She is wild, uncontrollable, both playful and deadly, beautiful and terrifying. Her appetite for men is insatiable and She often plucks them ripe from the boat, pulls them into Her watery maw, then spits them out when She is done with them.

When I was nine years old, long before I had heard the stories of my own birth and lineage, I adopted Her for my own. Most girls my age worshiped Amourna, but I had no use for Her and Her soft, gentle love that was naught but a lie told to keep girls hopeful and compliant. For a while, I turned to Arduinna, for She was the one goddess who carried a weapon, and that appealed to me greatly, but in the end, She let me down as well. As a protector of virgins, it seemed She failed as often as She succeeded.

And so I turned to Saint Mer. Her wildish nature called to me. I wished to dance with storms, like She did. I wished to pick and choose which men I allowed into my domain, then be done with them once I'd taken my pleasure. Not that I believed there was any pleasure to be had between a man and a woman, but the stories and poets spoke of it often, and if it existed, I would have my share of it.

Mostly, I wanted to be feared as Saint Mer was feared, to have men treat me with great respect and caution and be afraid of what might await them if they did not.

When we reach the abbey, we rein in our horses. As we dismount, the door opens and a shrunken old woman comes out. In her hand is the sacred trident of Saint Mer, and around her neck are nearly a dozen strands of cockle shells, which mark her as the abbess.

Beast bows low before her, as do Sir Lannion and Sir Lorril. I sink into a deep curtsy. The charbonnerie look uncertainly about them, then bob their knees.

"Come inside and be welcome," the abbess says. She motions with her trident, and two girls emerge from the abbey door and come forward to tend our horses: the daughters of Saint Mer, born of the goddess and drowning men.

I am filled with curiosity, as I have never met anyone said to be born of another god before. Saint Camulos does not count, for He makes no claim to have sired His dedicants, merely accepts those conceived in His name.

There is a translucent quality to the girls' skin, as if they spend more time beneath the waves than beneath the sun. Their hair is long and flowing, one light blond and the other dark. As they draw closer, I see that their feet are bare and they have the slightly webbed toes that mark them as one of Saint Mer's. When I hand one of the girls my reins, she smiles at me. Her teeth are slightly pointed.

I nod in greeting and thanks, then hurry to follow the abbess into the abbey.

Her receiving chamber is sparse, with none of the luxuries the abbess of Saint Mortain enjoys. She offers us cool, clear water to drink, and naught else.

"I bring thanks from the duchess herself for the aid you have given her," Beast says formally, and I am intrigued by this new side of him.

The abbess nods her head, causing the shells to rattle. "I am committed to doing whatever is in my power to keep our land free."

"Are there any new reports? Do the British remain anchored off the coast?"

"Yes, but they are running out of supplies. Some of the locals were rowing food and water out to them, but the French soldiers got wind of it and began picking them off with their archers, so that has stopped."

"And what of Morlaix itself?"

"There are near five hundred French soldiers stationed in the town, with another two hundred positioned along the estuary. Your biggest problem will be the cannon the French have positioned at the mouth of the bay. I do not know if they can reach the ships, but the captains seem to think they can, and they will not draw near."

Beast glances to the charbonnerie, who smile and nod. He turns back to the abbess. "Their cannon will not be a problem. We will take them out easily enough so the ships can get through. My bigger concern is disabling as many French in the town as possible so the British will not be massacred as they attempt to disembark."

The abbess moves to a table set up near one of the high windows. "Here is a map of the town," she says, and we join her.

"Here," the abbess says, pointing at the map. "This is where I am told the soldiers are being garrisoned."

We spend the rest of the afternoon plotting and planning, trying to come up with a strategy that has some hope of succeeding. All the while, I can feel time eating away at our chance of success, just as the waves eat away at the shore. D'Albret has likely reached Rennes by now. Hopefully, with no saboteurs to grant d'Albret access, the city will hold.

Chapter Forty

IT IS LATE AFTERNOON WHEN we rejoin the rest of our party. They have been busy during our absence and have the camp set up. It is abustle with activity: the rubbing down of saddles and tack, the sharpening of blades, and the checking of weapons. The air fair hums with the anticipation everyone is feeling, but there is none of the old acrimony that had been haunting us since we first left Rennes. Whether they have called a temporary truce or merely needed some common enemy to focus on, I do not know.

It is not until I dismount and hand my reins to Yannic that I see the marques. There, on that man-at-arm's brow—a man whose name I do not even know. Winnog too is marqued, I see, as he walks by and gives me a jaunty wave. Alarm clangs through me like a bell.

My gaze searches among the camp for the greenlings. I find them just beyond the clearing, practicing their skills. Henri and Claude also bear marques. As does Jacques. More than a dozen men bear the marque, and cold understanding creeps along my skin.

Ismae was right. These men cannot all be traitors to our country. Nor does it make sense for Mortain to have marqued them all at once if I am to be the one to kill them. It can only mean they are to die. Tonight, or more likely on the morrow, during our assault on Morlaix.

Even though I have eaten nothing all day, I fear I will be sick.

Beast.

Dreading what I will find, but desperate to know, I go in search of Beast. He has already called the captains to him and begun telling them what we have learned. I ignore the others, my eyes devouring the ugly face that has grown so dear to me. While it is not one whit prettier and is covered in dark stubble, it bears no marque.

It is all I can do not to whoop with joy, but the marques I see on de Brosse and Lorril sober me. While I knew that men would die in this battle, it is hard—so very hard—to know who will not be returning.

I join Beast and the others at the small map table that Yannic has set up. I glance once at d'Albret's former jailor and am relieved when I see that he too is unmarqued.

"There are three points of attack," Beast is saying. "We will send two parties north, to take out the cannon on either side of the bay. Erwan, I will want at least half the party to be your charbonnerie.

"The second defense we will hit is the massive chain they have strung across the narrow mouth of the bay. If we can cut that down, some of the smaller British ships will be able to sail directly into the town quay and disembark there.

"Last, the majority of our forces will strike here. Lazare and Graelon have developed a plan to immobilize most of the French troops."

Lazare's thin serious face breaks into a rare smile. "We will smoke them out," he says.

It is a bold and desperate plan, and because of that it just might work. Under the cover of night, the charbonnerie will bolt the sleeping garrison in, then set fires at two of the windows and direct the smoke to fill the room. That will leave one window—the one with a twenty-foot drop outside the city walls—through which they can escape. Many broken bones will ensue, and not nearly enough deaths to make the men happy, but it is the fastest way to free the town of the troops' presence so the British can land.

"Have your men catch some sleep," Beast tells them. "We will move at midnight so we are in place well before dawn and can strike while the French are still unsuspecting."

As the captains leave to give their men their orders, I move to stand beside Beast. "How do you do it?" I ask, my gaze on the departing men. "Send men to their deaths?"

Beast looks at me, surprised. "You know they will die?"

I nod without looking at him. "De Brosse and Lorril are marqued. As are a dozen other men, including Winnog and Jacques."

"They are not all traitors."

"No," I agree. "They are not. Which is why I ask you: How do you do it?"

He is silent, then, as he watches the men he will send to their deaths. "I have sworn to support the duchess with my life. I do not ask of anyone that which I am not also willing to do. I believe that this cause is worth fighting for."

"And is it?" I stare at Jacques, who is laughing with Samson and Bruno, boasting of his hoped-for valor in tomorrow's mission.

Beast is silent a long moment before he speaks. "That is one of the hardest things, and we will not know until later. Sometimes much later."

We are both quiet awhile, lost in our own separate thoughts. Finally, I turn to him. "What is my role in tomorrow's assault?"

At his blank look, I fold my arms and scowl at him. "You cannot think I will sit here quietly and wait with the other women?" But I see that is exactly what he had hoped I would do. So he will not suspect how much his concern touches me, I mock him. "You cannot tell a handmaiden of Death that it is too dangerous."

He sighs and runs his hand over his head. "I suppose I cannot, although I would like to." He turns to me then, his piercing blue eyes studying me intently. "Could you see a marque on yourself, if there was one?"

"I do not know," I admit, his question filling me with curiosity. "But you can be sure of one thing. I will not die until d'Albret is defeated. "

The two parties headed for the north of the bay are the first to leave, for they have the farthest to go. Sir Lannion is leading one group, Sir Lorril another. There are as many charbonnerie in the parties as soldiers, for the plan is not only to take out the men guarding the cannon, but also to find a way to disable the cannon themselves. We talk briefly about using them against the French, but there is no way to do that without also injuring the townspeople, and that we are not willing to do.

I cannot take my eyes off the cheerful, gangly Winnog and the faint black marque that sits on his forehead. Against my better judgment, I search out Lazare, who has also been placed on the cannon detail.

At my approach, he eyes me suspiciously. "What?" he asks.

"I want you to keep a close watch on Winnog."

"Winnog? You are daft if you suspect him of any trickery or deceit."

"I suspect him of no such thing," I say sharply. "I tell you because he is marqued for death."

Lazare's dark eyes widen in both fear and awe. "You can see such a thing?"

"Yes, that is one of the powers my god has given me."

Lazare's gaze drifts upward as if he would look upon his own forehead. I bite back a smile. "You bear no marque," I tell him. "I do not know if we can outsmart Death, but I am willing to try. Watch him carefully and keep him as safe as the mission allows."

Lazare gives me a fierce smile. "If there is anyone who can outsmart Death, it is the Dark Mother. I will watch out for Winnog. And thank you." Our eyes hold for a long moment, then he joins the main party, moving to stand near Winnog.

I cannot save them all, but the innocents, the ones who do not fully understand the duty they have signed up for, those I shall try to save.

My own party is next to leave. We are to travel west to where the river narrows just before reaching the town, where we will wrest control of the chain and lower it into the river so ships can get through. Sir de Brosse will lead our party, and while I hold no great love for him, it is an uncomfortable thing to see him marqued for death and say nothing. In the end, I cannot stay silent. Just before we leave, I approach him. He lifts one side of his mouth in a lazy smile. "My lady?"

"I just want to warn you to be careful," I say.

He lays his hand on his chest. "Have my lady's feelings for me softened?"

I roll my eyes. "No. Just do not do something stupid and get yourself killed."

He frowns in puzzlement. "I will try not to, my lady."

I give a curt nod, then fall back to check my knives and Ismae's rondelles and make certain the crossbow is secure upon its chain. Before I can join the others, Beast draws near. "Are you certain you will not stay here and wait?"

"I am certain. Besides, I must stick close to Jacques and the others. I do not want to be the one to tell his mother that she has lost her son."

He nods his understanding, and even though he is not marqued, my heart is in my throat, worried for him, for the danger that might find him while I am away from his side. His eyes have begun to burn with some eerie inner light so that they shine like twin blue flames.

He steps closer and places his hands on my arms. "We will meet again on the other side of this, for what is between us is not finished by half."

"Does your god tell you this?"

He grins. "No—yours does." Then he leans in and plants a quick, fierce kiss on my lips. A flash of heat and hunger and something so sweet I dare not name it, and then he is gone, striding off to lead the remainder of the men to town.

A quarter moon hangs in the sky, shedding just enough light that we can see where to put our feet but not so much as to expose us utterly, even once we step out of the shelter of the trees. We are most vulnerable while crossing the northbound road, but with the countryside occupied by French soldiers, most of the small folk keep to their beds with their doors and windows locked.

There are only eight of us, but still it feels like far too many. I have only ever fought alone or with Beast and Yannic at my side. I already miss the little jailor's excellent aim and keen timing.

The night has leached all the color from our surroundings so that everything around us is cast in shades of silver and gray and black. The tall trees are but darker shadows and smudges against the sky. The greenlings blend in well with the others, and I am proud that they make no more noise than do de Brosse and his soldiers. Their nervousness and excitement hangs in a thick cloud around them.

We finally come to a stop on a hillock overlooking the bay. A small copse of trees sits atop it, like a crown. We tie our horses up here and I suggest Claude be set to guard them. He accepts the assignment grudgingly, but up here, out of harm's way, he will be one less person I must watch after. Careful to stay hidden among the trees, we move to the edge of the hill, the hearty scrub grass cushioning our footsteps. Looking down, we can see the small, square rock shelter built for the chain winch. Beyond it, the water of the bay is flat and still and silver, like a mirror. The thick heavy chain spans the width of it, and on the other side, the full forest descends all the way to the water line.

De Brosse motions two of his men forward, and they disappear down the hill to learn how many guard the winch and where they are posted. Behind us, one of the horses blows gently, and I hear Claude move to quiet him.

Although we do not wait more than a few minutes, it feels like hours until the scouts return. They speak quietly to de Brosse. There are at least six soldiers and three archers, possibly more inside. I glance at the marqued Jacques and de Brosse and wonder what Mortain would think if He knew I was planning to thwart His will.

We ignore the footpath and, instead, approach slightly from the south, using a deer track through the bracken.

Bruno and Samson are to stay back, as we will need their strong arms to free the chain. Jacques and I are to slip down and take out as many of the sentries as we can before being noticed. Once the alarm goes up, de Brosse and the other soldiers will leap into the fray and engage the soldiers directly.

Luckily, it is near the end of the Frenchmen's watch, and they are tired. Perhaps even a little complacent as they lean against the trees, talking quietly among themselves. I shut my ears to their voices. Hearing them talk of their wine or dicing or women will not make them any easier to kill. I lean into Jacques. "You take the one on the left, I'll take the two on the right."

He nods, his whole body atremble, and begins creeping toward his target. I pull a crossbow bolt from the frame and stick it in my belt for quick access, then draw my knife.

As silent as one of the shadows, I approach my target. He is listening intently to some story the other fellow is telling him. Closer and closer I creep. When the man throws his head back to laugh, I step silently forward, reach around with my knife, and slit his throat. The soul bursts from him nearly as quickly as the blood that hits the other man in a wide arcing spray. While the second man is still staring in stunned amazement at his dying friend, I slap the bolt in place, lift the crossbow, and fire.

The bolt takes him between the eyes, and he falls backwards. There is a scuffling sound behind me, and I turn to find Jacques and his archer clasped together in some sort of lethal dance. Retrieving my knife, I hurry forward. The archer's hands are around Jacques's neck, and the boy's eyes bulge in fear. Bette's and Guion's faces float before me. I brush the vision away, take a step forward, and stab the archer in the back, then force the knife up as high as it will go to hurry his passing.

As his hands fall away from Jacques's neck and he slumps to the ground, his soul rises from his body like mist from a swamp. I ignore it and focus on Jacques, who is breathing hard and rubbing his neck. Our eyes meet over the dead man, and then Jacques turns and retches into the bushes.

To give him some privacy, I kneel down and clean my knife on the tabard of the Frenchman. Jacques may be embarrassed, but at least he is still alive.

There is a shout from the stone house and then the clang of metal as de Brosse and his men fall upon the guards. "Come," I tell Jacques. "We must—" My words are cut off by a cry of rage as a man—a fourth archer—emerges from the trees. He pauses long enough to unsling his bow from his shoulder, nock an arrow to the string, and aim directly at Jacques.

Luckily, he does not see me squatting in the shadows beside his dead friend. I shove to my feet and use the upward momentum to launch myself at Jacques's attacker.

I catch him completely unawares, the impact of my body knocking his bow from his fingers and his legs out from under him. As we hit the ground, I lever up, adjust my knife, sweep it across his throat, then roll out of the way of the mess that follows.

My pulse racing, I leap to my feet and peer into the shadows in case they should be hiding any other attackers. A long moment passes, then another, and no one else emerges. I turn to Jacques then, who is still on his knees, eyes wide, staring at the fallen archer.

The marque is gone from his brow. "Go." The fear still coursing through me makes my voice harsh. "Join Claude and the horses. The rest of us will be right behind you."

He does not question me but nods once and then goes to do what I ordered. When he is out of harm's way, I go to the winch house, where the clang of sword against sword is accompanied by the heavy, solid pounding of an ax as it chops.

When I reach the doorway, I see that all four guards lie dead, and Samson and Bruno have almost hacked the wooden winch from its mooring. It is not enough to simply lower the chain — we must ensure it cannot be raised again before the British get through.

I lean against the rough stones and catch my breath, keeping my gaze focused carefully on the shadows outside for any more of the French.

There is a great splintering as the winch finally gives way. Like a huge metal serpent, the giant chain slithers and writhes from the broken winch, each enormous link clanging like an immense bell as it hits the stone floor. Then there is a faint rumble as the chain slithers across the rocky shore and sinks to the bottom of the bay.

We all stare after it for a moment, the silence ringing in our ears. "It is done," de Brosse says. "Let's return to town and see if they need our help."

He pokes his head outside the winch house, then motions the rest of us to follow. Before he has taken two steps there is a hissing sound, followed by a thud, then de Brosse and the soldier behind him are flat on their backs with crossbow bolts rammed through their necks.

"Down," I shout to the others as I flatten myself on the floor. I belly-crawl to the door and peer out, but see no one. "Samson, give me your cloak," I order. Wordlessly, he pulls it from his shoulders and hands it to me. I wad it up, then toss it outside.

Before it lands there is another hiss of a crossbow bolt. "They are coming from across the river," I tell the others. "And we are caught like sitting ducks." We must find a way to shield ourselves long enough that we can reach the path behind the chain house. Once we do, we will be out of their direct line of sight, but until then we are ripe for the plucking.

I call to two of de Brosse's men. "Can you fire your arrows to the far side of the river?"

One of them shrugs. "We can, but I don't know how accurate they'll be."

"That's all right, I am only looking to slow their arrows down somewhat. Bruno and Samson?" The two boys step forward, their faces serious, all traces of adventure or games erased by the death of their comrades. "I want you to get down on your bellies and crawl over to the fallen French, just at the far side of the chain house. When you reach them"—this next part is hard to say, for all that they are our enemies—"I want you to lift the bodies and use them as shields against the arrows. Bring them back here and then we can all move together behind their screen."

It is a foul thing to do, to use a man's body thusly, and I will not dishonor our own fallen in such a way.

Bruno's eyes widen so that the white shows, and he makes the sign to ward off evil. I reach out and grab his thick, meaty arms and give him a shake. "I do not enjoy this one bit more than you, but I have five of us I wish to get out alive. Now, can you do it or must I ask someone else?"

When he finally nods, I relax my grip. "We can all say extra prayers for them later, if you'd like." I gesture to the two soldiers to take position. When their crossbows are aimed at the far side, I motion to the other two boys to hit the dirt. As they do, de Brosse's men begin firing their bolts to the far bank.

We all hold our breath as inch by painful inch Samson and Bruno make their way to the dead Frenchmen. Every moment brings the risk of an arrow strike, and I must keep reminding myself that neither of them was marqued. It does not make the wait any easier.

At last they return with their grisly burden. The rest of us step out into the night and use our enemies to shield our flight to safety. De Brosse's remaining soldiers drag him and the other fallen with them as we go.

We leave the bodies at the crest of the hillock where Claude and Jacques wait with our horses. It does not matter that we've been spotted — the chain cannot be raised again, not until a new winch is built. But it is possible that the Frenchmen may head for town, and we do not want them to raise a hue and cry before Beast and the charbonnerie have completed their task. The element of surprise is one of the few things we have going for us.

Once we are all mounted, I tell the greenlings to head back to camp with our dead and order de Brosse's remaining soldiers to come with me. If they think it strange to take orders from a woman, they wisely keep it to themselves. We ride hard to reach Morlaix before word of our nighttime activity does.

Chapter Forty-One

THE TOWN IS QUIET, AND the city gates are still closed. There is no sign of increased sentries, nor is there any cry of warning. I rein back hard before we ride into sight of the watchmen. "You stay here and intercept any archers from the far bank who think to warn the city," I tell the two remaining men-at-arms. "With luck, you at least injured a few with your blind shots." Hoping they will heed my orders, I leave my horse with them and make my way to the abbey window that was to be left open for us.

The night is quiet, not a whisper of activity or hint of warning. I cannot help but worry that something has gone wrong, that their plans fell through or that they were caught before they could reach the barracks.

At last I see a dark smudge of smoke rising up in a column over the city, and my fists unclench. The column grows thicker and is followed by a faint orange glow. The fires are set. I close my eyes and imagine the thick, choking smoke moving across the sleeping French, filling their mouths and noses as they sleep, the soldiers coming away coughing and choking, struggling for breath. "Fire!" some of them will yell, waking the rest, and a mad, chaotic scramble will ensue as they all try to break free from the hall.

But only one window will be open. All the others blocked or filled with churning smoke so the French will have no choice but to hurl themselves out the one escape route, a long drop to the hard ground below, outside the protection of the city walls.

I draw near the abbey. The abbess of Saint Mer had promised there would be a window left open for us, and there is. I quickly crawl through it and find no one about, so I hurry through the empty corridors to the city beyond.

Outside, the streets seems almost deserted, with only a few pockets of fighting here and there. I stop long enough to pick up a handful of bolts from a fallen soldier. Feeling better thus armed, I continue on my way.

As I draw near the soldiers' garrison, I hear the sounds of fighting. Hugging the wall, I creep forward. At first, I see no one, but as my eyes adjust to the darkened street, I see a knot of charbonnerie pinned behind an overturned wagon by three French archers.

Luckily, I have five bolts. But I will need to be quick and well hidden. I slip silently from the wall to kneel behind a water pump near the barracks building. I stick two bolts in my mouth, then load a third, take aim, and shoot. The man gives a surprised cry as he is struck. His two companions look around, but they were so focused on the charbonnerie they did not see where the arrow came from. I quickly load the second bolt and fire it off.

The second archer is down, but before I can load the third bolt, the last remaining archer turns and fires in my direction. I hear a clang as the bolt strikes the metal handle of the pump. Now—while he is reloading—I take my shot.

It catches him in the temple. I wait for a second to be certain there are no more archers, then give an all-clear wave to the charbonnerie.

The closer I draw to the quay, the louder the sound of fighting becomes. The French must have realized that the purpose of our attack was to allow the British through, and they have chosen to make a last stand by the dock.

I have only two quarrels left but take comfort in the weight of the knives.

When I reach the end of the street, I must step over three fallen bodies. Indeed, I follow a trail of fallen French soldiers the rest of the way to the dock. I emerge from the alley and pause midstep. Beast stands alone, hacking and swinging at nearly a dozen men. His bravery—or stupidity—is breathtaking. He has no regard for his own safety as he cuts through his enemies. Indeed, that may be what gives him such advantage over the others, for none would guess the risks he is willing to take with his own life.

Shaking my head in reluctant admiration, I load the last of my bolts and let them fly, taking down two of his opponents.

Beast does not so much as check his stride. I pull one of the knives from my ankle and send it whipping through the night to land in the neck of one of the French soldiers. He stumbles, giving Beast just the opening he needs to finish the man off.

In the moment that follows, I see a flurry of movement out of the corner of my eye. It is the British! The first of the boats has arrived. The pilot has not even secured the rope around the piling before the British soldiers begin spilling onto the dock. After all, they have had two long weeks cooped up aboard their ships to stoke their anger.

As the fresh troops pour into the town, the remaining French soldiers—those who have not already leaped from the city walls—realize they are outnumbered and quickly surrender their arms.

D'Albret will soon have six thousand British troops riding down his back, and he will be caught between them and the soldiers stationed at Rennes. The duchess now has a decent chance at victory.

And we have bought ourselves some time.

* * *

HIS FAIR ASSASSIN

Beast finds me back at camp, tending the wounded. He strides out of the night, filthy, bloody, and grinning. Unable to help myself, I smile back, for even though he was not marqued, I have been filled with visions of his death. I draw away from the injured men so our greeting will not disturb them. "You did it," I tell him, but my words are lost as he wraps his thick arms around me, picks me up, and swings me around. "We," he corrects me. "We did it. Me, you, the charbonnerie, all of us."

"Put me down," I say, biting back my laughter.

He places me on the ground but does not remove his arms. Instead, he leans in and sets his mouth to mine. It is a lusty kiss, full of joy and triumph and victory. But after a moment, triumph gives way to something else. Something wondrous and fragile.

Beast's hands slide up my waist, firm and solid at my back, a buttress that will not give way, no matter what comes.

One hand continues moving, reaching up to cup my face, and the feel of his rough, callused hands so gentle on my skin makes me want to weep. For all that I have kissed before, I have never felt anything like this. It is as if I have swallowed a tiny piece of the sun, its warmth and light reaching into every corner of my soul and chasing away the shadows.

I surrender to that kiss—surrender to the strength and the courage and the sheer goodness of the man.

A short while later, the rest of the men straggle in. I scan them nervously, looking for the thin, gangly figure of Winnog. Instead, I find Lazare. As our eyes meet, he gives a curt shake of his head. Winnog will not be returning, and Lazare's face is haunted by the unasked-for responsibility I placed on his shoulders. It was unfair of me, for who are we to stop Death? Even I, one of His handmaidens, could only save one of the three in my group.

In spite of our victory, the camp is in somber spirits that night, for it did not come without a cost. In addition to Winnog and de Brosse, we lost Sir Lorril, six soldiers, and seven charbonnerie. De Brosse and Lorril will be returned to their families' holdings for burial in their crypts. The six soldiers will be buried first thing in the morning, and now lie, carefully covered, sheltered by the trees.

However, it is Winnog's death that affects us the most — the awkward, gangly youth was always cheerful, blind to any ill will, and quick to smile. But the charbonnerie do not bury their dead. In keeping with their customs, they make an offering of the bodies to the Dark Mother. They select a clearing far away from the trees, close to an ancient standing stone, and begin building a funeral pyre with as much care and precision as they build their charcoal pits. As if by some silent agreement, one by one the soldiers and men-at-arms rise from their resting places to join the charbonnerie in honoring their dead. Erwan sets the torch to the wood, the fire crackling and hissing as it rushes through the dry kindling and branches.

Within moments, the entire pile is engulfed in flames of red and gold that lick at the bodies of the men. It is an especially hot fire. I do not know if this is some trick of the charbonnerie or simply due to the size of fire a funeral pyre needs. The heat is so intense that we must all step back or risk being roasted ourselves. Thick black smoke churns upward into the night sky, carrying the souls of the charbonnerie to the Dark Mother.

When at last nothing is left of the fire but smoldering ash and embers, we return to the camp. The men do not drift back into their separate groups but instead stay together, talking in quiet voices. Death has brought the fellowship that life could not. I cannot help but think

Winnog would be pleased with this outcome. Even the most arrogant of them, Sir Gaultier, is listening attentively to something Erwan is saying. It is as Beast promised them. Or perhaps it was their Dark Mother's promise—out of the ashes of despair, they have found forgiveness and acceptance.

If they can, perhaps so can I.

I find Beast standing apart from the others, watching the smoldering embers from the pyre. He is still filthy, covered in dirt and soot and blood, and his eyes are heavy and red. I cringe now at how I asked him how he could bear ordering men to their deaths, for clearly it weighs heavily on him.

At the sound of my approach, he looks up.

"Where do we go next?" I ask, pretending we have not just recently shared a kiss.

"Guingamp. A French garrison holds the town, and on the heels of this victory, I think we can fan an uprising to take back the city. But we will rest a day or two so we may finish burying our dead. It will also allow more time for the rumors of our victory here to reach the town."

"Would you be willing to ride out with me tomorrow?" I take a deep breath and clasp my hands together to hide their trembling. It has taken me this long to be certain that this final secret of mine is one he can accept unconditionally. "I have one last thing I must share with you. But this is one you must see."

Chapter Forty-Two

As much as I look forward to putting aside the last of the secrets between Beast and me, I am also looking forward to seeing my sisters. It has been nearly a year, and I miss them as much as any mother misses her babe, for they are the only bright spots in our family.

Near midday, we stop at a tavern to rest the horses and find a meal. It is a quiet enough place, in a sleepy hamlet of a village, and I am fairly certain no one will recognize me. Even so, I am careful to choose a table near the back.

It is not until we are halfway through our meal that other patrons arrive. Two farmers, by the look of them. I ignore them until their talk turns to recent activity in the area.

". . . troop of Lord d'Albret's men rode through here not five days ago . . ."

At these words, I feel as if the ground beneath my feet gives way. I stand up and stride over to their table. "What did you say?" I demand.

The man stares at me as if I am mad. "Around fifty of Lord d'Albret's men came galloping through here about five days ago. Headed to his holding, they were. At Tonquédec."

I turn and head for the door. *No, no, no* beats deep in my breast. Not Charlotte. Not Louise.

Beast leaps up from the table and follows me. "What? What is wrong?"

I barely spare him a glance as I take my cloak from the hook and draw it around my shoulders. "D'Albret and his men passed through here five days ago."

He frowns. "For what reason? Surely he needs all his men at Rennes?"

I shake my head. "I told you it is a foolish commander who puts all his hope in a single plan." I take a deep breath and turn to meet his eyes. "Tonquédec is where we grew up, but only my two younger sisters are in residence there now."

"Does he fear the duchess will try to ransom them?"

I laugh, a dry brittle sound that hurts my ears. "No. *He* plans to ransom them. To me."

I try to hold on to hope for the entire ride to Tonquédec, but the cruelties d'Albret might visit upon the two girls is limited only by my imagination. And my knowledge of him.

I put my horse to a full gallop, not caring if the others cannot keep up. Soon Yannic and the men-at-arms fall behind, but Beast still rides alongside me. The comfort of his presence is all that keeps me from splintering into a hundred broken pieces.

I spare a thought for how he must feel, approaching the place where his sister died, but that brings a fresh wave of despair, so I shove it aside. I pray—beg—Mortain to keep them safe. To let me be wrong. To let him only have sent to Tonquédec for more troops.

But I know in my heart it is a false hope.

When we reach the holding, the long winding road leading up to the castle walls is empty of any traffic. No hunting parties, no departing troops. There are no extra guards posted along the battlements, as there would be if d'Albret were still in residence.

The guard at the gate looks surprised to see me, but lets us pass. As we ride into the empty courtyard, the seneschal comes rushing out, eager to greet me. He takes my horse's rein. "Lady Sybella!"

I dismount, not bothering to wait for a groom. "My sisters, Charlotte and Louise. I must see them."

A look of confusion crosses the seneschal's face. "But they are gone, my lady. They have left for Nantes."

Chapter Forty-Three

THEY ARE GONE.

The truth of that hits my body before my mind can come to terms with it, and I double over. A faint trembling spreads throughout my limbs, making my hands shake and my knees wobble.

They are gone.

It feels as if some monster has just pried my rib cage open and scooped the very heart from my chest, leaving it empty and hollow.

"Demoiselle?" The voice seems to come from far away, and I can barely hear it as the jittery, liquid silver pain courses through me, roaring in my ears as it looks for a way out.

I must get them back.

Without thinking further than that, I turn toward the horses. A large hand clamps down on my arm, restraining me.

I whirl around, reaching for my knife. "Let go."

Beast ignores my knife and reels me closer, like a fish he has caught, until I am up against his armored chest. "They are many days gone," he says softly. "We cannot catch up to them on the open road."

Hiding the knife in the folds of my gown, I glance up at the seneschal. "How long ago did my lord father leave with my sisters?"

"Three days ago, my lady. Only it wasn't your lord father—it was the young master Julian."

This second shock sends me reeling, I even stumble back a step or two. "Julian?"

"Aye, my lady. He and fourscore of your father's men."

A cold dark seed of panic begins in my gut. My father could have taken my sisters for any number of reasons, but Julian? There is only one reason he would do so, and that is to bait a trap for me. He more than anyone knows of the love I bear Charlotte and Louise.

Or could he simply have collected them on our father's orders? As if in answer to my question, the seneschal says, "The young master asked me to give you something should you show up here."

I take a step toward the man. "What? Where is it?"

He sends a page to fetch the box from his office, and I wait impatiently, pacing back and forth. I start to tell the groom to saddle fresh horses, but Beast stops me. "No," he says, his voice low. "We cannot leave this minute. You need rest and time to compose yourself. You cannot clatter across the countryside like a poorly cocked arrow."

And though Beast has but said what I know deep inside to be true, I lash out at him. "How? How can I rest while they are in danger?" The sympathy in his eyes is like another blow, for of course he knows of this misery firsthand. It is precisely what he felt when Alyse went off to marry d'Albret.

And now he will have to endure it a second time.

I press the heels of my palms against my eyes, willing myself to cry, willing the nearly overwhelming pain to find a way out.

But it does not.

How can I tell him now? The last of the secrets between us, the one that I had hoped to lay before him like a gift. But no longer. Now I only have more despair to hand him.

Ignoring my attempt to put space between us, Beast draws close again. "They are not in danger while they are traveling, not with such a large escort," he says. "Nor by my reckoning are they in any true danger—they are merely being used as a means to compel you to your father's side. We have nearly foundered our horses trying to get here, and you yourself are swaying on your feet. Besides, we will need some sort of plan."

I am saved from arguing with him by the seneschal's return. He carries a small wooden casket, carved of lustrous ebony wood and inlaid with ivory. He hands it to me with a little bow, and I find I am terrified of opening it. I take a deep breath, then lift the lid.

Two locks of hair sit upon the red velvet lining. One is the golden brown of my sister Louise's hair and the other the much darker color of Charlotte's. They are braided together with a third lock—the shiny black of Julian's own hair.

I snap the lid closed and press the box to my stomach, as if to hide it, but the image is burned into my vision. It is a clear echo of our own two locks of hair that he carries in the hilt of his sword, a sign of his devotion to me. I think I will be sick.

"Is everything all right?" the seneschal asks in a worried voice.

It is Beast who answers. "We have ridden hard to reach here and my lady is nigh unto exhausted. That is all. Fetch some wine," he orders. "And a waiting woman."

I want to tell him I do not need such coddling, but I can barely breathe, let alone speak. Strong hands press me down so that I am sitting on a low wall. Beast leans over and whispers in my ear, "We have an audience."

His warning is like a pail of frigid water in my face. Of course, he is right. And even now I have no idea how many are blindly loyal to d'Albret or simply follow him out of fear.

As I straighten, I glance at the seneschal. Is that only concern over my well-being I see in his eyes? Or is there a trace of slyness as well? And the others. I glance around the courtyard at the men-at-arms. There are nearly a dozen of them, and they all appear relaxed enough. If they have been given any orders concerning me, the instructions do not seem to include restraining me on sight.

Avoiding Beast's eyes, I compose my face and stand up. "I am overwhelmed by the dearness of the gift my brother has left me," I tell the seneschal. "And tired besides. I would like to retire to my room, if I may. Oh, and our riders follow behind us. When they arrive, see that they and their horses are cared for."

"But of course, my lady." Just then, a serving woman bearing a tray comes into the courtyard, and I recognize Heloise. She greets me joyfully as she hands me a goblet. I take a sip and act as if it refreshes me. "See to the Baron de Waroch's comfort, if you please. We would both like to rest ourselves after our travels."

At the very least, I need to wash the taint of my brother's message from me, so that I am clean when I set out after my sisters.

For all the staff's faults and questionable loyalties, they are well trained, and the holding is in excellent order. My own room is as if I had never left it. "Put the baron in the south guest chamber," I instruct Heloise. It is one of the finest and will confer a certain amount of prestige upon him, and it is close by mine—a mere two doors away.

Once I'm settled in my chambers, Heloise directs two young maids to prepare a bath before the fire, then comes to help me undress. "How did you find my brother, Heloise? Was he in good spirits? I know my lord father is much distracted of late."

"Oh yes, my lady. Lord Julian was in gay spirits and overjoyed to see his sisters once more. Indeed, his pleasure at their reunion reminded me of how much pleasure he always takes in your company."

Her words are spoken innocently enough, but they cause my stomach to shrivel into a tiny knot. "And Louise? How is her health of late?"

There is a tiny pause, one that sets alarms clanging in my breast. "She has not grown any stronger, my lady, that is for certain. But hopefully, as spring comes, her health will return."

I turn to look at her so I may see the truth of her answer in her face. "Was she well enough to make the trip?" As I stare into her brown eyes, I can see a shadow of doubt lurking there.

"Of a certainty, Master Julian thought so. I made sure they placed extra blankets and furs around her and instructed him to be certain she had warm bricks at every opportunity. Lady Charlotte promised to look after her as well."

And she would, of that I had no doubt, but she was only ten years old and a mere child herself.

After I have bathed and dressed, I send my attendants from the room, claiming I need rest. Instead of resting, however, I begin pacing in front of the fire, trying to determine the best way to free my sisters. Will I have any allies on the inside? If Julian is only acting on my father's wishes, I could most likely coax him into giving me aid, but I fear that he may well have acted on his own, for how else to explain the locks of hair?

And even once I have them free—assuming I do not get us all killed in the process—where will I take them? Where will they be safe?

The convent. The answer comes to me like a whisper on a breeze.

But *will* they be safe there? What of the abbess? I think of Charlotte and Louise, so different from me, and then I think of all the younger girls at the convent and know they will be safe enough. Even I was safe for a few short years.

It is only the most rudimentary beginnings of a plan, but it is something.

I glance out the window, heartened to see that the sun has dropped low in the sky. The sooner night comes, the sooner I can depart. Even so, as the shadows lengthen in my room, old memories awaken. Dark memories. Having no wish to be alone with them, I decide to go in search of Beast. It is time for him to hear the last of the secrets between us. Perhaps it will make him as eager to be off as I.

I rap on his door, then let myself in. Beast is just pulling a clean doublet over his head and is scandalized. "Sybella! You cannot be in here. Your servants—"

"Shhh," I tell him. "You forget that these are d'Albret servants, much accustomed to all manner of indiscretion and wickedness. They would be more surprised if I did not visit your room."

He blinks, not sure what to say to that, and I see drops of water still cling to his lashes. He is quiet for a moment, then ask, "With no one else to hear, will you tell me the significance of the locks of hair?"

Just thinking of them is like a fist to my belly. "It is a message. From my brother Julian." My throat closes around the things I want to tell him. Instead, I say, "He carries a lock of my hair entwined with his in the hilt of his sword. It is a message . . ." And here I falter, for I cannot bring myself to say out loud what I fear it means.

But Beast is no fool, and when his large hands clench into fists, I know he has puzzled out the meaning. Now. I must tell him now before my courage fails me yet again.

"There is something you must know. My sister Louise—she is Alyse's daughter."

Chapter Forty-Four

BEAST STARES MUTELY AT ME, as if he has not heard a word I said. Color begins to rise in his face. "What did you say?" he whispers, his gaze fastening to mine like a starving man to a bone.

"Louise is your sister's child."

Beast stares at me a moment longer, his thoughts scudding across his face like storm clouds. Hope, as he realizes some small piece of Alyse still exists, then dismay—nay, anguish—as he realizes that she, too, has been taken from him. By yet another devil-spawned d'Albret. "Why did you not tell me sooner?"

"I had to be certain that you could accept that part of her was d'Albret. Once it was clear you did not hold that against me, I decided it was safe to tell you. I think I had some nascent thought about spiriting them away to safety. Louise, at least. To your own holding, perhaps? But once again, I am too late." Of a surety, my love is as good as a death sentence.

"You think he means to kill them straightaway?"

"There are other ways to hurt her," I say softly.

His head jerks around, his face gone white. "Like they hurt you." It is not a question but a moment of realization. His expression grows thunderous, and his eyes take on that feral light. A low rumble begins deep in his chest, but he chokes it back. Instead, he turns and slams his fist into the casement at the window, causing the leaded glass to rattle.

I wait, holding my breath, uncertain which part of him has control.

When he glances back at me, the fierce light has gone from his eyes, but his face looks as if it were set in gray stone. "I will kill them. All of them."

"I do not think the girls are in any true danger, not yet."

Beast's brows shoot up and he growls his disbelief. I take a deep breath then, for this is not a secret I ever planned to share with him. "Julian—Julian loves me, in his own twisted way. I think he simply sees them as a way to get my attention. Besides, what lies between my brother and me is as much my fault as it is his."

I move over to the window to stare out into the courtyard. Dusk is falling, and the castle retainers are making ready for the coming night. "It was my brother Pierre's fault, as most things often were. When I was but eleven years old he began scratching on my bedroom door, wanting to prove he was a man full grown. At first I thought it was ghosts, but then I realized it was Pierre, and his pinching, probing fingers and hungry mouth frightened me far more than any ghosts.

"The first night, I hid under my covers, wondering how I could keep him away from me. Then I did what I have always done to protect myself. I gave Fortune's wheel a mighty spin and decided to use his own move against him. The next night when he came scratching at my door—more loudly and insistent—it was Julian who called out, 'What do you want?'

"Of course, we nearly ruined the effect by bursting into a fit of giggles, but we pressed the pillows against our mouths to stifle them.

"You have to understand, Julian was my dearest friend as well as my brother. My first memory is of skirts—coarse woolen or linsey cloth skirts as I toddled in bare feet on the stone kitchen floor. But my second memory is of Julian. Of his small, four-year-old hand taking hold of mine and pulling me into the family proper. Of his kind eyes and a face that always held a smile for me. Of hours spent hiding and playing

331

our secret games, games that no one else understood, or cared to. It was Julian who risked much to hide me from the harm and cruelty of this household, and has since we were old enough to walk.

"So he was my friend first, before all else. We had always been stronger together; I thought this would be no exception.

"Would that I could swim back through time or somehow pour the sand through the hourglass backwards. To live one brief moment differently, make a different choice, set my life on a different path. Surely if gods or saints truly existed, they would have given me some warning, some inkling that my actions would send my life down a road I had no wish to take.

"Such was the moment when I invited Julian into my room, for I did not reckon on Julian's own ripening body, or that mine would affect him so. He had always had my best interests at heart, and I never imagined this would be any different."

Beast is still looking out the window, which makes it easier to continue. "But immediately it went wrong—horribly, deeply wrong. Inside, I felt as if some rot had taken hold of my soul. And yet, it made Julian so happy, and it gave him the courage to face down Pierre in all the challenges d'Albret set them. And I had not realized how beholden I felt to him for all the times he had saved me. So while I did not say yes, neither did I tell him no.

"Julian's fingers were not poking or prodding, but gentle, teasing—awakening sensations that I had never experienced before. And I had not imagined that I could ever hold such power over a man—I, who had been at their mercy since I was born.

"But I had not foreseen that our relationship would take a twisted turn and come close to erasing all the good that once lay between us."

I glance up at Beast's face, which is contorted with—horror? Despair? I cannot guess what he is thinking or feeling. He looks down at his enormous, scarred hands. "How you must hate us all," he says.

I stare at him, trying to understand what game he is playing. "But it was *my* fault," I whisper. "*My* weakness and my—"

His head snaps up. "Your need to be loved? Protected? And for that, your brother demanded such a tithe? That is not a price anyone should have to pay for such things. And so I say again, it is a wonder you do not hate us all on sight."

Marveling at how easily he has absolved me, I step forward and take his big hands into my own. "Not you, for you are as different from them as day is from night."

Something in my words has struck him as forcefully as his words did me, and I can see that he wants to kiss me. But he does not, and I—I cannot bring myself to kiss him, not while the confession of such wantonness and wickedness still clings to my lips. The moment draws out into a palpable awkwardness, something that has never existed between us.

Unable to bear it, I turn back to the room and begin straightening the bed curtains. "We leave at first light?"

"Yes," Beast says. "Do you think they are being brought to d'Albret's encampment in front of Rennes? Or to Nantes for safekeeping until he returns?"

"I suspect Nantes, for even d'Albret does not want the inconvenience of girl children on his battlefield."

"Very well. We leave for Nantes at daybreak."

Leaving Beast to his window, I pace the small chamber, forming a mental list of all the preparations we will need to make before we go. There are not many. Provisions and fresh horses. I will not even have to alert the holding that we are leaving; we can simply be gone when they arise in the morning.

"Is Alyse buried here?" Beast asks, still staring out the window.

My skin pulls tight across my bones. "Yes."

He turns from the window, his eyes bleak. "I would like to see her."

I can think of a thousand places I would rather go, for the idea of visiting that place fair sets a wild clang of alarm bells ringing inside me, but I cannot refuse him this chance to visit his sister's final resting place. "Wait here," I tell him. "I must fetch the key."

We step out of the castle into the raw spring evening, both of us quiet and lost in our own thoughts as we cross the inner courtyard and then go through the gate to the outbuildings beyond. Thick gray clouds scuttle across the sky, and I pray they will release their rain tonight rather than tomorrow, as a storm will greatly hamper our progress.

The closer we draw to the castle's cemetery, the more my muscles twitch and spasm, desperate to avoid this place. My knees tremble with the effort to keep walking and not turn and run.

I lift the latch on the old rusty gate and push it open, its rarely used hinges squeaking in protest. My heart begins pounding and my breath comes faster, as if I have just run some great race. Beast looks at me in question. "There," I say, pointing to the large mausoleum set near the back.

It is a grim and frightening place, not meant to bring comfort but to invoke all the demons of hell and damnation; that is what d'Albret is certain his wives deserve for having failed to please him in some way.

The building is made of gray marble, with devils and grotesques decorating its walls. The lintel over the doorway is a parade of cavorting gargoyles formed in darker stone.

"This looks like hell itself," Beast mutters.

"It is meant to." Pressure builds behind my brow as I lean down to fit the key to the rusty lock. I am filled with a violent urge to run away. I clamp down hard on my terror and turn the key. The lock falls open. I set my teeth, lift the latch, and put my shoulder to the door.

It swings open with ease. And then the ghosts are there, cold and lifeless, swirling about me—their whispering voices are no longer coherent, but I know their accusations by heart. There is his first wife, Jeanne, the one who thought to flee to her brother for sanctuary and instead brought death to them all. Next was Françoise, mother of Julian, Pierre, and Gabriel, who died while out riding alone with d'Albret. A fall from her horse broke her neck, some say, but few believe it.

My own mother, Iselle, whose only crime was that she bore him two daughters in a row. The first child was lucky, as she was stillborn. Then the next wife, Jehanne, who dared to take a lover, and then Blanche, whose belly grew great with child—only it was no babe, in the end, but a tumor. Once she was unable to bear children, d'Albret had no further use for her. And after that, Alyse.

One of the ghosts ignores me and floats toward Beast, circling him.

"What is that?" Beast asks as a shiver racks his great body.

"Alyse," I tell him. "It is your sister's ghost. Here." I point to a long white marble coffin. "This is her tomb."

Beast reaches out for my hand. In spite of his size, in spite of all the courage I know he possesses, he looks achingly vulnerable.

I take his offered hand; I cannot do otherwise.

I know I should look away, let him grieve in private, but I cannot. The sweet girl that I knew only briefly is the key to this gentle beast who has captured my heart. Besides, to look away smacks of cowardice, for I must bear witness to the misery my family has wrought.

When he is next to the coffin, he lets go of my hand, bows his great head, and closes his eyes, a spasm of grief distorting his face, his hands clenching into fists. I can feel the surge of his rage pound through his veins. He drops to his knees, and, unable to help myself, I go to him, but tentatively, afraid that after what my family has done to his, he will reject me.

But he does not. He grasps my hand in his and pulls me close until his head rests against my stomach. We stay like that a long time. How long, I do not know. But long enough for his heart to quiet and settle into a slow, steady rhythm, like a funeral drum. When he finally pulls away, I see he has found some measure of peace. But even so, the panic thrumming through my veins does not diminish.

At last he gets to his feet and brushes the dirt from his knees. Then he stops, his gaze falling on the tiny tomb to the right of Alyse's. He turns to me with a stricken look. "Did Alyse have a second babe?"

Slowly, with every muscle in my body screaming at me to stop, I force myself to turn my own gaze to the small tomb. The beating of my heart grows so fast I fear it will burst out of my chest. Fiercely locked-away memories come rushing up from deep inside. Like water through a dam that has broken, they roar in my ears as I read the name engraved on the stone. "No," I say with a voice I hardly recognize as my own. "That babe is mine."

Chapter Forty-Five

I REMEMBER THE SCREAMING . . .

It was as if someone opened her mouth and all the anguish of hell came pouring out. It wasn't until my father clouted me across the face—hard—that the sound stopped and I realized it was me.

And blood. I remember the blood. It was as if the bed had been dipped in a wide swath of dark crimson.

That has been all that I could remember of that day. But now, it all comes rushing back, a great black tide of despair and heartbreak.

My baby. Child of my womb. I have few memories of her, but they too have been locked behind this door.

"She stopped crying the moment they placed her in my arms. I remember her tiny hands, the even tinier fingernails, as she clutched my thumb in a surprisingly strong grip." Her pink rosebud lips rooted around, eager to suckle and draw the warmth of mother's milk into her tiny body.

We had but a hand span of moments together, my babe and I.

"I do not know how—from some unearthly power?—d'Albret heard her birthing cry and made his way to my chamber door. I looked up at his glowering form and bristling black beard and knew that if he let me keep this babe, I would do anything he asked of me. But even as I opened my mouth to tell him that, to give him my complete and unconditional surrender, he strode forward and grabbed the babe from my breast.

"She was so small, he could fit her head in one hand and it terrified me how carelessly he held her, but I said nothing for fear of antagonizing him. He carried her to the window, where he examined her small, dainty features in the light. I held my breath, hoping he was as bewitched by her perfect rosebud lips, her tiny little nose, and her dark blue eyes as I was.

"He lifted his eyes from the babe and turned them on me. 'I had hoped the whelp was Julian's.'

"In that moment, I saw what he meant to do. I struggled to get out of bed. 'Stop him!' I cried, but of course, none of the servants would dare cross him." I look up into Beast's stricken face. "Only Alyse. She was the only one who moved to save my baby. She threw herself at him, trying to grab the baby from his hands, but he struck her, knocking her to the ground, where she hit her head on the leg of the heavy wooden chair. I did not know until days later that she had died from the blow.

"Then he put his thick fingers around my baby's frail neck and broke it. When he was done, he tossed the baby to the floor, and left the room."

That was when the screaming started. And the blood, although I did not learn until later that it was my own birthing blood.

"After that, I remember very little. Strong, gentle hands pushing me back upon the bed. A sweet, bitter syrup being spooned down my throat. And then darkness. Blessed, blessed darkness. With not a drop of crimson in sight.

"I learned afterward that my father rode away two days later. That is what most likely saved my life, for old Nonne would never have taken the risks she did if my father were nearby. But he left me to the indifferent care of Madame Dinan, and she was not concerned that I would not rouse myself from my bed, nor eat a bite. But old Nonne was. She clucked and badgered, poked and scolded, trying so hard to coax me back to the land of the living that I thought I would go mad with it."

Mayhap I did.

"Was it madness that possessed me to slip into the stable one night, take a thick, stout rope from a hook, and knot it firmly around my neck? Was it madness that caused me to jump from the hayloft, hoping to end my life?

"I say it was courage. I said it then and I say it now. I had found the courage to rid the world of at least one of the dark, twisted d'Albrets, for if I was my father's daughter, then I was every bit the abomination he was, and I deserved death just as much as he did. If I could not kill him, I could at least rid the world of my own tainted presence.

"But it was not a long enough fall to break my neck, and as I lay dangling, wondering how long it would take me to die, old Nonne found me and cut me down.

"'Go away,' I told her. She could not stop me. I knew where there was more rope and I would devise a longer drop on my next attempt. There was nothing she could do to stop me, or so I thought. Until she spoke.

"'He is not your father.' Her words caused everything inside me to grow still, and for the first time in many days, a small bit of the despair lifted.

"She told me of my birth then, how I was my mother's last chance to bear a son. Her first child — a daughter — was stillborn. But my mother outsmarted d'Albret, for while giving birth to me, she left with Death, her lover.

"I tried to follow them, and I came from the womb cold and blue, the birth cord wrapped twice around my neck, but Death rejected me. So old Nonne rubbed my limbs and blew into my mouth, trying to force some spark of life back into my cold, limp body. It eventually worked."

"Is she the one who took you to the convent of Saint Mortain?" Beast asks. Somehow I am in his arms, standing with my back against his chest.

"Yes," I say. "That is when I was sent to the convent. I was wild at first; I do not blame the nuns for being exasperated. But eventually, I grew calmer and came to believe that I had found sanctuary there. That I would have a purpose, a place where my dark talents could be put to good use. And they were, at first. I killed several traitors before they could betray us to the French. But then . . ." Here my voice falters, for the truth is, I still cannot believe it happened. "The abbess sent me back into d'Albret's household. She said his aid—or lack thereof—had the power to turn the tides of the war, and I needed to be in place there to keep them apprised of d'Albret's intentions."

Beast says nothing, but his arms tighten around me, as if he would keep me safe even across the strands of time. "I argued with her. I fought. I begged and pleaded, but her mind and her heart were set. And then she dangled the one lure in front of me that she knew I would grasp for: she was certain Mortain would marque the count so that I could kill him. She even claimed Sister Vereda had Seen it. That is why I went, but it turned out that it was but another lie she told me."

"Who was the babe's father?" Beast asks.

"Josse, the blacksmith's boy. Alyse tried to help us run away. She helped us plan and prepare, even thought up the excuses she would give when I did not show up for days. But d'Albret found out anyway." I did not love Josse, but loved the freedom he offered me.

It was Julian who betrayed us to d'Albret.

"They rode Josse down like a dog on the road, then pierced him with a lance. They dragged me back tied in ropes because I fought them so."

I can feel Beast's anger moving through his limbs, but he says nothing. I focus on the fluttering ghosts who have drawn near as I talked.

There is Alyse, who gave me Louise and laughter. And Françoise, who gave me Julian, my first friend, and a true brother before he became my enemy. My own mother, who gave me life, and Jeanne, whose story, I now realize, was no cautionary tale, but one of courage—the courage to face death rather than the horrors life held for her.

For all the atrocities d'Albret has committed—and there have been many—it is these innocents he swore to love and protect that have been betrayed most grievously. These are the ones that deserve to be avenged.

Any doubts that I held about Beast being strong enough to bear all the horrors of my past are gone. The last of my secrets has been spilled, and still he holds me in his arms as if he will never let me go.

Something wakes me. At first I think it is the silvery moonlight streaming in the window and falling across the bed. And then I hear a faint sound, like barren winter branches rustling in the wind. Although I do not hear my name precisely, I know that the sound is calling me, beckoning me closer, and I am afraid. Afraid it is the ghosts of d'Albret's dead wives, calling me to account.

But the sound comes again, and I know I must go. Quietly, I lift the covers, swing my feet onto the floor, and rise from the bed.

The sound comes a third time, and it is as if there is a string tied to my heart that pulls me toward it. I step into my shoes, throw my cloak around my shoulders, and slip from the room.

It is the dead of night and all is quiet. For the first time that I can remember, I do not feel afraid in my father's house. Whether it is because of Beast, who sleeps nearby, or because of the otherworldly voice beckoning me, I do not know. Perhaps I simply have nothing more to lose.

The castle corridors are empty, as is the great hall. There are a few sentries posted at the door, but since I am born of darkness, the shadows are my friend, and I use them to hide my passing.

Outside, the night has turned bitterly cold. Mortain's freeze, the farmers call it, an unexpected cold snap that threatens the emerging spring crops.

And that's when I know who is calling me. I pull my cloak closer and hasten my steps, not surprised when the rustling leads me to the cemetery.

The waning moon casts the graveyard in pale silver light, but I am drawn to the darkest corner where the shadows are the deepest. As I approach, a tall, dark figure emerges. He is dressed all in black and smells of the earth in early spring, when the fields have just been tilled. With a jolt that pierces my heart, I recognize my true father. Every doubt I have had that He existed, every fear that I have possessed that I am tainted by d'Albret's dark blood, falls away from me in that moment. Like a lamb in a field that trots unerringly to its own mother, I know that I am His. At first, the wave of gratitude and humility this brings makes me want to fall on my knees before Him and bow my head. But as I look upon Him, the years of anguish and terror unfurl inside me, and a great whip of anger lashes out. "Now? You come to me now? Where were You all those times when I was small and terrified and truly needed You? Where were You when d'Albret cut down the innocent time and time again?"

Then, just as suddenly as it came, the anger is gone. "And why did You abandon me? When You came for my mother, why did You not take me with You?" The last question comes out in a whisper.

"It was your own mother's wish, that you live." When He speaks, His voice is like a cold wind from the north, bringing snow and frost. "She prayed not only to be delivered from her husband but that other women be spared her fate. That prayer brought Me to her so that I was there when you were born, to see you safely into this world as well as to carry your mother away, as I had promised."

"So You did not reject me?"

His voice, like the rustle of dying leaves, fills my head. "Never."

"But I have sinned against You and acted on my will alone, rather than Yours. Do I not deserve Your retribution?"

"No, for you are My daughter and I would no more punish you for plucking flowers from My garden than I would for your drawing breath. Besides, the men you killed had earned their deaths. If they had not, the knife would have missed, the quarrel gone wide, or the cup laced with poison remained untouched."

"Are the marques not meant for us to act upon?"

I realize I do not so much as hear Him speak as feel Him inside my mind, as if He is unfurling some great tapestry before me, filling me with understanding.

As a person's death draws near, his soul ripens and readies itself for plucking. That ripening can be seen by some. As souls ripen, they begin to loosen from their bodies, much as fruit makes ready to leave the branch. But even the same fruits on the same tree fall at different times—occasionally defying all odds and clinging throughout the entire winter.

And just like one who toils in the orchards, He does not control everything. Not the wind, nor the rain, nor the sun. And just as those elements shape the fruit on the tree, so do many factors shape a man's life, and therefore his death.

Then He reaches out and lays His cold hand on my head, and His grace and understanding fill me, burning away all vestiges of d'Albret's evil darkness weighing on my soul until the only darkness that remains is that of beauty. The darkness of mystery, and questions, and the endless night sky, and the deep caverns of the earth. I know then that what Beast said was true: I am a survivor, and the taint of the d'Albrets was but a disguise I wore so that I could pass among them. It is no more a true part of me than the cloak on my back or the jewels I wear. And just as love has two sides, so too does Death. While Ismae will serve as His mercy, I will not, for that is not how He fashioned me.

Every death I have witnessed, every horror I have endured, has forged me to be who I am—Death's justice. If I had not experienced these things firsthand, then the desire to protect the innocent would not burn so brightly within me.

There in the darkness, shielded by my father's grace, I bow my head and weep. I weep for all that I have lost, but also for what I have found, for there are tears of joy mixed in with those of sorrow. I let the light of His great love fill me, burning away all the tendrils and traces of d'Albret's darkness, until I am clean, and whole, and new.

Beast finds me just before daybreak. Asking no questions, he helps me to my feet. The small circle of frost on the ground is all that remains of Mortain's presence.

No. That is not true. For I am utterly transformed by His presence. All the fear and doubt and shame has been stripped away, like dead leaves in a winter storm. Only the clean, strong branches remain.

I know now why d'Albret bore no marque, and I also know why he has not yet died. Even better, I now possess something I never had before: faith. Faith in myself, faith in Mortain. But most of all, faith in love. Hate cannot be fought with hate. Evil cannot be conquered by darkness. Only love has the power to conquer them both.

With the strength of that love flowing strong within me, we make ready to go rescue my sisters.

Chapter Forty-Six

WE RIDE HARD FOR NANTES, stopping only when it is so dark we cannot see the road in front of us, then start again as soon as there is light enough to continue. Beast brings Yannic and Lazare and two of his men-at-arms. There is little time for talking, and we collapse bone tired into our bedrolls each night and fall into a dreamless sleep.

When we draw near Rennes, Beast dispatches the two men-at-arms with messages for Duval and the duchess. As we turn and head south, I wonder if this was my destiny all along, to face d'Albret with Beast at my side, for surely it will take the power of our two gods to bring him down. Or—I glance at the silent Lazare, whose rouncey struggles to keep up with our stronger horses—two gods and the Dark Mother Herself.

By the time we draw near Nantes, we have a plan firmly in place. The desire to ride off straightaway and storm through the gates of the city to the palace is nearly overwhelming. But we will have no prayer of success if we face d'Albret in our current exhausted state. Indeed, we barely have a prayer of success if we are rested and fully prepared, so we stop at the abandoned hunting lodge, the very one where this journey first began, hoping that it is still abandoned.

"Empty," Beast says when he returns. "It does not look like anyone has been here since we left."

That is all the rest of us need to hear. We put our heels to our horses' flanks and head for the stable. They hardly need any steering, for they are as exhausted as we and go eagerly to the scent of hay and the promise of rest.

For all my exhaustion, I cannot sleep. I toss and turn, causing the bed ropes to creak in protest. I can think only of the morrow and getting my sisters to safety. I wonder where they are being kept and who is guarding them. Hopefully, they are in one of the palace's many chambers rather than in the dungeon, for Louise's health will quickly fail if she is kept in such a foul, damp place. And while d'Albret might not care for her, he would not want to lose a bargaining piece in this game he plays.

The desire to leave now is so overpowering I fear I will have to tie myself to the bed. To wait here all alone for morning when I can finally act is agony.

But you are not alone, a small voice whispers inside my heart. A great, giant-sized love waits in the next room.

Suddenly, I wish to drown myself in that love, don it like a shield or a suit of armor to keep my doubts at bay. Without stopping to think, I throw aside the covers, get to my feet, and step out into the hall.

When I pause at the door, my doubts catch up to me. Will he think me wanton or depraved? Surely not, for he has learned every horrible secret I possess and has not flinched. It is impossible not to be humbled by the sheer immensity of that gift.

I knock once on the door, then open it.

The room is dark but for a trickle of moonlight coming in from the window onto the bed. At my entrance, Beast starts to reach for his sword, then stops. "Sybella?"

I shut the door softly behind me. "I have slept with five men, not dozens. Three because I had to, one because I thought he could save me, and the fifth so I could get close enough to kill him."

He says nothing, but watches my fingers as they unlace my chemise.

"I have never lain with a man out of love." I meet his gaze steadily. "I would like to do so at least once before I die."

"You love me?"

"Yes, you great lummox. I love you."

He lets out a sigh. "Sweet Camulos! It's about time."

I cannot help it. I laugh. "What do you mean?"

"I have loved you since you first slapped that vile mud on my leg and ordered me to heal."

"As far back as that?"

"I was too stupid to know it, but yes."

"When did you realize you felt that way?" I am embarrassed to ask such a pitiable question, but I yearn to know.

He tilts his head in thought. "When the abbess announced you were d'Albret's daughter."

I gape. "*That* is when you decided you loved me?"

He lifts his hands, as if in surrender. "There was no *deciding* about it. It was just *there*. A great, unlooked-for complication. It is why I grew so angry, thinking the gods were having a rich jape at my expense." He shakes his head in disbelief.

"So does that mean you will lie with me?" My voice sounds far more vulnerable than seductive.

He swings his legs over the side of the bed, his face growing serious. "Sybella, with all that you have endured at the hands of men, you do not have to do this. You do not have to give your body to earn my love. It is already yours."

"I know," I whisper. "But I would go to my death having truly loved at least once."

He rises to his feet and crosses the short distance between us. I always forget how much he towers over me. Most likely because I never look upon him with fear. His hand comes up to smooth the hair back from my face, as if he would see it—*me*—more clearly. That simple gesture makes me feel more exposed than standing here in naught but my shift.

"I want you to be with me for the right reasons. Not because you feel you must or because you fear we will die, but because you want it with your heart and your body."

I stare into his eyes—eyes that are only part human, just as I feel only partly human. If ever there was a man who could understand—and accept—the darkness in me, it is Beast. "Who better to entrust both to than the mighty Beast of Waroch?"

He pulls me closer, his gaze drifting down to my lips. I am surrounded by the heat from his body, can feel his heart thundering in his chest. He lowers his head until our lips are almost touching. When he hesitates, I rise up on my toes to close the distance between us and press my lips to his. Our kiss is sweet and raw and full of hunger. My hunger. His hunger. A hunger born of two lifetimes.

It is also full of rightness. Such blessed *rightness*. No dark ribbon of shame unfurls inside me. No voice screams *No* inside my head. I do not have to close my eyes and pretend I am a hundred leagues away.

His hand moves downward, his fingers trailing along my neck, and I savor the rough feel of his callused hand, marvel that a hand that has such a capacity for killing can also be so gentle. His other hand encircles my waist, then slowly skims up my ribs, stopping just before he reaches my breast. He rests his forehead against mine, breathing hard. "Are you certain?" he whispers.

That is when I hear it, the faint note of disbelief in his voice. "I have rarely been more certain than I am in this moment," I say.

Then his mouth is back on mine and the carefully banked heat that has smoldered between us for so long erupts. Still, no darkness threatens to claim me. Instead, true desire, as uncertain and ungainly as a newborn colt, awakens in my body. My own limbs become unfamiliar, my movements uncertain. I, who have only ever been practiced and skilled. But I do not care, for all that has come before is but a distant memory. All that matters is us. Only us. This moment. His hand on my body. The mingling of our breath. Our hearts that are so close they now beat as one.

With a dizzying swoop, he picks me up and cradles me in his arms, surprising a laugh out of me. "What are you doing?"

He grins. "I've always wanted to carry a fair maid away and ravish her."

"Methinks you should reconsider who is ravishing whom," I murmur, surprised at how much I enjoy the sensation of his arms around me, of being carried.

When we reach the bed, he gently lays me down, his eyes drinking me in. And even though it is his trick, to see into my soul, in this moment I see into his—his doubts and uncertainties—and see that I want this. That I want *him*. I reach up and take his hand, pulling him down beside me. "If you do not know how to ravish, I will gladly teach you."

He laughs then, and once again I place my mouth on his, letting his laughter fill all the dark places inside me.

And then the laughter fades, and for a brief moment, I am reminded of the charbonnerie's stories and feel certain that it is not Amourna, or even Arduinna, who blesses our night together, but the Dark Mother Herself, with Her gift for new beginnings.

I awake in the morning with Beast's thick arm wrapped tightly around me. It reminds me for a moment of one of the roots of the great trees in the forest that anchor them to the earth.

I know I should wake him, that we have an urgent, impossible task before us, but I am hungry for one more moment, wanting to savor the magic that has taken place between us. Oh, it is not the magic that the poets speak of in their love poems, but a different, far stronger magic.

I stare down at his face. It has not grown more beautiful since I first found him, festering in the dungeon, and yet it is more dear to me than my own.

His eyes open just then, and he catches me studying him. "What?" His early-morning voice is gruff, like two rocks being rubbed together.

"I was wondering, since I have kissed you three times now, if you might turn into a handsome prince."

At the sight of his quick, easy grin, I feel my heart dance in my chest. "Alas, you are still stuck with a toad, my lady."

"Ah, but it turns out I am quite fond of toads." I lean down and kiss his nose, surely one of the silliest things I have ever done, but I do not care. "Even toads who sleep the entire day away." I plant one more kiss upon his face, then force myself from the bed.

I do not even mind that he watches me dress.

When I reach the kitchen, Lazare looks up from the knife he is sharpening, his keen eyes missing nothing, so that I feel almost naked before him.

"Someone is happy this morning," he smirks.

"Someone is eager to feel the kiss of cold steel before he's even broken his fast."

His smile widens, for the fact that I have not already pulled my knife on him only serves to prove him right.

"Don't you have a cart to fetch or something?" I ask.

He nods toward the window. "It's here already. Some of us didn't laze about all morning."

I look outside and see three other charbonnerie and a cart full of charcoal. Our means to gain access to the city has arrived. "Well then. Let's get going."

The strategy that worked so well when we traveled to Rennes serves us equally well here. In no time at all, I have tucked my hair up under a coif and smeared a thin film of coal dust over my face and hands. My altered appearance will render me nearly invisible, for guards pay little attention to lowly peasants and even less attention to the shunned charbonnerie.

But Beast's huge stature is far too recognizable. This time he is laid in the cart, covered with rough hempen cloth, then buried under a layer of charcoal. Lazare fashions some sort of vent through which he can breathe.

We pass through the city gates and receive nary a second glance, and Lazare steers us directly to a blacksmith he knows, a fellow, he assures us, who will be most happy to give us aid. Even though he is not closely allied with the charbonnerie, he certainly does not bear any love for d'Albret or his occupation of the city.

With the first part of our plan successfully behind us, it is time for me to get cleaned up so I may pay a visit to the convent of Saint Brigantia that sits just across from the palace.

Chapter Forty-Seven

I AM SHOWN IMMEDIATELY TO the abbess's chamber, where she waits for me at her desk. She is a large woman, nearly as tall as a man, with a high, intelligent brow and heavy-lidded eyes. I am shown in, and she motions for the novitiate to close the door on her way out, then leans back in her chair and studies me.

"What does one of Mortain's own daughters want from those who serve Brigantia?"

"I do not come on official business, Reverend Mother, but to ask for your aid in rescuing two young girls. They have been taken by Count d'Albret and I fear for their welfare."

"As well you should," she mutters.

"In order to get them to safety, I must gain access to the castle. A Brigantian habit would provide a most excellent disguise and allow me to enter the palace without scrutiny."

"Do you plan to go alone?"

"No, I will have assistance."

"Then you will need more than one."

Unable to help myself, I smile at the thought. "No, Reverend Mother. I will be accompanied by two men."

She raises one eyebrow. "And who are they?"

"One of them is the Beast of Waroch."

"The same Beast of Waroch who stood so nobly before our own duchess but a few weeks ago?"

"The very one."

"Then I have something else I would share with you. There is a secret passage that runs from the convent to the palace. It was built by the late duke. After he and his family narrowly avoided capture by the French when they stormed the city in one of the many skirmishes, he had his engineers build a secret escape route out of the palace so his daughters would never come that close to capture again. You can use that to free the girls."

It appears all the gods are in favor of this venture, and it is all I can do to keep from leaping over the desk and hugging her. "'Tis a great solution to a most vexing problem. Thank you."

"So it is but a rescue mission?" Her sharp eyes study me.

I hold her gaze. "That is the focus of our foray."

"Good. Although if there are other opportunities that present themselves, I hope that you will seize them. You will need to be most careful. D'Albret and his troops returned three days ago, he and his forces riding hard from Rennes. Whatever he had hoped to accomplish there did not happen, and he and his men are in a foul humor."

That is good news, then, for surely that must mean that his saboteurs were not able to help him gain entrance to the city.

"That is why things are so quiet here. The townsfolk have taken to their homes and closed their shops, not wanting to come into contact with d'Albret or his men when this mood is upon them."

For some reason, my thoughts go to the silversmith who fashioned the key for me. "That is most wise of them."

She pushes herself to her feet and crosses to the window that overlooks the moat. "There is something else you should know. There are reports, reliable reports, that the French regent and a large fighting force are encamped a mere five leagues upriver."

So close! "Did they think to take advantage of d'Albret's absence by invading the city while he was making war on Rennes?"

She shakes her head. "I do not know, for messengers have been flying fast and furious between d'Albret and the French for the last fortnight. Whatever it is, they may be planning it together."

She turns to face me. "I do not tell you this to dissuade you but so that you will keep your eyes and ears open. If you were to catch wind of what is afoot while you are moving these girls to safety, I am sure the duchess would be most grateful. Now, go fetch your companion, and when you return, I will escort you to the passage myself."

The tunnel is long and dark, and the oil lantern the abbess gave us casts just enough light so that we do not trip and fall. The walls are of dank stone, dripping with damp from the nearby river and the moat overhead. The darkness swallows up most of the light from the lantern. It feels as if we have stepped into the long, murky throat of some monstrous serpent from the legends of old.

When finally the meager light shows a stone staircase, we quicken our pace and hurry up the stairs. According to the abbess, since the duke was aware that his own chamber might well be the first taken in any hostilities, the door opens into the room the duchess and Isabeau shared as children.

I quietly lift the latch, then slowly pull the door open—only to be met by another wall of wood. No, not a wall, but the back of a huge wooden headboard. The door is set into the wall behind the room's bed and further hidden from view by the bed curtains. There is just enough space for a person to pass through, although Beast will have to turn himself sideways, and even then it will be a tight fit.

Yannic will wait in the passageway armed with his slingshot and a long dagger, as we do not dare risk having our avenue of escape sealed off by our enemies.

The bedchamber opens onto a small receiving room, and even though I sense no hearts beating in there, I pause. It is as if some invisible barrier holds me back, my mind remembering all that I have endured within these walls, even while my heart sings that it is different now. *I* am different now. I had been forced to disguise my true nature even from myself—for what hounds would not be terrified by the wolf that stalks among them? And even a baby wolf must be given a chance to grow. That thought allows me to step into the chamber. Beast follows silently on my heels.

At the door, I peer out to see if there are any guards or sentries posted, but the hallway is empty. "You have to wait here," I tell Beast. "At least until I know where they are, and how heavily guarded." His eyes burn with frustration, for he is not used to standing idly by while others put themselves in danger, but he knows that for now, stealth is our best weapon, not brute force.

In the hall, I am careful to keep my head down and hope the wimple I wear will shield my features from any casual passersby. The farther I move away from the door, the more it feels as if some great weight is pressing down upon me. Instead of making it hard to breathe like it once did, the force propels me forward, much like a crashing wave hurls a boat toward shore.

I have not gone two doors down before I hear voices—the clear, high voices of children. They come from inside the third chamber. There are no guards posted, so I take a deep breath, remind myself that I am Mortain's daughter, then rap on the open door. The voices stop.

"Come in." It is Tephanie, and I breathe a sigh of relief. I had half feared Madame Dinan or Julian himself would be guarding the girls.

But no doubt they did not expect me to come gamboling into the lion's den unannounced.

I enter the room, careful to keep my eyes lowered, and slip my hands inside my sleeves to my hidden knives, in case I need them quickly. "Hello." I pitch my voice deeper than normal. "I am Sister Widona, from the convent of Saint Brigantia, and I have been sent to see to the child they call Louise. She is said to have contracted lung fever."

Tephanie draws closer until I can see the tips of her plain brown shoes poking out from under her skirt. "Not lung fever, no. But she coughs all the time and her lungs seem weak. We would be very grateful for any healing skill you care to offer."

"But of course," I say as I shut the door behind me and then slowly look up.

It is Louise who recognizes me first. She leaps from the couch where she has been playing with her doll and runs forward, flinging herself at me. I pull her close, savoring the feel of her small arms wrapped around my neck. She has grown thin and frail, and her cheeks bear an unhealthy flush. Tephanie watches her with a mixture of surprise and dismay until her startled gaze moves up to my face. Her mouth drops open and her hand flies to her face. "My lady."

I hold my finger to my lips and pray she is loyal to me and the girls.

Slowly, Charlotte rises from the couch, her solemn brown eyes never leaving my face. "I knew you'd come," she says, and I open my arms to her as well. Stiffly, she walks over to me, but she does not throw herself at me like Louise. She has always been more formal, so I reach out and pull her close. Only then does she relax into my embrace.

Tephanie glances to the door. "My lady. It is not safe for you here. They say . . . they say the most horrible things about you."

I smile at her. "Some of them may even be true," I tell her. "But for now, I have come to get the girls to safety."

Tephanie crosses herself. "Then my prayers have not been in vain."

"You must come with us, Tephanie, or else you will be gravely punished for their disappearance."

Her earnest gaze meets mine. "My lady, I would follow you anywhere."

"Good. Then follow us to safety." I set the girls from me, but Louise sways on her feet. I let go of Charlotte's hand and pick up Louise so I may carry her in my arms. "Grab their cloaks. And boots. And any warm clothing you can find quickly. We do not have much time."

She nods and hurries to the chest at the far side of the room.

I turn my attention back to the girls. "We must be very, very quiet. If anyone sees us, they will try to stop us, and we may never see one another again. Do you understand?"

Both nod solemnly, and Tephanie returns with her arms full of garments. "Shall I dress them now, my lady?"

"No, there will be time enough when we reach safety. Can you carry all that?"

"Yes, but what about you? Can you carry Louise the whole way?"

"I will not have to." Just as we are ready to leave, there is a sound at the door. I whirl around to find Jamette staring at us.

"You're back? I had hoped you would never return."

"A minute more and I won't," I tell her. "The girls and I are leaving, and you will never have to see me again."

Indecision flits across her pretty, shallow face and I find that all the hatred I once felt for her is gone. "Come with us if you like. You do not need to stay here."

"No." She all but spits the word. "I will not betray my lord father. Or yours."

Suddenly, I am afraid for her, afraid the full force of our fathers' anger will land on her silly head. "Do not be a fool, for they do not bear you the same loyalty and would wring your neck as soon as listen to your prattle. Come with us. You can have a new life, free of all this lying and deceit."

Bitterness flashes in her eyes and she takes a step closer to me, her hands gripping her skirts. "I do not want a new life. I have always only wanted your life. All the admiration you commanded, all the attention you garnered, all the riches heaped upon you—those would be mine if you were gone."

"If that is what you want, then all you must do is let us go."

She shakes her head. "It is not that simple, and well you know it. I will be horribly punished if I do not stop you."

And she is right. As she turns to go, I reach out to grab her, but Louise is heavy and I am not fast enough. Jamette steps beyond my grasp and dashes down the hallway.

I turn to the others. "We must go. *Now.*"

The hallway is still clear, but it will be only a matter of minutes before others arrive. I clasp Louise tightly, hold Charlotte's hand, and pull them toward the bedchamber and Beast. If the guards find us before we reach safety, Beast will be our only hope.

Chapter Forty-Eight

WHEN WE ENTER THE ROOM, he looks up, the ferocity of his expression startling even to me. Then his gaze goes unerringly to Louise. Charlotte shrinks into my skirts, but Louise studies him curiously. "Who are you?" she asks in her high, clear voice. Beast glances at me, helpless, and I see agony in his eyes.

"Do not be afraid of him, Louise."

"I'm not," she says, sounding faintly affronted.

"Good. For he was very close to your mother and will see you to safety, no matter what happens. You, too," I tell Charlotte. Then I turn my full attention to Beast. "We must hurry," I warn him. "I was spotted, and Jamette has gone to raise the alarm."

He nods, then looks surprised as I thrust Louise into his arms. "We will need a diversion so they do not discover your escape route. I must stay behind," I say.

At his horrified expression, I rush to explain. "They cannot come anywhere near this room, else the passageway will be discovered and they will find you within minutes."

"I will not leave you here!"

His eyes! Oh, his eyes! The fury and the anguish in them rob me of my breath. Two things define him — his honor and his loyalty — and he is being asked to abandon one of them.

Sensing his anger, Louise shifts restlessly in his arms, drawing his attention back to her. Using that to my advantage, I thrust Charlotte's hand in his, quickly kiss both girls, then begin pushing them toward the bedchamber. "You must get them safely away. Everything else can wait."

"I will be back," he says, then leans forward and plants a savage, desperate kiss upon my lips, as if he would have me feel the force of his promise.

I do not indulge myself by watching them go but instead turn and take off the distinctive blue habit so d'Albret will not think to punish the Brigantian convent. I stuff it in one of the chests in the room and then peer out into the hall. I can hear approaching footsteps in the distance, but no one is within sight yet, so I step into the corridor and begin running in the opposite direction.

The sounds behind me draw closer, but if I can gain the main floor, I may be able to slip out the doors and lose myself among the servants in the courtyard. I hit the stairs at a full run, but my hope is quickly crushed by the sound of boots rushing toward me.

It is not the guards or soldiers or even Captain de Lur, but Julian. "Sybella!" His voice is full of both hope and caution. "You're back!"

"I came for our sisters."

"Sybella." He reaches out to grab my arms.

I jerk away. "No. *No.*" And now that I am telling him no, I cannot stop. It is as if there is a great storm of noes that have been building inside me for years. "No, no, no."

His brow furrows in concern and he tries again to take my arm. "Don't touch me!" I pull out of his grip, breathing hard.

He stares at me in dismay. "What is wrong?"

"You. Us. The love you think is between us."

He shakes his head gently, as if something is amiss with his hearing. "You don't mean that."

The confusion in his voice reminds me of when he was a young boy, and it pierces my heart. "I do," I whisper.

"Why did you run away?" Even though he tries to hide it, the pain in his voice is clear.

What do I tell him? Do I speak of the convent, and my work there? Or do I simply say what is in my heart, the reason I went to the convent in the first place? "Because I was dying inside, Julian. I could not bear this life one moment longer."

"But we had plans. I have been working to gain our father's trust so he will grant me a holding of my own. Then we will have a life together. The life we have dreamed of since we were children."

"That you dreamed of Julian, not me." In spite of the gentleness of my voice, he acts as if he has been struck.

"But we talked of it, planned it together . . ."

"When we were young, Julian, too young to know that sisters and brothers did not marry and have babies together. What was between us was wrong—"

"Why should we care what the world thinks? They do not understand the bond we share. The horrors we have endured together. I wouldn't have survived if not for you, Sybella."

I close my eyes. "Nor I without you, but that does not make what you asked of me right. I only did it because I was afraid of losing you, afraid that you would no longer protect me or be my friend."

He stares at me in silence, as if he has never truly seen me before. "I was always your friend and would never have stopped protecting you."

"Julian, you betrayed me! You told on the blacksmith's boy and had him killed!"

His eyes are wild and his breath grows ragged. "I saved you from a life as a blacksmith's whore—bearing his dirty little brats and living an existence of toil and labor. I saved you from a lifetime of looking over your shoulder wondering when our father would find you, for he would never have stopped searching. Surely you know that."

"If all that is true, as you say, then how could you ever have used our sisters against me?"

"I was sent to collect them on Father's orders."

"And the locks of hair? What were those, Julian, if not a threat?"

"Is that what you think? That I would do such a thing?"

"Yes," I whisper. "I think you would wrap it up in fine excuses and pretty lies, but only to hide from yourself what you truly intended."

"I just wanted you to know that I would keep them safe, as I kept you safe all those years. And this is how you thank me."

But even now, I do not know if he tells the truth or only thinks he does.

In the silence that follows, I hear once more the sound of booted feet fast approaching. I step toward Julian. "When they come, tell them you have found me and stopped me. Here, take out your sword to convince them."

Julian shakes his head and steps away from me.

I reach out and wrest his sword from his scabbard, then shove the hilt into his hand. "Do it." Just as I step in front of his sword point, Captain de Lur, Jamette, and half a dozen men-at-arms reach the landing.

"There she is," Jamette says. "But where are the others?"

"What others?" Julian asks, looking from me to Jamette and back again.

"Tephanie and the girls," Jamette says. "Sybella said they would all be leaving together."

"I found only her. Where did you last see them?"

"In the small solar."

De Lur jerks his head, and half the men retrace their steps to the solar. Then he turns back to Julian. "Were you stopping her? Or aiding her? One can never quite tell with you."

Julian's eyes are colder than frost on stone. "Are you so very certain of that, de Lur? What if my lord father has trusted me above all others and we have but played a deep game to draw her out?"

My gaze snaps to Julian's face, but even I cannot tell if he is bluffing. Ignoring him, de Lur turns to me. "Your lord father knew just what bait to use to set the trap, and now here you are. Unfortunately, you have chosen an inconvenient time to make your reappearance, as Lord d'Albret has pressing business elsewhere at the moment."

I arch one eyebrow in disbelief, hoping my scorn will goad him into telling me d'Albret's business. "More pressing than exacting revenge on his prodigal daughter?"

"More pressing even than that."

My mind scrambles, trying to find a way to turn this to my advantage. "Take me to Marshal Rieux, then." For he has at least some small shard of decency and honor. Or at least, he did.

De Lur smiles. "The good marshal is no longer with us. He didn't have the stomach for what was required."

I do not know if he means that they have parted ways or that Rieux is dead.

"You will have to avail yourself of the castle dungeon's hospitality until your father returns." He turns to his men. "Bring her."

Two men step forward to grab hold of my arms. Desperate to keep my knives, I jerk my arms out of their reach before they can touch me. "I do not need to be dragged like a sack of wheaten flour."

De Lur smiles, then fingers the faint white scar on his cheek. "Oh, but you do, my lady."

I do not like what I see in his eyes, and I shoot Julian a desperate gaze, but he is lost in his own thoughts, painful ones, by the look on his face. The men reach for me again, and this time they grab my arms and feel the knives at my wrists. De Lur orders them removed and then searches me for any other weapons.

Once again I must endure his touch, must feel his hot breath against the back of my neck, must listen as his breathing grows heavier. I say nothing, only watch him. I am not certain that I could best him in a fight, but it would be close, and I would certainly cause him grave injury. At the very least, he or his men would have to kill me in self-defense. But I am not certain I am willing to embrace death just yet. Not while there is still a chance I can get to d'Albret.

As they escort me to the dungeon — the very dungeon Beast once occupied — my heart begins to pound like a drum and I can hear my own blood beating in my ears, for this is the stuff of every nightmare I have ever had — being helpless and at d'Albret's mercy once more.

Chapter Forty-Nine

IT IS A LONG, DARK night. Panic and terror do their best to stalk me, but I keep them at bay, knowing that if I succumb, I will only be the weaker for it. Terror is as much one of d'Albret's weapons as his sword or fists, and he wields it with deadly accuracy, using it to sap the will and crush the spirit.

The tower ghosts flutter near me, drawn to my warmth. To distract myself, I force my mind to stillness, curious if these ghosts will tell me their stories.

But there is nothing other than a faint restless rippling in my mind, no cries of anguish, no begging for revenge, no whispered tales of the horror that was inflicted upon them. These ghosts are far older than the others, here long before d'Albret. Maybe they were not wronged in death, but simply died.

Quiet understanding comes, like a soft breeze, and I finally realize why I am able to see not just the souls that depart from their earthly bodies but the restless ghosts who linger. If I am Death's justice, I must be able to hear their stories.

I turn my attention to the living and what wrongs they might whisper to me. Jamette is naught but a victim, too frightened to see the bars of her own cage. And Madame Dinan? She was innocent once, but no longer. She chose to look away from the truth of d'Albret's actions once too often, thus crossing the boundary from innocent to guilty.

And Julian? He was not a child of Mortain and did not inherit that extra measure of strength, and yet he rejected so much of what d'Albret wanted him to be, fought so hard against the taint that marred him. Unlike Pierre, who embraced it all.

Julian always offered me kindness and love where Pierre and d'Albret offered only cruelty and pain. We had survived so many horrors together, our life was awash in so much wrongness, that the warped love he held out to me felt almost right. Almost. And in his own way, Julian was protecting me—from Pierre.

I know that love is required to defeat the monster before me, but I am at a loss as to how to manifest that love. I face him secure in Mortain's love, and Beast's love, and love for my sisters, but I do not know how to turn that into a weapon that I can use against him.

I must trust now in the god whose blood flows in my veins and in my own true nature. And while it is not as dark and twisted as d'Albret's, it *is* dark. And strong. And will hopefully offer some small chance of victory. I must have faith, but having faith is hard, so very much harder than despair.

The sound of a key in the lock wakes me with a jolt, and it is all I can do to keep from leaping to my feet and rushing over to peer through the bars. Slowly, I stand.

When the door is flung open, two soldiers stride in, then drag me into the outer chamber. De Lur is there. "It is time to face your father's justice."

I am escorted to a chamber where Madame Dinan herself is waiting for me, along with Jamette. Two servants are filling a tub with water. Dinan does not even bother to look at me, just stares out the window. "Get her out of those rags," she orders.

The two servants step forward, eyeing me warily, but I do not make their job difficult, for none of this is their fault. I watch Jamette the whole time, hoping to unnerve her, for it is her duplicity that has brought me here. "All you had to do was turn the other way," I tell her under my breath, "and I would have been out of your life forever. Julian might even have come to hate me eventually, leaving the way clear for you. But now—now I will be a martyr in his eyes, and my memory much more difficult to compete with."

Her eyes widen and she glances at Madame Dinan to see if she has heard, but the older woman is still staring out the window.

She has aged much since I last saw her. The skin is sagging off her delicate bones. Her eyes are no longer merely nervous but haunted-looking. As if feeling my gaze on her, she turns, but even then she will not meet my eyes. "Burn the rags she was wearing," she tells the maid. "And get her into the tub."

"There is no need. I will do it myself," I say, stepping into the warm water and taking up the soap.

Once the servants have left, Dinan turns to me. "You foolish girl! You have ruined everything!"

"What do you mean?"

"Since d'Albret wasn't able to take Rennes as he'd planned, he had to resort to other options."

"Options that have driven Marshal Rieux from his side?"

She ignores my question. "With the duchess's marriage to the Holy Roman emperor, he has been left with no choice but to . . ." She trails off with a glance in Jamette's direction. "Go fetch her gown," she orders. Jamette curtsies then hurries to do as she is told.

Remembering the abbess of Saint Brigantia's words, I stare at her, the soap in my hand forgotten. "Is this option why my father has been communicating with the French regent?"

She stops twisting the linen handkerchief she holds and I see that her nails are bitten to the quick. "What do you know of that?"

I shrug. "Simply that there are rumors."

She smiles thinly. "You must realize there are other ways he can gain control of the kingdom if the duchess will not honor her promises."

I look away so she will not see how much her words disturb me, for if d'Albret is conspiring with the French regent, it can only mean disaster for the duchess. And why is Dinan telling me this? Is it because she knows I will die and take this knowledge with me? Or is there some small spark of loyalty left in her that abhors the choice d'Albret has made?

But there is no opportunity to ask further questions because Jamette returns carrying one of my gowns. It is of crimson velvet trimmed with gold braid, and I wonder if she has chosen it because the blood will not show.

Chapter Fifty

DE LUR TAKES GREAT PLEASURE in binding my hands behind my back and prodding me forward into the great hall. As I am ushered in, I hold my head high. The chamber is stuffed full of d'Albret's retainers and vassals. Looking among them, I see that there are none of the Nantes lords who were recent allies of d'Albret's. Have they left? Has he killed them all out of suspicion? Or perhaps any of his soldiers with a scrap of decency left with Marshal Rieux. I know not, but the soldiers and vassals here are wholly his and have been for years. They are the ones who stood silently by as he murdered each of his six wives, who eagerly carried out his order to terrorize the town into submission by raping their women and burning their homes. They are the ones who chased down and slayed any servants who remained loyal to the duchess, hunting them with as much feeling as if they were hunting rats. Whatever d'Albret plans for me, there will be no help from them.

De Lur shoves me forward, and, with my wrists bound, I am barely able to keep my balance. D'Albret sprawls in the great chair on the dais, his cold fury lurking just beneath a thin veneer of civility. But my newfound purpose burns so bright within me that there is no room for fear. Or maybe I no longer care. Especially knowing that Death will not—has never—rejected me, but will welcome me home when my time here is done.

Besides, even if I were terrified, I would not give d'Albret the one thing he wants—me cowering at his feet. Instead, I stare coolly at him, as if *he* has been brought before *me* to be held to account for his crimes.

He straightens, his eyes studying me with cold appraisal. "You have much to answer for. You have betrayed my plans to the duchess—twice—run off with my prisoner, and kidnapped my own children from under my roof. Surely no father has ever had to suffer such treachery at the hands of his own daughter." He rises up from his chair and crosses the small space between us. "What did you do with my prisoner? I had plans for him, you know. Did you let him bed you, like you let the blacksmith's boy?"

Hearing him talk of what is between Beast and me this way sickens me. "The prisoner was nothing to me. An assignment, nothing more."

"An assignment?" He circles me slowly, assessing. "Are you truly a whore, then?"

Suddenly, I want him to know. *Need* him to know whom I truly serve and all that I have done to thwart him. "Have you not guessed? I am not your daughter. My mother invited Death into her bed rather than suffer life with you, and I was sired by Mortain Himself."

A loud silence rises up in the room, broken only by the crack of his hand as it strikes my face. My head snaps back, and I taste blood.

"Then clearly returning you to Death will not be a punishment. I shall have to find some other way to repay you for all the grief you have caused me."

I know I should stop. Keep my mouth closed and leave well enough alone, but I have stood silent witness in his household for too long. I will not be silent any longer. "I am not merely Death's daughter, but His handmaiden as well. All the accidents that have befallen your allies and trusted commanders have not truly been accidents but my own hand carrying out Death's orders and, through Him, the duchess's."

D'Albret smiles then, surprising me. He leans in close to my ear. "For all that you wrap your killing in some saint of old, you are just like me," he says with something akin to pride. "You fool only yourself. It is a shame we could not have come to terms, you and I."

As he gives voice to the very fear that has dogged me all my life, I smile. D'Albret may play with Death. He may even be good at it, but I am Death's true daughter. "No," I say, my voice strong and sure. "I am not like you. I have never been like you. For while you think to control Death and bend it to your will, I *am* His will. I have never killed an innocent, or to serve my own pleasure. I have killed only men like you who are a blight upon the earth."

"A blight, am I? We shall see." He reaches for a strand of my hair and then rubs it between two of his fingers. "I find I am quite taken with the idea of mixing my bloodline with Death's own. Then, surely, nothing could withstand my will."

The mere thought of d'Albret's touch sickens me, and the idea of the abomination that would result fills me with unspeakable terror. I struggle against the rope at my wrists, but it does not so much as budge. I curse myself for throwing my true parentage in his face, for I should have remembered just how shrewd he is at finding the thing one values most and using it as a weapon.

D'Albret smiles, and his hand leaves my hair to trail down my face, like a caress. I cannot help it: I shudder at his touch, at what I see in his eyes. "Since you are not my daughter, I could even make you my seventh wife, hmm?"

I glance at Madame Dinan, but her face is a brittle mask.

D'Albret winks at me, then pats my cheek. "She will not mind. She is barren and understands I must have sons to secure my holdings." Then he grabs my chin, locking me in place, and presses his mouth on mine in a brutal, crushing kiss. Bile rises in my throat as his teeth grind against my swollen lip. When he licks the cut on my lip, I shudder violently, every nerve in my body screaming at the wrongness of it, the sheer horror of it. With no other way to fight back, I bite him.

He jerks away, fury darkening his eyes. He raises his hand to strike me again—

"No!" Julian's voice rings throughout the hall.

D'Albret turns his cold, flat eyes to Julian. "I will take my vengeance as I please."

"No, my lord," Julian says again.

D'Albret tilts his head and studies his son. "You cannot bear for others to touch her, can you?"

"It is not that."

"Do you wish her for yourself? If you will breed me heirs with Death's own blood in their veins, I would forgive you much."

I hold my breath and wonder if Julian will take what is being offered. "No," he says, looking not at d'Albret but at me. As our eyes meet across the distance, I know that he has made his choice—he has chosen to be my brother rather than my lover, and I am filled with a quiet joy. We were always strongest when we faced our tormentors with one mind. But in the next moment, my happiness trickles away, as I see what that choice will cost him. A marque has begun to form on his brow.

"Wait, Julian." I start to go to him, but de Lur yanks me back.

Julian steps away from d'Albret and comes to stand before me until we are but a handbreadth apart. "Do you remember when we were children and you were afraid of the dark? Do you remember what I promised you?"

"Yes." My throat is so constricted with grief that the word comes out in a whisper. He promised that when he grew up, he would slay all the monsters.

"I meant it. I am only sorry I did not do it sooner."

"If you do this, you will die."

His mouth wrenches into a wistful smile that nearly breaks my heart in two. "I fear a part of me—the best part—has been dead for years." He presses a quick kiss upon my brow—that of an older brother—then steps back and turns toward d'Albret.

"Are you truly willing to die for her, boy?"

In answer, Julian draws his sword. He is an excellent swordsman, but he does not have the ruthless skill nor the cruelty that d'Albret possesses. I cannot believe that I must stand here helplessly and watch the one person who loved me the longest, now die for that love. That could even have been d'Albret's intention all along, for surely he knows that watching Julian die trying to defend me is the most crushing punishment he could devise.

There is a ring of steel as d'Albret draws his sword, and Captain de Lur pulls me out of the circle the other men have formed. The entire room grows silent. Then Julian advances with a rapid succession of blows, but d'Albret counters with a brutal thrust that causes Julian to leap back to avoid being impaled.

As they eye each other warily, I strain my wrists trying to bring my fingers within reach of the knot, but I am unable to reach it. I turn my gaze to the room, at all the hard and unsympathetic faces.

Beast will come.

But he will be too late.

The crowd murmurs in approval, and I look back to the fighting men in time to see d'Albret deliver two quick blows, one on either side of Julian's head. That is when I suspect d'Albret is only toying with Julian and does not wish to kill him. Or at least, does not wish to kill him yet.

Julian is disoriented just long enough for d'Albret to step inside his guard and deliver a vicious hack to his ribs. I bite down on my swollen lip to keep from crying out, fearing it will only distract Julian more. He doubles over, grimacing with the pain, breathing hard, as blood begins to seep through the cut and onto his doublet.

Pleased by this drawing of first blood, the men break into grim smiles. As they shift on their feet, I feel a hand on my bound wrists. I pull away, fearing one of the soldiers has decided to act on his own, then realize these are a woman's hands that have touched me. A moment later, something hard and sharp is slipped into my fingers.

A knife.

I glance over my shoulder and see Jamette silently slipping back among the crowd. While she does not love me, she *does* love Julian. But what can I do with one puny knife? Does she wish that I put him out of his misery? Or hope that I will use it on myself and stop the fight?

Keeping my eyes on the men in front of me, I slip the knife up so that it is hidden between my hands, then maneuver it until I feel its tip meet the resistance of the rope. Then I begin sawing at the bindings.

D'Albret is openly toying with Julian now; a quick blow here, a nick there, a sudden cut to the arm. Frustrated, Julian sidesteps and swings his blade upward, coming inside d'Albret's guard and almost—*almost*—plunging his sword into the other man's gut, but d'Albret sidesteps at the last possible moment. The mood of the watching men shifts again, their displeasure palpable, for they bear Julian no love. He has never been one of them like Pierre has.

Julian is growing tired now and is no longer quick on his feet. I saw frantically at the ropes, my fingers cramping and slick with blood where I have nicked myself.

Pressing his advantage, D'Albret takes a mighty swing. Julian ducks so that the blade whistles through empty air, then uses d'Albret's brief moment of surprise to deliver a stroke that crunches so loudly I am sure he has broken at least one of d'Albret's ribs. Although I feel like cheering, I keep silent, for it would only draw attention my way.

Then Julian gives up all pretense of fighting fairly or with honor and rushes, lifting his sword so that it will catch d'Albret square in the face, but the older man steps back and stumbles as the crowd gives way, and the blow misses. Even if by some miracle Julian survives the fight, I am not sure the men will let him walk away.

And still I cannot cut through the be-damned rope.

Julian is bleeding from a dozen different cuts, and if he ever owed a debt for having loved me, he has surely paid it.

At the next flurry of blows, I must look away, for Julian's fatigue is so great that I fear each blow will be his last. I pull against the rope once more, hoping I have frayed it enough that I can free my hands, but still it holds.

When the sound of clashing blades stops, I look up. Julian is breathing hard, and I can feel the labored beating of his heart as it tries to keep up with the strain of attacks and fuel his flagging body, and my own heart aches for him. Then d'Albret comes on hard and fast, but incredibly Julian is able to block each blow, until a savage swing that nearly decapitates him. He jerks back just in time, but the tip of the blade opens his right cheek to the bone. I long to run to them, to put myself in front of Julian and stop this game of d'Albret's. I do not even realize I have taken a step forward until de Lur yanks me back. I glance at him and pray I live long enough to kill him after I kill d'Albret.

If I kill d'Albret. The fight is winding down. Julian is staggering, his sword arm drooping, his blade dragging on the floor.

But d'Albret does not press his attack. Instead, he says, "By God, I will end this now." Then he raises his sword high over his head. But instead of lunging toward Julian, he pivots, aiming the blow in my direction, and some small part of me is glad. Glad that he has chosen Julian over me and that I do not have to watch another loved one die.

But Julian, ever quick-witted Julian, sees what d'Albret's intends. He leaps in front of me, and the sword plunges through his chest. His dark eyes widen with surprise—and pain. As I cry out, doubling over in anguish, the rope around my wrists finally gives way.

As Julian falls, the entire hall grows quiet and all the men step back. Not out of respect for Julian, but out of fear for their own skins, for it is hard to know how d'Albret will react to this.

In the ensuing silence, I drop to my knees beside Julian. The force of his leap wrenched the sword from d'Albret's grip, and it is still impaled in his chest. He is soaked in crimson, his face is even whiter than Death's own. His soul beats frantically against the trappings of his mortal body, desperate to be free of the pain that consumes him. He tries to speak, but his pale lips cannot form the words.

"Dearest brother, you were wrong. The best part of you still lives." I lean down and place my lips upon his brow. In forgiveness, and in farewell.

No sooner have I done so than his soul bursts from his body, as if it needed only my permission to be free. And it *is* free. It is finally, finally free from the dark world it has inhabited for so long.

There is the sound of boots on the marble floor, then d'Albret stands over us. He nudges Julian's body with his foot. "We must add the death of my son to your list of crimes."

As I stare down at Julian's poor, wounded body, true understanding dawns. In order to defeat d'Albret, I have only to *love* more than he hates.

And I do. My heart is filled with the love I bear, love that I was too terrified to give voice to for fear d'Albret would use it against others in order to hurt me. But they are all gone, far beyond his reach. Only I remain.

Julian's sword is but inches from my hand. *Now*, I think. *Now*. Fueled by all the fierce love inside me, I reach out, grasp the sword hilt still slick with my brother's blood, then surge upward, aiming to drive it deep into d'Albret's belly.

D'Albret discerns my intent just in time. He kicks out with his foot, knocking the sword from my fingers, then his hand reaches out and closes around my throat.

I smile. I know d'Albret will not kill me this way, for I was born with the birth cord wrapped twice around my neck and did not die. And I still have the knife Jamette gave me—the very one I once gave her.

Still smiling, I lean in toward d'Albret as if welcoming his hands around my neck. I grip the knife handle firmly and, fueled by seventeen years of the despair I have felt on behalf of those I love, whip the knife out from behind my back and plunge it into his belly, driving it upward.

D'Albret's eyes widen in surprise, and his hold around my neck loosens. He looks faintly puzzled, as if unable to believe what I have done. I shove upward again and twist, willing the knife to damage every organ it touches, just as he has damaged every life he has touched.

As my hand grows wet with his blood, and I watch his eyes dull, I want to throw my head back and howl with victory. Instead, I yank my knife out, and he starts to slump to the ground.

Even now, with his guts spilling out onto the fine white marble, Death does not claim him and no marque rests upon his brow. It never will. That is another thing I learned from my true father that night: d'Albret is not welcome in Death's realm. That is the promise Mortain made to all d'Albret's victims, that d'Albret will be barred from the Underworld, his flesh fated to linger until it rots, his soul to wander restlessly until the end of time.

Madame Dinan rushes to his side and tries to shove his guts back into his belly, staining her slender white hands with blood and gore. As she calls for the surgeons, I have a vision of her new life as it spreads before her, tending to d'Albret and his unnatural wound for all the rest of her days.

I glance again at the fallen Julian's face, as white and still as marble.

That is when I understand that it was Julian's love that was the key to this victory. His love for me, Beast's love for Alyse, my own love for my sisters — even Jamette's love for Julian — has driven all of us to this moment in time, each strand wrapped around the next like links in a chain.

And now d'Albret is as good as dead. And I am finally free.

Dinan looks up to glare at me. "Seize her!"

Ah, but I am not free yet. There are still over fifty men in here, and all of them are staring at me with eyes bright with the promise of violence and their own brutal nature. What did I hope? That with d'Albret's death, they would be released from their own dark impulses and rejoice in their freedom? No, for they were drawn to him as like is drawn to like, and they eye me now with a hunger for blood and vengeance. Besides, they will have to answer to Pierre for what happened here. I grip the knife I still hold in my hand. D'Albret cannot hurt anyone again — my destiny has been fulfilled. I will not surrender to what I see lurking in the enraged faces around me. Slowly, I lift the knife and press the tip of it to my own throat.

One of the men, seeing what I intend, leaps forward. He looms over me, the helm he wears shadowing his face. I try to pull away from his grasp, but he is as quick as he is tall. When his hand closes around my wrist — the moment our skin touches — I *know*.

My head snaps up, and I look into a pair of light blue eyes that burn with an unholy light.

Beast.

Chapter Fifty-One

THE SIGHT OF BEAST FILLS my heart with such joy that I fear it will burst. He is dressed in d'Albret's colors and shoves a rolled-up leather packet into my hands. His disguise buys us some time, and while his body blocks me from the other men's view, I quickly unroll my knives. Since there is no time to don the sheaths, I stab them through my skirt, threading the blades through the thick fabric so they will not fall out.

"Bring her over here!" Captain de Lur orders.

When I am fully armed, Beast flashes one of his fierce grins at me. "Cut the tabard off, for I will not besmirch my god by fighting in d'Albret's colors."

I cannot blame him. I put the tip of my knife to the tabard and cut it in half, careful that the blade does not go too far. Beast shrugs out of it and pulls his sword from its sheath. For a brief moment, the men think he means to use it on me. "You ready?" he asks.

"I've only been waiting on you."

He smiles again, then turns to face the surrounding men, and confusion erupts. As Captain de Lur takes a step toward us, there is a faint whisper of sound, then his eyes roll up and he crumples. A small rock pings to the floor.

Yannic.

Then Beast gives one of his bloodcurdling yells as the battle lust engulfs him. He raises his sword and lunges to his left to get his body and his weapon between me and the bulk of d'Albret's soldiers.

I kick out, my foot connecting with the nearest man's gut, up high where it will knock all the air from his lungs. Gripping a knife in each hand, I realize that all the hate in this room is no match for the love that fills me. And fill me it does, its effervescence racing along my limbs, chasing away the sorrow and fatigue, as if some holy light rather than mere blood flows in my veins.

But it is no holy light, simply me, whole and unafraid of who and what I am, eager to do the work I was born to do.

D'Albret's men have regrouped and are rushing toward Beast. He meets the first parry, and the sound of their swords is deafening.

I tighten my grip on my knives as another soldier rushes toward me, sword drawn. As easily as if I were practicing with Annith, I duck under his blade, get inside his guard, and shove my knife into his throat. Before he has even begun to fall to the ground, I turn to meet another. But this one has witnessed my trick just now and lowers his own sword to block another such maneuver. So instead, I flip my knife around, grab it by the point, and hurl it toward him. It takes him straight through the eye, and he drops to his knees.

Two more guards approach and I turn to meet them. Time slows, like a drop of honey suspended from the tip of a knife. As I feint and parry, every move comes without conscious thought. It feels as if my body has been filled with something as cool and dark and unerring as a shadow. I am whole now. Whole and unbroken and filled with an unearthly grace that moves through me with unspeakable joy.

From out of the corner of my eye I see that the battle fever has completely consumed Beast, and he churns through the rushing guards like a plow tills through earth. Truly, we are the gods' own children, forged in the fire of our tortured pasts, but also blessed with unimaginable gifts.

How long we fight, I do not know, but slowly, as if I am being drawn up from the bottom of some deep well, I become aware of my surroundings. Now that I have stopped fighting, I feel as thin and empty as a discarded glove. Over half of d'Albret's men lay dead at our feet. The other half show no signs of retreating. Indeed, two of the men have gone for reinforcements.

Out of knives, I bend over and pluck a sword from one of the dead soldiers who litter the ground, then turn to Beast, who is breathing hard.

The light in his eyes is only half feral now. He opens his mouth to say something, but an explosion rocks the building—indeed, the very earth beneath our feet. It sounds as if a dozen cannon have been shot at once. Beast grabs my hand and begins pulling me toward the door.

"What was that?" I ask.

"Lazare and his charbonnerie."

"Here?"

"He thought we might need a diversion. Nor did we think it necessary to leave the duchess's own weapons in the hands of her enemy to be used against her." Another explosion follows.

"And the girls?"

"At the convent of Brigantia. The abbess swore she would not release them to anyone but you or me or on the duchess's own orders."

As the soldiers recover and regroup, they spot us moving toward the door.

We break into a run.

At the main door to the palace, small knots of servants huddle, peeking out the door and watching, whispering among themselves, but they make no move to stop us.

Outside, in the courtyard, I blink against the bright light. Clusters of soldiers stand, trying to discern the direction of the attack, not realizing it is their very own artillery that has been destroyed. Beast uses their confusion and heads for the east gate. Not wanting to draw any more attention to ourselves, we walk rather than run. But he is a head taller than most men and I am dressed in crimson; it does not take them long to notice us. Besides, they are d'Albret's men, and they know too well the punishment that will be exacted if they fail to stop us. They quickly shift their attention from the unknown attackers to us and begin moving toward the gate, blocking our escape.

Beast does not so much as check his stride, merely switches direction and begins running toward the stairs that lead to the battlements. I do not know what he has planned, but I follow him blindly. Behind us another shout goes up.

I glance over my shoulder to see that the archers have been summoned and are forming a line in the middle of the courtyard.

Luckily, the stairway is covered with a stone arch, which will afford us some protection, and its narrow width will force the soldiers to go two abreast and slow their pursuit.

However, when we emerge on the battlements, I quickly realize there is nowhere for us to go. I throw a questioning look at Beast, who says nothing but continues running until we reach the farthest tower — the one that looms over the river.

More shouts ring out from below and I look down to see the archers are loading their crossbows. Beast stops and turns to me. "We must jump."

I stare down at the swollen, roiling river below. "We will be leaping to our deaths."

"Do I bear a marque?"

I glance up at his forehead, relieved to see there is no dark smudge upon it. "No," I say in wonder.

"Then we will make it. Trust me." As he holds out his hand, three crossbow bolts arc by, flying wide.

The sounds of our pursuers grow louder as they gain the stairs. Soon they will be on the battlement behind us and close enough that their arrows will not miss.

I reach out and take Beast's offered hand. A glorious smile spreads across his face, making it almost beautiful. He lifts my hand and kisses it. "Do not let go," he says, "and kick your feet to get us well clear of the wall."

I nod, then he tugs us several paces back from the edge. We take deep breaths, filling our lungs with air. There is a shout as one of the men gains the parapet. It is an archer, and he is raising his crossbow.

We take a running start, and then we jump.

The wall drops away beneath us and we are flying through the air. We do not let go of each other but kick and windmill with our free arms, trying to get as far away from the shallows as we can. Beast grins maniacally, as if he will keep us alive by sheer will.

Then a cold, hard shock jars my teeth and sends the rest of the air whooshing from my lungs as the water closes over my head.

Chapter Fifty-Two

THE FRIGID WATER SUCKS ME down into its murky depths. It is dark and disorienting, and I cannot tell which way is up. I remember every story I have ever heard of Saint Mer and how she lures sailors deeper and deeper into her realm until they cannot find their way back.

But this is a river, not the sea.

I try to kick to the surface, but my rich, heavy skirt is already filled with water and has turned to lead, pulling me down like an anchor. Even so, I struggle desperately to swim free. The water is dark and cloudy, and my vision is filled with bubbles swirling, much like snow in a blizzard. And still I am pulled down. I push off my shoes, then fumble at the ribbons around my waist so I can be free of my skirt, but they are wet and my hands clumsy, and no matter how I struggle, they are stuck fast in a tight, wet knot. My lungs burn with the effort of not breathing, and I am not sure how much longer I can hold my breath. Black spots dance before my eyes.

At least I have been spared the fate d'Albret had planned for me. And the fierce retribution of his men. I will die knowing that Charlotte and Louise are safe and that d'Albret will never be able to hurt anyone again.

My feet touch the soft, silty bottom of the river, and still I am too stubborn to take a breath, knowing it will be water that fills my lungs, not the air I crave.

Just as my lungs are ready to spasm, ready to gasp for air when there is nothing but water, an icy hand grabs mine. At first, my heart leaps in joy because I think it is Beast, but surely it is far too cold for any human hand. Has my father come to escort me home?

But it matters not. I kick and strain, letting the hand pull me to the surface, hoping we will make it before my lungs give way. But I am cold, so cold. My own hands no longer work properly, and I lose my grip.

I flounder for a moment, then begin to sink again, until the hand — warmer this time — grabs hold and pulls as I kick frantically for the surface.

Up, up, up he pulls. Just when I am certain my lungs will burst, I break through the surface with a loud splash. I take in great gulping breaths of air as I tread water. I look over to see Beast doing the same, but it is harder for him because he cannot stop smiling. When we finally catch our breath, he reaches down and cuts the ribbons that hold my heavy skirt, and it slowly drifts to the bottom. Then we turn and kick off, letting the strong current of the river begin to carry us away.

I think once more of all those I have loved and lost, and I know that they have found peace at last. And I — I have my whole life before me, and for the first time, it is filled not with fear and darkness, but with love and promise.

And a beast. I cannot help it. I smile, finally able to appreciate the gentle laughter of the gods.

Epilogue

WE STAY WITH THE RIVER'S current until we can barely keep our heads up. It would not do to have the river cast us out into the wide open ocean, for then we would never gain land. Slowly, with leaden limbs and exhausted bodies, we begin swimming for the shore. There are no houses here, nothing but forest and stone. When at last I feel the riverbed under my feet, I nearly sob with relief as my tired, trembling legs are able to stop swimming. Slowly, leaning against each other for support, we stumble out of the river onto the bank and collapse, sodden and shivering and gasping for air.

"You came back," I finally manage to get out.

Beast rolls his head to look at me, the intensity of his gaze searing itself into my soul. "I told you I would."

He did, but how do I confess that I did not believe him? Not that I thought he was lying, but that I did not believe the gods would allow him to return. They have never answered my prayers for aid before.

I say nothing, but lie on the rough rocky shore, relishing being alive and on dry land. As I stare up at the blue sky, I remember that it was Julian who taught me to swim. For all the ill he has done me, he has saved my life twice in one day.

My heart twists in pain. That is when the tears come. Not for Julian my lover, nor even for Julian my savior, as he was in the end, but for my brother. A young boy who protected and comforted me through all the horrors we endured together before the darkness claimed him, too. But in the end, he was able to reject that darkness.

Saying nothing, Beast gathers me into his arms—arms that are full of the promise of the future—and holds me as I say goodbye to the past that has haunted me for so long.

When I have finished, he gently brushes the tears from my cheeks. "I thought you'd been hit by an arrow, just before we jumped."

"I was."

He scowls in concern, running his hands along my back, then my shoulders, searching. "But the arrow . . ."

"Came out in the river." I am unsure how to explain what happened. Was it a miracle? Or something my own mind created as it faced death?

Beast will not rest until he has seen the wound with his own eyes and is assured it does not need tending. Slowly, I sit up and present my back to him. There is silence, then his finger comes down and touches a tiny hole in my gown. "There is no blood," he says, with awe in his voice. "Just a white scar."

"I think it was a miracle," I whisper. One of many this day. When I tell him of the cold hand that grabbed mine and pulled me up into Beast's own grip, he grows quiet and sober. In that silence, there is a faint sound behind us where the trees meet the shore. Beast leaps up, hand going for the knife at his hip, then relaxes. When I turn to see who it is, my heart lifts.

Lazare sits atop a small cart, his white teeth chewing on a stem of grass. Yannic is driving. "Thought you might want some dry clothes," he calls out as Yannic brings the mules to a halt.

Lazare hops out and saunters toward us, eyeing my scarlet gown. "It's not as fancy as your current fare, but since that's as good as a target painted on your back, I'm guessing you won't mind."

"You guessed right." I rise to my feet and take the drab gown he holds out to me. Once I have taken it, he hands a similar bundle to Beast.

Only too eager to be rid of my finery, I step behind the trees for privacy. I remove the lone knife that is still woven into its skirts, then quickly don the charbonnerie gear, welcoming the dust-colored skirt and the dark gray bodice. After I have tucked my hair up under the linen coif, I gather up the gown Madame Dinan dressed me in and return to the shore, where the others are talking. Before joining them, I pause long enough to take my knife and stab it into the red dress, relishing the shredding sound the silk makes.

When I am done and the entire thing is naught but ribbons, I feel Beast, Lazare, and Yannic watching me. I meet their gaze steadily. "As you said, it is as good as a target. Best if it is never seen again. Or if it is, let it be mistaken for all that remains of me." I adjust my grip on the shredded dress, carry it back down to the river's edge, and toss the whole of it into the raging waters.

The long scarlet strips swirl on the surface for a moment, like a pool of blood, before the current catches hold and carries them, swirling and churning, toward the sea.

When they are finally out of sight, I return to the others. "Now, let us fetch my sisters."

Fetching my sisters is easier said than done, for the convent sits right across from the palace, the palace that is still teeming with angry, confused soldiers who are trying to come to grips with the attack on their armory as well as the mortal wound to their lord. While we are well disguised, they will all be on high alert, scanning for any unusual activity in the area.

But even convents need charcoal for burning.

We pull up before the Brigantian convent just as dusk is falling. There is still enough light to drive the cart by, but too little to be easily recognized. Or so we hope.

Like before, Beast is hidden in the bed of the cart. Just as I alight from the seat to let him know it is safe to come out, the clattering of hoofbeats comes within hearing. As it grows louder, I put my hands on Beast and press down, letting him know it is not safe to come out.

Twenty riders come into view, galloping toward us along the avenue that runs between the convent and the palace. With a sick twisting in my gut, I recognize their leader—Pierre. He has returned from whatever business he was conducting with the French.

I smear my hands in some of the charcoal dust from the cart, then casually wipe them across my face, before busying myself with stacking the charcoal into a bundle. Every muscle in my body remains tense as Pierre rides by. I do not relax until the column of riders crosses the moat and disappears from view into the palace yard.

"Dark Mother, that was close!" Lazare mutters.

"Too close," I agree. "We need to get off the road. Pull the cart around to the side. Beast and I will collect the girls and meet you over there."

The abbess greets us at the door herself. "I've been waiting, hoping and praying," she says.

"And we thank you for your prayers. We needed every one of them." I give her a quick report of what transpired. When I have finished, she crosses herself. "Well, you have wrested the dice from their hands and given them a toss of your own. Now we must see how they land. But come, the girls have been asking for you."

We are ushered into a spare clean room where Tephanie sits on the floor playing with Louise and Charlotte. Charlotte sees us first and hops to her feet. "You are back." There is an unmistakable note of relief in her voice.

"I told you I would be."

She glances behind me at Beast. "And so is he." Charlotte's voice is decidedly less welcoming. Fortunately, Louise bounces up from the floor and she throws herself at me.

"I was scared you weren't coming back."

I don't know what to tell her. I ventured into the very heart of darkness to save them—and in saving them, I somehow also managed to free myself. Instead, I simply hold on to her, letting her feel the truth of my presence. When she starts to wriggle in impatience, I slowly let go. She casts a sly glance at Beast.

I look from Beast back to Louise, then kneel so that I am eye to eye with her. "This is your mother's brother, Louise. He is your uncle."

I can feel Beast holding his breath, bracing himself for disbelief or revulsion or any of the dozens of reactions he is used to. But Louise's face brightens. "He is?" She turns immediately to him. "Are you older or younger?"

He blinks a moment at the unexpected question. "She was my older sister, like Charlotte is yours."

"You don't look like her."

"No, I am much prettier."

Charlotte scowls at this joke—and, mayhap, at being excluded from this bond—but Louise giggles, her face breaking into a smile. "No, you're not."

Beast runs his hand along his chin. "Are you certain?"

"Yes," Louise says. "Momma was beautiful."

Beast grows serious. "Yes, little one. She was. Both of face and, more importantly, of spirit. I see much of her in you."

It is there, I realize, staring at her face. The faint traces of Alyse.

"Do you have any stories of her?" The hunger in Louise's eyes is unmistakable.

"Oh, many!" Beast says.

"Tell me."

I stand up and take her hand. "He will, sweeting. Once we are in the cart and on the road, he will tell you all about your mother."

I reach out to Charlotte. "And you," I tell her, grasping her fingers tightly in my own. In truth, I am not sure I will ever be able to let go. For now, it is enough that I do not have to.

AUTHOR'S NOTE

WHILE *GRAVE MERCY* TOOK PLACE against a historical and political back-drop, Sybella's story is a much more personal one, touching only on the fringes of the political happenings of the time. Because of that, I have taken a bit more creative license with this book.

As with *Grave Mercy*, many of the characters in the book are actual historical figures, and the broad strokes of the politics have been taken directly from history. The duchess did retreat to Rennes with her council, and the French did invade Brittany's borders and conquer a number of towns.

One of the greatest liberties I have taken is that I have greatly compressed the time frames involved. While many of the events of this story did happen in the spring of 1489, there was then a large gap of about a year and a half when nothing significant happened politically. The French took towns that were then reclaimed by Bretons. Ambassadors met and political protocols were observed, all of which makes for fairly dry story-telling. Anne traveled around the countryside, visiting her people, while France kept sniffing around Brittany's borders, looking for a way in. It came at the end of 1490, when Anne married the Holy Roman emperor by proxy and thereby broke the Treaty of Vergers. So essentially I have compressed the events that occurred in 1490 and 1491 and pulled them all together into one year for ease of storytelling.

I have probably taken the most grievous liberties with the historical figure of Count Alain d'Albret, one of Anne's most ardent suitors. It is true that he was in his fifties, large and rough-looking, with an uncouth manner. Madame Dinan, Anne's governess, was indeed his half sister and pressured the young duchess constantly, trying to get her to agree to the match. All of that has been taken from historical chronicles of the time. It is also true that Anne was so repelled by him that she issued a decree stating she would never marry him, no matter what documents she may have signed as a child. This strong revulsion in one so dedicated to her country captured my imagination.

This came together with my research into the folklore of Brittany, where two of the historical kernels for the Bluebeard tales are said to have originated. One is the story of Conomor the Cursed, and the other was about Gilles de Rais. When Sybella first showed up in *Grave Mercy* so damaged and broken, I knew that she had to have suffered some horrible trauma, and so all those elements swirled together and coalesced into *Dark Triumph*.

After the events at the end of 1491, Count d'Albret seems to disappear from the annals of historical record, except for the recording of his death in 1528. He would have been more than eighty years old, an extraordinary age for that time.

Jean d'Albret, Count d'Albret's oldest son, became King of Navarre, and d'Albret's daughter, Charlotte d'Albret, later went on to marry Cesare Borgia.

For the most part, I have tried to stick with words that were in use at the time the story takes place, but that wasn't always possible. The word *saboteur* did not come into English usage until the early part of the twentieth century; however, the root word, *sabot*, was in use in the fifteenth century. Since *saboteur* has such a distinctly different nuance of meaning from the closest historically accurate word, *conspirator*, I have decided to stick with *saboteur* and hang what little justification I could on the French roots of the word.

Such are the problems that keep historical fantasy writers awake at night.

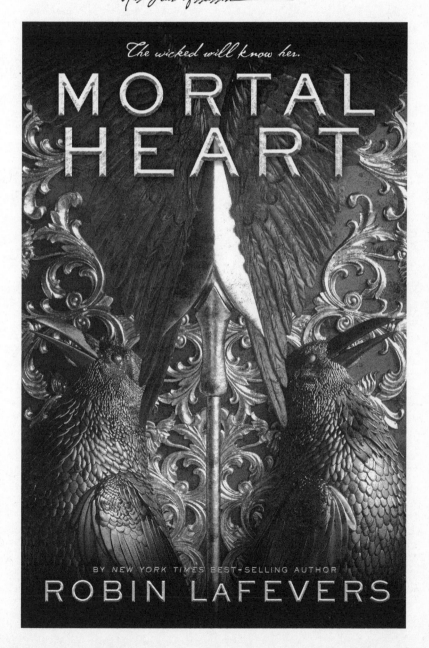

The wicked will know her.

MORTAL HEART

BY *NEW YORK TIMES* BEST-SELLING AUTHOR

ROBIN LAFEVERS

Chapter One

FOR MOST, THE BLEAK DARK months when the black storms come howling out of the north is a time of grimness and sorrow as people await the arrival of winter, which brings death, hunger, and bitter cold in its wake. But we at the convent of Saint Mortain welcome winter with open arms and hearts, for it is Mortain's own season, when He is full upon us. In such a way does the Wheel of Life turn, with every ending but a new beginning; that is the promise Mortain has made us.

So while most people bar their doors and shut their windows tight, we have cause for celebration and go traipsing through the wood, gathering the sacred yew branches and collecting holly with its bright red berries that remind us of the three drops of blood spilled when Mortain was pierced by love and Arduinna's own arrow.

And while Mortain is a far more gentle god than most people give Him credit for, I do not think He would look kindly upon His youngest handmaidens jousting with the sacred branches that are intended for His holy fire.

"Audri! Aveline! Stop that!"

"She started it," Aveline says, peering out from under the pale red hair that has fallen across her eyes.

"No, I didn't! You did. You always do. Because you're good with swords and knives and fighting, you always want to fight."

"Girls!" I clap my hands, wincing at how very much I remind myself of Sister Beatriz when she loses control of the womanly-charms lessons. "Enough. Audri, go help Florette. Aveline, you come over here with me."

Thinking the other girl in trouble, Audri sticks her tongue out at Aveline, then hurries over to help Florette. Instead of scolding Aveline, I take her hand, lead her to a holly bush, and give her a knife. "You will fill that basket, and I will fill this one."

Pleased at being given a blade, something normally reserved for older girls or the training yard, Aveline turns to the bush and begins cutting.

I keep my eyes on the leaves in front of me as I speak to her. "You are the oldest of the group, Aveline. There is no honor in besting those younger than you."

She stops her cutting and turns her strange, solemn gaze on me. "Are you saying I should pretend to be weak so they can feel strong? Is that not telling a lie?" Before I can untangle her knotted logic, she shrugs. "Besides, she is nearly as old as I am and likes to show off by going without her cloak and shoes."

I hide a smile, for it is true that Audri is quite proud of her ability to withstand cold. Not only does she not feel the wintry chill, but she does not suffer chilblains or deadened limbs when exposed to it. That is her gift for being pulled from the womb of a woman who had frozen to death in one of winter's most savage storms. She is as impervious to the cold as one of the great white bears of the far north, and proud of it. "That may be true," I concede, "but you have gifts every bit as glorious as hers and you constantly pick fights so that you may show them off."

For a moment, the old familiar wave of loss and longing rears up and I catch my breath at the pain of it. Among the handmaidens of Death our birth stories are our most treasured possessions, marking us as they do as Death's true daughters. But on the day that I was born, no cuckolded husband paced nearby, no herbwitch pulled me from a cold, dead womb, nor did any hedge priest administer the last rites to a dying mother while I rooted futilely at her breast.

Or at least, I think not, for the truth is that I do not even know the day on which I was born. I do not know the manner of my birth, the name of my mother, or even if she still lives, although we think she must not, else I would not have ended up on the convent's doorstep when I was less than a week old. Of all the women whose feet have pattered along these stone floors, I am the only one to have no inkling of the circumstances of my own birth.

It is like an itching, festering wound I have trained myself not to scratch. But some days the pain and burn of it are nearly beyond bearing. Especially when I am confronted with a cocksure nine-year-old who is blessed with reflexes so fast she has been known to snatch arrows from their flight.

Aveline keeps her attention on the holly but watches me from the corner of her eye. "Does that mean you will let me fight you sometime?"

I cannot help it—I laugh. "You think you can best me?"

She lifts one shoulder. "I think I would like to know if I could or could not."

At her words, my smile wobbles and it is all I can do to keep from throwing my knife down in defeat. Even this *child* thinks I am no longer a match for her. I carefully avoid looking out at the ocean, just beyond the trees. It is too painful a reminder that both Ismae and Sybella have been sent to places I have not, have begun to fulfill their destinies while I am stuck here playing nursemaid to a gaggle of budding assassins.

I feel a tug at the corner of my gown and look down to find Florette standing there with wide eyes. "We did not mean to make you sad, Annith."

"Oh, you didn't, sweeting. I am just"—what? Feeling sorry for myself? Pining for my friends? Wishing fate had dealt me a different hand? —"eager to finish up with these branches so we can begin decorating."

Her small face clears and she goes back to her own work while I move on to the next branch. It is hard—so hard—not to feel wasted, like a new sword that has been allowed to rust before it has ever been used. I tighten my grip on my blade, reminding myself that the abbess has assured me it is just one of Mortain's many mysteries, why He has called the others first. If I ever come face to face with Him again, I shall ask why.

Politely, of course.

"Annith?" Aveline says.

"Hmmm?"

"Are we supposed to chop at our branches like that?"

I look down, appalled to see the gouges and scars where I have hacked my knife, again and again, against the pale silver bark of the yew. Saints! "No! Of course not. It is simply that this knife needs to be sharpened."

She arches one of her pale red brows at me, looking far older than her nine years.

"Annith! Look!" At the sound of Florette's shouting, I turn around to find her pointing through the small copse of trees. Is it a crow? For I have promised to pay Florette if she alerts me whenever she sees one approaching. It is our little secret. In exchange, I change the sheets on her bed when she wets it and I tell no one, although I think many of the others suspect.

I hurry to the trees, my eyes scanning the sky, but I see nothing.

"No, not in the sky, in the water. It's a *boat*."

I jerk my gaze down to the horizon, where I see that Florette is correct: a boat is making its way to the island. There is a quick, sharp stab of fear in my gut until I see that the boat does not bear one of the ominous black sails that portend death. "Aveline, go find Sister Thomine and Sister Widona. Tell them a night rower has arrived. Audri, you stay here with the other girls and continue gathering the greenery."

I slip my knife into the sheath at my waist, lift my skirts, and hurry across the rocky beach to the landing. There are two men in the boat, the rower and one other—a hedge priest, I presume. A girl sits between them. She is small, small enough that I do not think she can be older than Audri or Florette. As the boat comes steadily closer, I see that her hands are tied, and a rope is around her waist, securing her to the boat.

The night rower meets my furious gaze. "You can quit yer glaring, missy. We tied 'er up only so she wouldn't jump into the water. Thinks she's a fish, she does." I blink in surprise and turn to the hedge priest for an explanation.

He nods in greeting. "It's true. The locals sent her to Saint Mer at first, thinking she was one of theirs. But the abbess took one look at her and knew she wasn't. Turns out, her mother drowned, but they found her in time to cut the child from her womb. Except then the father wanted nothing to do with her. Thought she'd caused the mother's death."

Her story, like most of the girls' stories, twists my heart. So many mothers dead, so many daughters blamed. It is almost enough to make me glad I do not know the circumstances of my own birth. What sort of death did my mother suffer? What sins were blamed on me for daring to come into this world?

"Well, you're ashore now, so untie her at once. What's her name?"

The hedge priest shoots an uneasy glance at the rower as he unties her. "Melusine," he says. The sailor lifts the sacred conch shell he wears around his neck to his lips.

When I roll my eyes, it is his turn to glare at me. "'Tis a bad-luck name, miss. Especially for us sailors."

"It is a foolish name," the hedge priest mutters.

Ignoring them both, I turn my attention to Melusine herself. "What do you think of your name?"

She looks up at me with eyes the exact color of the sea, and nearly as fathomless. "I like my name. I picked it myself."

I smile. "Then I like it too. The names we give ourselves are always the best. Now, come." I hold out my hand to her. The hedge priest carefully helps her to the bow, then over the side and onto the beach. The girl glances longingly over her shoulder to the sparkling blue water. I quickly grab her hand and pull her toward me. "You can go swimming later," I tell her. "When it is not so cold."

When I turn to escort Melusine back to the convent, I find a small knot of three girls watching us with large, curious eyes. Aveline arrives just then, breathless from her running. "Sister Thomine is teaching the others right now, and Sister Widona is tending to a mare who is foaling. They said you can see to the new arrival. You've done it often enough."

And so I have.

I shoo the younger girls on to their next lesson a little early — comportment with Sister Beatriz. She will be annoyed, but her petty annoyances are a lesser concern than getting this newest girl settled. I do not think Melusine is injured or ill, but it is customary to have new arrivals thoroughly examined, for many come to us malnourished, beaten, or in other ways physically abused.

As I lead her down the hall, I try not to think of all the other novitiates I have escorted this way, novitiates who are even now serving Mortain in a much more glorious manner than I. I try not to think of Ismae, ensconced at court with her finery and weapons, doing the work she was born to do. I push away thoughts of Sybella, currently on her fourth assignment, with no word for well over six months. Although *I* did not escort Sybella down the hall—it took four full-grown nuns, two on either side of her, to be certain she did not injure herself or bolt.

No, I will not think of that now. I will not indulge in the weakness of doubt and self-pity. Even though the infirmary door is open, I rap softly on it so that our presence will not startle Sister Serafina. She often becomes so absorbed in her work that she forgets to eat or sleep or even, sometimes, where she is. "Sister? We have a new arrival today."

Sister Serafina looks up from a long, complex series of tubing and flasks, a contraption of her own design she built in order to streamline her making of simples and tinctures. She peers over a coil of copper tube at us.

"Her name is Melusine, and she was mistakenly sent to the convent of Saint Mer. Apparently, she has an affinity for water." I smile down at the girl so she will know this is meant without judgment.

Sister Serafina sets down a glass flask, wipes her hands on a linen towel, and studies Melusine. "Fond of the sea, are you?"

"Yes, ma'am."

Once I have placed the girl in Sister Serafina's capable hands, I leave the infirmary to inform the abbess of our new addition.

As I draw near her chambers, I hear voices coming from within. Hoping they have gotten word of Sybella or, better yet, word of some new assignment for me, I stand near the door as if merely waiting my turn to see the abbess, then lean my ear close.

"That is dire news indeed." It is Sister Eonette who is speaking.

"It is most unwelcome," the abbess agrees. "And could not come at a worse time."

"Does it not worry you for *other* reasons?" Sister Eonette puts an odd emphasis on the word *other,* an emphasis that has me pressing my ear closer to the door.

"You mean other than Sister Vereda's illness leaving us Sightless at a time when our young duchess is fending off angry suitors and trying to keep the French from sweeping in and claiming our duchy as their own? When our country is threatened by civil war and risking outright invasion?" The reverend mother's voice is drier than the week-old bread we feed the pigs. My thoughts fly immediately to Ismae and Sybella and countless others out in the world. Without a seeress, how will we guide their hands? This will leave them exposed and instructionless when they can least afford to be.

"I should not have to point out to you that it is rare enough for one of Mortain's handmaidens to take ill, even one as old as Sister Vereda. Does that not hint at some—"

"Enough!" The abbess's voice slices through the air, cutting short the words I was so breathlessly waiting to hear. "You are not to share your doubts or concerns with anyone. Have Sister Thomine sent to my office immediately."

There is a long, heavy pause that is finally broken by Sister Eonette. "But of course, Reverend Mother." Her voice drips with sarcasm so sharp it is almost mockery. I expect the abbess to take her to task for it, to slap her or order her to do penance for showing such disrespect, but she does not.

The soft tread of Sister Eonette's footsteps approaching the chamber door spurs me to action. Quickly, before she exits, I scamper down the hall, then begin walking toward the office so I am a good six paces away when Sister Eonette steps out. She glances at me. "She has a meeting with Sister Thomine," she tells me.

"Is Sister Thomine in there already?" I ask innocently.

"No, I am to fetch her."

"I will only take a minute." I give her a quick, cheerful smile meant to appease her, but she simply jerks one shoulder in an annoyed shrug.

"Very well, but I warn you, she is not in good humor this morning."